Selected Folktales

Ausgewählte Märchen

JACOB & WILHELM GRIMM

A Dual-Language Book

Edited and Translated by
STANLEY APPELBAUM

DOVER PUBLICATIONS, INC.
Mineola, New York

Copyright

Bibliographical Note

This Dover edition, first published in 2003, includes unabridged German texts of 27 tales from the definitive seventh edition (Verlag der Dieterichschen Buchhandlung, Göttingen, 1857, 3 volumes) of the *Kinder- und Hausmärchen;* see Introduction for further bibliographical data. The German texts are accompanied by new English translations by Stanley Appelbaum, who also made the selection, wrote the Introduction, and provided the footnotes.

Library of Congress Cataloging-in-Publication Data

Kinder- und Hausmärchen. English & German. Selections.
   Selected folktales = Ausgewählte Märchen : a dual-language book / [collected by] Jacob & Wilhelm Grimm ; edited and translated by Stanley Appelbaum.
      p. cm.
   "Includes unabridged German texts of 27 tales from the definitive seventh edition (Verlag der Dieterichschen Buchhandlung, Göttingen, 1857, 3 volumes) of the Kinder- und Hausmärchen . . . The German texts are accompanied by new English translations by Stanley Appelbaum, who also made the selection, wrote the Introduction, and provided the footnotes"—T.p. verso.
   ISBN-13: 978-0-486-42474-3 (pbk.)
   ISBN-10: 0-486-42474-X (pbk.)
   1. Fairy tales—Germany. I. Title: Ausgewählte Märchen. II. Grimm, Jacob, 1785–1863. III. Grimm, Wilhelm, 1786–1859. IV. Appelbaum, Stanley. V. Title.
GR166 .K54 2003
398.2'0943—dc21

2002041125

Manufactured in the United States by Courier Corporation
42474X08   2013
www.doverpublications.com

Contents

The numbers in brackets are the numbers of the tales in the definitive 1857 edition of the *Kinder- und Hausmärchen*.

Introduction   v

Der Froschkönig oder der eiserne Heinrich / The Frog King; or, Iron Henry [The Frog Prince] [1]   2/3

Märchen von einem, der auszog, das Fürchten zu lernen / Tale of One Who Set Out to Learn Fear [4]   8/9

Der Wolf und die sieben jungen Geißlein / The Wolf and the Seven Kids [5]   24/25

Brüderchen und Schwesterchen / Brother and Sister [11]   28/29

Rapunzel / Rampion [12]   38/39

Die drei Spinnerinnen / The Three Spinners [14]   44/45

Hänsel und Gretel / Hänsel and Gretel [15]   48/49

Strohhalm, Kohle und Bohne / Straw, Coal, and Bean [18]   60/61

Das tapfere Schneiderlein / The Brave Little Tailor [20]   64/65

Aschenputtel / Ash-Wallower [Cinderella] [21]   76/77

Frau Holle / Mother Holle [24]   90/91

Rotkäppchen / Little Red Hood [Little Red Riding Hood] [26]   94/95

Die Bremer Stadtmusikanten / The Bremen Town Musicians [27]   100/101

Tischchendeckdich, Goldesel und Knüppel aus dem Sack / Table-Set-Yourself, Gold-Donkey, and Cudgel-Out-of-the-Sack [36]   106/107

Daumesdick / Big-as-a-Thumb [Tom Thumb] [37]   122/123

Die sechs Schwäne / The Six Swans [49] 132/133

Dornröschen / Little Briar Rose [Sleeping Beauty] [50] 140/141

Sneewittchen / Snow White [53] 146/147

Rumpelstilzchen / Rumpelstiltskin [55] 160/161

Der goldene Vogel / The Golden Bird [57] 164/165

Allerleirauh / All-Kinds-of-Fur [Catskin; Cap o' Rushes] [65] 178/179

Sechse kommen durch die ganze Welt / Six Men Make Their Way in Life [71] 186/187

Hans im Glück / Hans in Luck [83] 194/195

Die Gänsemagd / The Goose Girl [89] 202/203

Die zertanzten Schuhe / The Danced-Out Shoes [133] 214/215

Schneeweißchen und Rosenrot / Snow White and Rose Red [161] 220/221

Der Meisterdieb / The Master Thief [192] 230/231

INTRODUCTION

The Brothers Grimm: Life and Work

The lives of the Brothers Grimm, Jacob (born 1785) and Wilhelm (born 1786) were so closely linked, and their careers so similar, that it is possible to sketch a joint biography. Though their father was a lawyer who filled responsible municipal posts, and their mother was from a cultured family, in the rank-conscious atmosphere of the pre-unification German petty princedoms their social position was humble, and more than once they were passed over for preferment, or required a special dispensation to get ahead.[1] Jacob and Wilhelm, always staunch Hessians, were born in the little town of Hanau, not far from Frankfurt-am-Main. In 1791 the family moved to Steinau, near Kassel.

After the head of the family died in 1796, the survivors were aided by the widow's sister, a lady-in-waiting at the court in Kassel, who arranged for Jacob and Wilhelm to attend a prestigious secondary school in that city beginning in 1798; Jacob graduated in 1802, and Wilhelm in 1803, but not before he had suffered a breakdown in his health—he was to be plagued by severe asthma all his life. Next, Jacob studied at the University of Marburg from 1802 to 1805 (Wilhelm was there from 1803 to 1806), following in his father's footsteps with a concentration on law. His most inspiring teacher was the great Friedrich Karl von Savigny (1779–1861), founder of the historical "school" of jurisprudence;[2] Savigny became an active mentor, training Jacob in archival research, instilling in him a love for the lore of the past, and, on a more personal but hardly less significant level, introducing him to his brother-in-law, the poet Clemens Brentano (1778–1842), who was to preside over the Grimms' early collecting of

---

1. There were five siblings, another of whom was to become famous: Ludwig Grimm (1790–1863) was an eminent artist.   2. This historical approach viewed the law as a body of material that had grown organically over the ages. Savigny, only six years older than Jacob, had begun teaching at Marburg a mere two years before Jacob arrived; he married a sister of the poet Brentano (not the famous Bettina) in 1803.

folktales. Jacob accompanied Savigny to Paris on an archival treasure hunt in 1805.

In 1806 Napoleon invaded Germany and abolished the thousand-year-old Holy Roman Empire; the following year, he set up his brother Jérôme as the puppet ruler of a large part of northwestern Germany, the so-called Kingdom of Westphalia. These events traumatized all patriotic Germans (leading to wars of liberation), and surely influenced the Grimms' lifelong mission of investigating and glorifying the German past. Both brothers had articles published for the first time in 1807. In 1808 (the year in which his mother died) Jacob became private librarian to Jérôme. In 1809 Wilhelm visited various cities, including Berlin, where he struck up a great friendship with Brentano's literary partner Achim von Arnim (1781–1831), who also encouraged the brothers to collect folklore. In 1811 each of the brothers had his first book-length work published.

By 1813 Jacob was working for the government of no-longer-occupied Hessia. In 1814 Wilhelm became a secretary at the Elector's library in Kassel; Jacob, who had been traveling in 1814 and 1815 (to Paris, to recover items looted from Germany, and to the Congress of Vienna), joined his brother there in a similar post in 1816. Meanwhile, the publication of the first edition of the folktales, *Kinder- und Hausmärchen* (Children's and Household Tales), begun with one volume in 1812, had been completed by a second volume in 1815. (The remaining sections of the Introduction are exclusively concerned with all aspects of the folktales.)

In 1816 and 1818 the Grimms published the two volumes of their invaluable *Deutsche Sagen* (German Legends; legends are tales that may be just as imaginative as *Märchen,* but are firmly linked to a specific locality, historical personality, or event). Among their major publications of the 1810s and 1820s are: Jacob's *Deutsche Grammatik* (German Grammar) of 1819 (continued in further volumes until 1837), in which he enunciated some of the fundamental sound-change "laws" in the development of the Indo-European languages; his *Deutsche Rechtsalterthüme* (German Legal Antiquities) of 1828; and Wilhelm's *Die deutsche Heldensage* (The German Heroic Legend) of 1829, generally considered his scholarly masterpiece. (Wilhelm concentrated on literature, whereas Jacob's interests were more wide-ranging.) In 1825 Wilhelm married one of the young women in the Wild family, who had been friends of the brothers for many years and had provided a number of their earliest folktales; Jacob, a confirmed bachelor, moved in with them.

After a decided snub in Kassel in 1829, when neither brother received a well-merited promotion at their library, in 1830 they both accepted an invitation to teach at the major University of Göttingen. The most important product of the seven Göttingen years was Jacob's mammoth *Deutsche Mythologie* (Teutonic Mythology) of 1835. In 1837, in a *cause célèbre*, the brothers became two of the "Göttingen Seven," a group of professors who were expelled after denouncing the revocation of an 1833 liberal charter by the new king of Hanover, Ernst August II;[3] they went into "exile" at Kassel, outside the boundaries of Hanover.

In 1840 both brothers were invited to Berlin, and they moved there in 1841. In that bustling cosmopolitan city, their home for the rest of their lives, they were members of the distinguished Prussian Royal Academy of Sciences, and lectured at the University. They both continued to contribute scholarly books and articles, to review new publications in their fields, including folklore, and to correspond with learned men all over Europe. As early as 1838 they had begun working jointly on a vast German dictionary; the first volume of the famous *Deutsches Wörterbuch* appeared in 1852; the protracted (but well-worth-the-wait) publication wasn't completed until 1960.

Jacob traveled to Italy in 1843, to Denmark and Sweden in 1844. After the contagious Parisian revolution of 1848, which toppled King Louis-Philippe at home and then spread to a number of other European countries, Jacob was a vocal member of the major liberal political convention at the Paulskirche in Frankfurt; but after the swift and brutal stamping out of the movement in German lands, he abandoned politics. Both brothers died in Berlin, Wilhelm in 1859, Jacob in 1863.

The Grimm Folktale Collection

The *Kinder- und Hausmärchen* collection is probably the best-known German-language book worldwide. It has been translated into more

---

3. Hanover (Hannover in German) was an electorate of the Holy Roman Empire from 1692 until the dissolution of the Empire in 1806. After Napoleon was ousted from Germany, it was a separate kingdom from 1814 until the unification of Germany in 1866. A seventeenth-century marriage into English royalty led to joint kingships over England and Hanover from George I through William IV. In 1837 William's brother, the Duke of Cumberland, succeeded him as king of Hanover only (Hanoverian law didn't recognize female succession), while William's niece Victoria was given the throne of England—occupying it for 64 years.

than 70 languages; it has influenced storytellers and collectors of all lands; it has provided reference models and frameworks for all professional folklorists; it has inspired retellings and adaptations in all public media; and it has become an integral part of the childhood experience of millions.

Through Jacob Grimm's mentor Savigny, the brothers became part of what is known as the Second (German) Romantic School, a group of like-minded writers chiefly associated with the University of Heidelberg (the group included Brentano, Arnim, Joseph Görres, and Joseph von Eichendorff; the movement was active from 1804 to 1809).[4] Brentano and Arnim are most famous for their monumental verse collection *Des Knaben Wunderhorn* (The Boy's Magic Horn; published in 1806 and 1808), which contains the texts of real German folksongs, as well as texts heavily altered or even manufactured out of folk-style whole cloth by the compilers. The *Wunderhorn* creators were interested in following up with a collection of prose folktales, and employed the young Brothers Grimm as scouts and collectors. The Grimms handed over a certain amount of material to Brentano, who finally decided not to pursue the project himself. But Brentano and Arnim encouraged the Grimms to persevere on their own, and eventually the *Kinder- und Hausmärchen* became a more successful folklore product of the Second Romantic School than the *Wunderhorn* or Tieck's stories in a folk vein.

The first edition of the KHM[5] appeared in two volumes, one in 1812, containing 86 tales, and the other in 1815, with an additional 70 tales; both volumes were published by a schoolbook firm in Berlin, the Realschulbuchhandlung; the original edition of 900 sold poorly, perhaps because of weak distribution, perhaps for other reasons offered below. The tide began to turn with the second, one-volume edition of 1819, which contained 170 tales and had a separate section of annotations. The third edition, 1837, contained 177 tales; the fourth, 1840, had 187 tales; the fifth, 1843, had 203 tales, as did the sixth, 1850. The definitive seventh edition, the last in the brothers' lifetime, was published in Göttingen by the Verlag der Dieterichschen Buchhandlung, 1857, in three volumes (the third being a separate volume of annotations). The 1857 edition, the textual source for this

---

4. The First Romantic School, 1797–1801, was associated with the University of Jena, and included Friedrich and August Wilhelm Schlegel, Ludwig Tieck, Friedrich Wilhelm Schelling, Friedrich Schleiermacher, and Novalis.   5. This convenient abbreviation of *Kinder- und Hausmärchen*, familiar to folklorists all over the world, will be used for the remainder of this Introduction.

Dover volume, contains 211 folktales, numbered 1 to 200 with an additional no. 151°, and ten religious legends. The Grimms' folktale corpus also includes 28 tales dropped from editions subsequent to the first; six fragments; and numerous items recounted at length or in part, or merely summarized, in their annotations. In 1825 Wilhelm published a shorter edition (Kleine Ausgabe) of the 50 tales most suitable for children (these included the most popular stories); naturally this shorter volume sold even better than the main one, and enjoyed ten editions by 1858.

The Grimms did not pioneer the folktale-collecting field in Germany. Not to mention the innumerable folk motifs that inevitably found their way into much earlier literature of all types, at least since the late stages of the eighteenth-century Enlightenment (*Aufklärung*) and "Storm and Stress" (*Sturm und Drang*) movement there had been voices calling out for the collection of folklore (notably Johann Gottfried Herder, 1744–1803), and extensively adapted or totally invented folktales, often heavily indebted to the prevailing French school, had been published singly or in volumes. The outstanding pre-Grimm collection is that of Johann Karl August Musäus, *Volksmährchen der Deutschen* (1782–86). (In addition, such members of the First and Second Romantic Schools as Tieck, Novalis, and Brentano had written excellent *Kunstmärchen*, "artistic folktales" that were obviously the product of elegant literary craftsmen.)

The Brothers Grimm, however, by their fresh approach, gave new life and impetus to folktale collecting everywhere, not merely in Germany—and yet some of their practices, which have only become known through scholarly research in the last few decades, dismay modern practitioners. For one thing, they destroyed their raw notes; it was only the preservation among Brentano's papers of the early batch of material they sent to him that has allowed twentieth-century scholars to investigate their sources and methods more thoroughly. They never credited their sources sufficiently. Even more significant is the fact that, contrary to some readers' notions, they never collected in the field, let alone from humble rural or proletarian folk in the field. Many of the tales were told to them by middle-class friends (who may possibly have heard them from nannies or servants), and some of these friends were of Huguenot ancestry, with a knowledge of French, and thus even more susceptible than the average German to French influences (since the late seventeenth century, the period of Perrault, a long series of French writers, especially women, had dominated the fairy-tale market in Europe; some of these writers will

be mentioned in the commentary on the individual tales in the next section of this Introduction). Even the now celebrated Dorothea Viehmann, the source of some of the best Grimm tales, though she indeed was a village inhabitant (from Zwehrn, near Kassel), was the wife of a well-to-do master tailor, an artisan entrepreneur. The Grimms received other stories in written form in response to circulars and other requests for material. Even more drastically, they didn't hesitate to appropriate already published tales, new or old, that they considered suitable for their collection, from medieval Latin poems to items in current magazines and volumes.

Jacob was the guiding spirit behind the first edition of 1812–15; this rather more pedantic of the brothers didn't conceive the collection as children's reading matter, despite its title, and included some horrific reports of village blood baths, as well as some tales he didn't recognize at the time as being direct retellings of French ones; this point of view must have contributed to the slow sales of the first edition. Beginning with the second, of 1819, the more literary Wilhelm more or less took over the brothers' folktale publishing for the rest of their lives. He had a child audience more clearly in mind, he weeded out the duds from the first edition, and he rewrote some of the material that remained; in fact, he never stopped rewriting, adapting, and recombining tales, so that the definitive edition of 1857 is his masterpiece as an author and literary editor, but is furthest removed from "pure sources" from a folklorist's standpoint. Nevertheless, every skillful teller of folktales, oral or written, contributes his (more often: her) own "spin," and literary merit is nothing to be despised.[6] (Many European governments have honored their truly gifted national storytellers, and well-known folktale bards have even entertained front-line troops.)

Not all the Grimm tales are magical tales of transformations, wish-fulfilling objects, and other preternatural elements. Their collection also includes animal tales, tales of animated objects, cumulative tales, anecdotes, jokes, aetiological stories, tall tales, farcical tales of numbskulls and others, tales of horror, religious and moral tales, and more. Among the characters are gnomes and dwarfs who dwell and/or labor underground, and there are also brownies who aid cottagers at night,

---

6. Some current folklorists who posthumously rap the Grimms' knuckles with plastic rulers are themselves guilty of the amazing belief that any version of a tale is as good as any other; they fail to recognize obvious retellings from standard sources, and they are evidently only happy when recording the stammerings of untalented narrators who have half-forgotten what they never learned correctly and are blissfully unaware of how they are mangling the story line.

but there are virtually *no fairies* as fairies are understood in the French folktale tradition.[7] The first English translation of the Grimm stories (1823–26) called them "fairy tales" because the French school had made that term so popular (and there *were* obvious plot resemblances), but it was a misnomer that has unfortunately stuck to these tales out of inertia (and publishers' unwillingness to sacrifice "recognition value" in their labeling); all self-respecting recent translations use the terms "tale" or "folktale."

The Grimms were convinced that folktales were largely based on (or: debased from) ancient mythology. In some cases, such as "Frau Holle," they can hardly be contradicted, but their overall view is now outmoded, and these days there are any number of competing explanations of folktale elements. The sorry political situation in Germany in the Grimms' pre-unification era must always be kept in mind: their belief that the tales represented an unbroken tradition dating back to the "childhood of humanity" endowed the tales with a pan-German unifying force. In addition, their trust in a monolithic ultimate source for the stories in the remote German past justified in their eyes their sometimes drastic adaptation and recombination ("contamination," in folklore terms) of their immediate sources.

In the early and middle nineteenth century the Grimms' collection was not the most popular set of local stories in Germany. Their star went into the ascendant toward the end of the century, and by 1900 the KHM was second only to the Bible in German book sales. During the Weimar Republic, their tales were sometimes viewed as dangerously jingoistic, and indeed they were heavy-handedly exploited by the Nazis as Aryan treasures; this led to their being banned in West Germany for some time after World War II; in East Germany they were reprinted in softened versions by sanctimonious Communists.

Stylistically, in German, the tales are delightful. Wilhelm Grimm was a skilled craftsman who deliberately simplified vocabulary and syntax (though he allowed a sprinkling of picturesque regional and archaic words and expressions)[8] to achieve the folk atmosphere his researches had made him so familiar with. He also enlivened his versions

---

7. Even where real fairies are prominent in other versions of well-known tale-types, they are absent in Grimm: the Grimms' Cinderella has no fairy godmother (the transformation of the heroine is effectuated differently), and their Sleeping Beauty receives her natural gifts from "wise-women" (presented as a sort of benevolent sybils in the service of royalty).   8. In the 1857 edition there are 20 tales not in standard ("High") German, but in various dialects; none of these has been included in this volume. (Some of the standard-German tales include verses in dialect.)

with lots of colorful dialogue. Countless German children have learned to read by way of the Grimm stories, and pedagogically these tales are also a good approach to the language for foreign beginners.

The Individual Selections in This Volume

"Der Froschkönig oder der eiserne Heinrich." Already appeared in the first volume of the first edition (1812). The Grimms' own annotations say that the tale came from Hessia (Hessen); more specifically, scholars have discovered that it was told to them by the Wild family[9] in Kassel (the father was a druggist; they were personal friends of Jacob and Wilhelm, and Wilhelm was to marry one of the daughters); the interpolated verses, however, are from earlier sources. Amphibians or reptiles as guardians of bodies of water occur in many world folktales (another frog appears at the beginning of "Dornröschen," in this volume); in their annotations the Grimms indicated a fairly close Scottish parallel to the Frog Prince plot. But, even more fundamentally, this tale is an example of a beast-marriage type most famously represented by the Cupid and Psyche story in the *Metamorphoses* of Apuleius (Roman, 2nd century A.D.) and by "La belle et la bête" (Beauty and the Beast) by Marie Leprince (or: Le Prince) de Beaumont (1711–1780); psychologically, these stories reflect the mindset of a virgin female afraid of marriage and intercourse. The fact that the Grimm heroine is repeatedly called "youngest daughter" (this is irrelevant to the Grimm plot) would point to the existence of longer versions in which her elder sisters fail to come to terms with the frog. The Iron Henry part of the story, loosely tacked on at the end, is obviously a separable motif; it has very old parallels in folklore.

"Märchen von einem, der auszog, das Fürchten zu lernen." An earlier version, containing just a few of the episodes in the castle and lacking the motif of learning to fear, appeared in the 1812 volume under the title "Gut Kegel- und Kartenspiel" (Good Games of Bowls and Cards; source of this version unclear). The 1819 second edition contained the revised and expanded version that was retained (it had already been printed by Wilhelm in the magazine *Die Wünschelruthe* [The Magic Wand], published by the Haxthausen family of

---

9. For simplicity, the present commentary refrains from specifying family members who supplied stories even when this is known.

Westphalia, friends of the Grimms); the Grimms got this second version from a teacher in Kassel, Ferdinand Siebert, but subsequently added material gleaned from Dorothea Viehmann and others (their annotations, which seldom credit individuals, merely state that the sources were in Mecklenburg, Hessia, and Zwehrn). Similar plot elements in the Grimm collection occur in "Bruder Lustig" (Brother Merry; KHM 81) and "De Spielhansl" (Johnny the Gambler; KHM 82). The boy who didn't understand fear (this is itself a well-known motif, which Wagner adapted in his opera *Siegfried*) is one of folklore's numerous "unpromising heroes" who ultimately succeed (other examples in this anthology occur in "Das tapfere Schneiderlein" and "Der goldene Vogel"); the motif of competition between brothers goes back at least to early-A.D. India. The moving bed in the castle is a feature of medieval courtly romances; Gawa(i)n has a similar experience in Wolfram von Eschenbach's *Parzival,* ca. 1200.

"Der Wolf und die sieben jungen Geißlein." Already in the 1812 volume. The Grimms said it was from "the Main [river] area"; the specific source was the Hassenpflug (or: Hasenpflug) family in Kassel, friends of the Grimms since 1808 (their sister, Lotte Grimm, married a son of the family in 1822). This tale comes from old fable literature, a particularly noteworthy version being that of Jean de La Fontaine, "Le loup, la chèvre et le chevreau" (The Wolf, the Nanny-goat, and the Kid; Book IV, no. 15, 1668). Folklorists include this tale, as well as the Grimms' version of Little Red Riding Hood (in this volume, and also a story told by the Hassenpflugs) as examples of the universal Big Swallow motif, in which victims are gulped down whole. The stones sewed into the wolf's belly in both tales are reminiscent of the stones in Greek mythology fed to Kronos (in Rome: Saturn) by his wife when she didn't want him to eat their children. The Disney cartoon *Three Little Pigs* (1933) owes a great deal to the tale under discussion. Cultural historians are amused by the *gemütlich,* bourgeois interior furnishings of the goats' home in the Grimm story.

"Brüderchen und Schwesterchen."[10] This tale appeared in 1812, but was expanded for the 1819 edition; the source both times

---

10. Both nouns bear the diminutive suffix -*chen,* and so the tale (and, indeed, even the tale-type that folklorists have named after it) has been called "Little Brother and Little Sister" in English. The "little" has been omitted in this translation, not merely to avoid tediousness (it occurs so often), but also because what the -*chen* conveys here in German is not relative size or age (the immediate connotation of "little sister" in English is "younger sister") but endearment. (Indications in the tale itself are that the girl is the elder sibling.)

was the Hassenpflug family (the Grimms: "Main area"). Among the folktale motifs in this story are the medieval Genoveva (Genevieve) legend (an unjustly disowned wife and her baby live in the forest with a kindly deer), the substituted bride, and the mother returning from the dead to care for her child. The most notable literary antecedent is the story "Nennillo e Nennella" (V, 8) in the *Pentameron* (or: *Cunto de li cunti;* 1634–36) by Giambattista Basile (in Neapolitan dialect). A twentieth-century Hungarian version contains some elements that may possibly be closer to the "primitive" original form of this extremely widespread story: the children leave home to avoid being eaten by their father, who has accidentally acquired a taste for human flesh; the only water sources in the forest are accumulations in the tracks of various animals, and whoever drinks from a given track turns into that animal (the stepmother is not responsible for this *or* for the bride substitution, which is all to the good: she's much too overworked in the Grimm version, and the Hassenpflugs, who also supplied the Grimms with "Sneewittchen," may have been influenced by the omnipresent queen in that story).

"Rapunzel." In the 1812 volume. The Grimms said they used an oral source, but scholars claim that they found the story in the 1798 volume *Kleine Romane* (Short Novels) by Friedrich Schulz (moreover, Schulz derived *his* story from "Persinette" in *Les fées* [The Fairies], 1692, by Charlotte-Rose de la Force). An even older antecedent is Basile's story "Petrosinella" (II, 1). The French and Italian heroines are named after parsley. The term *Rapunzel* has been translated into English in various ways, sometimes as "rapunzel lettuce" or "lamb's lettuce"; but surely "rampion" (an herbaceous flowering plant of which the stems can be eaten in salads) is correct, because the garden in question is an ornamental one, not a truck garden. Note: the illustrations in children's books that show the sorceress and the prince climbing up by means of flowing hair are incorrect; it should be braided.

"Die drei Spinnerinnen." A version of this tale, called "Von dem bösen Flachsspinnen" (On the Obnoxious Spinning of Flax), told by the Hassenpflugs, appeared in 1812, but was replaced in 1819 by the present story, as told by Paul Wigand, a schoolmate of the Grimms from Kassel (their own annotations say: from the Princedom of Corvei, with elements from Hessia). A notable literary antecedent is Basile's "Le sette cotenelle" (The Seven Bacon Rinds; IV, 4). The popularity of the story in more recent folktale collections may stem directly from the Grimms' version. The setting of tasks is an

immemorial folktale motif; just think of Hercules. Other task-setting Grimm stories in this anthology alone are: "Das tapfere Schneiderlein," "Aschenputtel," "Rumpelstilzchen," "Der goldene Vogel," and "Der Meisterdieb."

"Hänsel und Gretel." The definitive 1857 version, credited by the Grimms to various sources in Hessia, was actually a combination of a story told by the Wild family, possibly as early as 1809, with the story "Das Eierkuchenhäuslein" (The Little House Made of Omelets) in August Stöber's *Elsässisches Volksbüchlein* (Little Book of Alsatian Folktales) of 1842. Like "Brüderchen und Schwesterchen," it is a tale of deserted children, this time with outspoken cannibalism. A very early literary antecedent occurs in the *Gartengesellschaft* (Garden Party) of Martin Montanus, ca. 1559. The above-mentioned "Nennillo e Nennella" by Basile also counts as an antecedent, as does the very beginning of Charles Perrault's Tom Thumb story, "Le Petit Poucet," in *Histoires ou contes du temps passé, avec des moralités* (Stories or Tales of Olden Days, with Morals; 1697). There are various printed sources besides Stöber for the edible-house motif, which scholars believe entered the literature in late Enlightenment days. It is needless to recall the immense popularity of this Grimm story, enhanced by Engelbert Humperdinck's 1893 opera.

"Strohhalm, Kohle und Bohne." In the 1812 volume, collected from the Wild family (Grimms: "from Kassel"). Beginning with the third (1837) edition, they also indicated as sources old Latin poems and fable 97 in the 1548 *Esopus* by Burkard Waldis. This is one of several Grimm stories about inanimate objects, or small or barnyard animals, living or traveling together; some meet misfortune through carelessness, as here, others achieve success aggressively, like the Bremen town musicians.

"Das tapfere Schneiderlein." A shorter version was printed in 1812, the definitive version from 1819 on. The Grimms declared that half the tale was from Hessia, the other half from *Der Wegkürtzer* (The Journey-Shortener; i.e., pleasurable reading while traveling) by Martin Montanus, ca. 1557. The clear dividing line between the two parts comes after the tailor's escape from the giants' cave (an episode strikingly reminiscent of the Polyphemus adventure in the *Odyssey*). Details of the story are found in many old sources; the Grimm tale itself has been widely imitated. It received a new boost in popularity in the United States (at least) from the 1938 Disney cartoon starring Mickey Mouse as the tailor.

"Aschenputtel." Appeared in the 1812 volume, as told by an old

woman in a hospital in Marburg. From the 1819 edition on, the story contained additional elements contributed by Dorothea Viehmann (the Grimms' statement: based on three sources in Hessia, one in Zwehrn). Cinderella is the world's most popular tale-type. Very similar stories in the Grimm collection alone are "Allerleirauh," in this anthology, and "Einäuglein, Zweiäuglein und Dreiäuglein" (Little One Eye, Little Two Eyes, and Little Three Eyes; KHM 130). The archetypal literary antecedent is Basile's "La gatta cenerentola" (The Cat Dirty with Ashes; I, 6). The version with the greatest currency nowadays is Charles Perrault's from the 1697 *Contes du temps passé*. In striking contrast to Perrault (and some other versions), in Grimm there is no fairy godmother, the sisters are beautiful (in Perrault they are elegant, but not described physically), and there are three sets of gowns and slippers, none of the slippers being of glass (an invention of Perrault's?).[11] Just as *Hamlet* has humorously been called a vast collection of quotations, so the Grimms' version of Cinderella can be seen as a veritable showcase of different folktale motifs: the humble gift requested by the youngest daughter as her father sets out on a journey seems to be more in place in the above-mentioned "Beauty and the Beast," where it sets the entire plot in motion (in "Aschenputtel" it does provide the mechanism for the heroine's transformation, in the absence of a fairy godmother); the picking out of the spilled lentils by the birds usually occurs in folktales about grateful animals repaying a human benefactor; and so on. The *Aschen-* in the German heroine's name indubitably means "ashes" (the "ash" prefix to a name or noun frequently designates a drudge, or someone sulking asocially, in such Nordic literature as the Icelandic sagas and Scandinavian folktales; and such Scottish equivalents as Ashiepattle may have been influenced by Viking occupiers), but the *-puttel* is not so clear.[12] The translation in this volume, Ash-Wallower, is based on what the Grimms thought the term meant: they derived it from the local Hessian verb *putteln* (possibly cognate with English "puddle"). In two other Grimm tales, *Aschenputtel* is used as a common noun for a (female) drudge or scullion. In earlier German literature, terms equivalent to "ash-person" (the commonest is *Aschenbrödel*) referred to a male (as in many of the Scandinavian examples), and some scholars believe that the change of sex in Grimm was due to a progressive

---

11. Incidentally, there is a story about an Egyptian king searching for the obviously beautiful owner of a dainty shoe that came into his possession, and marrying her, in the *Varia Historia* of Aelian (Claudius Aelianus; second century A.D.)   12. A truly drastic etymology based on a modern Greek term has even been suggested.

feminization of folktales based on sociological factors; this is dubious, however.

"Frau Holle." The Grimms' source indication as "from Hessia and Westphalia" reflects the fact that in the 1819 edition more material was added to the original Wild family contribution as first published in the 1812 volume. In Teutonic mythology Holle (or: Holde, Hulda, Helle, Holl) was a sky goddess (hence the feather-snow) who was also associated with the underworld and with bodies of water (the entrance to her abode was down a well—shades of the rabbit hole in *Alice!*); she was also maternal, presiding over the hearth, and diabolical, associated with the Wild Host (stormy meteorological phenomena); in the later folk mentality, she was sometimes a kind of bogey to frighten children with (cf. her long teeth in this story). Though Frau Holle figures so prominently in the Grimm tale, it is basically one of the thousand or so exemplars (known since at least the fifteenth century) of the tale-type contrasting a good and a bad little girl. Basile's story "Le doie pizzelle" (The Two Pies; IV, 7) includes this element (as well as a substituted bride and a Goose Girl–like strand). Other likely influences on the Grimm version are Perrault's "Les fées" in *Contes du temps passé*, later French stories, and Benedikte Naubert's "Der kurze Mantel" (The Short Cape) in her *Neue Volksmährchen der Deutschen* (New Folktales of the Germans) of 1789.

"Rotkäppchen." In the 1812 volume, as told by the Hassenpflug family; even the Grimms acknowledged the influence of Perrault's "Le Petit Chaperon Rouge" (Little Red Hood, in *Contes du temps passé*), and Ludwig Tieck's closet drama *Leben und Tod des kleinen Rothkäppchens* (Life and Death of Little Red Hood; 1800), in addition to one of their code terms for the Hassenpflugs, "Main area." The heroine of these stories always wore a mere hood until the first English translation of Perrault in 1729 introduced her durable "riding hood" (but why?). The Perrault version ends abruptly with the definitive deglutition of both the grandmother and the girl; it was Tieck who brought the hunter (or: gamekeeper) into the story. The Grimm version is unique in their collection in adding a second adventure (for the two ladies and another wolf); this appendage was related by a different member of the Hassenpflug family. Like the Grimm story of the wolf and the young goats, this is a Big Swallow tale (and another example of a wolf masquerading). Modern folklorists, especially those psychoanalytically inclined, have had a field day with Little Red Riding Hood, evoking werewolves, menstruation (the red hood), and an initiatory rite for seamstresses.

"Die Bremer Stadtmusikanten." First appeared in the 1819 edition. According to the Grimms, a mixture of two sources in the Paderborn area; actually, a mixture of one story from the Haxthausen family and one from Dorothea Viehmann. Animal stories were probably told in the Old Stone Age. Setting aside the ancient Aesopic corpus, there are major medieval and Renaissance models for this particular story: in the Latin poem *Ysengrimus* (ca. 1150, a forerunner of the *Roman de Renard* cycle), a group of animals take up residence in a cabin in the woods, and in Georg Rollenhagen's *Froschmeuseler* (Tale of Frogs and Mice; 1571) a gang of domestic animals attack and occupy a similar cabin (these references are in the Grimms' notes). Other Grimm tales of bonded small animals and/or inanimate objects that assail people are "Das Lumpengesindel" (The Bunch of Bums; KHM 10) and "Herr Korbes" (KHM 41). Faithful animals ill used by man are a feature of another, enormously popular tale-type in which they spitefully defend the snake that wants to kill a man who has warmed it under his shirt.

"Tischchendeckdich, Goldesel und Knüppel aus dem Sack." A Hassenplug story published in the 1812 volume (Grimms: "from Hessia"). This is an excellent example of the widespread tale-types about miraculous wish-fulfilling objects replaced by inoperative substitutes, about inexhaustible supplies of food, and about three brothers setting out in life, the last of whom is the most successful. Similar plot elements occur in KHM 54, "Der Ranzen, das Hütlein und das Hörnlein" (The Knapsack, the Little Hat, and the Little Horn) and in KHM 130, "Einäuglein, Zweiäuglein und Dreiäuglein" (Little One Eye, Little Two Eyes, and Little Three Eyes). Such stories already appear in the Buddhist birth legends (*Jātakas*) by the fifth century A.D. Basile's first story, "L'uerco" (The Ogre, or Wild Man) is a notable forerunner of the Grimm version, and Perrault's 1694 verse tale "Peau d'Ane" (Donkey-Skin) includes a gold-defecating donkey. The goat story in the Grimm version, though used nicely as a frame, is obviously irrelevant to the main plot; at the end, it exemplifies the tale-type in which an innocuous creature terrifies more ferocious, but stupid animals.

"Daumesdick." In the 1819 edition, from an informant in "Mühlheim" (today, the suburb of Cologne called Köln-Mülheim). The Grimm collection includes a second, quite different Tom Thumb story, "Daumerlings Wanderschaft" (The Travels of Thumbling; KHM 45). Tales of tiny people date back to very ancient times (cf. the Pygmies mentioned in the *Iliad*). Sayings about Tom Thumb types

occur in sixteenth-century literature, and Reginald Scot's 1584 *Discoverie of Witchcraft* mentions such a person; chapbooks helped to preserve the subject matter in the following centuries. Perrault's "Le Petit Poucet" is very different from either of the two Grimm tales; his Tom Thumb story is a combination of deserted-child and giant-killer themes. Caroline (or: Karoline) Stahl (1776–1837), an important German predecessor of the Grimms, published a Tom Thumb story. The Grimms provide many other parallels in their annotations.

"Die sechs Schwäne." In the 1812 volume. Grimms: "from Hessia." Actually a combination of a Wild family story with the story "Die sieben Schwäne" in the 1801 volume *Feenmärchen* (Fairy Tales). Extremely similar shape-shifting tales in the Grimms' own collection are "Die zwölf Brüder" (The Twelve Brothers; KHM 9) and "Die sieben Raben" (The Seven Ravens; KHM 25). The bird-people motif is very old and literally universal (the Japanese Nō play *Hagoromo* [The Feather Robe; fourteenth century] and the Swan Lake story instantly spring to mind). The oldest written European version seems to be that of Jean de Haute-Seille in his Latin-language *Dolopathos* (ca. 1200), in which the motif is already connected with the later Swan Knight theme (Lohengrin; the *French Crusade Cycle;* etc.).[13] The Grimm tale under discussion also includes the well-known folktale themes of children in concealment and a girl seeking her lost brothers, a theme exploited in Basile's "Le sette palommielle" (The Seven Little Doves; IV, 8). (Versions of the story in which the girl, the last-born, is to inherit her father's entire fortune have been seen as a residual trace of ultimogeniture and a matrilineal society.) The statement in the Grimm story that the swan-boys' cabin is a den of thieves leads nowhere and is apparently due to confusion with other woodland huts in folktales.

"Dornröschen." In the 1812 volume, as told by the Hassenpflug family, but altered in the 1819 edition to resemble Perrault's Sleeping Beauty version ("La belle au bois dormant," *Contes du temps passé,* 1697) even more closely (the Grimm annotation: "from Hessia"). The Grimms were convinced that this story was a bit of flotsam coming from the wreck of Teutonic mythology, and connected it with Brünnhilde's magic sleep after she was pricked by the soporific thorn, and with the protective wall of fire around her. Modern interpreters point to an allegory of seasonal changes; the fear of loss of virginity

---

13. English translations of this tale and others from *Dolopathos* may be found in: Appelbaum (ed. & trans.), *Medieval Tales and Stories*, Dover, 2000.

(with the spindle as an obvious phallic symbol); etc. Apparently, the oldest written version is an episode in the vast French prose romance *Perceforest* (ca. 1340). Basile has a version of the story, "Sole, Luna e Talia" (Sun, Moon, and Talia; V, 5). Perrault was the direct source for the Grimm version, but there are two main differences: Perrault's story goes on and on after the Grimms' ends, and the Grimms' is much more concise and homespun. (The awakening of a dormant princess by her lover is also to be found in the Grimms' "Sneewittchen," in this volume.) Folklorists have noted the resemblance between the neglected wise-woman's actions and those of Eris (Discord) at the wedding of Peleus and Thetis, which eventually led to the Trojan War. Preternatural birth gifts and kisses that dissolve enchantments are stock folktale motifs.

"Sneewittchen." In the 1812 volume, as told by the Hassenpflug family in 1808, but altered from 1819 on; the Grimms: "from several sources in Hessia." Ever since Disney's first feature-length cartoon, *Snow White and the Seven Dwarfs* (1937), this has been the most popular worldwide of all the folktales originating in the Grimm collection. The standard German form of the heroine's name (which actually occurs in another tale in this anthology) would be "Schneeweiß-chen," but the Low (Northern) German form was already indelibly associated with this story by 1812. It is easy to recognize such standard folktale characters as the compassionate executioner and the subterranean dwarfs, here guardian spirits of mines. The three drops of blood on the snow are strikingly reminiscent of a passage in Wolfram's *Parzival*.

"Rumpelstilzchen." In the 1812 volume, as told by the Wild family in 1808, but from 1819 on combined with material from the Hassenpflug family and others. The Grimms credit, without names, four sources in Hessia, but also mention such literary forerunners as Caroline Stahl, the Baroness d'Aulnoy (Marie Catherine Le Jumel de Barneville, ca. 1650–1705; from a section of her book *La chatte blanche* [The White Cat]), and Marie-Jeanne L'Héritier (1664–1734; a niece of Perrault; from her story "Ricdin-Ricdon"). The little man's name in Grimm is taken from Johann Fischart's *Gargantua* (1582 edition). Some folklorists believe that this tale-type had its origins in Britain, where the humorous villain is generally called Tom-Tit-Tot. Among the folktale motifs in the Grimm version are: the malicious dwarf (see also "Schneeweißchen und Rosenrot," in this volume); the guessing of a name, which is sometimes a ridiculous one; the claiming of a new-born infant (this has led some commentators to view

Rumpelstiltskin as a demon of childhood diseases); and distress caused by spinning (compare "Die drei Spinnerinnen," in this volume), a motif with a vast extension.

"Der goldene Vogel." In the 1812 volume, as told by the Wild family, but from 1819 on combined with material from Dorothea Viehmann and others; Grimms: "from Hessia." A very early printed version appears in the *Scala coeli* (Ladder [or: Stairway] to Heaven) of Johann Gabius, 1480. The Grimm story is amazingly close to what is perhaps the most famous Russian folktale, "Prince Ivan, the Firebird, and the Gray Wolf" (the source of Stravinsky's ballet; in Russia, the wolf assumes the role of the Grimms' fox), from Aleksandr Nikolaevich Afanas'iev's *Narodnïe Russkie skazki* (Russian Folktales; 1855–1863); Russian folklorists recognize the potential influence of Western European sources on their story, which has other Slavic counterparts. Among the well-known folktale motifs in the Grimm version are: the unpromising hero, often a third brother; the grateful animal helper (in this particular case, also enchanted) that aids a helpless hero; the accumulation of acquisitions through tests and adventures; and the treacherous brothers, companions, or associates who take undue credit for an exploit and enforce silence on the maiden in their power.

"Allerleirauh." In the 1812 volume. The Grimms: "from Hessia and the Paderborn area." Actually from the Wild family and from a subplot of the novel *Schilly* by Karl Nehrlich (1798). This is one of the tales of a beauty disguised as an ugly creature that folklorists categorize under the tale-type Catskin or Cap o' Rushes. A notable predecessor of the Grimm version is Perrault's verse tale "Peau d'Ane" (Donkey-Skin) of 1694; a very important difference is that, whereas Grimm's heroine makes her own decisions in the face of her father's lust, Perrault's has a fairy godmother to advise her. Even earlier versions of the tale appear in Gianfrancesco Straparola's *Le piacevoli notti* (1550–53)[14] and in Basile ("L'orsa" [The She-Bear]; II, 6). After Allerleirauh arrives at the strange palace, her story is very similar to Cinderella's. The cubbyhole under the stairs where she lodges is reminiscent of the plight of Saint Alexis in the group of stories concerning him (a very early version is a French narrative poem of the mid eleventh century).[15]

---

14. This famous collection also includes the earliest known version of the Puss in Boots story, which may have been invented by Straparola.   15. A translation of the Saint Alexis story, as it appears in the *Gesta Romanorum* (Deeds of the Romans; ca. 1300), may be found in the work cited in footnote 13.

"Sechse kommen durch die ganze Welt." In the 1819 edition, as told by Dorothea Viehmann (in the Grimms' code: "from Zwehrn"). This story, and the Grimms' "Die sechs Diener" (The Six Servants; KHM 134), are examples of the universal tale-type of the band of companions who possess remarkable talents. Basile has two similar stories, "Lo polece" (The Flea) and "Lo gnorante" (The Ignorant Man). The Grimms' foot race against a princess, with her hand in marriage at stake, is reminiscent of the race with Atalanta recounted by Ovid in his *Metamorphoses* (and by several other ancient writers), and naturally also recalls the wooing of the athletic Brünnhilde in the *Nibelungenlied* (ca. 1200) and other medieval Germanic texts.

"Hans im Glück." In the 1819 edition. The Grimms acknowledged that they had taken this story from a printed source by August Wernicke, in the belief that he had recorded an oral tale; actually, Wernicke's story, "Hans Wolgemut" (Johnny Cheerful), published in the above-mentioned magazine *Die Wünschelruthe* in 1818, was probably his own invention. This Grimm story is an example of their nonmagical, humorous tales, often dealing with a "noodle" or a "numbskull"; the most important other such tale in their collection is "Die goldene Gans" (The Golden Goose; KHM 64). "Hans im Glück" became wildly successful in Germany, and was frequently printed separately. Its folksy dialogue and assortment of village characters are quite endearing.

"Die Gänsemagd." In the 1815 second volume of the first edition, as told by Dorothea Viehmann (Grimms' code: "from Zwehrn"). It has been compared thematically to another Grimm tale, "Die weiße und die schwarze Braut" (The White Bride and the Black; KHM 135). It has some very primitive-appearing features: the oath under the open sky, the talking head, and the archaic morphology and syntax in the verses. Among the celebrated folktale motifs it includes: the substituted bride; the beauty of the heroine that is concealed under duress but inevitably becomes known; and the Speaking Horsehead motif (brilliantly exploited by Jean Cocteau in his 1927 play *Orphée*). Folklorists have linked this Grimm tale to a group of Scandinavian stories of unchaste brides. In their annotations the Grimms point out that the name of the horse, Falada, resembles the names of steeds ridden by Roland and William of Orange in medieval epic poems and their derivatives.

"Die zertanzten Schuhe." In the 1815 volume. The Grimms gave "the Münster region" as their source. Actually, they acquired the

story from the highly cultured Droste-Hülshoff family, who belonged to the same "Bökendorf Circle" as the Haxthausen family. (Annette von Droste-Hülshoff, 1797–1848, was the greatest German woman poet of the nineteenth century, and perhaps of all time.)

"Schneeweißchen und Rosenrot." First appeared in the third edition, 1837. Wilhelm Grimm had already summarized the story in annotations, he had printed it *in toto* in an 1826 annual album, and in 1833 he had already included it in the second edition of the Kleine Ausgabe of the KHM (Shorter Edition; the one with 50 stories aimed at children). His version is a total retelling and expansion of "Der undankbare Zwerg" (The Ungrateful Dwarf) by the above-mentioned Caroline Stahl, who included it in her *Fabeln, Mährchen und Erzählungen für Kinder* (Fables, Tales, and Stories for Children), 1819 and 1821. Stahl's story, typical of the moralistic Enlightenment trend, is told baldly, with practically no dialogue. It begins when Schneeweißchen, one of several impoverished siblings, first meets the dwarf, who has gotten his beard wedged in a tree. Then, with her sister Rosenrot joining her, she meets him again when he has trouble with the fish and the eagle. At the end, a bear appears for the first time and deals a sort of divine retribution to the ill-mannered, selfish dwarf by eating him; there is no relationship between the bear and the girls. Wilhelm, adding a verse couplet that he borrowed from Friedrich Kind (1768–1843; best known as the librettist of Weber's opera *Der Freischütz*), enlivened Stahl's story with racy dialogue and numerous deft touches, and added from whole cloth the almost too charmingly idyllic picture of the girls' homelife and their wooing by the bear. In so doing, he created what has been called the only *Kunstmärchen* ("artistic folktale," one consciously bedizened with literary graces and values) in the Grimm corpus. The animal-suitor theme occurs in folktales of all eras and climes; it is an aspect of early man's egocentrically anthropomorphic view of animals.

"Der Meisterdieb." This story didn't appear in the Grimm collection until the fifth edition, 1843, for the excellent reason that it wasn't available until that year, when it was published in the *Zeitschrift für deutsches Alterthum* (Journal of German Antiquities); the Grimms acknowledged its authorship by Friedrich Stertzing, adding that it came from Thuringia, but without mentioning the direct source. Researchers believe that Clemens Brentano had discovered an oral tradition for the tale in Bohemia in 1810. The Master Thief tale-complex encompasses stories like the Grimms', in which the thief is tested, and others in which he dies and his relatives must

conceal their grief and give him a decent burial by means of various ruses in order to escape detection.[16] Written Master Thief stories go back to the Greek historian Herodotus (5th century B.C.), who retells a version he heard in Egypt, purporting to be historical fact.[17] An Arabic version is found among the works of the Iraqi polymath Mas'ūdī (ca. 900–ca. 956). The Grimms' version is close to one by the above-mentioned Italian *novella* writer Straparola. The parson in the sack is a separate folktale motif that occurs elsewhere. Some scholars believe that an actual religious practice underlies the motif of the candles stuck to little crawling creatures, which first appears in a story in the Florentine short-story writer Franco Sacchetti's *Il Trecentonovelle* (Three Hundred Stories; ca. 1400).[18]

Features of This Edition

The basis of selection was fame and literary merit, with a secondary interest in representing different types of folktales (the deficiencies for folklorists of the 1857 edition that was the source for the texts have already been mentioned).[19] Each tale is printed complete, without alterations of any sort. The original paragraphing is retained, though some paragraphs may seem inordinately long to a modern reader.

As in practically every edition, the spelling has been mildly modernized, without altering the phonological or morphological shape of any word. German given names have been retained in their original, even to the (really essential) umlaut in "Hänsel." It shouldn't be too difficult for any reader to recognize Heinrich, Hans, and Konrad as being equivalent to Henry, John, and Conrad; and, after all, no one has ever translated "Hänsel and Gretel" as "Johnny and Maggie (or: Madge, Peggy, etc.)."

---

16. An example of this type of Master Thief story, from the above-mentioned *Dolopathos,* may be found in English in the work cited in footnote 13.   17. Egypt was a home of great storytelling as early as the second millennium B.C.   18. Sacchetti's story, and others from his important collection, may be found in English in the work cited in footnote 13.   19. Two stories printed by the Grimms in a Pomeranian variety of *Plattdeutsch* ("Low" or Northern German) just as they were submitted by the eminent painter Philipp Otto Runge (1777–1810) have been most regretfully omitted from this anthology despite their real merit both as literature and as folklore; this omission was due entirely to the pedagogical aims of Dover's dual-language series, for which it was felt that the German texts should all be in the standard language. These two stories are "Von dem Fischer un syner Fru" (Of the Fisherman and His Wife; KHM 19) and "Von dem Machandelboom" (Of the Juniper Tree; KHM 47).

The translation is very literal, but always within the limitations of good English. One major exception is the verses that are featured in many of the stories: it seemed foolish not to retain the jingles that are so much a part of their appeal. But even here, the translations are basically accurate; it should be easy to spot the handful of added or altered words that made it possible to achieve a rhyme, however clunky. True idioms—that is, expressions which would be nonsensical if translated word-for-word into another language (such a translation wouldn't even convey the basic meaning)—are represented here by English counterparts.[20] On the other hand, the numerous colorful, racy expressions that some translators have altered into standard English sayings, even though they are quite understandable (and entertaining) when rendered literally, have been retained here.[21] In general, every effort has been made to match the German in level of colloquiality, diction, and overall spirit.

---

20. For example, the idiom *ins Bockshorn jagen*, which occurs toward the end of "Die Bremer Stadtmusikanten," translates word-for-word as "to chase into the billygoat's horn"; its proper English equivalent is "to throw a scare into; to intimidate," or the like.   21. For instance (in "Hänsel und Gretel"): *wer A sagt, muß auch B sagen* has been translated in this volume as "Whoever says 'A' must also say 'B,'" the purport being that an initial decision determines subsequent ones.

Selected Folktales

Ausgewählte Märchen

Der Froschkönig oder der eiserne Heinrich

In den alten Zeiten, wo das Wünschen noch geholfen hat, lebte ein König, dessen Töchter waren alle schön, aber die jüngste war so schön, daß die Sonne selber, die doch so vieles gesehen hat, sich verwunderte, sooft sie ihr ins Gesicht schien. Nahe bei dem Schlosse des Königs lag ein großer dunkler Wald, und in dem Walde unter einer alten Linde war ein Brunnen; wenn nun der Tag recht heiß war, so ging das Königskind hinaus in den Wald und setzte sich an den Rand des kühlen Brunnens; und wenn sie Langeweile hatte, so nahm sie eine goldene Kugel, warf sie in die Höhe und fing sie wieder; und das war ihr liebstes Spielwerk.

Nun trug es sich einmal zu, daß die goldene Kugel der Königstochter nicht in ihr Händchen fiel, das sie in die Höhe gehalten hatte, sondern vorbei auf die Erde schlug und geradezu ins Wasser hineinrollte. Die Königstochter folgte ihr mit den Augen nach, aber die Kugel verschwand, und der Brunnen war tief, so tief, daß man keinen Grund sah. Da fing sie an zu weinen und weinte immer lauter und konnte sich gar nicht trösten. Und wie sie so klagte, rief ihr jemand zu: »Was hast du vor, Königstochter, du schreist ja, daß sich ein Stein erbarmen möchte.« Sie sah sich um, woher die Stimme käme, da erblickte sie einen Frosch, der seinen dicken häßlichen Kopf aus dem Wasser streckte. »Ach, du bist's, alter Wasserpatscher«, sagte sie, »ich weine über meine goldene Kugel, die mir in den Brunnen hinabgefallen ist.« »Sei still und weine nicht«, antwortete der Frosch, »ich kann wohl Rat schaffen, aber was gibst du mir, wenn ich dein Spielwerk wieder heraufhole?« »Was du haben willst, lieber Frosch«,

The Frog King; or, Iron Henry [The Frog Prince]

In olden days, when wishing still did some good, there lived a king whose daughters were all beautiful; but the youngest was so beautiful that the sun itself, which after all has seen so much, was astonished every time it shone in her face. Near the king's castle lay a big, dark forest, and in that forest, beneath an old linden tree, there was a well;[1] now, when the day was good and hot, the princess used to go out into the forest and sit on the rim of the cool well; and when she was bored, she took a golden ball, threw it in the air, and caught it; that was her favorite pastime.

Now, on one occasion the princess's golden ball didn't fall into the little hand she had been holding up, but hit the ground alongside it and rolled right into the water. The princess watched it go, but the ball disappeared, and the well was deep, so deep that you couldn't see the bottom. Then she started to cry, and cried louder and louder, unable to console herself. And as she was lamenting that way, someone called out to her: "What are you up to, princess? You're yelling so, that a stone would take pity." She looked around to see where the voice came from, and she caught sight of a frog that was sticking its big, ugly head out of the water. "Oh, it's you, old water-slapper," she said; "I'm crying over my golden ball, which has fallen into the well." "Be quiet and stop crying," the frog replied; "I can help you out, but what will you give me if I bring your toy up again?" "Whatever you like, frog dear," she said, "my gowns, my pearls and jewels,

---

1. In accordance with the best modern English translations, *Brunnen* has been generally translated as "well" in this volume, though when the *Brunnen* is in a forest, "spring" or "fountain" may possibly be a better rendering.

3

sagte sie, »meine Kleider, meine Perlen und Edelsteine, auch noch die goldene Krone, die ich trage.« Der Frosch antwortete: »Deine Kleider, deine Perlen und Edelsteine, und deine goldene Krone, die mag ich nicht; aber wenn du mich liebhaben willst, und ich soll dein Geselle und Spielkamerad sein, an deinem Tischlein neben dir sitzen, von deinem goldenen Tellerlein essen, aus deinem Becherlein trinken, in deinem Bettlein schlafen: wenn du mir das versprichst, so will ich hinuntersteigen und dir die goldene Kugel wieder herauf- holen.« »Ach ja«, sagte sie, »ich verspreche dir alles, was du willst, wenn du mir nur die Kugel wiederbringst.« Sie dachte aber: Was der einfältige Frosch schwätzt, der sitzt im Wasser bei seinesgleichen und quakt und kann keines Menschen Geselle sein.

Der Frosch, als er die Zusage erhalten hatte, tauchte seinen Kopf unter, sank hinab, und über ein Weilchen kam er wieder her- aufgerudert, hatte die Kugel im Maul und warf sie ins Gras. Die Königstochter war voll Freude, als sie ihr schönes Spielwerk wieder erblickte, hob es auf und sprang damit fort. »Warte, warte«, rief der Frosch, »nimm mich mit, ich kann nicht so laufen wie du.« Aber was half ihm, daß er ihr sein quak, quak so laut nachschrie, als er konnte! Sie hörte nicht darauf, eilte nach Haus und hatte bald den armen Frosch vergessen, der wieder in seinen Brunnen hinabsteigen mußte.

Am andern Tage, als sie mit dem König und allen Hofleuten sich zur Tafel gesetzt hatte und von ihrem goldenen Tellerlein aß, da kam, plitsch platsch, plitsch platsch, etwas die Marmortreppe her- aufgekrochen, und als es oben angelangt war, klopfte es an der Tür und rief: »Königstochter, jüngste, mach mir auf.« Sie lief und wollte sehen, wer draußen wäre, als sie aber aufmachte, so saß der Frosch davor. Da warf sie die Tür hastig zu, setzte sich wieder an den Tisch, und war ihr ganz angst. Der König sah wohl, daß ihr das Herz gewaltig klopfte, und sprach: »Mein Kind, was fürchtest du dich, steht etwa ein Riese vor der Tür und will dich holen?« »Ach nein«, antwortete sie, »es ist kein Riese, sondern ein garstiger Frosch.« »Was will der Frosch von dir?« »Ach lieber Vater, als ich gestern im Wald bei dem Brunnen saß und spielte, da fiel meine goldene Kugel ins Wasser. Und weil ich so weinte, hat sie der Frosch wieder heraufgeholt, und weil er es durchaus verlangte, so versprach ich ihm, er sollte mein Geselle wer- den, ich dachte aber nimmermehr, daß er aus seinem Wasser heraus könnte. Nun ist er draußen und will zu mir herein.« Indem klopfte es zum zweitenmal und rief:

even the golden crown that I'm wearing." The frog replied: "I don't want your gowns, your pearls and jewels, or your golden crown; but if you're willing to love me, and I can be your companion and playmate, sit next to you at your little table, eat out of your little golden plate, drink out of your little goblet, sleep in your little bed: if you promise me that, I'll go down and bring the golden ball back up to you." "Oh, yes," she said, "I promise you everything you want, if only you bring me back the ball." But she was thinking: "My, how that silly frog babbles; it sits in the water with its own kind and croaks; it can't be a companion to any person."

When the frog had received her consent, it plunged its head in and sank down; after a while it came paddling up again with the ball in its mouth, and threw it onto the grass. The princess was overjoyed when she saw her pretty toy again; she picked it up and dashed away with it. "Wait! Wait!" called the frog; "take me along, I can't run as fast as you." But it did the frog no good to croak after her as loud as it could! She paid no attention to it, but hastened homeward, and soon forgot all about the poor frog, which had to plunge down into its well again.

The next day, when she had sat down at table with the king and all the courtiers, and was eating out of her little golden plate, something came creeping up the marble stairs—slip, slop, slip, slop—and when it had reached the top, it knocked on the door and called: "Youngest princess, open up!" She ran over, wishing to see who was outside; but when she opened the door, the frog was sitting on the other side. Then she quickly slammed the door shut, sat back down at the table, and was terribly upset. The king naturally saw that her heart was pounding violently, and said: "My child, why are you so afraid? Can it be a giant standing outside the door, trying to take you away?" "Oh, no," she replied, "it isn't a giant, but a disgusting frog." "What does the frog want of you?" "Oh, father dear, yesterday when I was sitting by the well in the forest playing, my golden ball fell into the water. And because I was crying so, the frog brought it up again, and because he insisted on it, I promised it that it could be my companion. But I never thought that it could come out of its water. Now it's right outside and wants to come in to me." Meanwhile there was a second knock, and the call:

»Königstochter, jüngste,
mach mir auf,
weißt du nicht, was gestern
du zu mir gesagt
bei dem kühlen Brunnenwasser?
Königstochter, jüngste,
mach mir auf.«

Da sagte der König: »Was du versprochen hast, das mußt du auch halten; geh nur und mach ihm auf.« Sie ging und öffnete die Türe, da hüpfte der Frosch herein, ihr immer auf dem Fuße nach, bis zu ihrem Stuhl. Da saß er und rief: »Heb mich herauf zu dir.«. Sie zauderte, bis es endlich der König befahl. Als der Frosch erst auf dem Stuhl war, wollte er auf den Tisch, und als er da saß, sprach er: »Nun schieb mir dein goldenes Tellerlein näher, damit wir zusammen essen.« Das tat sie zwar, aber man sah wohl, daß sie's nicht gerne tat. Der Frosch ließ sich's gut schmecken, aber ihr blieb fast jedes Bißlein im Halse. Endlich sprach er: »Ich habe mich satt gegessen und bin müde, nun trag mich in dein Kämmerlein und mach dein seiden Bettlein zurecht, da wollen wir uns schlafen legen.« Die Königstochter fing an zu weinen und fürchtete sich vor dem kalten Frosch, den sie nicht anzurühren getraute und der nun in ihrem schönen reinen Bettlein schlafen sollte. Der König aber ward zornig und sprach: »Wer dir geholfen hat, als du in der Not warst, den sollst du hernach nicht verachten.« Da packte sie ihn mit zwei Fingern, trug ihn hinauf und setzte ihn in eine Ecke. Als sie aber im Bett lag, kam er gekrochen und sprach: »Ich bin müde, ich will schlafen so gut wie du: heb mich herauf, oder ich sag's deinem Vater.« Da ward sie erst bitterböse, holte ihn herauf und warf ihn aus allen Kräften wider die Wand. »Nun wirst du Ruhe haben, du garstiger Frosch.«

Als er aber herabfiel, war er kein Frosch, sondern ein Königssohn mit schönen und freundlichen Augen. Der war nun nach ihres Vaters Willen ihr lieber Geselle und Gemahl. Da erzählte er ihr, er wäre von einer bösen Hexe verwünscht worden, und niemand hätte ihn aus dem Brunnen erlösen können als sie allein, und morgen wollten sie zusammen in sein Reich gehen. Dann schliefen sie ein, und am andern Morgen, als die Sonne sie aufweckte, kam ein Wagen herangefahren, mit acht weißen Pferden bespannt, die hatten weiße Straußfedern auf dem Kopf und gingen in goldenen Ketten, und hinten stand der Diener des jungen Königs, das war der treue Heinrich. Der treue Heinrich hatte sich so betrübt, als sein Herr war in einen Frosch verwandelt worden, daß er drei eiserne

"Youngest princess,
open the door!
Don't you remember what you said
to me yesterday
by the cool well water?
Youngest princess,
open the door!"

Then the king said: "Whatever promise you made you must keep; go over and let it in." She went and opened the door; then the frog hopped in, following always at her heels, all the way to her chair. There it sat, calling: "Lift me up to you!" She hesitated, until the king finally ordered her to. Once the frog was on the chair, it wanted to be on the table; when it was sitting there, it said: "Now shove your little golden plate closer, so we can eat together." She did do so, but it was obvious that she did it unwillingly. The frog enjoyed its food, but nearly every morsel she ate stuck in her throat. Finally the frog said: "Now I'm full and tired, so carry me into your little bedroom and make up your little silk bed, so we can lie down to sleep." The princess started to cry; she was afraid of the cold frog, which she didn't dare to touch, but which was now to sleep in her beautiful, clean little bed. But the king got angry and said: "When someone has helped you when you were in distress, you mustn't despise him afterwards." Then she picked up the frog with two fingers, carried it upstairs, and placed it in a corner. But when she was lying in bed, it came crawling over and said: "I'm tired; I want to sleep just as much as you do: pick me up, or I'll tell your father." This time she became wildly angry; she picked it up and hurled it against the wall with all her might. "Now you can rest, you disgusting frog!"

But when it fell down, it was no longer a frog, but a prince with lovely, friendly eyes. Now, by her father's wishes, he was her loving companion and husband. He then told her that he had been placed under a spell by an evil witch, and that no one could have delivered him from the well except her; the next day, they would journey together to his kingdom. Then they fell asleep, and the following morning, when the sun awakened them, a carriage drove up drawn by eight white horses, which had white ostrich plumes on their heads and were harnessed with golden chains; in the back stood the young king's servant, faithful Heinrich. Faithful Heinrich had been so downcast after his master had been turned into a frog that he had had three iron bands

Bande hatte um sein Herz legen lassen, damit es ihm nicht vor Weh und Traurigkeit zerspränge. Der Wagen aber sollte den jungen König in sein Reich abholen; der treue Heinrich hob beide hinein, stellte sich wieder hinten auf und war voller Freude über die Erlösung. Und als sie ein Stück Wegs gefahren waren, hörte der Königssohn, daß es hinter ihm krachte, als wäre etwas zerbrochen. Da drehte er sich um und rief:

>Heinrich, der Wagen bricht.«
>Nein, Herr, der Wagen nicht,
es ist ein Band von meinem Herzen,
das da lag in großen Schmerzen,
als Ihr in dem Brunnen saßt,
als Ihr eine Fretsche (Frosch) wast (wart).«

Noch einmal und noch einmal krachte es auf dem Weg, und der Königssohn meinte immer, der Wagen bräche, und es waren doch nur die Bande, die vom Herzen des treuen Heinrich absprangen, weil sein Herr erlöst und glücklich war.

Märchen von einem, der auszog, das Fürchten zu lernen

Ein Vater hatte zwei Söhne, davon war der älteste klug und gescheit und wußte sich in alles wohl zu schicken, der jüngste aber war dumm, konnte nichts begreifen und lernen: und wenn ihn die Leute sahen, sprachen sie:»Mit dem wird der Vater noch seine Last haben!« Wenn nun etwas zu tun war, so mußte es der älteste allzeit ausrichten: hieß ihn aber der Vater noch spät oder gar in der Nacht etwas holen und der Weg ging dabei über den Kirchhof oder sonst einen schaurigen Ort, so antwortete er wohl:»Ach nein, Vater, ich gehe nicht dahin, es gruselt mir!« Denn er fürchtete sich. Oder wenn abends beim Feuer Geschichten erzählt wurden, wobei einem die Haut schaudert, so sprachen die Zuhörer manchmal:»Ach, es gruselt mir!« Der jüngste saß in einer Ecke und hörte das mit an und konnte nicht begreifen, was es heißen sollte.»Immer sagen sie: Es gruselt mir! Es gruselt mir! Mir gruselt's nicht: das wird wohl eine Kunst sein, von der ich auch nichts verstehe.«

Nun geschah es, daß der Vater einmal zu ihm sprach:»Hör du, in der Ecke dort, du wirst groß und stark, du mußt auch etwas lernen,

placed around his heart to keep it from bursting with pain and sorrow. But the carriage was now going to return the young king to his kingdom; faithful Heinrich helped the couple get in, took his place in back again, and was filled with joy at the deliverance. And after they had traveled some distance, the prince heard a snapping sound behind him, as if something had broken. So he turned around and called:

> "Heinrich, I hear the carriage break."
> "No, my lord, that's a mistake.
> It's a band from around my heart,
> which always felt a painful smart
> all the time that in the well
> as a frog you used to dwell."

Again, and once again, there was a snap as they rode, and each time the prince thought the carriage was breaking; but it was really only the bands coming off faithful Heinrich's heart, because his master was rescued and happy.

Tale of One Who Set Out to Learn Fear

A father had two sons, of whom the elder was intelligent and clever and could handle every situation, but the younger was stupid and unable to grasp or learn anything: when people saw him, they said: "His father's going to have his hands full with that one!" So whenever something needed to be done, it was always the elder son who had to take care of it; but if his father told him to fetch something late in the day, or especially at night, and the path led across the churchyard or some other scary place, he'd reply: "Oh, no, father, I'm not going there, it gives me the creeps!" Because he was frightened. Or else, when by the fire in the evening, folks told stories that make your flesh crawl, the listeners sometimes said: "Oh, it gives me the creeps!" The younger son sat in the corner and heard it, but couldn't understand what they meant. "They always say: 'It gives me the shudders! It gives me the shudders!' I don't get any shudders: that must be another accomplishment I have no idea of."

Now, it came about that his father once spoke to him: "Listen, you in the corner there, you're getting big and strong; you too

womit du dein Brot verdienst. Siehst du, wie dein Bruder sich Mühe gibt, aber an dir ist Hopfen und Malz verloren.« »Ei, Vater«, antwortete er, »ich will gerne was lernen; ja, wenn's anginge, so möchte ich lernen, daß mir's gruselte; davon verstehe ich noch gar nichts.« Der älteste lachte, als er das hörte, und dachte bei sich: »Du lieber Gott, was ist mein Bruder ein Dummbart, aus dem wird sein Lebtag nichts: was ein Häkchen werden will, muß sich beizeiten krümmen.« Der Vater seufzte und antwortete ihm: »Das Gruseln, das sollst du schon lernen, aber dein Brot wirst du damit nicht verdienen.«

Bald danach kam der Küster zum Besuch ins Haus, da klagte ihm der Vater seine Not und erzählte, wie sein jüngster Sohn in allen Dingen so schlecht beschlagen wäre, er wüßte nichts und lernte nichts. »Denkt euch, als ich ihn fragte, womit er sein Brot verdienen wollte, hat er gar verlangt, das Gruseln zu lernen.« »Wenn's weiter nichts ist«, antwortete der Küster, »das kann er bei mir lernen; tut ihn nur zu mir, ich will ihn schon abhobeln.« Der Vater war es zufrieden, weil er dachte: »Der Junge wird doch ein wenig zugestutzt.« Der Küster nahm ihn also ins Haus, und er mußte die Glocke läuten. Nach ein paar Tagen weckte er ihn um Mitternacht, hieß ihn aufstehen, in den Kirchturm steigen und läuten. »Du sollst schon lernen, was Gruseln ist«, dachte er, ging heimlich voraus, und als der Junge oben war und sich umdrehte und das Glockenseil fassen wollte, so sah er auf der Treppe, dem Schalloch gegenüber, eine weiße Gestalt stehen. »Wer da?« rief er, aber die Gestalt gab keine Antwort, regte und bewegte sich nicht. »Gib Antwort«, rief der Junge, »oder mache, daß du fortkommst, du hast hier in der Nacht nichts zu schaffen.« Der Küster aber blieb unbeweglich stehen, damit der Junge glauben sollte, es wäre ein Gespenst. Der Junge rief zum zweitenmal: »Was willst du hier? Sprich, wenn du ein ehrlicher Kerl bist, oder ich werfe dich die Treppe hinab.« Der Küster dachte: »Das wird so schlimm nicht gemeint sein«, gab keinen Laut von sich und stand, als wenn er von Stein wäre. Da rief ihn der Junge zum dritten Male an, und als das auch vergeblich war, nahm er einen Anlauf und stieß das Gespenst die Treppe hinab, daß es zehn Stufen hinabfiel und in einer Ecke liegenblieb. Darauf läutete er die Glocke, ging heim, legte sich, ohne ein Wort zu sagen, ins Bett und schlief fort. Die Küsterfrau wartete lange Zeit auf ihren Mann, aber er wollte nicht wiederkommen. Da ward ihr endlich angst, sie weckte den Jungen und fragte: »Weißt du nicht, wo mein Mann geblieben ist? Er ist vor dir auf den Turm gestiegen.« »Nein«, antwortete der Junge, »aber da hat einer dem Schalloch

have to learn some trade by which to earn your bread. See how hard your brother works, but hops and malt are wasted on you." "Oh, father," he replied, "I'm perfectly willing to learn something; in fact, if it were possible, I'd like to learn how to get the shudders; I still don't understand a thing about it." The elder son laughed on hearing that, and he said to himself: "Dear God, what a dumbbell my brother is; he'll never amount to anything: if something's going to become a hook, its got to start curving early on." Their father sighed and answered: "All right, you'll learn how to shudder, but it won't help you earn your bread."

Soon afterwards, the sexton paid a visit to the family, and the father complained to him about his unpleasant situation, telling him that his younger son was so poorly endowed for any trade; he didn't know and couldn't learn a thing. "Just imagine, when I asked him how he wanted to earn his bread, he actually wanted to learn how to get the shudders." "If that's all there is to it," the sexton replied, "he can learn that from me; just hand him over to me, and I'll plane off his rough edges." The father was contented, because he thought: "The boy will surely be licked into shape a little." So the sexton took him home with him, and set him to ringing the church bell. After a couple of days, he woke him up around midnight and told him to get up, climb into the belfry, and ring. "Now you'll find out what the shudders are," he thought, as he secretly started out ahead of him; when the boy was up there and turned around, about to grasp the bell rope, he saw a white figure standing on the staircase opposite the louver through which the sound escaped. "Who's there?" he shouted, but the figure made no reply; it didn't stir or budge. "Answer me," shouted the boy, "or get out of here! You have no business here at night." But the sexton remained standing there motionless, so that the boy would think it was a ghost. The boy shouted a second time: "What do you want here? Speak up, if you're an honest fellow, or I'll throw you down the stairs." The sexton thought: "He doesn't really mean it"; he uttered no sound but just stood there as if he were made of stone. Then the boy addressed him a third time, and when even that did no good, he made a sprint and pushed the ghost down the staircase, so that it fell ten steps and lay still in a corner. Then he rang the bell, went back to the house, lay down in bed without saying a word, and went back to sleep. The sexton's wife waited a long time for her husband, but he didn't return. So she finally got nervous, woke up the boy, and asked him: "Do you

gegenüber auf der Treppe gestanden, und weil er keine Antwort geben und auch nicht weggehen wollte, so habe ich ihn für einen Spitzbuben gehalten und hinuntergestoßen. Geht nur hin, so werdet Ihr sehen, ob er's gewesen ist, es sollte mir leid tun.« Die Frau sprang fort und fand ihren Mann, der in einer Ecke lag und jammerte und ein Bein gebrochen hatte.

Sie trug ihn herab und eilte dann mit lautem Geschrei zu dem Vater des Jungen. »Euer Junge«, rief sie, »hat ein großes Unglück angerichtet, meinen Mann hat er die Treppe hinabgeworfen, daß er ein Bein gebrochen hat: schafft den Taugenichts aus userm Hause.« Der Vater erschrak, kam herbeigelaufen und schalt den Jungen aus. »Was sind das für gottlose Streiche, die muß dir der Böse eingegeben haben.« »Vater«, antwortete er, »hört nur an, ich bin ganz unschuldig: er stand da in der Nacht, wie einer, der Böses im Sinne hat. Ich wußte nicht, wer's war, und habe ihn dreimal ermahnt, zu reden oder wegzugehen.« »Ach«, sprach der Vater, »mit dir erleb ich nur Unglück, geh mir aus den Augen, ich will dich nicht mehr ansehen.« »Ja, Vater, recht gerne, wartet nur, bis Tag ist, da will ich ausgehen und das Gruseln lernen, so versteh ich doch eine Kunst, die mich ernähren kann.« »Lerne, was du willst«, sprach der Vater, »mir ist alles einerlei. Da hast du funfzig Taler, damit geh in die weite Welt und sage keinem Menschen, wo du her bist und wer dein Vater ist, denn ich muß mich deiner schämen.« »Ja, Vater, wie Ihr's haben wollt, wenn Ihr nicht mehr verlangt, das kann ich leicht in Acht behalten.«

Als nun der Tag anbrach, steckte der Junge seine funfzig Taler in die Tasche, ging hinaus auf die große Landstraße und sprach immer vor sich hin: »Wenn mir's nur gruselte! Wenn mir's nur gruselte!« Da kam ein Mann heran, der hörte das Gespräch, das der Junge mit sich selber führte, und als sie ein Stück weiter waren, daß man den Galgen sehen konnte, sagte der Mann zu ihm: »Siehst du, dort ist der Baum, wo siebene mit des Seilers Tochter Hochzeit gehalten haben und jetzt das Fliegen lernen: setz dich darunter und warte, bis die Nacht kommt, so wirst du schon das Gruseln lernen.« »Wenn weiter nichts dazu gehört«, antwortete der Junge, »das ist leicht getan; lerne ich aber so geschwind das Gruseln, so sollst du meine funfzig Taler haben: komm nur morgen früh wieder zu mir.« Da ging der Junge zu dem Galgen, setzte sich darunter und wartete, bis der Abend kam. Und weil ihn fror, machte er sich ein Feuer an: aber um Mitternacht ging der Wind so kalt, daß er trotz des Feuers nicht warm werden wollte. Und als der Wind die Gehenkten gegeneinander stieß, daß sie

have any idea where my husband might be? He climbed the belfry before you did." "No," the boy replied, "but when I was there, someone was standing on the staircase opposite the louver, and because he refused either to answer or to go away, I thought he was a crook and I pushed him down. Go up there and you'll see if that was him; I'd be sorry if it was." The woman dashed away and found her husband lying in a corner howling; he had broken a leg.

She carried him down and then hastened to the boy's father with a loud outcry. "Your boy," she shouted, "has caused a great misfortune; he threw my husband down the stairs, and he's broken a leg: get that good-for-nothing out of our house!" The father was alarmed, came running, and scolded the boy. "What sort of wicked pranks are these? The Evil One must have put them into your head." "Father," he replied, "just listen: I'm completely innocent: he was standing there at night like someone with bad intentions. I didn't know who it was, and I ordered him three times to speak or go away." "Alas," said his father, "you bring me only misfortune; get out of my sight, I don't want to look at you anymore." "Yes, father, most gladly; just wait until daylight, and I'll set out to learn what the shudders are; that way I'll finally understand a craft that can earn me a living." "Learn whatever you like," his father said; "it's all the same to me. Here are fifty thalers, take them and go out into the world, but never tell a soul where you're from or who your father is, because I'm forced to be ashamed of you." "Yes, father, just as you wish; if that's all you ask of me, I can easily keep that in mind."

So, when day broke the boy put his fifty thalers in his pocket, went out onto the main highway, and kept saying to himself: "If I could only get the creeps! If I could only get the creeps!" A man came by and heard the conversation the boy was having with himself; and when they had walked a bit further, so that the gallows was visible, the man said to him: "See that? That's the tree on which seven men have married the ropemaker's daughter and are now learning how to fly: sit down under it and wait till night comes, and I'm sure you'll learn how to have the creeps." "If that's all there is to it," the boy replied, "it's easily done; but if I learn how to have the creeps as quickly as that, you can have my fifty thalers: just come back to me tomorrow morning." Then the boy went to the gallows, sat down under it, and waited until evening came. And because he felt cold, he made a fire: but around midnight there was such a cold wind that, in spite of the fire, he couldn't get warm. And when the wind blew the hanged men against one another, so

sich hin und her bewegten, so dachte er: »Du frierst unten bei dem Feuer, was mögen die da oben erst frieren und zappeln.« Und weil er mitleidig war, legte er die Leiter an, stieg hinauf, knüpfte einen nach dem andern los und holte sie alle siebene herab. Darauf schürte er das Feuer, blies es an und setzte sie ringsherum, daß sie sich wärmen sollten. Aber sie saßen da und regten sich nicht, und das Feuer ergriff ihre Kleider. Da sprach er: »Nehmt euch in acht, sonst häng ich euch wieder hinauf.« Die Toten aber hörten nicht, schwiegen und ließen ihre Lumpen fortbrennen. Da ward er bös und sprach: »Wenn ihr nicht achtgeben wollt, so kann ich euch nicht helfen, ich will nicht mit euch verbrennen«, und hing sie nach der Reihe wieder hinauf. Nun setzte er sich zu seinem Feuer und schlief ein, und am andern Morgen, da kam der Mann zu ihm, wollte die funfzig Taler haben und sprach: »Nun, weißt du, was Gruseln ist?« »Nein«, antwortete er, »woher sollte ich's wissen? Die da droben haben das Maul nicht aufgetan und waren so dumm, daß sie die paar alten Lappen, die sie am Leibe haben, brennen ließen.« Da sah der Mann, daß er die funfzig Taler heute nicht davontragen würde, ging fort und sprach: »So einer ist mir noch nicht vorgekommen.«

Der Junge ging auch seines Weges und fing wieder an, vor sich hin zu reden: »Ach, wenn mir's nur gruselte! Ach, wenn mir's nur gruselte!« Das hörte ein Fuhrmann, der hinter ihm her schritt, und fragte: »Wer bist du?« »Ich weiß nicht«, antwortete der Junge. Der Fuhrmann fragte weiter: »Wo bist du her?« »Ich weiß nicht.« »Wer ist dein Vater?« »Das darf ich nicht sagen.« »Was brummst du beständig in den Bart hinein?« »Ei«, antwortete der Junge, »ich wollte, daß mir's gruselte, aber niemand kann mir's lehren.« »Laß dein dummes Geschwätz«, sprach der Fuhrmann, »komm, geh mit mir, ich will sehen, daß ich dich unterbringe.« Der Junge ging mit dem Fuhrmann, und abends gelangten sie zu einem Wirtshaus, wo sie übernachten wollten. Da sprach er beim Eintritt in die Stube wieder ganz laut: »Wenn mir's nur gruselte! Wenn mir's nur gruselte!« Der Wirt, der das hörte, lachte und sprach: »Wenn dich danach lüstet, dazu sollte hier wohl Gelegenheit sein.« »Ach schweig stille«, sprach die Wirtsfrau, »so mancher Vorwitzige hat schon sein Leben eingebüßt, es wäre Jammer und Schade um die schönen Augen, wenn die das Tageslicht nicht wiedersehen sollten.« Der Junge aber sagte: »Wenn's noch so schwer wäre, ich will's einmal lernen, deshalb bin ich ja ausgezogen.« Er ließ dem Wirt auch keine Ruhe, bis dieser erzählte, nicht weit davon stände ein verwünschtes Schloß, wo einer wohl lernen könnte, was Gruseln wäre, wenn er nur

that they moved to and fro, he thought: "You're freezing down here by the fire; just think how cold those people up there are, they're squirming so." And because he was compassionate, he stood the ladder against the gallows, climbed up, untied one man after the other, and carried all seven down. Then he stirred up the fire, blew on it, and seated them around it to get warm. But they just sat there without moving, and their clothing caught on fire. So he said: "Watch out, or I'll hang you up again." But the dead men didn't hear him; they remained silent and let their rags keep burning. Then he got angry and said: "If you refuse to watch out, I can't help you; I'm not going to burn up along with you." And he hung them back up again in turn. Now he sat down by his fire and fell asleep, and the next morning, the man came to him and asked for the fifty thalers, saying: "Well, do you know what the creeps are?" "No," he replied, "how should I know? Those men up there never opened their yap, and they were so dumb that they allowed the few old scraps they're wearing to burn." Then the man saw that he wouldn't carry away the fifty thalers that day; he left, saying: "I've never run across anyone like *him* before."

The boy also continued on his journey, beginning to talk to himself again: "Oh, if I only had the creeps! Oh, if I only had the creeps!" That was overheard by a wagoner who was walking behind him; he asked: "Who are you?" "I don't know," the boy replied. The wagoner next asked: "Where are you from?" "I don't know." "Who is your father?" "I'm not allowed to say." "What are you constantly muttering under your breath?" "Oh," the boy replied, "I'd like to have the creeps, but no one can teach me how." "Leave off your stupid babbling," said the wagoner; "come with me, and I'll see to it that you're instructed." The boy went with the wagoner, and in the evening they reached an inn where they intended to stay the night. Then, as he entered the public room, the boy again said aloud: "If I could only get the creeps! If I could only get the creeps!" The innkeeper, hearing this, laughed and said: "If that's what you crave, there ought to be a good chance for it here." "Oh, be quiet," said the innkeeper's wife; "so many cheeky fellows have already paid with their lives; it would be a crying shame if those beautiful eyes were never to see the daylight again." But the boy said: "No matter how hard it is, I'm determined to learn how; after all, that's what I set out to do." And he gave the innkeeper no peace until the innkeeper informed him that, not far away, there was an enchanted castle where someone could surely learn what the shudders were if

drei Nächte darin wachen wollte. Der König hätte dem, der's wagen wollte, seine Tochter zur Frau versprochen, und die wäre die schönste Jungfrau, welche die Sonne beschien; in dem Schlosse steckten auch große Schätze, von bösen Geistern bewacht, die würden dann frei und könnten einen Armen reich genug machen. Schon viele wären wohl hinein-, aber noch keiner wieder herausgekommen. Da ging der Junge am andern Morgen vor den König und sprach: »Wenn's erlaubt wäre, so wollte ich wohl drei Nächte in dem verwünschten Schlosse wachen.« Der König sah ihn an, und weil er ihm gefiel, sprach er: »Du darfst dir noch dreierlei ausbitten, aber es müssen leblose Dinge sein, und das darfst du mit ins Schloß nehmen.« Da antwortete er: »So bitt ich um ein Feuer, eine Drehbank und eine Schnitzbank mit dem Messer.«

Der König ließ ihm das alles bei Tage in das Schloß tragen. Als es Nacht werden wollte, ging der Junge hinauf, machte sich in einer Kammer ein helles Feuer an, stellte die Schnitzbank mit dem Messer daneben und setzte sich auf die Drehbank. »Ach, wenn mir's nur gruselte!« sprach er. »Aber hier werde ich's auch nicht lernen.« Gegen Mitternacht wollte er sich sein Feuer einmal aufschüren; wie er so hineinblies, da schrie's plötzlich aus einer Ecke: »Au, miau! Was uns friert!« »Ihr Narren«, rief er, »was schreit ihr? Wenn euch friert, kommt, setzt euch ans Feuer und wärmt euch.« Und wie er das gesagt hatte, kamen zwei große schwarze Katzen in einem gewaltigen Sprunge herbei, setzten sich ihm zu beiden Seiten und sahen ihn mit ihren feurigen Augen ganz wild an. Über ein Weilchen, als sie sich gewärmt hatten, sprachen sie: »Kamerad, wollen wir eins in der Karte spielen?« »Warum nicht?« antwortete er. »Aber zeigt einmal eure Pfoten her.« Da streckten sie die Krallen aus. »Ei«, sagte er, »was habt ihr lange Nägel! Wartet, die muß ich euch erst abschneiden.« Damit packte er sie beim Kragen, hob sie auf die Schnitzbank und schraubte ihnen die Pfoten fest. »Euch habe ich auf die Finger gesehen«, sprach er, »da vergeht mir die Lust zum Kartenspiel«, schlug sie tot und warf sie hinaus ins Wasser. Als er aber die zwei zur Ruhe gebracht hatte und sich wieder zu seinem Feuer setzen wollte, da kamen aus allen Ecken und Enden schwarze Katzen und schwarze Hunde an glühenden Ketten, immer mehr und mehr, daß er sich nicht mehr bergen konnte; die schrien greulich, traten ihm auf sein Feuer, zerrten es auseinander und wollten es ausmachen. Das sah er ein Weilchen ruhig mit an, als es ihm aber zu arg ward, faßte er sein Schnitzmesser und rief: »Fort mit dir, du Gesindel«, und haute auf sie los. Ein Teil sprang weg, die andern schlug er tot und warf sie hinaus in den Teich. Als er

he were only willing to sit up three nights there. The king had promised that anyone who risked it could marry his daughter, who was the most beautiful girl the sun shone on; besides, the castle contained great treasures, which were now guarded by evil spirits, but which would then be ready for the taking and were sufficient to make a poor man quite rich. Many men had already gone in, but no one yet had come out again. The next morning the boy appeared before the king and said: "If it's allowed, I'd like to sit up three nights in the enchanted castle." The king looked at him, and because he liked him, he said: "You may request three items—but they must be inanimate objects—which you can take along into the castle." The boy replied: "In that case, I ask for a fire, a lathe, and a carpenter's bench with the knife that goes with it."

The king had all of that conveyed into the castle for him during the day. When night was about to fall, the boy went up, made a bright fire in one bedroom, placed the carpenter's bench and knife next to it, and sat down at the lathe. "Oh, if I could only get the shudders!" he said. "But I won't learn how here, either." Toward midnight he wanted to stir up his fire; as he was blowing on it, a cry suddenly came from a corner: "Oh, meow! How cold we are!" "You fools," he shouted, "what are you yelling for? If you're cold, come sit down by the fire and yet warm." As soon as he said that, two big black cats arrived with a mighty bound, sat down on either side of him, and glared at him fiercely with their blazing eyes. After a while, when they had warmed themselves, they said: "Buddy, how about a game of cards?" "Why not?" he replied; "but first show me your paws." They stretched out their claws. "My," he said, "what long nails you have! Wait, I have to clip them for you first." Then he grabbed them by the scruff of the neck, lifted them onto the carpenter's bench, and fastened their paws tightly in the vise. "I've taken a good look at you," he said, "and I've lost my desire for a card game"; he killed them and threw them out into the pond. But once he had sent those two to their rest and was about to sit back down by the fire, from every nook and cranny there emerged black cats and black dogs on fiery chains, more and more of them, so that he could no longer take shelter; they yelled horribly, trod on his fire, scattered it, and tried to put it out. For a while he watched this calmly, but when it got too much for him, he seized his carpenter's knife and shouted: "Away with you, you bums!" And he lit into them. Some of them jumped away, the others he killed and

wieder gekommen war, blies er aus den Funken sein Feuer frisch an und wärmte sich. Und als er so saß, wollten ihm die Augen nicht länger offen bleiben, und er bekam Lust zu schlafen. Da blickte er um sich und sah in der Ecke ein großes Bett. »Das ist mir eben recht«, sprach er und legte sich hinein. Als er aber die Augen zutun wollte, so fing das Bett von selbst an zu fahren und fuhr im ganzen Schloß herum. »Recht so«, sprach er, »nur besser zu.« Da rollte das Bett fort, als wären sechs Pferde vorgespannt, über Schwellen und Treppen auf und ab: auf einmal, hopp, hopp! warf es um, das unterste zuoberst, daß es wie ein Berg auf ihm lag. Aber er schleuderte Decken und Kissen in die Höhe, stieg heraus und sagte: »Nun mag fahren, wer Lust hat«, legte sich an sein Feuer und schlief, bis es Tag war. Am Morgen kam der König, und als er ihn da auf der Erde liegen sah, meinte er, die Gespenster hätten ihn umgebracht und er wäre tot. Da sprach er: »Es ist doch schade um den schönen Menschen.« Das hörte der Junge, richtete sich auf und sprach: »So weit ist's noch nicht!« Da verwunderte sich der König, freute sich aber und fragte, wie es ihm gegangen wäre. »Recht gut«, antwortete er, »eine Nacht wäre herum, die zwei andern werden auch herumgehen.« Als er zum Wirt kam, da machte der große Augen. »Ich dachte nicht«, sprach er, »daß ich dich wieder lebendig sehen würde; hast du nun gelernt, was Gruseln ist?« »Nein«, sagte er, »es ist alles vergeblich: wenn mir's nur einer sagen könnte!«

Die zweite Nacht ging er abermals hinauf ins alte Schloß, setzte sich zum Feuer und fing sein altes Lied wieder an: »Wenn mir's nur gruselte!« Wie Mitternacht herankam, ließ sich ein Lärm und Gepolter hören, erst sachte, dann immer stärker, dann war's ein bißchen still, endlich kam mit lautem Geschrei ein halber Mensch den Schornstein herab und fiel vor ihn hin. »Heda!« rief er, »noch ein halber gehört dazu, das ist zu wenig.« Da ging der Lärm von frischem an, es tobte und heulte und fiel die andere Hälfte auch herab. »Wart«, sprach er, »ich will dir erst das Feuer ein wenig anblasen.« Wie er das getan hatte und sich wieder umsah, da waren die beiden Stücke zusammengefahren, und saß da ein greulicher Mann auf seinem Platz. »So haben wir nicht gewettet«, sprach der Junge, »die Bank ist mein.« Der Mann wollte ihn wegdrängen, aber der Junge ließ sich's nicht gefallen, schob ihn mit Gewalt weg und setzte sich wieder auf seinen Platz. Da fielen noch mehr Männer herab, einer nach dem andern, die holten neun Totenbeine und zwei Totenköpfe, setzten auf und spielten Kegel. Der Junge bekam auch Lust und fragte: »Hört ihr, kann ich mit sein?« »Ja, wenn du Geld

threw out into the pond. When he returned, he blew a new fire out of the embers and warmed himself. And as he sat there, his eyes refused to stay open any longer, and he felt an urge to sleep. Then he looked all around and saw a big bed in one corner. "Just what I needed," he said, and lay down on it. But when he tried to close his eyes, the bed started to move by itself, and traveled through the entire castle. "Fine," he said; "keep it up!" Then the bed rolled on as if pulled by six horses, up and down over thresholds and stairs: all at once, presto, it turned over upside down, so that it lay on top of him like a mountain. But he flung the blankets and pillows in the air, climbed out, and said: "Let anyone with a mind to it take that trip!" He lay down beside his fire and slept until day. In the morning the king came; when he saw him lying there on the floor, he thought that the ghosts had killed him and he was dead. Then he said: "It really is too bad about that good-looking fellow." The boy heard that, sat up, and said: "It's not as bad as all that!" Then the king was amazed, but happy, and he asked him how he had spent the night. "Just fine," he replied; "one night is over, and the other two will pass also." When he got to the inn, the innkeeper's eyes bulged. "I didn't think," he said, "that I'd ever see you alive again; have you learned now what the shudders are?" "No," he said, "it was all for nothing: if only someone could tell me!"

On the second night he went back up to the old castle, sat down by the fire, and repeated his old refrain: "If I only had the creeps!" When midnight arrived, a noisy racket was heard, first softly, then more and more loudly; then it was quiet for a bit; finally, with a piercing scream, half of a human body came down the chimney and landed in front of him. "Ho there!" he cried; "another half-man should come with this one; this isn't enough." Then the noise picked up again, there was ranting and howling, and the second half fell down as well. "Wait," he said, "first I want to blow on the fire for you a little." After doing that, he looked around again and the two pieces had joined; a hideous man was sitting in the boy's regular place. "That wasn't part of our bargain," the boy said; "the lathe is for me." The man tried to shove him away, but the boy would have none of it, pushed him away violently and sat back down on his spot. Then more men came falling down, one after the other; they fetched nine human leg bones and two skulls, set the bones up as pins, and played bowls. The boy felt like playing, too, and asked: "Listen, can I join in?" "Yes, if you've got money."

hast.« »Geld genug«, antwortete er, »aber eure Kugeln sind nicht
recht rund.« Da nahm er die Totenköpfe, setzte sie in die Drehbank
und drehte sie rund. »So, jetzt werden sie besser schüppeln«, sprach
er, »heida, nun geht's lustig!« Er spielte mit und verlor etwas von
seinem Geld, als es aber zwölf Uhr schlug, war alles vor seinen
Augen verschwunden. Er legte sich nieder und schlief ruhig ein. Am
andern Morgen kam der König und wollte sich erkundigen. »Wie ist
dir's diesmal gegangen?« fragte er. »Ich habe gekegelt«, antwortete
er, »und ein paar Heller verloren.« »Hat dir denn nicht gegruselt?«
»Ei was«, sprach er, »lustig hab ich mich gemacht. Wenn ich nur
wüßte, was Gruseln wäre.«

In der dritten Nacht setzte er sich wieder auf seine Bank und
sprach ganz verdrießlich: »Wenn es mir nur gruselte!« Als es spät
ward, kamen sechs große Männer und brachten eine Totenlade
hereingetragen. Da sprach er: »Haha, das ist gewiß mein Vetterchen,
das erst vor ein paar Tagen gestorben ist«, winkte mit dem Finger und
rief: »Komm, Vetterchen, komm!« sie stellten den Sarg auf die Erde,
er aber ging hinzu und nahm den Deckel ab: da lag ein toter Mann
darin. Er fühlte ihm ans Gesicht, aber es war kalt wie Eis. »Wart«,
sprach er, »ich will dich ein bißchen wärmen«, ging ans Feuer, wärmte
seine Hand und legte sie ihm aufs Gesicht, aber der Tote blieb kalt.
Nun nahm er ihn heraus, setzte sich ans Feuer und legte ihn auf
seinen Schoß und rieb ihm die Arme, damit das Blut wieder in
Bewegung kommen sollte. Als auch das nichts helfen wollte, fiel ihm
ein: Wenn zwei zusammen im Bett liegen, so wärmen sie sich, brachte
ihn ins Bett, deckte ihn zu und legte sich neben ihn. Über ein
Weilchen ward auch der Tote warm und fing an, sich zu regen. Da
sprach der Junge: »Siehst du, Vetterchen, hätt ich dich nicht
gewärmt!« Der Tote aber hub an und rief: »Jetzt will ich dich erwür-
gen.« »Was«, sagte er, »ist das mein Dank? Gleich sollst du wieder in
deinen Sarg«, hub ihn auf, warf ihn hinein und machte den Deckel zu;
da kamen die sechs Männer und trugen ihn wieder fort. »Es will mir
nicht gruseln«, sagte er, »hier lerne ich's mein Lebtag nicht.«

Da trat ein Mann herein, der war größer als alle andere und sah
fürchterlich aus; er war aber alt und hatte einen langen weißen Bart.
»O du Wicht«, rief er, »nun sollst du bald lernen, was Gruseln ist,
denn du sollst sterben.« »Nicht so schnell«, antwortete der Junge,
»soll ich sterben, so muß ich auch dabeisein.« »Dich will ich schon
packen«, sprach der Unhold. »Sachte, sachte, mach dich nicht so
breit; so stark wie du bin ich auch, und wohl noch stärker.« »Das
wollen wir sehn«, sprach der Alte, »bist du stärker als ich, so will ich

"Money enough," he replied, "but your bowling balls aren't perfectly round." Then he took the skulls, put them on the lathe, and turned them till they were spherical. "There, now they'll roll better," he said; "oh boy, now we'll have fun!" He joined in the game and lost some of his money; but when the clock struck twelve, everyone vanished from his sight. He lay down and fell asleep peacefully. The next morning the king came, eager to make inquiries. "How did it go with you this time?" he asked. "I played bowls," he replied, "and I lost a couple of farthings." "But didn't you get the creeps?" "You're kidding," he said; "I was having a good time! If I only knew what the shudders were!"

On the third night he sat down at his lathe again and said in great vexation: "If I only had the creeps!" When it got late, six tall men came in, carrying in a coffin. Then he said: "Oh, ho, that's surely my poor cousin, who died only a few days ago"; he beckoned with his finger and called: "Come, cousin, come!" They placed the coffin on the floor, and he went over and lifted off the lid: there was a dead man inside. He felt his face, but it was cold as ice. "Wait," he said, "I'll warm you up a little"; he went to the fire, warmed his hand, and placed it on the man's face, but the corpse remained cold. Now he took him out, sat down by the fire, laid him on his lap, and rubbed his arms to get the blood circulating again. When that didn't help, either, he got an idea: When two people share a bed, they warm each other. He carried him onto the bed, covered him with blankets, and lay down beside him. After a while the dead man got warm, too, and began to move. Then the boy said: "See, cousin? What if I hadn't warmed you?" But the dead man began to shout: "Now I'm going to throttle you!" "What?" the boy said; "is this the thanks I get? You're going right back to your coffin"; he picked him up, threw him in, and closed the lid; then the six men came and carried him out again. "I just can't get the creeps," he said; "I'll never learn how in this place as long as I live."

Then a man came in who was taller than all the rest and looked fearsome; but he was old and had a long white beard. "Oh, you runt," he shouted, "now you'll soon learn what the shudders are, for you must die." "Not so fast," the boy replied; "if I'm to die, I have to be present." "I'll grab you now," the monster said. "Easy, easy, don't show off like that; I'm as strong as you are, and probably even stronger." "We'll see," said the old man; "if you're stronger than I am, I'll let you go; come on, let's

dich gehn lassen; komm, wir wollen's versuchen.« Da führte er ihn durch dunkle Gänge zu einem Schmiedefeuer, nahm eine Axt und schlug den einen Amboß mit einem Schlag in die Erde. »Das kann ich noch besser«, sprach der Junge und ging zu dem andern Amboß; der Alte stellte sich nebenhin und wollte zusehen, und sein weißer Bart hing herab. Da faßte der Junge die Axt, spaltete den Amboß auf einen Hieb und klemmte den Bart des Alten mit hinein. »Nun hab ich dich«, sprach der Junge, »jetzt ist das Sterben an dir.« Dann faßte er eine Eisenstange und schlug auf den Alten los, bis er wimmerte und bat, er möchte aufhören, er wollte ihm große Reichtümer geben. Der Junge zog die Axt raus und ließ ihn los. Der Alte führte ihn wieder ins Schloß zurück und zeigte ihm in einem Keller drei Kasten voll Gold. »Davon«, sprach er, »ist ein Teil den Armen, der andere dem König, der dritte dein.« Indem schlug es zwölfe, und der Geist verschwand, also daß der Junge im Finstern stand. »Ich werde mir doch heraushelfen können«, sprach er, tappte herum, fand den Weg in die Kammer und schlief dort bei seinem Feuer ein. Am andern Morgen kam der König und sagte: »Nun wirst du gelernt haben, was Gruseln ist?« »Nein«, antwortete er, »was ist's nur? Mein toter Vetter war da, und ein bärtiger Mann ist gekommen, der hat mir da unten viel Geld gezeigt, aber was Gruseln ist, hat mir keiner gesagt.« Da sprach der König: »Du hast das Schloß erlöst und sollst meine Tochter heiraten.« »Das ist all recht gut«, antwortete er, »aber ich weiß noch immer nicht, was Gruseln ist.«

Da ward das Gold heraufgebracht und die Hochzeit gefeiert, aber der junge König, so lieb er seine Gemahlin hatte und so vergnügt er war, sagte doch immer: »Wenn mir nur gruselte, wenn mir nur gruselte.« Das verdroß sie endlich. Ihr Kammermädchen sprach: »Ich will Hilfe schaffen, das Gruseln soll er schon lernen.« Sie ging hinaus zum Bach, der durch den Garten floß, und ließ sich einen ganzen Eimer voll Gründlinge holen. Nachts, als der junge König schlief, mußte seine Gemahlin ihm die Decke wegziehen und den Eimer voll kalt Wasser mit den Gründlingen über ihn herschütten, daß die kleinen Fische um ihn herumzappelten. Da wachte er auf und rief: »Ach was gruselt mir, was gruselt mir, liebe Frau! Ja, nun weiß ich, was Gruseln ist.«

try it out." Then he led him through dark passageways to a forge, picked up an axe, and with one blow drove one of the anvils into the ground. "I can do better than that," said the boy, going over to the other anvil; the old man took his stand beside it, wanting to watch, and his white beard hung down. Then the boy seized the axe, split the anvil with one blow, and wedged the old man's beard inside it. "Now I've got you," said the boy; "now it's your turn to die." Then he seized a crowbar and hit the old man with it until he whimpered and begged him to stop; he'd give him enormous riches. The boy pulled out the axe and freed him. The old man led him back into the castle and, in a cellar, showed him three crates full of gold. "One third of this," he said, "is for the poor, one third is for the king, and one third is for you." Meanwhile, the clock struck twelve and the spirit vanished, so that the boy was left in the dark. "I'll find my way out of here anyway," he said; he groped around and found the path to the bedroom, where he fell asleep beside his fire. The next morning the king came and said: "Now you must have learned what the shudders are?" "No," he replied; "what can they be? My dead cousin was here, and a bearded man came, who showed me a lot of money downstairs, but nobody told me what the shudders are." Then the king said: "You've lifted the spell off the castle, and you shall marry my daughter." "That's all well and good," he replied, "but I still don't know what the shudders are."

Then the gold was brought up, and the wedding was celebrated, but the young king, as much as he loved his wife, and as contented as he was, kept on saying: "If I only had the creeps! If I only had the creeps!" That finally grieved his wife. Her maid said: "I'll help you out; he'll finally learn what the shudders are." She went out to the brook that flowed through the garden and had a pailful of minnows[2] caught. At night, while the young king was sleeping, his wife, following her instructions, pulled the blanket off him and poured the pail full of cold water and minnows over him, so that the little fish wriggled all around him. Then he woke up and shouted: "Oh, wife dear, how I'm shuddering, how I'm shuddering! Yes, now I know what the shudders are!"

---

2. Literally: "gudgeons."

Der Wolf und die sieben jungen Geißlein

Es war einmal eine alte Geiß, die hatte sieben junge Geißlein und hatte sie lieb, wie eine Mutter ihre Kinder liebhat. Eines Tages wollte sie in den Wald gehen und Futter holen, da rief sie alle sieben herbei und sprach:»Liebe Kinder, ich will hinaus in den Wald, seid auf eurer Hut vor dem Wolf, wenn er hereinkommt, so frißt er euch alle mit Haut und Haar. Der Bösewicht verstellt sich oft, aber an seiner rauhen Stimme und an seinen schwarzen Füßen werdet ihr ihn gleich erkennen.« Die Geißlein sagten:»Liebe Mutter, wir wollen uns schon in acht nehmen, Ihr könnt ohne Sorge fortgehen.« Da meckerte die Alte und machte sich getrost auf den Weg.

Es dauerte nicht lange, so klopfte jemand an die Haustür und rief: »Macht auf, ihr lieben Kinder, eure Mutter ist da und hat jedem von euch etwas mitgebracht.« Aber die Geißerchen hörten an der rauhen Stimme, daß es der Wolf war.»Wir machen nicht auf«, riefen sie, »du bist unsere Mutter nicht, die hat eine feine und liebliche Stimme, aber deine Stimme ist rauh; du bist der Wolf.« Da ging der Wolf fort zu einem Krämer und kaufte sich ein großes Stück Kreide: die aß er und machte damit seine Stimme fein. Dann kam er zurück, klopfte an die Haustür und rief:»Macht auf, ihr lieben Kinder, eure Mutter ist da und hat jedem von euch etwas mitgebracht.« Aber der Wolf hatte seine schwarze Pfote in das Fenster gelegt, das sahen die Kinder und riefen: »Wir machen nicht auf, unsere Mutter hat keinen schwarzen Fuß wie du: du bist der Wolf.« Da lief der Wolf zu einem Bäcker und sprach: »Ich habe mich an den Fuß gestoßen, streich mir Teig darüber.« Und als ihm der Bäcker die Pfote bestrichen hatte, so lief er zum Müller und sprach:»Streu mir weißes Mehl auf meine Pfote.« Der Müller dachte: »Der Wolf will einen betrügen«, und weigerte sich, aber der Wolf sprach:»Wenn du es nicht tust, so fresse ich dich.« Da fürchtete sich der Müller und machte ihm die Pfote weiß. Ja, das sind die Menschen.

Nun ging der Bösewicht zum drittenmal zu der Haustüre, klopfte an und sprach:»Macht mir auf, Kinder, euer liebes Mütterchen ist heimgekommen und hat jedem von euch etwas aus dem Walde mitgebracht.« Die Geißerchen riefen:»Zeig uns erst deine Pfote, damit wir wissen, daß du unser liebes Mütterchen bist.« Da legte er die Pfote ins Fenster, und als sie sahen, daß sie weiß war, so glaubten sie, es wäre alles wahr, was er sagte, und machten die Türe auf. Wer aber hereinkam, das war der Wolf. Sie erschraken und wollten sich verstecken. Das eine sprang unter den Tisch, das zweite ins Bett,

The Wolf and the Seven Kids

There was once an old nanny goat who had seven kids; she loved them the way a mother loves her children. One day she wanted to go to the woods to gather forage, so she summoned all seven and said: "Children dear, I want to go out to the forest; be on your guard against the wolf; if he gets in, he'll eat you all, hide and hair. The villain often disguises himself, but you'll recognize him at once by his husky voice and his black feet." The kids said: "Mother dear, we'll pay close attention. You can leave without worrying." Then the old goat bleated and set out, her mind at peace.

Before very long someone knocked at the door to the house and called: "Open up, children dear, your mother is back and she's brought something with her for each of you." But the little goats heard by the husky voice that it was the wolf. "We're not opening," they called, "you're not our mother; she has a high, sweet voice, but your voice is husky; you're the wolf." Then the wolf went to a grocer's and bought a big piece of chalk: he ate it and it made his voice high and soft. Then he returned, knocked at the door to the house, and called: "Open up, children dear, your mother is back and she's brought something with her for each one of you." But the wolf had placed his black paw in the window; the children saw this and called: "We're not opening; our mother doesn't have black feet like you: you're the wolf." Then the wolf ran to a baker's and said: "I've banged my foot, smear dough on it." And when the baker had smeared his paw, he ran to the miller's and said: "Sprinkle white flour on my paw." The miller thought: "The wolf wants to trick somebody," and he refused, but the wolf said: "If you don't do it, I'll eat you." So the miller got scared and made his paw white. Yes, that's how people are.

Now the villain went to the house door for the third time, knocked, and said: "Open up, children, your dear mother has come home and has brought along something for each one of you from the forest." The little goats called: "First show us your paw, so we know that you're our dear mother." Then he placed his paw in the window, and when they saw that it was white, they believed that everything he said was true, and they opened the door. But it was the wolf that came in. They got frightened and tried to hide. One of them leaped under the table, the second

das dritte in den Ofen, das vierte in die Küche, das fünfte in den Schrank, das sechste unter die Waschschüssel, das siebente in den Kasten der Wanduhr. Aber der Wolf fand sie alle und machte nicht langes Federlesen: eins nach dem andern schluckte er in seinen Rachen; nur das jüngste in dem Uhrkasten, das fand er nicht. Als der Wolf seine Lust gebüßt hatte, trollte er sich fort, legte sich draußen auf der grünen Wiese unter einen Baum und fing an zu schlafen.

Nicht lange danach kam die alte Geiß aus dem Walde wieder heim. Ach, was mußte sie da erblicken! Die Haustüre stand sperrweit auf: Tisch, Stühle und Bänke waren umgeworfen, die Waschschüssel lag in Scherben, Decke und Kissen waren aus dem Bett gezogen. Sie suchte ihre Kinder, aber nirgend waren sie zu finden. Sie rief sie nacheinander bei Namen, aber niemand antwortete. Endlich als sie an das jüngste kam, da rief eine feine Stimme: »Liebe Mutter, ich stecke im Uhrkasten.« Sie holte es heraus, und es erzählte ihr, daß der Wolf gekommen wäre und die andern alle gefressen hätte. Da könnt ihr denken, wie sie über ihre armen Kinder geweint hat.

Endlich ging sie in ihrem Jammer hinaus, und das jüngste Geißlein lief mit. Als sie auf die Wiese kam, so lag da der Wolf an dem Baum und schnarchte, daß die Äste zitterten. Sie betrachtete ihn von allen Seiten und sah, daß in seinem angefüllten Bauch sich etwas regte und zappelte. »Ach Gott«, dachte sie, »sollten meine armen Kinder, die er zum Abendbrot hinuntergewürgt hat, noch am Leben sein?« Da mußte das Geißlein nach Haus laufen und Schere, Nadel und Zwirn holen. Dann schnitt sie dem Ungetüm den Wanst auf, und kaum hatte sie einen Schnitt getan, so streckte schon ein Geißlein den Kopf heraus, und als sie weiter schnitt, so sprangen nacheinander alle sechse heraus, und waren noch alle am Leben und hatten nicht einmal Schaden gelitten, denn das Ungetüm hatte sie in der Gier ganz hinuntergeschluckt. Das war eine Freude! Da herzten sie ihre liebe Mutter und hüpften wie ein Schneider, der Hochzeit hält. Die Alte aber sagte: »Jetzt geht und sucht Wackersteine, damit wollen wir dem gottlosen Tier den Bauch füllen, solange es noch im Schlafe liegt.« Da schleppten die sieben Geißerchen in aller Eile die Steine herbei und steckten sie ihm in den Bauch, soviel sie hineinbringen konnten. Dann nähte ihn die Alte in aller Geschwindigkeit wieder zu, daß er nichts merkte und sich nicht einmal regte.

Als der Wolf endlich ausgeschlafen hatte, machte er sich auf die Beine, und weil ihm die Steine im Magen so großen Durst erregten, so wollte er zu einem Brunnen gehen und trinken. Als er aber anfing,

one into bed, the third into the stove, the fourth into the kitchen, the fifth into the closet, the sixth under the washbasin, the seventh into the case of the wall clock. But the wolf found them all and didn't beat around the bush: he gulped one after the other into his maw; the youngest one, in the clock case, was the only one he didn't find. When the wolf had satisfied his appetite, he toddled away, lay down outdoors on the green meadow under a tree, and fell asleep.

Not long afterward the old goat came back home from the forest. Alas, the sight that met her eyes! The door to the house was wide open; the table, chairs, and benches were overturned, the washbasin was in pieces, the blanket and pillows were pulled out of the bed. She looked for her children, but they were nowhere to be found. She called them by name, one by one, but nobody answered. Finally, when she came to the youngest, a piping voice called: "Mother dear, I'm in the clock case." She took the little goat out, and it told her that the wolf had come and had eaten all the others. So you can imagine how she wept over her poor children.

Finally, in her sorrow, she went out, and the youngest kid ran along. When she got to the meadow, there was the wolf lying by the tree and snoring so loud that the boughs were trembling. She observed him from all sides, and saw that something was moving and wriggling in his bloated belly. "Oh, God," she thought, "is it possible that my poor children, whom he gulped down for supper, are still alive?" Then the kid was sent running back home to fetch scissors, needle, and thread. Then she cut open the monster's paunch; and scarcely had she made a cut when one kid already popped its head out; and as she kept on cutting, all six leaped out, one after another; they were all still alive, and hadn't even been injured because in his greed the monster had swallowed them whole. What a joy that was! Then they hugged their dear mother and hopped around like a tailor on his wedding day. But the old goat said: "Now go and find big stones, with which we'll fill this wicked beast's belly, while he's still sleeping." So the seven little goats quickly dragged over the stones and put in his belly as many as they could get in. Then in great haste the old goat sewed him up again so skillfully that he didn't notice a thing or even budge.

When the wolf had finally slept his fill, he got on his legs; and because the stones in his stomach made him extremely thirsty, he wanted to go to a well and drink. But when he started

zu gehen und sich hin und her zu bewegen, so stießen die Steine in
seinem Bauch aneinander und rappelten. Da rief er:

> Was rumpelt und pumpelt
> in meinem Bauch herum?
> Ich meinte, es wären sechs Geißlein,
> so sind's lauter Wackerstein.«

Und als er an den Brunnen kam und sich über das Wasser bückte
und trinken wollte, da zogen ihn die schweren Steine hinein, und er
mußte jämmerlich ersaufen. Als die sieben Geißlein das sahen, da
kamen sie herbeigelaufen, riefen laut:»Der Wolf ist tot! Der Wolf ist
tot!«, und tanzten mit ihrer Mutter vor Freude um den Brunnen
herum.

Brüderchen und Schwesterchen

Brüderchen nahm sein Schwesterchen an der Hand und sprach:»Seit
die Mutter tot ist, haben wir keine gute Stunde mehr; die Stiefmutter
schlägt ans alle Tage, und wenn wir zu ihr kommen, stößt sie uns mit
den Füßen fort. Die harten Brotkrusten, die übrigbleiben, sind unsere
Speise, und dem Hündlein unter dem Tisch geht's besser: dem wirft
sie doch manchmal einen guten Bissen zu. Daß Gott erbarm, wenn das
unsere Mutter wüßte! Komm, wir wollen miteinander in die weite
Welt gehen.« Sie gingen den ganzen Tag über Wiesen, Felder und
Steine, und wenn es regnete, sprach das Schwesterchen:»Gott und
unsere Herzen, die weinen zusammen!« Abends kamen sie in einen
großen Wald und waren so müde von Jammer, Hunger und dem langen Weg, daß sie sich in einen hohlen Baum setzten und einschliefen.
Am andern Morgen, als sie aufwachten, stand die Sonne schon hoch
am Himmel und schien heiß in den Baum hinein. Da sprach das
Brüderchen:»Schwesterchen, mich dürstet, wenn ich ein Brünnlein
wüßte, ich ging' und tränk' einmal; ich mein, ich hört eins rauschen.«
Brüderchen stand auf, nahm Schwesterchen an der Hand, und sie wollten das Brünnlein suchen. Die böse Stiefmutter aber war eine Hexe und
hatte wohl gesehen, wie die beiden Kinder fortgegangen waren, war
ihnen nachgeschlichen, heimlich, wie die Hexen schleichen, und hatte
alle Brunnen im Walde verwünscht. Als sie nun ein Brünnlein fanden,
das so glitzerig über die Steine sprang, wollte das Brüderchen daraus
trinken; aber das Schwesterchen hörte, wie es im Rauschen sprach:

walking and moving to and fro, the stones in his belly bumped one another and rattled. So he cried:

> "What's rumbling and bumbling
> around in my tummy?
> 'I'll eat six baby goats,' I said;
> now it feels like boulders instead."

And when he reached the fountain, leaned over the water, and tried to drink, the heavy stones pulled him in, and he had to drown miserably. When the seven kids saw that, they came running over, loudly shouting: "The wolf is dead! The wolf is dead!" And they danced around the well for joy along with their mother.

Brother and Sister

Brother took his Sister by the hand and said: "Since our mother died, we haven't had one good moment; our stepmother beats us every day, and when we come to her she shoves us away with her feet. The hard bread crusts that are left over are our food, and the little dog under the table is better off: after all, she sometimes throws *him* a tasty morsel. God pity us: if our mother knew all this! Come, let's go out together into the wide world." All day long they walked over meadows, fields, and stones, and when it rained, Sister said: "God and our hearts are weeping together!" In the evening they entered a big forest, and were so weary from sorrow, hunger, and their long journey that they sat down in a hollow tree and fell asleep.

The next morning, when they awoke, the sun was already high in the sky and was shining hotly into the tree. Then Brother spoke: "Sister, I'm thirsty; if I knew where there was a spring, I'd go to it and take a drink; I believe I hear one babbling." Brother stood up, took Sister by the hand, and they set out to find the spring. But their evil stepmother was a witch and had taken good notice of the two children's departure; she had skulked after them—secretly, the way that witches do—and she had cast a spell over all the springs in the forest. When they now found a spring, glittering as it leapt over the stones, Brother wanted to drink from it; but Sister heard it saying as it babbled: "Whoever

»Wer aus mir trinkt, wird ein Tiger; wer aus mir trinkt, wird ein Tiger.«
Da rief das Schwesterchen: »Ich bitte dich, Brüderchen, trink nicht,
sonst wirst du ein wildes Tier und zerreißest mich.« Das Brüderchen
trank nicht, ob es gleich so großen Durst hatte, und sprach: »Ich will
warten bis zur nächsten Quelle.« Als sie zum zweiten Brünnlein kamen,
hörte das Schwesterchen, wie auch dieses sprach: »Wer aus mir trinkt,
wird ein Wolf; wer aus mir trinkt, wird ein Wolf.« Da rief das
Schwesterchen: »Brüderchen, ich bitte dich, trink nicht, sonst wirst du
ein Wolf und frissest mich.« Das Brüderchen trank nicht und sprach:
«Ich will warten, bis wir zur nächsten Quelle kommen, aber dann muß
ich trinken, du magst sagen, was du willst: mein Durst ist gar zu groß.«
Und als sie zum dritten Brünnlein kamen, hörte das Schwesterlein, wie
es im Rauschen sprach: »Wer aus mir trinkt, wird ein Reh; wer aus mir
trinkt, wird ein Reh.« Das Schwesterchen sprach: »Ach Brüderchen, ich
bitte dich, trink nicht, sonst wirst du ein Reh und läufst mir fort.« Aber
das Brüderchen hatte sich gleich beim Brünnlein niedergekniet, hin-
abgebeugt und von dem Wasser getrunken, und wie die ersten Tropfen
auf seine Lippen gekommen waren, lag es da als ein Rehkälbchen.

Nun weinte das Schwesterchen über das arme, verwünschte
Brüderchen, und das Rehchen weinte auch und saß so traurig neben
ihm. Da sprach das Mädchen endlich: »Sei still, liebes Rehchen, ich
will dich ja nimmermehr verlassen.« Dann band es sein goldenes
Strumpfband ab und tat es dem Rehchen um den Hals, und rupfte
Binsen und flocht ein weiches Seil daraus. Daran band es das
Tierchen und führte es weiter und ging immer tiefer in den Wald
hinein. Und als sie lange, lange gegangen waren, kamen sie endlich an
ein kleines Haus, und das Mädchen schaute hinein, und weil es leer
war, dachte es: »Hier können wir bleiben und wohnen.« Da suchte es
dem Rehchen Laub und Moos zu einem weichen Lager, und jeden
Morgen ging es aus und sammelte sich Wurzeln, Beeren und Nüsse,
und für das Rehchen brachte es zartes Gras mit, das fraß es ihm aus
der Hand, war vergnügt und spielte vor ihm herum. Abends, wenn
Schwesterchen müde war und sein Gebet gesagt hatte, legte es seinen
Kopf auf den Rücken des Rehkälbchens, das war sein Kissen, darauf
es sanft einschlief. Und hätte das Brüderchen nur seine menschliche
Gestalt gehabt, es wäre ein herrliches Leben gewesen.

Das dauerte eine Zeitlang, daß sie so allein in der Wildnis waren. Es
trug sich aber zu, daß der König des Landes eine große Jagd in dem
Wald hielt. Da schallte das Hörnerblasen, Hundegebell und das lustige
Geschrei der Jäger durch die Bäume, und das Rehlein hörte es und
wäre gar zu gerne dabei gewesen. »Ach«, sprach es zum Schwesterlein,

drinks of me will become a tiger; whoever drinks of me will become a tiger." So Sister called: "Please, Brother, don't drink, or you'll become a wild animal and tear me apart." Brother didn't drink, in spite of his awful thirst, but said: "I'll wait until the next spring." When they got to the second spring, Sister heard this one, too, speaking: "Whoever drinks of me will become a wolf; whoever drinks of me will become a wolf." So Sister called: "Brother, please don't drink, or you'll become a wolf and eat me." Brother didn't drink, but said: "I'll wait until we reach the next spring, but then I have to drink, say whatever you will: my thirst is just too great." And when they came to the third spring, Sister heard it say as it babbled: "Whoever drinks of me will become a roe deer; whoever drinks of me will become a roe deer." Sister said: "Alas, Brother, please don't drink, or you'll become a roe deer and run away from me." But Brother had immediately knelt down by the spring, had leaned over, and had drunk of the water; and as soon as the first drops touched his lips, he lay there in the shape of a roe deer fawn.

Now Sister wept over her poor enchanted Brother, and the fawn wept also as it sat so sadly next to her. Then the girl finally said: "Be calm, dear fawn, I'll never leave you." Then she undid her golden garter and put it around the fawn's neck, and she pulled out some rushes and braided them into a soft cord. She tied the little animal to this and led him away, moving deeper and deeper into the forest. And when they had walked for a long, long time, they finally reached a little house; the girl looked inside, and because it was empty, she thought: "We can stay and live here." Then she looked for leaves and moss to make a soft bed for the fawn, and every morning she went out and gathered roots, berries, and nuts for herself and brought back tender grass for the fawn, which ate it out of her hand, became contented, and sported around her. In the evening, when Sister was tired and had said her prayers, she would lay her head on the fawn's back; that was her pillow, on which she quietly went to sleep. And if only Brother had had his human form, it would have been a splendid life.

That lasted awhile, their lonely existence in the wilderness. But it came about that the king of the country held a great hunt in the forest. Then the blowing of horns, the barking of hounds, and the merry shouts of the hunters resounded through the trees, and the fawn heard it and was dreadfully eager to

»laß mich hinaus in die Jagd, ich kann's nicht länger mehr aushalten«, und bat so lange, bis es einwilligte. »Aber«, sprach es zu ihm, »komm mir ja abends wieder, vor den wilden Jägern schließ ich mein Türlein; und damit ich dich kenne, so klopf und sprich: Mein Schwesterlein, laß mich herein; und wenn du nicht so sprichst, so schließ ich mein Türlein nicht auf.« Nun sprang das Rehchen hinaus und war ihm so wohl und war so lustig in freier Luft. Der König und seine Jäger sahen das schöne Tier und setzten ihm nach, aber sie konnten es nicht einholen, und wenn sie meinten, sie hätten es gewiß, da sprang es über das Gebüsch weg und war verschwunden. Als es dunkel ward, lief es zu dem Häuschen, klopfte und sprach: »Mein Schwesterlein, laß mich herein.« Da ward ihm die kleine Tür aufgetan, es sprang hinein und ruhete sich die ganze Nacht auf seinem weichen Lager aus. Am andern Morgen ging die Jagd von neuem an, und als das Rehlein wieder das Hüfthorn hörte und das Hoho! der Jäger, da hatte es keine Ruhe und sprach: »Schwesterchen, mach mir auf, ich muß hinaus.« Das Schwesterchen öffnete ihm die Türe und sprach: »Aber zu Abend mußt du wieder da sein und dein Sprüchlein sagen.« Als der König und seine Jäger das Rehlein mit dem goldenen Halsband wieder sahen, jagten sie ihm alle nach, aber es war ihnen zu schnell und behend. Das währte den ganzen Tag, endlich aber hatten es die Jäger abends umzingelt, und einer verwundete es ein wenig am Fuß, so daß es hinken mußte und langsam fortlief. Da schlich ihm ein Jäger nach bis zu dem Häuschen und hörte, wie es rief: »Mein Schwesterlein, laß mich herein«, und sah, daß die Tür ihm aufgetan und alsbald wieder zugeschlossen ward. Der Jäger behielt das alles wohl im Sinn, ging zum König und erzählte ihm, was er gesehen und gehört hatte. Da sprach der König: »Morgen soll noch einmal gejagt werden.«

Das Schwesterchen aber erschrak gewaltig, als es sah, daß sein Rehkälbchen verwundet war. Es wusch ihm das Blut ab, legte Kräuter auf und sprach: »Geh auf dein Lager, lieb Rehchen, daß du wieder heil wirst.« Die Wunde aber war so gering, daß das Rehchen am Morgen nichts mehr davon spürte. Und als es die Jagdlust wieder draußen hörte, sprach es: »Ich kann's nicht aushalten, ich muß dabei sein; so bald soll mich keiner kriegen.« Das Schwesterchen weinte und sprach: »Nun werden sie dich töten, und ich bin hier allein im Wald und bin verlassen von aller Welt: ich laß dich nicht hinaus.« »So sterb ich dir hier vor Betrübnis«, antwortete das Rehchen, »wenn ich das Hüfthorn höre, so mein ich, ich müßt aus den Schuhen springen!« Da konnte das Schwesterchen nicht anders und schloß ihm mit schwerem Herzen die Tür auf, und das Rehchen sprang gesund und

participate. "Oh," he said to Sister, "let me go out and join the
hunt, I can't resist any longer." He pleaded so long that she consented. "But," she said to him, "come back here in the evening;
I'm going to lock my door, with those wild hunters around; so I
can recognize you, knock and say: 'Sister, let me in.' If you don't
say that, I won't unlock my door." Now the fawn leapt out and
felt so good and so cheerful in the open air! The king and his
hunters saw the pretty animal and pursued him, but were unable
to overtake him; whenever they thought they surely had him, he
would leap away over the bushes and vanish. When it got dark,
he ran to the little house, knocked, and said: "Sister, let me in."
Then the little door was opened for him, he leapt in, and he re-
posed on his soft bed all night long. The next morning the hunt
resumed, and when the fawn heard the hunting horn and the
hunters' hallooing again, he couldn't rest, and said: "Sister, open
the door, I must go out!" Sister opened the door for him, saying:
"But you must be back here by evening and speak your little
speech." When the king and his hunters saw the fawn with the
golden collar again, they all pursued him, but he was too fast and
nimble for them. That lasted the whole day, but finally in the
evening the hunters had him surrounded, and one of them
wounded him slightly in the foot, so that he had to limp, and he
got away slowly. Then a hunter sneaked after him up to the little house and heard him call: "Sister, let me in." He saw the door
being opened for him and immediately locked again. The hunter
kept this all in mind, went to the king, and told him what he had
seen and heard. Then the king said: "Tomorrow we'll hunt
again."

But Sister was terribly frightened when she saw that her fawn
was wounded. She washed off the blood, applied herbs, and
said: "Go to bed, fawn dear, so you can get better again." But the
wound was so trifling that in the morning the fawn no longer felt
a thing. And when he heard the merriment of the chase outside
again, he said: "I can't resist it; I must take part; no one's going
to catch me as soon as all that." Sister wept and said: "Now
they'll kill you, and I'll be left alone in the woods here, totally
abandoned by everyone: I won't let you out." Then I'll die here
from melancholy," the fawn replied; "when I hear the hunting
horn, I feel like jumping out of my shoes!" So Sister had no other
choice than to unlock the door for him, though her heart was
heavy, and the fawn leapt into the forest, hale and happy. When

fröhlich in den Wald. Als es der König erblickte, sprach er zu seinen Jägern:»Nun jagt ihm nach den ganzen Tag bis in die Nacht, aber daß ihm keiner etwas zuleide tut.« Sobald die Sonne untergegangen war, sprach der König zum Jäger:»Nun komm und zeige mir das Waldhäuschen.« Und als er vor dem Türlein war, klopfte er an und rief:»Lieb Schwesterlein, laß mich herein.« Da ging die Tür auf, und der König trat herein, und da stand ein Mädchen, das war so schön, wie er noch keins gesehen hatte. Das Mädchen erschrak, als es sah, daß nicht sein Rehlein, sondern ein Mann hereinkam, der eine goldene Krone auf dem Haupt hatte. Aber der König sah es freundlich an, reichte ihm die Hand und sprach:»Willst du mit mir gehen auf mein Schloß und meine liebe Frau sein?«»Ach ja«, antwortete das Mädchen,»aber das Rehchen muß auch mit, das verlaß ich nicht.« Sprach der König:»Es soll bei dir bleiben, solange du lebst, und soll ihm an nichts fehlen.« Indem kam es hereingesprungen, da band es das Schwesterchen wieder an das Binsenseil, nahm es selbst in die Hand und ging mit ihm aus dem Waldhäuschen fort.

Der König nahm das schöne Mädchen auf sein Pferd und führte es in sein Schloß, wo die Hochzeit mit großer Pracht gefeiert wurde, und war es nun die Frau Königin und lebten sie lange Zeit vergnügt zusammen; das Rehlein ward gehegt und gepflegt und sprang in dem Schloßgarten herum. Die böse Stiefmutter aber, um derentwillen die Kinder in die Welt hineingegangen waren, die meinte nicht anders, als Schwesterchen wäre von den wilden Tieren im Walde zerrissen worden und Brüderchen als ein Rehkalb von den Jägern totgeschossen. Als sie nun hörte, daß sie so glücklich waren und es ihnen so wohl ging, da wurden Neid und Mißgunst in ihrem Herzen rege und ließen ihr keine Ruhe, und sie hatte keinen andern Gedanken, als wie sie die beiden doch noch ins Unglück bringen könnte. Ihre rechte Tochter, die häßlich war wie die Nacht und nur ein Auge hatte, die machte ihr Vorwürfe und sprach:»Eine Königin zu werden, das Glück hätte mir gebührt.«»Sei nur still«, sagte die Alte und sprach sie zufrieden:»Wenn's Zeit ist, will ich schon bei der Hand sein.« Als nun die Zeit herangerückt war und die Königin ein schönes Knäblein zur Welt gebracht hatte und der König gerade auf der Jagd war, nahm die alte Hexe die Gestalt der Kammerfrau an, trat in die Stube, wo die Königin lag, und sprach zu der Kranken:»Kommt, das Bad ist fertig, das wird Euch wohltun und frische Kräfte geben: geschwind, eh es kalt wird.« Ihre Tochter war auch bei der Hand, sie trugen die schwache Königin in die Badstube und legten sie in die Wanne; dann schlossen sie die Tür ab und liefen davon. In der Badstube aber

the king caught sight of him, he said to his hunters: "Now pursue him all day until nighttime, but no one is to do him the least harm." As soon as the sun had set, the king said to that hunter: "Now come and show me the little house in the woods." And when he was in front of the door, he knocked and called: "Sister dear, let me in." Then the door opened and the king stepped in, and there stood a girl who was more beautiful than any other he had ever seen. The girl was frightened on seeing that it wasn't her fawn but a man who had come in, a man with a golden crown on his head. But the king looked at her with a friendly expression and gave her his hand, saying: "Will you come to my palace with me and be my beloved wife?" "Oh, yes," the girl replied, "but the fawn must come along; I won't desert him." The king said: "He can stay with you as long as you live, and he will lack for nothing." Meanwhile the fawn came bounding in, and Sister tied it to the rush cord again, took the cord in her own hand, and led him out of the little house in the woods.

The king lifted the beautiful girl onto his horse and rode with her to his palace, where their wedding was celebrated with great splendor; now she was the queen, and they lived contentedly together for a long time; the fawn was protected and nourished, and used to leap around in the palace garden. But the evil stepmother, because of whom the children had left home, was convinced that Sister had been torn apart by the wild animals in the forest and that Brother, in the shape of a fawn, had been shot and killed by the hunters. When she now heard that they were so happy and well off, envy and ill will stirred in her heart and gave her no rest; her only thought was how she could still bring misfortune on the two of them. Her own daughter, who was ugly as night and had only one eye, reproached her, saying: "The good fortune to become a queen should have been mine." "Just relax," said the old woman, and satisfied her mind, saying: "At the right time I'll be on hand." Now, when the time had come around, and the queen had brought a pretty little boy into the world, the king being away on a hunt, the old witch assumed the appearance of the lady of the bedchamber; entering the room where the queen lay in bed, she said to the new mother: "Come, your bath is ready; it will do you good and restore your strength; quick, before it gets cold." Her daughter was also present; they carried the weak queen into the bathroom and placed her in the tub; then they locked the door and ran away. But in the

hatten sie ein rechtes Höllenfeuer angemacht, daß die schöne junge Königin bald ersticken mußte.

Als das vollbracht war, nahm die Alte ihre Tochter, setzte ihr eine Haube auf und legte sie ins Bett an der Königin Stelle. Sie gab ihr auch die Gestalt und das Ansehen der Königin, nur das verlorene Auge konnte sie ihr nicht wiedergeben. Damit es aber der König nicht merkte, mußte sie sich auf die Seite legen, wo sie kein Auge hatte. Am Abend, als er heimkam und hörte, daß ihm ein Söhnlein geboren war, freute er sich herzlich und wollte ans Bett seiner lieben Frau gehen und sehen, was sie machte. Da rief die Alte geschwind: »Beileibe, laßt die Vorhänge zu, die Königin darf noch nicht ins Licht sehen und muß Ruhe haben.« Der König ging zurück und wußte nicht, daß eine falsche Königin im Bette lag.

Als es aber Mitternacht war und alles schlief, da sah die Kinderfrau, die in der Kinderstube neben der Wiege saß und allein noch wachte, wie die Türe aufging und die rechte Königin hereintrat. Sie nahm das Kind aus der Wiege, legte es in ihren Arm und gab ihm zu trinken. Dann schüttelte sie ihm sein Kißchen, legte es wieder hinein und deckte es mit dem Deckbettchen zu. Sie vergaß aber auch das Rehchen nicht, ging in die Ecke, wo es lag, und streichelte ihm über den Rücken. Darauf ging sie ganz stillschweigend wieder zur Türe hinaus, und die Kinderfrau fragte am andern Morgen die Wächter, ob jemand während der Nacht ins Schloß gegangen wäre, aber sie antworteten: »Nein, wir haben niemand gesehen.« So kam sie viele Nächte und sprach niemals ein Wort dabei; die Kinderfrau sah sie immer, aber sie getraute sich nicht, jemand etwas davon zu sagen.

Als nun so eine Zeit verflossen war, da hub die Königin in der Nacht an zu reden und sprach:

»Was macht mein Kind? Was macht mein Reh?
Nun komm ich noch zweimal und dann nimmermehr.«

Die Kinderfrau antwortete ihr nicht, aber als sie wieder verschwunden war, ging sie zum König und erzählte ihm alles. Sprach der König: »Ach Gott, was ist das! Ich will in der nächsten Nacht bei dem Kinde wachen.« Abends ging er in die Kinderstube, aber um Mitternacht erschien die Königin wieder und sprach:

»Was macht mein Kind? Was macht mein Reh?
Nun komm ich noch einmal und dann nimmermehr.«

Und pflegte dann des Kindes, wie sie gewöhnlich tat, ehe sie

bathroom they had lit a fire truly as hot as hell, so that the beautiful young queen soon suffocated.

When that was accomplished, the old woman took her daughter, placed a nightcap on her, and put her in bed in place of the queen. She also gave her the form and appearance of the queen, but was unable to restore her lost eye. But, to prevent the king from noticing this, she had to lie on the side where the eye was missing. In the evening, when he came home and heard that a son had been born to him, he was extremely happy, and insisted on visiting his dear wife's bedside to see how she was doing. Then the old woman quickly called: "By all means keep the bed curtains closed; the queen mustn't look into bright light yet, and she has to rest." The king returned, not knowing that a false queen lay in the bed.

But when midnight came and everyone was asleep, the dry-nurse, who was sitting in the nursery next to the cradle, and who was the only person still awake, saw the door open and the true queen enter. She lifted the child from the cradle, took him on her arm, and suckled him. Then she shook out his pillow, put him back in the cradle, and covered him with the feather quilt. Nor did she forget the fawn; she went to the corner where he lay and caressed his back. Then, in complete silence, she went out the door again; the next morning the nurse asked the guards whether anyone had entered the palace during the night, but they replied: "No, we didn't see anyone." She came many nights in that manner, never uttering a word; the nurse saw her each time, but didn't dare tell anyone about it.

Well, after some time had gone by, the queen began to speak at night; she said:

> "How is my child? How is my fawn?
> I come but twice again, and then I'm gone!"

The nurse didn't answer her, but after she had disappeared again, she went to the king and made a full report. The king said: "Oh, God, what's this? This coming night I'll sit up with my child." In the evening he went to the nursery; about midnight the queen appeared again, and said:

> "How is my child? How is my fawn?
> I come but once again, and then I'm gone!"

Then she nursed the child, as she usually did, before disappearing.

verschwand. Der König getraute sich nicht, sie anzureden, aber er wachte auch in der folgenden Nacht. Sie sprach abermals:

>Was macht mein Kind? Was macht mein Reh?
Nun komm ich noch diesmal und dann nimmermehr.«

Da konnte sich der König nicht zurückhalten, sprang zu ihr und sprach: »Du kannst niemand anders sein als meine liebe Frau.« Da antwortete sie: »Ja, ich bin deine liebe Frau«, und hatte in dem Augenblick durch Gottes Gnade das Leben wiedererhalten, war frisch, rot und gesund. Darauf erzählte sie dem König den Frevel, den die böse Hexe und ihre Tochter an ihr verübt hatten. Der König ließ beide vor Gericht führen, und es ward ihnen das Urteil gesprochen. Die Tochter ward in Wald geführt, wo sie die wilden Tiere zerrissen, die Hexe aber ward ins Feuer gelegt und mußte jammervoll verbrennen. Und wie sie zu Asche verbrannt war, verwandelte sich das Rehkälbchen und erhielt seine menschliche Gestalt wieder; Schwesterchen und Brüderchen aber lebten glücklich zusammen bis an ihr Ende.

Rapunzel

Es war einmal ein Mann und eine Frau, die wünschten sich schon lange vergeblich ein Kind, endlich machte sich die Frau Hoffnung, der liebe Gott werde ihren Wunsch erfüllen. Die Leute hatten in ihrem Hinterhaus ein kleines Fenster, daraus konnte man in einen prächtigen Garten sehen, der voll der schönsten Blumen und Kräuter stand; er war aber von einer hohen Mauer umgeben, und niemand wagte hineinzugehen, weil er einer Zauberin gehörte, die große Macht hatte und von aller Welt gefürchtet ward. Eines Tags stand die Frau an diesem Fenster und sah in den Garten hinab, da erblickte sie ein Beet, das mit den schönsten Rapunzeln bepflanzt war; und sie sahen so frisch und grün aus, daß sie lüstern ward und das größte Verlangen empfand, von den Rapunzeln zu essen. Das Verlangen nahm jeden Tag zu, und da sie wußte, daß sie keine davon bekommen konnte, so fiel sie ganz ab, sah blaß und elend aus. Da erschrak der Mann und fragte: »Was fehlt dir, liebe Frau?« »Ach«, antwortete sie, »wenn ich keine Rapunzeln aus dem Garten hinter unserm Hause zu essen kriege, so sterbe ich.« Der Mann, der sie liebhatte, dachte: »Eh du deine Frau sterben lässest, holst du ihr von den Rapunzeln, es mag

The king didn't dare address her, but he sat up the following night as well. She spoke once more:

"How is my child? How is my fawn?
I come only this time, and then I'm gone!"

Then the king was unable to restrain himself any longer; he leapt to her side, saying: "You can be no one else than my beloved wife." Then she answered: "Yes, I am your beloved wife." And at that moment, by the grace of God, she had been restored to life; she was hearty, red-cheeked, and healthy. Next, she told the king about the vicious crime that the evil witch and her daughter had committed against her. The king had both of them haled into court, where they were sentenced. The daughter was led out into the forest, where the wild animals tore her apart, but the witch was thrown on a fire and burned to death miserably. As soon as she was burnt to ashes, the fawn was transformed, recovering his human shape; and Sister and Brother lived happily together till the end of their lives.

Rampion

There once lived a husband and wife who had long been wishing in vain for a child; finally, the woman had reason to believe that God was granting her wish. In the back part of their house the couple had a small window from which they could see a splendid garden that was full of the most beautiful flowers and herbs; but it was enclosed by a high wall, and no one ventured inside it because it belonged to a sorceress, who had great powers and was universally feared. One day the woman was standing at that window looking down at the garden, when she caught sight of a flowerbed that was planted with the most beautiful rampions; they looked so fresh and green that she got a craving for them and felt the strongest desire to eat a rampion salad. Her desire increased daily, and since she knew she wouldn't get any of them, she became gaunt and looked pale and wretched. Then her husband became frightened and asked her: "What's wrong with you, wife dear?" "Ah," she replied, "if I don't get any rampions to eat from the garden in back of our house, I'll die." The man, who loved her, thought: "Before you let your wife die, you'll get some

kosten, was es will.« In der Abenddämmerung stieg er also über die Mauer in den Garten der Zauberin, stach in aller Eile eine Handvoll Rapunzeln und brachte sie seiner Frau. Sie machte sich sogleich Salat daraus und aß sie in voller Begierde auf. Sie hatten ihr aber so gut, so gut geschmeckt, daß sie den andern Tag noch dreimal soviel Lust bekam. Sollte sie Ruhe haben, so mußte der Mann noch einmal in den Garten steigen. Er machte sich also in der Abenddämmerung wieder hinab, als er aber die Mauer herabgeklettert war, erschrak er gewaltig, denn er sah die Zauberin vor sich stehen. »Wie kannst du es wagen«, sprach sie mit zornigem Blick, »in meinen Garten zu steigen und wie ein Dieb mir meine Rapunzeln zu stehlen? Das soll dir schlecht bekommen.« »Ach«, antwortete er, »laßt Gnade für Recht ergehen, ich habe mich nur aus Not dazu entschlossen: meine Frau hat Eure Rapunzeln aus dem Fenster erblickt und empfindet ein so großes Gelüsten, daß sie sterben würde, wenn sie nicht davon zu essen bekäme.« Da ließ die Zauberin in ihrem Zorne nach und sprach zu ihm: »Verhält es sich so, wie du sagst, so will ich dir gestatten, Rapunzeln mitzunehmen, soviel du willst, allein ich mache eine Bedingung: Du mußt mir das Kind geben, das deine Frau zur Welt bringen wird. Es soll ihm gut gehen, und ich will für es sorgen wie eine Mutter.« Der Mann sagte in der Angst alles zu, und als die Frau in Wochen kam, so erschien sogleich die Zauberin, gab dem Kinde den Namen *Rapunzel* und nahm es mit sich fort.

Rapunzel ward das schönste Kind unter der Sonne. Als es zwölf Jahre alt war, schloß es die Zauberin in einen Turm, der in einem Walde lag und weder Treppe noch Türe hatte, nur ganz oben war ein kleines Fensterchen. Wenn die Zauberin hinein wollte, so stellte sie sich unten hin und rief:

> »Rapunzel, Rapunzel,
> laß mir dein Haar herunter.«

Rapunzel hatte lange prächtige Haare, fein wie gesponnen Gold. Wenn sie nun die Stimme der Zauberin vernahm, so band sie ihre Zöpfe los, wickelte sie oben um einen Fensterhaken, und dann fielen die Haare zwanzig Ellen tief herunter, und die Zauberin stieg daran hinauf.

Nach ein paar Jahren trug es sich zu, daß der Sohn des Königs durch den Wald ritt und an dem Turm vorüberkam. Da hörte er einen Gesang, der war so lieblich, daß er stillhielt und horchte. Das war Rapunzel, die in ihrer Einsamkeit sich die Zeit damit vertrieb, ihre süße Stimme erschallen zu lassen. Der Königssohn wollte zu ihr hin-

of the rampions for her, cost what it may." So at twilight he climbed over the wall into the sorceress's garden, rapidly pulled up a handful of rampions, and brought them to his wife. She immediately made a salad of them and devoured them greedily. But they tasted so good, so good, to her that by the following day her desire for them had tripled. If her mind was to be at rest, her husband had to climb into the garden again. So at twilight he made his way down there again, but after climbing down the wall he got a terrible fright because he saw the sorceress standing in front of him. "How dare you climb into my garden," she said with an angry gaze, "and steal my rampions like a thief? You'll be sorry you did!" "Oh," he replied, "show mercy; I resolved to do it only because it was an emergency: my wife caught sight of your rampions through the window, and has such a strong craving for them that she'd die if she didn't get some to eat." Then the sorceress's anger abated, and she said to him: "If matters are as you say, I'll allow you to take along as many rampions as you like, but I make one condition: you must give me the child your wife will give birth to. It will be well treated, and I'll care for it like a mother." In his dread, the man agreed to everything, and when his wife went into confinement, the sorceress immediately appeared, gave the child the name Rampion, and took it away.

Rampion became the most beautiful child under the sun. When she was twelve years old, the sorceress shut her into a tower that stood in a forest and had neither stairs nor a door; there was just a tiny window near the top. When the sorceress wanted to go in, she would stand at the foot of the tower and call:

> "Rampion, Rampion,
> let down your hair for me."

Rampion had splendid long hair as fine as spun gold. Whenever she heard the sorceress's voice, she unwound her braids and wrapped them around the casement handle up there, and then her hair descended twenty ells down, and the sorceress climbed up it.

After a few years it came about that a king's son was riding through the forest and passed by the tower. He heard singing so lovely that he stopped and listened. It was Rampion, who in her loneliness was passing the time by letting her sweet voice be heard abroad. The prince wanted to climb up to her and looked

aufsteigen und suchte nach einer Türe des Turms, aber es war keine
zu finden. Er ritt heim, doch der Gesang hatte ihm so sehr das Herz
gerührt, daß er jeden Tag hinaus in den Wald ging und zuhörte. Als er
einmal so hinter einem Baum stand, sah er, daß eine Zauberin herankam und hörte, wie sie hinaufrief:

>>Rapunzel, Rapunzel,
laß dein Haar herunter.<<

Da ließ Rapunzel die Haarflechten herab, und die Zauberin stieg zu
ihr hinauf. >>Ist das die Leiter, auf welcher man hinaufkommt, so will
ich auch einmal mein Glück versuchen.<< Und den folgenden Tag, als
es anfing, dunkel zu werden, ging er zu dem Turme und rief:

>>Rapunzel, Rapunzel,
laß dein Haar herunter.<<

Alsbald fielen die Haare herab, und der Königssohn stieg hinauf.

Anfangs erschrak Rapunzel gewaltig, als ein Mann zu ihr
hereinkam, wie ihre Augen noch nie einen erblickt hatten, doch der
Königssohn fing an, ganz freundlich mir ihr zu reden, und erzählte
ihr, daß von ihrem Gesang sein Herz so sehr sei bewegt worden, daß
es ihm keine Ruhe gelassen und er sie selbst habe sehen müssen. Da
verlor Rapunzel ihre Angst, und als er sie fragte, ob sie ihn zum
Manne nehmen wollte, und sie sah, daß er jung und schön war, so
dachte sie: >>Der wird mich lieber haben als die alte Frau Gothel<<, und
sagte ja und legte ihre Hand in seine Hand. Sie sprach: >>Ich will gerne
mit dir gehen, aber ich weiß nicht, wie ich herabkommen kann. Wenn
du kommst, so bring jedesmal einen Strang Seide mit, daraus will ich
eine Leiter flechten, und wenn die fertig ist, so steige ich herunter,
und du nimmst mich auf dein Pferd.<< Sie verabredeten, daß er bis
dahin alle Abend zu ihr kommen sollte, denn bei Tag kam die Alte.
Die Zauberin merkte auch nichts davon, bis einmal Rapunzel anfing
und zu ihr sagte: >>Sag Sie mir doch, Frau Gothel, wie kommt es nur,
Sie wird mir viel schwerer heraufzuziehen als der junge Königssohn,
der ist in einem Augenblick bei mir.<< >>Ach du gottloses Kind<<, rief die
Zauberin, >>was muß ich von dir hören, ich dachte, ich hätte dich von
aller Welt geschieden, und du hast mich doch betrogen!<< In ihrem
Zorne packte sie die schönen Haare der Rapunzel, schlug sie ein paar-
mal um ihre linke Hand, griff eine Schere mit der rechten, und ritsch,
ratsch waren sie abgeschnitten, und die schönen Flechten lagen auf
der Erde. Und sie war so unbarmherzig, daß sie die arme Rapunzel in

for a door to the tower, but there was none to be found. He rode home, but the singing had touched his heart so tenderly that he went out into the woods to listen every day. Once, while he was standing behind a tree that way, he saw a sorceress arrive and heard her shout upward:

> "Rampion, Rampion,
> let down your hair."

Then Rampion let her braids down, and the sorceress climbed up to her. "If that's the ladder by which people get up there, I'll go try my luck, too." And the next day, when it began to grow dark, he went to the tower and called:

> "Rampion, Rampion,
> let down your hair."

At once the hair descended, and the prince climbed up.

At first Rampion was terribly frightened at seeing a man come in, a man unlike any other her eyes had ever seen; but the prince began to speak to her quite amiably, telling her that his heart had been so affected by her singing that it gave him no peace and he had to see her in person. Then Rampion was no longer afraid, and when he asked her whether she would accept him as her husband, and she saw that he was young and handsome, she thought: "He will love me more than old lady Gothel does"; she consented and placed her hand in his. She said: "I will gladly go with you, but I don't know how to get down. When you visit me, bring along a skein of silk each time; I'll braid a ladder out of it, and when it's ready, I'll climb down, and you'll lift me onto your horse." They agreed that, until that time, he would visit her every evening, because the old woman came by day. And the sorceress noticed nothing of all this, until, one time, Rampion opened the conversation by saying: "Please tell me, Mother Gothel, how is it that you're becoming much harder to pull up than the young prince, who's with me in a minute?" "Oh, you wicked child," shouted the sorceress, "what's this I hear? I thought I had isolated you from the whole world, and all the same you've tricked me!" In her anger she seized Rampion's beautiful hair, wrapped it around her left hand a couple of times, grasped a pair of scissors in her right, and—snip, snip—it was cut off, and her beautiful braids were lying on the floor. And she

eine Wüstenei brachte, wo sie in großem Jammer und Elend leben mußte.

Denselben Tag aber, wo sie Rapunzel verstoßen hatte, machte abends die Zauberin die abgeschnittenen Flechten oben am Fensterhaken fest, und als der Königssohn kam und rief:

>»Rapunzel, Rapunzel,
>laß dein Haar herunter«,

so ließ sie die Haare hinab. Der Königssohn stieg hinauf, aber er fand oben nicht seine liebste Rapunzel, sondern die Zauberin, die ihn mit bösen und giftigen Blicken ansah. »Aha«, rief sie höhnisch, »du willst die Frau Liebste holen, aber der schöne Vogel sitzt nicht mehr im Nest und singt nicht mehr, die Katze hat ihn geholt und wird dir auch noch die Augen auskratzen. Für dich ist Rapunzel verloren, du wirst sie nie wieder erblicken.« Der Königssohn geriet außer sich vor Schmerz, und in der Verzweiflung sprang er den Turm herab: das Leben brachte er davon, aber die Dornen, in die er fiel, zerstachen ihm die Augen. Da irrte er blind im Walde umher, aß nichts als Wurzeln und Beeren und tat nichts als jammern und weinen über den Verlust seiner liebsten Frau. So wanderte er einige Jahre im Elend umher und geriet endlich in die Wüstenei, wo Rapunzel mit den Zwillingen, die sie geboren hatte, einem Knaben und Mädchen, kümmerlich lebte. Er vernahm eine Stimme, und sie däuchte ihn so bekannt; da ging er darauf zu, und wie er herankam, erkannte ihn Rapunzel und fiel ihm um den Hals und weinte. Zwei von ihren Tränen aber benetzten seine Augen, da wurden sie wieder klar, und er konnte damit sehen wie sonst. Er führte sie in sein Reich, wo er mit Freude empfangen ward, und sie lebten noch lange glücklich und vergnügt.

Die drei Spinnerinnen

Es war ein Mädchen faul und wollte nicht spinnen, und die Mutter mochte sagen, was sie wollte, sie konnte es nicht dazu bringen. Endlich übernahm die Mutter einmal Zorn und Ungeduld, daß sie ihm Schläge gab, worüber es laut zu weinen anfing. Nun fuhr gerade die Königin vorbei, und als sie das Weinen hörte, ließ sie anhalten, trat in das Haus und fragte die Mutter, warum sie ihre Tochter schlüge, daß man draußen auf der Straße das Schreien hörte. Da

was so merciless that she brought poor Rampion into a wilderness, where she was forced to live in great sorrow and want.

But on the evening of the same day that she had cast out Rampion, the sorceress tied the cut-off braids firmly to the casement handle, and when the prince arrived and called:

"Rampion, Rampion,
let down your hair,"

she let down the hair. The prince climbed up, but at the top he found not his darling Rampion but the sorceress, who glared at him with evil, poisonous eyes. "Aha," she shouted scornfully, "you want to fetch Miss Darling, but the pretty bird is no longer on her nest and she isn't singing anymore; the cat got her and is going to scratch out your eyes, too. Rampion is lost to you; you'll never see her again." The prince was beside himself with sorrow, and in his despair he jumped down from the tower: he got off with his life, but the thorns that he fell into pierced his eyes. Then he roamed blindly through the forest, eating nothing but roots and berries, and doing nothing but lamenting and weeping over the loss of his beloved wife. He wandered around in misery that way for a few years, and finally arrived in the wilderness where Rampion eked out a poor existence along with the twins that she had borne, a boy and a girl. He heard a voice, which seemed so familiar to him; so he walked toward it, and when he reached it, Rampion recognized him, embraced him, and wept. But two of her tears moistened his eyes, which were healed again, and he could see out of them the way he used to. He led her to his kingdom, where he was given a joyous reception, and they lived in happiness and contentment for a long time afterward.

The Three Spinners

There was a lazy girl who didn't want to spin, and no matter what her mother said, she couldn't make her do it. Finally her mother was overcome with anger and impatience, so that she hit her, which made her start weeping loudly. Now, just at that moment the queen was driving by, and when she heard the weeping, she ordered her carriage halted, she entered the house, and asked the mother why she was beating her daughter so hard that her

schämte sich die Frau, daß sie die Faulheit ihrer Tochter offenbaren sollte, und sprach: »Ich kann sie nicht vom Spinnen abbringen, sie will immer und ewig spinnen, und ich bin arm und kann den Flachs nicht herbeischaffen.« Da antwortete die Königin: »Ich höre nichts lieber als Spinnen und bin nicht vergnügter, als wenn die Räder schnurren: gebt mir Eure Tochter mit ins Schloß, ich habe Flachs genug, da soll sie spinnen, soviel sie Lust hat.« Die Mutter war's von Herzen gerne zufrieden, und die Königin nahm das Mädchen mit. Als sie ins Schloß gekommen waren, führte sie es hinauf zu drei Kammern, die lagen von unten bis oben voll vom schönsten Flachs. »Nun spinn mir diesen Flachs«, sprach sie, »und wenn du es fertig bringst, so sollst du meinen ältesten Sohn zum Gemahl haben; bist du gleich arm, so acht ich nicht darauf, dein unverdroßner Fleiß ist Ausstattung genug.« Das Mädchen erschrak innerlich, denn es konnte den Flachs nicht spinnen, und wär's dreihundert Jahr alt geworden und hätte jeden Tag vom Morgen bis Abend dabei gesessen. Als es nun allein war, fing es an zu weinen und saß so drei Tage, ohne die Hand zu rühren. Am dritten Tage kam die Königin, und als sie sah, daß noch nichts gesponnen war, verwunderte sie sich, aber das Mädchen entschuldigte sich damit, daß es vor großer Betrübnis über die Entfernung aus seiner Mutter Hause noch nicht hätte anfangen können. Das ließ sich die Königin gefallen, sagte aber beim Weggehen: »Morgen mußt du mir anfangen zu arbeiten.«

Als das Mädchen wieder allein war, wußte es sich nicht mehr zu raten und zu helfen und trat in seiner Betrübnis vor das Fenster. Da sah es drei Weiber herkommen, davon hatte die erste einen breiten Platschfuß, die zweite hatte eine so große Unterlippe, daß sie über das Kinn herunterhing, und die dritte hatte einen breiten Daumen. Die blieben vor dem Fenster stehen, schauten hinauf und fragten das Mädchen, was ihm fehlte. Es klagte ihnen seine Not, da trugen sie ihm ihre Hülfe an und sprachen: »Willst du uns zur Hochzeit einladen, dich unser nicht schämen und uns deine Basen heißen, auch an deinen Tisch setzen, so wollen wir dir den Flachs wegspinnen, und das in kurzer Zeit.« »Von Herzen gern«, antwortete es, »kommt nur herein und fangt gleich die Arbeit an.« Da ließ es die drei seltsamen Weiber herein und machte in der ersten Kammer eine Lücke, wo sie sich hinsetzten und ihr Spinnen anhuben. Die eine zog den Faden und trat das Rad, die andere netzte den Faden, die dritte drehte ihn und schlug mit dem Finger auf den Tisch, und sooft sie schlug, fiel eine Zahl Garn zur Erde, und das war aufs feinste gesponnen. Vor der Königin verbarg sie die drei Spinnerinnen und zeigte ihr, sooft sie

screams could be heard out in the street. Then the woman was ashamed to make her daughter's laziness public, and she said: "I can't make her stop spinning, she wants to go on spinning eternally, and I'm poor and can't provide the flax." Then the queen replied: "The sound of spinning is my favorite sound, and I'm never happier than when the wheels hum: let me take your daughter to the palace; I have enough flax and she can spin to her heart's content." The mother was extremely satisfied, and the queen took along the girl. When they arrived at the palace, she led her upstairs to three rooms that were filled from top to bottom with the most beautiful flax. "Now spin this flax for me," she said, "and if you accomplish this, you shall have my eldest son for your husband; even if you're poor, I don't mind that; your tireless industry is enough of a dowry." The girl was frightened in her heart, because she couldn't spin the flax even if she lived three hundred years, sitting at the job every day from morning to evening. So when she was alone, she started weeping, and she sat that way for three days without lifting a finger. On the third day the queen came, and when she saw that no spinning had yet been done, she was amazed, but the girl made the excuse that she hadn't been able to begin yet because she was so melancholy about being taken away from her mother's house. The queen was satisfied with that, but said as she left: "Tomorrow you must start working."

When the girl was alone again, she was at her wits' end; in her dejection she stepped over to the window. There she saw three women arriving, the first of whom had a huge flat foot, the second had a lower lip so big that it hung down over her chin, and the third had a wide thumb. They stopped in front of the window, looked up, and asked the girl what was wrong with her. She described her distress, and they offered her their help, saying: "If you agree to invite us to your wedding, not to be ashamed of us, and to say we're your cousins, also to seat us at your table, we'll spin all the flax for you, and quickly too." "Most gladly," she replied; "please come in and start working right away." Then she let in the three peculiar women and made a space in the first room where they sat down and began their spinning. One of them drew the thread and trod the treadle, the second one moistened the thread, the third one twisted it and hit the table with her finger; and every time she hit it, a reel of yarn fell to the floor, and it was as fine as can be. She concealed the three spinners from the queen whenever she came, and showed her the

kam, die Menge des gesponnenen Garns, daß diese des Lobes kein
Ende fand. Als die erste Kammer leer war, ging's an die zweite,
endlich an die dritte, und die war auch bald ausgeräumt. Nun nahmen
die drei Weiber Abschied und sagten zum Mädchen: »Vergiß nicht,
was du uns versprochen hast, es wird dein Glück sein.«

Als das Mädchen der Königin die leeren Kammern und den großen
Haufen Garn zeigte, richtete sie die Hochzeit aus, und der Bräutigam
freute sich, daß er eine so geschickte und fleißige Frau bekäme, und
lobte sie gewaltig. »Ich habe drei Basen«, sprach das Mädchen, »und
da sie mir viel Gutes getan haben, so wollte ich sie nicht gern in
meinem Glück vergessen: erlaubt doch, daß ich sie zu der Hochzeit
einlade und daß sie mit an dem Tisch sitzen.« Die Königin und der
Bräutigam sprachen: »Warum sollen wir das nicht erlauben?« Als nun
das Fest anhub, traten die drei Jungfern in wunderlicher Tracht
herein, und die Braut sprach: »Seid willkommen, liebe Basen.« »Ach«,
sagte der Bräutigam, »wie kommst du zu der garstigen Freundschaft?« Darauf ging er zu der einen mit dem breiten Platschfuß und
fragte: »Wovon habt Ihr einen solchen breiten Fuß?« »Vom Treten«,
antwortete sie, »vom Treten.« Da ging der Bräutigam zur zweiten und
sprach: »Wovon habt Ihr nur die herunterhängende Lippe?« »Vom
Lecken«, antwortete sie, »vom Lecken.« Da fragte er die dritte:
»Wovon habt Ihr den breiten Daumen?« »Vom Faden drehen«,
antwortete sie, »vom Faden drehen.« Da erschrak der Königssohn
und sprach: »So soll mir nun und nimmermehr meine schöne Braut
ein Spinnrad anrühren.« Damit war sie das böse Flachsspinnen los.

Hänsel und Gretel

Vor einem großen Walde wohnte ein armer Holzhacker mit seiner
Frau und seinen zwei Kindern; das Bübchen hieß Hänsel und das
Mädchen Gretel. Er hatte wenig zu beißen und zu brechen, und einmal, als große Teuerung ins Land kam, konnte er auch das täglich
Brot nicht mehr schaffen. Wie er sich nun abends im Bette Gedanken
machte und sich vor Sorgen herumwälzte, seufzte er und sprach zu
seiner Frau: »Was soll aus uns werden? Wie können wir unsere armen
Kinder ernähren, da wir für uns selbst nichts mehr haben?« »Weißt du
was, Mann«, antwortete die Frau, »wir wollen morgen in aller Frühe
die Kinder hinaus in den Wald führen, wo er am dicksten ist: da
machen wir ihnen ein Feuer an und geben jedem noch ein Stückchen

quantity of spun yarn, so that the queen praised her to the skies. When the first room was empty, they proceeded to the second, then to the third, and it, too, was soon cleared. Now the three women took their leave, saying to the girl: "Don't forget your promise to us, it will bring you happiness."

When the girl showed the queen the empty rooms and the big heap of yarn, she arranged for the wedding; the groom was happy at getting such a skillful, diligent wife, and he gave her no end of praise. "I have three cousins," the girl said, "and since they've been very good to me, I wouldn't want to forget them now that I'm happy: please let me invite them to the wedding and let them sit at our table." The queen and the groom said: "Why shouldn't we let you?" Now, when the party began, the three spinners came in wearing odd clothes, and the bride said: "Welcome, dear cousins!" "Oh," said the groom, "where did you get such ghastly friends?" Then he went over to the one with the huge flat foot and asked: "How did you get such a wide foot?" "From treading," she replied, "from treading." Then the groom went over to the second one and said: "How in the world did you get that drooping lip?" "From licking," she replied, "from licking." Then he asked the third one: "How did you get that wide thumb?" "From twisting thread," she replied, "from twisting thread." Then the prince was frightened and said: "If that's the case, my beautiful bride must never ever touch a spinning wheel!" And that's how she was saved from that tiresome flax spinning.

Hänsel and Gretel

Just outside a large forest there lived a poor woodchopper with his wife and his two children; the boy was called Hänsel and the girl, Gretel. He didn't have much to put between his teeth, and once, when prices rose sharply in the land, he couldn't even procure his daily bread. Now, as he was worrying in bed one evening, tossing and turning in his anxiety, he sighed and said to his wife: "What's to become of us? How can we feed our poor children when we have nothing for ourselves anymore?" "Do you know what, husband," his wife replied, "tomorrow very early we'll take the children out to the forest where it's at its densest: there we'll make a fire for them, and give each of them one more

Brot, dann gehen wir an unsere Arbeit und lassen sie allein. Sie finden den Weg nicht wieder nach Haus, und wir sind sie los.« »Nein, Frau«, sagte der Mann, »das tue ich nicht; wie sollt' ich's übers Herz bringen, meine Kinder im Walde allein zu lassen, die wilden Tiere würden bald kommen und sie zerreißen.« »O du Narr«, sagte sie, »dann müssen wir alle viere Hungers sterben, du kannst nur die Bretter für die Särge hobeln«, und ließ ihm keine Ruhe, bis er einwilligte. »Aber die armen Kinder dauern mich doch«, sagte der Mann.

Die zwei Kinder hatten vor Hunger auch nicht einschlafen können und hatten gehört, was die Stiefmutter zum Vater gesagt hatte. Gretel weinte bittere Tränen und sprach zu Hänsel: »Nun ist's um uns geschehen.« »Still, Gretel«, sprach Hänsel, »gräme dich nicht, ich will uns schon helfen.« Und als die Alten eingeschlafen waren, stand er auf, zog sein Röcklein an, machte die Untertüre auf und schlich sich hinaus. Da schien der Mond ganz helle, und die weißen Kieselsteine, die vor dem Haus lagen, glänzten wie lauter Batzen. Hänsel bückte sich und steckte so viel in sein Rocktäschlein, als nur hinein wollten. Dann ging er wieder zurück, sprach zu Gretel: »Sei getrost, liebes Schwesterchen, und schlaf nur ruhig ein, Gott wird uns nicht verlassen«, und legte sich wieder in sein Bett.

Als der Tag anbrach, noch ehe die Sonne aufgegangen war, kam schon die Frau und weckte die beiden Kinder: »Steht auf, ihr Faulenzer, wir wollen in den Wald gehen und Holz holen.« Dann gab sie jedem ein Stückchen Brot und sprach: »Da habt ihr etwas für den Mittag, aber eßt's nicht vorher auf, weiter kriegt ihr nichts.« Gretel nahm das Brot unter die Schürze, weil Hänsel die Steine in der Tasche hatte. Danach machten sie sich alle zusammen auf den Weg nach dem Wald. Als sie ein Weilchen gegangen waren, stand Hänsel still und guckte nach dem Haus zurück und tat das wieder und immer wieder. Der Vater sprach: »Hänsel, was guckst du da und bleibst zurück, hab acht und vergiß deine Beine nicht.« »Ach, Vater«, sagte Hänsel, »ich sehe nach meinem weißen Kätzchen, das sitzt oben auf dem Dach und will mir ade sagen.« Die Frau sprach: »Narr, das ist dein Kätzchen nicht, das ist die Morgensonne, die auf den Schornstein scheint.« Hänsel aber hatte nicht nach dem Kätzchen gesehen, sondern immer einen von den blanken Kieselsteinen aus seiner Tasche auf den Weg geworfen.

Als sie mitten in den Wald gekommen waren, sprach der Vater: »Nun sammelt Holz, ihr Kinder, ich will ein Feuer anmachen, damit ihr nicht friert.« Hänsel und Gretel trugen Reisig zusammen, einen kleinen Berg hoch. Das Reisig ward angezündet, und als die Flamme

piece of bread, then we'll go to our work and leave them alone. They won't find their way back home again, and we'll be rid of them." "No, wife," said the man, "I won't do it; how could I have the heart to abandon my children in the forest? The wild animals would soon come and tear them apart." "Oh, you fool," she said, "then all four of us have to die of hunger; go right ahead and plane the boards for our coffins"; and she gave him no peace until he agreed. "But I feel sorry for the poor children all the same," the man said.

Because they were hungry, the two children hadn't been able to fall asleep, either, and they had heard what their stepmother had said to their father. Gretel shed bitter tears and said to Hänsel: "Now we're done for." "Quiet, Gretel," said Hänsel, "don't grieve, I'll find a way." And when their parents had fallen asleep, he got up, put on his little jacket, opened the lower half of the door, and sneaked out. The moon was shining very brightly, and the white pebbles lying in front of the house were shining just like coins. Hänsel stooped down and put as many in his jacket pocket as he could get in. Then he went back inside and said to Gretel: "Cheer up, dear little sister, and sleep peacefully; God won't desert us." And he went back to his bed.

When day broke, even before the sun rose, the woman was already there waking up the two children: "Get up, you lazybones, we have to go to the forest and fetch wood." Then she gave each of them a piece of bread and said: "Here's something for lunch, but don't eat it in advance, because that's all you're getting." Gretel tucked the bread under her apron, because Hänsel had the pebbles in his pocket. Then all of them together set out for the forest. After they had walked awhile, Hänsel halted and gazed back at the house; he did so time and again. His father said: "Hänsel, why are you gazing and hanging back? Pay attention and remember you have legs." "Oh, father," Hänsel said, "I'm looking at my white kitten, who's sitting up on the roof saying good-bye to me." The woman said: "Fool, that's not your kitten, it's the morning sun shining on the chimney." But Hänsel hadn't been looking at the kitten; rather, each time he had taken one of the bright pebbles out of his pocket and thrown it onto the path.

When they reached the middle of the forest, the father said: "Now gather wood, children; I'll make a fire so you aren't cold." Hänsel and Gretel gathered brushwood, making a small mountain of it. The brushwood was kindled, and when the flame was

recht hoch brannte, sagte die Frau: »Nun legt euch ans Feuer, ihr
Kinder, und ruht euch aus, wir gehen in den Wald und hauen Holz.
Wenn wir fertig sind, kommen wir wieder und holen euch ab.«

Hänsel und Gretel saßen am Feuer, und als der Mittag kam, aß
jedes sein Stücklein Brot. Und weil sie die Schläge der Holzaxt
hörten, so glaubten sie, ihr Vater wäre in der Nähe. Es war aber nicht
die Holzaxt, es war ein Ast, den er an einen dürren Baum gebunden
hatte und den der Wind hin und her schlug. Und als sie so lange
gesessen hatten, fielen ihnen die Augen vor Müdigkeit zu, und sie
schliefen fest ein. Als sie endlich erwachten, war es schon finstere
Nacht. Gretel fing an zu weinen und sprach: »Wie sollen wir nun aus
dem Wald kommen!« Hänsel aber tröstete sie: »Wart nur ein
Weilchen, bis der Mond aufgegangen ist, dann wollen wir den Weg
schon finden.« Und als der volle Mond aufgestiegen war, so nahm
Hänsel sein Schwesterchen an der Hand und ging den Kieselsteinen
nach, die schimmerten wie neu geschlagene Batzen und zeigten
ihnen den Weg. Sie gingen die ganze Nacht hindurch und kamen bei
anbrechendem Tag wieder zu ihres Vaters Haus. Sie klopften an die
Tür, und als die Frau aufmachte und sah, daß es Hänsel und Gretel
war, sprach sie: »Ihr bösen Kinder, was habt ihr so lange im Walde
geschlafen, wir haben geglaubt, ihr wolltet gar nicht wiederkommen.«
Der Vater aber freute sich, denn es war ihm zu Herzen gegangen, daß
er sie so allein zurückgelassen hatte.

Nicht lange danach war wieder Not in allen Ecken, und die Kinder
hörten, wie die Mutter nachts im Bette zu dem Vater sprach: »Alles
ist wieder aufgezehrt, wir haben noch einen halben Laib Brot, hernach hat das Lied ein Ende. Die Kinder müssen fort, wir wollen sie
tiefer in den Wald hineinführen, damit sie den Weg nicht wieder her-
ausfinden; es ist sonst keine Rettung für uns.« Dem Mann fiel's
schwer aufs Herz, und er dachte: »Es wäre besser, daß du den letzten
Bissen mit deinen Kindern teiltest.« Aber die Frau hörte auf nichts,
was er sagte, schalt ihn und machte ihm Vorwürfe. Wer A sagt, muß
auch B sagen, und weil er das erstemal nachgegeben hatte, so mußte
er es auch zum zweitenmal.

Die Kinder waren aber noch wach gewesen und hatten das
Gespräch mit angehört. Als die Alten schliefen, stand Hänsel wieder
auf, wollte hinaus und Kieselsteine auflesen, wie das vorigemal, aber
die Frau hatte die Tür verschlossen, und Hänsel konnte nicht heraus.
Aber er tröstete sein Schwesterchen und sprach: »Weine nicht,
Gretel, und schlaf nur ruhig, der liebe Gott wird uns schon helfen.«

Am frühen Morgen kam die Frau und holte die Kinder aus dem

nice and high, the woman said: "Now lie down by the fire and rest, children; we're going into the forest to cut trees. When we're done we'll come back and pick you up."

Hänsel and Gretel sat by the fire, and when noon came each one ate his piece of bread. And because they heard the blows of the axe, they thought their father was close by. But it wasn't the axe, it was a bough that he had tied to a dead tree and that the wind was blowing back and forth. And after sitting there so long, their eyes closed with drowsiness, and they fell fast asleep. When they finally awoke, it was already pitch dark. Gretel started to cry, saying: "How can we get out of the forest now?" But Hänsel comforted her: "Just wait awhile until the moon rises, then we'll find the way back." And when the full moon had risen, Hänsel took his little sister by the hand and followed the pebbles, which were gleaming like freshly minted coins, showing them the way. They walked all night long and arrived back at their father's house when day was breaking. They knocked at the door, and when the woman opened it and saw that it was Hänsel and Gretel, she said: "You wicked children, why did you sleep so long in the woods? We thought you were never coming back." But their father was happy, because he had felt bad about abandoning them that way.

Not long afterward, there was a shortage of food everywhere, and the children heard their mother saying to their father in bed at night: "Everything has been eaten up again; all we have left is half a loaf of bread; after that, we've had it! The children must go; we'll take them deeper into the woods so they can't find their way out again; otherwise there's no way to save ourselves." The man was sad at heart, and he said to himself: "It would be better if you shared your last morsel with your children." But his wife wouldn't listen to anything he said; she scolded him and reproached him. Whoever says "A" must also say "B," and because he had yielded the first time, he had to do so the second time as well.

But the children had still been awake and had overheard the conversation. When their parents were asleep, Hänsel once more got up, intending to go out and gather pebbles as he had done that earlier time, but the woman had locked the door, and Hänsel couldn't get out. But he comforted his little sister, saying: "Don't cry, Gretel, and sleep peacefully; God will surely help us."

Early in the morning the woman came and rousted the

Bette. Sie erhielten ihr Stückchen Brot, das war aber noch kleiner als
das vorigemal. Auf dem Wege nach dem Wald bröckelte es Hänsel in
der Tasche, stand oft still und warf ein Bröcklein auf die Erde.
»Hänsel, was stehst du und guckst dich um«, sagte der Vater, »geh
deiner Wege.« »Ich sehe nach meinem Täubchen, das sitzt auf dem
Dache und will mir ade sagen«, antwortete Hänsel. »Narr«, sagte die
Frau, »das ist dein Täubchen nicht, das ist die Morgensonne, die auf
den Schornstein oben scheint.« Hänsel aber warf nach und nach alle
Bröcklein auf den Weg.

Die Frau führte die Kinder noch tiefer in den Wald, wo sie ihr
Lebtag noch nicht gewesen waren. Da ward wieder ein großes Feuer
angemacht, und die Mutter sagte: »Bleibt nur da sitzen, ihr Kinder,
und wenn ihr müde seid, könnt ihr ein wenig schlafen: wir gehen in
den Wald und hauen Holz, und abends, wenn wir fertig sind, kommen
wir und holen euch ab.« Als es Mittag war, teilte Gretel ihr Brot mit
Hänsel, der sein Stück auf den Weg gestreut hatte. Dann schliefen sie
ein, und der Abend verging, aber niemand kam zu den armen
Kindern. Sie erwachten erst in der finstern Nacht, und Hänsel
tröstete sein Schwesterchen und sagte: »Wart nur, Gretel, bis der
Mond aufgeht, dann werden wir die Brotbröcklein sehen, die ich aus-
gestreut habe, die zeigen uns den Weg nach Haus.« Als der Mond
kam, machten sie sich auf, aber sie fanden kein Bröcklein mehr, denn
die vieltausend Vögel, die im Walde und im Felde umherfliegen, die
hatten sie weggepickt. Hänsel sagte zu Gretel: »Wir werden den Weg
schon finden«, aber sie fanden ihn nicht. Sie gingen die ganze Nacht
und noch einen Tag von Morgen bis Abend, aber sie kamen aus dem
Wald nicht heraus, und waren so hungrig, denn sie hatten nichts als
die paar Beeren, die auf der Erde standen. Und weil sie so müde
waren, daß die Beine sie nicht mehr tragen wollten, so legten sie sich
unter einen Baum und schliefen ein.

Nun war's schon der dritte Morgen, daß sie ihres Vaters Haus verlassen hatten. Sie fingen wieder an zu gehen, aber sie gerieten immer
tiefer in den Wald, und wenn nicht bald Hilfe kam, so mußten sie ver-
schmachten. Als es Mittag war, sahen sie ein schönes schneeweißes
Vöglein auf einem Ast sitzen, das sang so schön, daß sie stehenblieben
und ihm zuhörten. Und als es fertig war, schwang es seine Flügel und
flog vor ihnen her, und sie gingen ihm nach, bis sie zu einem
Häuschen gelangten, auf dessen Dach es sich setzte, und als sie ganz
nah herankamen, so sahen sie, daß das Häuslein aus Brot gebaut war
und mit Kuchen gedeckt; aber die Fenster waren von hellem Zucker.
»Da wollen wir uns dranmachen«, sprach Hänsel, »und eine

children out of bed. They received their pieces of bread, but they were even smaller than the last time. On the way to the forest Hänsel crumbled the bread in his pocket, halted many times, and threw a crumb on the ground. "Hänsel, why are you stopping and looking around?" his father said; "keep moving." "I'm looking at my little dove, who's sitting on the roof saying goodbye to me," Hänsel replied. "Fool," the woman said, "that's not your dove, it's the morning sun shining on the chimney top." But little by little Hänsel threw all the crumbs onto the path.

The woman led the children even deeper into the woods, where they had never been in their lives. Then once more a big fire was made, and their mother said: "Just keep sitting here, children, and if you're tired you can sleep a little: we're going into the forest to cut trees; in the evening, when we're done, we'll come and pick you up." When it was noon, Gretel shared her bread with Hänsel, who had scattered the crumbs of his piece on the path. Then they fell asleep, and the evening passed, but no one came for the poor children. They didn't wake up until it was pitch dark; Hänsel comforted his little sister, saying: "Just wait, Gretel, until the moon rises; then we'll see the bread crumbs that I scattered, and they'll show us the way home." When the moon rose, they set out, but they didn't find a single crumb, because the many thousands of birds that fly about in forest and field had eaten them up. Hänsel said to Gretel: "We'll find the way anyhow"; but they didn't. They walked all night long, and one more day from morning to evening, but they couldn't get out of the woods and they were extremely hungry because all they had were the few berries on the ground. And because they were so weary that their legs could no longer carry them, they lay down under a tree and fell asleep.

By now it was the third morning since they had left their father's house. They began walking again, but they got deeper and deeper into the woods; if no help arrived soon, they'd surely perish. When it was noon, they saw a beautiful, snow-white bird sitting on a branch; it sang so sweetly that they halted and listened to it. When it had ended its song, it beat its wings and flew ahead of them, and they followed it until they reached a little house and the bird perched on the roof. When they were quite close to it, they saw that the house was made of bread and roofed with cake, while its windows were of gleaming sugar. "Let's have a go at it," said Hänsel, "and have a hearty meal. I'll

gesegnete Mahlzeit halten. Ich will ein Stück vom Dach essen, Gretel,
du kannst vom Fenster essen, das schmeckt süß.« Hänsel reichte in
die Höhe und brach sich ein wenig vom Dach ab, um zu versuchen,
wie es schmeckte, und Gretel stellte sich an die Scheiben und knu-
perte daran. Da rief eine feine Stimme aus der Stube heraus:

>Knuper, knuper, kneischen,
wer knupert an meinem Häuschen?«

Die Kinder antworteten:

>Der Wind, der Wind,
das himmlische Kind«,

und aßen weiter, ohne sich irremachen zu lassen. Hänsel, dem das
Dach sehr gut schmeckte, riß sich ein großes Stück davon herunter,
und Gretel stieß eine ganze runde Fensterscheibe heraus, setzte sich
nieder und tat sich wohl damit. Da ging auf einmal die Türe auf, und
eine steinalte Frau, die sich auf eine Krücke stützte, kam heraus-
geschlichen. Hänsel und Gretel erschraken so gewaltig, daß sie fallen
ließen, was sie in den Händen hielten. Die Alte aber wackelte mit
dem Kopfe und sprach: »Ei, ihr lieben Kinder, wer hat euch hier-
hergebracht? Kommt nur herein und bleibt bei mir, es geschieht euch
kein Leid.« Sie faßte beide an der Hand und führte sie in ihr
Häuschen. Da ward gutes Essen aufgetragen, Milch und Pfanne-
kuchen mit Zucker, Äpfel und Nüsse. Hernach wurden zwei schöne
Bettlein weiß gedeckt, und Hänsel und Gretel legten sich hinein und
meinten, sie wären im Himmel.

Die Alte hatte sich nur so freundlich angestellt, sie war aber eine
böse Hexe, die den Kindern auflauerte, und hatte das Brothäuslein
bloß gebaut, um sie herbeizulocken. Wenn eins in ihre Gewalt kam,
so machte sie es tot, kochte es und aß es, und das war ihr ein Festtag.
Die Hexen haben rote Augen und können nicht weit sehen, aber sie
haben eine feine Witterung, wie die Tiere, und merken's, wenn
Menschen herankommen. Als Hänsel und Gretel in ihre Nähe
kamen, da lachte sie boshaft und sprach höhnisch: »Die habe ich, die
sollen mir nicht wieder entwischen.« Frühmorgens, ehe die Kinder
erwacht waren, stand sie schon auf, und als sie beide so lieblich ruhen
sah, mit den vollen roten Backen, so murmelte sie vor sich hin: »Das
wird ein guter Bissen werden.« Da packte sie Hänsel mit ihrer dürren
Hand und trug ihn in einen kleinen Stall und sperrte ihn mit einer
Gittertüre ein; er mochte schreien, wie er wollte, es half ihm nichts.
Dann ging sie zur Gretel, rüttelte sie wach und rief: »Steh auf,

eat a piece of the roof; Gretel, you can have some of the window, it'll taste sweet." Hänsel reached up and broke off a little of the roof to see how it tasted, and Gretel stood next to the windowpanes and nibbled at them. Then a piping voice called from inside:

"Nibble, nibble, mousie;
who's nibbling at my housie?"

The children replied:

"The wind so wild,
that heavenly child,"

and went on eating, without being distracted. Hänsel, who found the roof delicious, pulled off a big piece of it, and Gretel pushed out an entire circular windowpane, sat down, and enjoyed it. Then the door suddenly opened and an old, old woman, leaning on a crutch, came slinking out. Hänsel and Gretel were so terribly frightened that they dropped whatever they were holding. But the old woman shook her head and said: "Oh, you dear children, who brought you here? Please come in and stay with me; no harm will come to you." She took both of them by the hand and led them into her little house. There she served them good food, milk and pancakes with sugar, apples, and nuts. Afterwards, white bedclothes were placed on two pretty little beds, and Hänsel and Gretel lay down on them, thinking they were in heaven.

But the old woman had only pretended to be so friendly; in reality she was an evil witch who lay in wait for children; she had built the little bread house merely to lure them. Whenever one fell into her hands, she'd kill it, cook it, and eat it, and that was a holiday for her. Witches have red eyes and can't see far, but they have a keen sense of smell, like animals, and are aware of the arrival of human beings. When Hänsel and Gretel had approached her house, she had laughed maliciously and said mockingly: "I've got them; they won't get away from me!" Early in the morning, before the children were awake, she was already up; when she saw the two of them sleeping so charmingly, with their round, red cheeks, she muttered to herself: "That will be a tasty morsel." Then she seized Hänsel with her withered hand and carried him to a small pen, where she locked him in behind a barred door; no matter how loud he yelled, it did him no good. Then she went

Faulenzerin, trag Wasser und koch deinem Bruder etwas Gutes, der sitzt draußen im Stall und soll fett werden. Wenn er fett ist, so will ich ihn essen.« Gretel fing an, bitterlich zu weinen, aber es war alles vergeblich, sie mußte tun, was die böse Hexe verlangte.

Nun ward dem armen Hänsel das beste Essen gekocht, aber Gretel bekam nichts als Krebsschalen. Jeden Morgen schlich die Alte zu dem Ställchen und rief: »Hänsel, streck deine Finger heraus, damit ich fühle, ob du bald fett bist.« Hänsel streckte ihr aber ein Knöchlein heraus, und die Alte, die trübe Augen hatte, konnte es nicht sehen, und meinte, es wären Hänsels Finger, und verwunderte sich, daß er gar nicht fett werden wollte. Als vier Wochen herum waren und Hänsel immer mager blieb, da übernahm sie die Ungeduld, und sie wollte nicht länger warten. »Heda, Gretel«, rief sie dem Mädchen zu, »sei flink und trag Wasser: Hänsel mag fett oder mager sein, morgen will ich ihn schlachten und kochen.« Ach, wie jammerte das arme Schwesterchen, als es das Wasser tragen mußte, und wie flossen ihm die Tränen über die Backen herunter! »Lieber Gott, hilf uns doch«, rief sie aus, »hätten uns nur die wilden Tiere im Wald gefressen, so wären wir doch zusammen gestorben.« »Spar nur dein Geplärre«, sagte die Alte, »es hilft dir alles nichts.«

Frühmorgens mußte Gretel heraus, den Kessel mit Wasser aufhängen und Feuer anzünden. »Erst wollen wir backen«, sagte die Alte, »ich habe den Backofen schon eingeheizt und den Teig geknetet.« Sie stieß das arme Gretel hinaus zu dem Backofen, aus dem die Feuerflammen schon herausschlugen. »Kriech hinein«, sagte die Hexe, »und sieh zu, ob recht eingeheizt ist, damit wir das Brot hineinschießen können.« Und wenn Gretel darin war, wollte sie den Ofen zumachen, und Gretel sollte darin braten, und dann wollte sie's auch aufessen. Aber Gretel merkte, was sie im Sinn hatte, und sprach: »Ich weiß nicht, wie ich's machen soll; wie komm ich da hinein?« »Dumme Gans«, sagte die Alte, »die Öffnung ist groß genug, siehst du wohl, ich könnte selbst hinein«, krappelte heran und steckte den Kopf in den Backofen. Da gab ihr Gretel einen Stoß, daß sie weit hineinfuhr, machte die eiserne Tür zu und schob den Riegel vor. Hu! da fing sie an zu heulen, ganz grauselich; aber Gretel lief fort, und die gottlose Hexe mußte elendiglich verbrennen.

Gretel aber lief schnurstracks zum Hänsel, öffnete sein Ställchen und rief: »Hänsel, wir sind erlöst, die alte Hexe ist tot.« Da sprang Hänsel heraus, wie ein Vogel aus dem Käfig, wenn ihm die Türe aufgemacht wird. Wie haben sie sich gefreut, sind sich um den Hals gefallen, sind herumgesprungen und haben sich geküßt! Und weil sie

over to Gretel, shook her awake, and shouted: "Get up, lazy-bones, carry in water and cook something good for your brother, who's out in the pen and needs to be fattened up. When he's fat, I'm going to eat him." Gretel began to shed bitter tears, but it was all in vain; she had to do what the evil witch wanted.

Now the finest food was cooked for poor Hänsel, but Gretel got only crayfish shells. Every morning the old woman skulked out to the little pen and called: "Hänsel, stick out your fingers so I can feel whether you're getting fat enough." But Hänsel would stick out a little bone, and the old woman, who had weak eyes, couldn't see it, and thought it was Hänsel's fingers; she was amazed that he just wasn't getting fat. When four weeks had gone by and Hänsel was still skinny, she was overcome with impatience and refused to wait any longer. "Hey, Gretel," she shouted to the girl, "look alive there and carry in water: whether Hänsel is fat or thin, tomorrow I'm going to slaughter him and cook him." Oh, how sorrowful his poor little sister was when she had to fetch the water, and how the tears flowed down her cheeks! "Dear God, please help us!" she exclaimed; "if only the wild animals had eaten us in the forest! At least we would have died together." "Save your whimpering," the old woman said, "none of it will do you any good."

Early in the morning Gretel had to go out, hang up the kettle full of water, and light a fire. "First we'll bake," said the old woman; "I have already heated the oven and kneaded the dough." She pushed poor Gretel out to the oven, from which flames were already shooting. "Creep in," the witch said, "and see if it's properly heated, so we can shove in the bread." Once Gretel was inside, she was going to shut the oven door so Gretel would be baked in there; then she intended to eat her up, too. But Gretel realized what she had in mind, and said: "I don't know how to do it; how do I get in?" "Silly goose," the old woman said, "the opening is big enough; just look, I could get in there myself"; she hobbled over and put her head in the oven. Then Gretel gave her a push, so that she fell all the way in; then she shut the iron door and shot the bolt. Oooh! She started to howl hideously: but Gretel ran away, and the wicked witch burned up in misery.

But Gretel ran straight to Hänsel, opened his little pen, and called: "Hänsel, we're saved; the old witch is dead!" Then Hänsel jumped out, like a bird from its cage when its door is opened. How they rejoiced, hugged each other, capered around, and kissed each other! And because they had no more reason to

sich nicht mehr zu fürchten brauchten, so gingen sie in das Haus der
Hexe hinein, da standen in allen Ecken Kasten mit Perlen und
Edelsteinen. »Die sind noch besser als Kieselsteine«, sagte Hänsel und
steckte in seine Taschen, was hinein wollte, und Gretel sagte: »Ich will
auch etwas mit nach Haus bringen«, und füllte sich sein Schürzchen
voll. »Aber jetzt wollen wir fort«, sagte Hänsel, »damit wir aus dem
Hexenwald herauskommen.« Als sie aber ein paar Stunden gegangen
waren, gelangten sie an ein großes Wasser. »Wir können nicht hinüber«,
sprach Hänsel, »ich sehe keinen Steg und keine Brücke.« »Hier fährt
auch kein Schiffchen«, antwortete Gretel, »aber da schwimmt eine
weiße Ente, wenn ich die bitte, so hilft sie uns hinüber.« Da rief sie:

>   »Entchen, Entchen,
>   da steht Gretel und Hänsel.
>   Kein Steg und keine Brücke,
>   nimm uns auf deinen weißen Rücken.«

Das Entchen kam auch heran, und Hänsel setzte sich auf und bat
sein Schwesterchen, sich zu ihm zu setzen. »Nein«, antwortete Gretel,
»es wird dem Entchen zu schwer, es soll uns nacheinander hinüber-
bringen.« Das tat das gute Tierchen, und als sie glücklich drüben
waren und ein Weilchen fortgingen, da kam ihnen der Wald immer
bekannter und immer bekannter vor, und endlich erblickten sie von
weitem ihres Vaters Haus. Da fingen sie an zu laufen, stürzten in die
Stube hinein und fielen ihrem Vater um den Hals. Der Mann hatte
keine frohe Stunde gehabt, seitdem er die Kinder im Walde gelassen
hatte, die Frau aber war gestorben. Gretel schüttete sein Schürzchen
aus, daß die Perlen und Edelsteine in der Stube herumsprangen, und
Hänsel warf eine Handvoll nach der andern aus seiner Tasche dazu.
Da hatten alle Sorgen ein Ende, und sie lebten in lauter Freude
zusammen. Mein Märchen ist aus, dort lauft eine Maus, wer sie fängt,
darf sich eine große, große Pelzkappe daraus machen.

Strohhalm, Kohle und Bohne

In einem Dorfe wohnte eine arme alte Frau, die hatte ein Gericht
Bohnen zusammengebracht und wollte sie kochen. Sie machte also
auf ihrem Herd ein Feuer zurecht, und damit es desto schneller brennen sollte, zündete sie es mit einer Hand voll Stroh an. Als sie die
Bohnen in den Topf schüttete, entfiel ihr unbemerkt eine, die auf

be afraid, they went into the witch's house, where there were chests full of pearls and jewels in every corner. "These are even better than pebbles," said Hänsel, and he stuffed his pockets with as many as would go in. And Gretel said: "I want to take something home with me, too," as she filled her apron with them. "But now we should leave," said Hänsel, "so we can get out of the witch's forest." But after they had walked a few hours, they reached a wide river. "We can't cross," said Hänsel; "I don't see any plank or any bridge." "And there's no boat around, either," Gretel replied, "but a white duck is swimming there; if I ask her, she'll help us cross." Then she called:

> "Little duck, little duck,
> Hänsel and Gretel are out of luck!
> Of planks and bridges there's a lack:
> carry us on your snow-white back!"

And the duck did come over; Hänsel took a seat on it and asked his little sister to join him. "No," Gretel replied, "it would be too heavy for the little duck; it must take us across one at a time." The kindly little creature did so, and when they were safely across and had walked a little farther, the forest became more and more familiar to them, and they finally caught sight of their father's house in the distance. Then they started to run; they burst through the door and hugged their father. The man hadn't had a happy moment since abandoning his children in the forest; and his wife had died. Gretel shook out her little apron, so that the pearls and jewels bounced around in the room, and Hänsel tossed one handful after another out of his pocket as well. Then all their worries were over, and they lived together in untroubled joy. My story is done, there's a mouse on the run, whoever catches it can make a big, big fur cap out of it!

Straw, Coal, and Bean

In a village there lived a poor old lady who had assembled enough beans for a meal and was ready to cook them. So she made a fire in her hearth, and to make it flare up faster, she ignited it with a handful of straw. When she poured the beans into the pot, one of them got away from her, without her

dem Boden neben einen Strohhalm zu liegen kam; bald danach sprang auch eine glühende Kohle vom Herd zu den beiden herab. Da fing der Strohhalm an und sprach: »Liebe Freunde, von wannen kommt ihr her?« Die Kohle antwortete: »Ich bin zu gutem Glück dem Feuer entsprungen, und hätte ich das nicht mit Gewalt durchgesetzt, so war mir der Tod gewiß: ich wäre zu Asche verbrannt.« Die Bohne sagte: »Ich bin auch noch mit heiler Haut davongekommen, aber hätte mich die Alte in den Topf gebracht, ich wäre ohne Barmherzigkeit zu Brei gekocht worden, wie meine Kameraden.« »Wäre mir denn ein besser Schicksal zuteil geworden?« sprach das Stroh. »Alle meine Brüder hat die Alte in Feuer und Rauch aufgehen lassen, sechszig hat sie auf einmal gepackt und ums Leben gebracht. Glücklicherweise bin ich ihr zwischen den Fingern durchgeschlüpft.« »Was sollen wir aber nun anfangen?« sprach die Kohle. »Ich meine«, antwortete die Bohne, »weil wir so glücklich dem Tode entronnen sind, so wollen wir uns als gute Gesellen zusammenhalten und, damit uns hier nicht wieder ein neues Unglück ereilt, gemeinschaftlich auswandern und in ein fremdes Land ziehen.«

Der Vorschlag gefiel den beiden andern, und sie machten sich miteinander auf den Weg. Bald aber kamen sie an einen kleinen Bach, und da keine Brücke oder Steg da war, so wußten sie nicht, wie sie hinüberkommen sollten. Der Strohhalm fand guten Rat und sprach: »Ich will mich querüber legen, so könnt ihr auf mir wie auf einer Brücke hinübergehen.« Der Strohhalm streckte sich also von einem Ufer zum andern, und die Kohle, die von hitziger Natur war, trippelte auch ganz keck auf die neugebaute Brücke. Als sie aber in die Mitte gekommen war und unter ihr das Wasser rauschen hörte, ward ihr doch angst: sie blieb stehen und getraute sich nicht weiter. Der Strohhalm aber fing an zu brennen, zerbrach in zwei Stücke und fiel in den Bach; die Kohle rutschte nach, zischte, wie sie ins Wasser kam, und gab den Geist auf. Die Bohne, die vorsichtigerweise noch auf dem Ufer zurückgeblieben war, mußte über die Geschichte lachen, konnte nicht aufhören und lachte so gewaltig, daß sie zerplatzte. Nun war es ebenfalls um sie geschehen, wenn nicht zu gutem Glück ein Schneider, der auf der Wanderschaft war, sich an dem Bach ausgeruht hätte. Weil er ein mitleidiges Herz hatte, so holte er Nadel und Zwirn heraus und nähte sie zusammen. Die Bohne bedankte sich bei ihm aufs schönste, aber da er schwarzen Zwirn gebraucht hatte, so haben seit der Zeit alle Bohnen eine schwarze Naht.

noticing, and landed on the floor next to a wisp of straw; soon afterwards, a glowing coal leaped out of the hearth, too, and joined them. Then the straw began speaking: "Dear friends, where have you come from?" The coal replied: "I fortunately escaped from the fire, and if I hadn't exerted myself to do that, I would certainly have died: I would have burned to ashes." The bean said: "I've managed to save my skin, too, but if the old woman had put me in the pot, I would have been mercilessly cooked to gruel, like my buddies." "Would I have enjoyed a better fate?" said the straw. "The old woman made all my brothers go up in fire and smoke; she grabbed sixty at one time and killed them. Luckily I slipped through her fingers." "But what should we do now?" said the coal. "I think," the bean replied, "that, since we have so luckily escaped death, we should stick together like good companions and, to avoid a new catastrophe here, we should emigrate together and go to another country."

The suggestion pleased the other two, and they set out together. But soon they came to a small brook, and since there was no bridge or plank over it, they didn't know how to get across. The straw had an idea and said: "I'll lie down across it, and you can walk over on me as if on a bridge." So the straw stretched out from one bank to the other, and the coal, which had a fiery temperament, toddled quite boldly onto the new-made bridge. But when it reachd the middle and heard the water babbling beneath it, it got scared all the same: it stopped short and didn't dare continue. But the straw started to burn, broke in two, and fell into the brook; the coal slid after it, hissed as it hit the water, and gave up the ghost. The bean, which had cautiously remained on the bank, had to laugh at the event; it couldn't stop, and laughed so hard that it burst. Now the bean, too, would have been done for, had not a tailor on his journeyman travels fortunately been resting on the bank. Because he had a compassionate heart, he took out his needle and thread and sewed the bean together again. The bean thanked him most politely, but, since he had used black thread, ever since then beans have had a black seam.

Das tapfere Schneiderlein

An einem Sommermorgen saß ein Schneiderlein auf seinem Tisch am Fenster, war guter Dinge und nähte aus Leibeskräften. Da kam eine Bauersfrau die Straße herab und rief: »Gut Mus feil! Gut Mus feil!« Das klang dem Schneiderlein lieblich in die Ohren, er steckte sein zartes Haupt zum Fenster hinaus und rief: »Hier herauf, liebe Frau, hier wird sie ihre Ware los.« Die Frau stieg die drei Treppen mit ihrem schweren Korbe zu dem Schneider herauf und mußte die Töpfe sämtlich vor ihm auspacken. Er besah sie alle, hob sie in die Höhe, hielt die Nase dran und sagte endlich: »Das Mus scheint mir gut, wieg sie mir doch vier Lot ab, liebe Frau, wenn's auch ein Viertelpfund ist, kommt es mir nicht darauf an.« Die Frau, welche gehofft hatte, einen guten Absatz zu finden, gab ihm, was er verlangte, ging aber ganz ärgerlich und brummig fort. »Nun das Mus soll mir Gott gesegnen«, rief das Schneiderlein, »und soll mir Kraft und Stärke geben«, holte das Brot aus dem Schrank, schnitt sich ein Stück über den ganzen Laib und strich das Mus darüber. »Das wird nicht bitter schmecken«, sprach er, »aber erst will ich den Wams fertig machen, eh ich anbeiße.« Er legte das Brot neben sich, nähte weiter und machte vor Freude immer größere Stiche. Indes stieg der Geruch von dem süßen Mus hinauf an die Wand, wo die Fliegen in großer Menge saßen, so daß sie herangelockt wurden und sich scharenweis darauf niederließen. »Ei, wer hat euch eingeladen?« sprach das Schneiderlein und jagte die ungebetenen Gäste fort. Die Fliegen aber, die kein Deutsch verstanden, ließen sich nicht abweisen, sondern kamen in immer größerer Gesellschaft wieder. Da lief dem Schneiderlein endlich, wie man sagt, die Laus über die Leber, es langte aus seiner Hölle nach einem Tuchlappen, und »Wart, ich will es euch geben!« schlug es unbarmherzig drauf. Als es abzog und zählte, so lagen nicht weniger als sieben vor ihm tot und streckten die Beine. »Bist du so ein Kerl?« sprach er und mußte selbst seine Tapferkeit bewundern. »Das soll die ganze Stadt erfahren.« Und in der Hast schnitt sich das Schneiderlein einen Gürtel, nähte ihn und stickte mit großen Buchstaben darauf: Siebene auf einen Streich! »Ei was, Stadt!« sprach er weiter. »Die ganze Welt soll's erfahren!« Und sein Herz wackelte ihm vor Freude wie ein Lämmerschwänzchen.

Der Schneider band sich den Gürtel um den Leib und wollte in die

The Brave Little Tailor

One summer morning a little tailor was sitting on his table by the window; he was in a good mood and he was sewing with all his might. Then a farmer's wife came down the street crying: "Good jam for sale! Good jam for sale!" That was music to the little tailor's ears; he thrust his delicate head out the window and called: "Up here, dear lady, here you'll sell your wares!" The woman climbed the three flights up to the tailor's with her heavy basket, and had to take out every one of the pots for him. He inspected them all, lifted them up, put his nose to them, and finally said: "The jam looks good to me; give me two ounces of it, dear lady—I don't care if it's even a quarter pound!" The woman, who had hoped to make a good sale, gave him what he asked for, but left vexed and muttering. "Now, may God bless this jam for me," cried the little tailor, "and give me power and strength!" He fetched bread from the cupboard, cut himself a slice the full width of the loaf, and spread the jam on it. "This won't taste bitter," he said; "but first I want to finish the jerkin before I sink my teeth in." He placed the bread next to him, went on sewing, and in his joy took bigger and bigger stitches. Meanwhile, the aroma of the sweet jam ascended to the wall, where a large number of flies were resting, so that they were tempted to come down, and they settled on the bread in swarms. "Say, who invited you?" asked the little tailor as he chased away the unbidden guests. But the flies, which didn't understand German, refused to be ejected, and returned in an increasingly numerous party. Then, as the saying goes, the little tailor had had it up to there;[3] from the space under his table he reached for a rag, and crying: "Wait, now you're going to get it!" he lammed into the mass unmercifully. When he moved back and counted the victims, no fewer than seven lay dead before him with rigid legs. "Is that the great fellow you are?" he said, compelled to admire his own bravery. "The whole town has to hear about this!" And in his haste the little tailor cut out material for a belt, sewed it together, and embroidered on it in big letters: "Seven at one blow!" "What do I mean, town?" he continued. "The whole world has to hear!" And his heart jumped for joy like the wagging of a lamb's tail.

The tailor tied the belt around his waist and determined to go

---

3. Literally: "The louse ran across his liver."

Welt hinaus, weil er meinte, die Werkstätte sei zu klein für seine Tapferkeit. Eh er abzog, suchte er im Haus herum, ob nichts da wäre, was er mitnehmen könnte, er fand aber nichts als einen alten Käs, den steckte er ein. Vor dem Tore bemerkte er einen Vogel, der sich im Gesträuch gefangen hatte, der mußte zu dem Käse in die Tasche. Nun nahm er den Weg tapfer zwischen die Beine, und weil er leicht und behend war, fühlte er keine Müdigkeit. Der Weg führte ihn auf einen Berg, und als er den höchsten Gipfel erreicht hatte, so saß da ein gewaltiger Riese und schaute sich ganz gemächlich um. Das Schneiderlein ging beherzt auf ihn zu, redete ihn an und sprach: »Guten Tag, Kamerad, gelt, du sitzest da und besiehst dir die weitläuftige Welt? Ich bin eben auf dem Wege dahin und will mich versuchen. Hast du Lust, mitzugehen?« Der Riese sah den Schneider verächtlich an und sprach: »Du Lump! Du miserabler Kerl!« »Das wäre!« antwortete das Schneiderlein, knöpfte den Rock auf und zeigte dem Riesen den Gürtel. »Da kannst du lesen, was ich für ein Mann bin.« Der Riese las: »Siebene auf einen Streich«, meinte, das wären Menschen gewesen, die der Schneider erschlagen hätte, und kriegte ein wenig Respekt vor dem kleinen Kerl. Doch wollte er ihn erst prüfen, nahm einen Stein in die Hand und drückte ihn zusammen, daß das Wasser heraustropfte. »Das mach mir nach«, sprach der Riese, »wenn du Stärke hast.« »Ist's weiter nichts?« sagte das Schneiderlein. »Das ist bei unsereinem Spielwerk«, griff in die Tasche, holte den weichen Käs und drückte ihn, daß der Saft herauslief. »Gelt«, sprach er, »das war ein wenig besser?« Der Riese wußte nicht, was er sagen sollte, und konnte es von dem Männlein nicht glauben. Da hob der Riese einen Stein auf und warf ihn so hoch, daß man ihn mit Augen kaum noch sehen konnte. »Nun, du Erpelmännchen, das tu mir nach.« »Gut geworfen«, sagte der Schneider, »aber der Stein hat doch wieder zur Erde herabfallen müssen, ich will dir einen werfen, der soll gar nicht wiederkommen«; griff in die Tasche, nahm den Vogel und warf ihn in die Luft. Der Vogel, froh über seine Freiheit, stieg auf, flog fort und kam nicht wieder. »Wie gefällt dir das Stückchen, Kamerad?« fragte der Schneider. »Werfen kannst du wohl«, sagte der Riese, »aber nun wollen wir sehen, ob du imstande bist, etwas Ordentliches zu tragen.« Er führte das Schneiderlein zu einem mächtigen Eichbaum, der da gefällt auf dem Boden lag, und sagte: »Wenn du stark genug bist, so hilf mir den Baum aus dem Walde heraustragen.« »Gerne«, antwortete der kleine Mann, »nimm du nur den Stamm auf deine Schulter, ich will die Äste mit dem Gezweig aufheben und tragen, das ist doch das Schwerste.« Der Riese nahm den Stamm auf die Schulter, der

out into the world, because he thought his workshop was too small for his bravery. Before he left, he looked around the house to see if there was anything there that he could take along, but all that he found was an old cheese, which he put in his pocket. Outside the town gate he noticed a bird that had gotten caught in the bushes; into his pocket went the bird, too. Now he set out bravely on his journey, and because he was lightweight and nimble, he felt no weariness. His path led him up a mountain, and when he had reached the highest peak, there sat an enormous giant who was looking around, completely at his ease. The little tailor went up to him confidently, and addressed him as follows: "Hello, pal, I guess you're sitting here and looking at the great big world. I'm just on my way there, to try my wings. Do you feel like going along?" The giant looked at the tailor with contempt, saying: "You bum! You good-for-nothing!" "That's what you think!" replied the little tailor, unbuttoning his jacket and showing the giant his belt. "You can read here what kind of man I am." The giant read: "Seven at one blow!" and thought it referred to people the tailor had killed; then he felt some respect for the little fellow. But he wanted to test him first; he picked up a stone and squeezed it until water came out of it in drops. "Do the same thing," said the giant, "if you're strong enough." "Is that all?" said the little tailor. "For my sort that's child's play." He reached into his pocket, took out the soft cheese, and pressed it until the liquid ran out. "I imagine that that was a little better," he said. The giant didn't know what to say, and didn't think it possible of that small man. Then the giant picked up a stone and threw it so high that it was hardly visible to the eye. "Now, little drake, do the same thing." "Nice throw," said the tailor, "but the stone did eventually fall to the ground again; I'll throw one that won't return at all"; he reached into his pocket, took out the bird, and threw it in the air. Happy to be free, the bird ascended, flew away, and never returned. "How do you like that feat, pal?" the tailor asked. "Yes, you are good at throwing," the giant said, "but now let's see if you're capable of carrying a decent weight." He led the little tailor to a mighty oak tree that had been cut down and was lying on the ground, and he said: "If you've got the strength, help me carry the tree out of the forest." "Sure," the little man replied; "just take the trunk on your shoulder, I'll lift and carry the boughs and branches; after all, that's the heavier part." The giant took the trunk on his shoulder, but

Schneider aber setzte sich auf einen Ast, und der Riese, der sich nicht umsehen konnte, mußte den ganzen Baum und das Schneiderlein noch obendrein forttragen. Es war dahinten ganz lustig und guter Dinge, pfiff das Liedchen »Es ritten drei Schneider zum Tore hinaus«, als wäre das Baumtragen ein Kinderspiel. Der Riese, nachdem er ein Stück Wegs die schwere Last fortgeschleppt hatte, konnte nicht weiter und rief: »Hör, ich muß den Baum fallen lassen.« Der Schneider sprang behendiglich herab, faßte den Baum mit beiden Armen, als wenn er ihn getragen hätte, und sprach zum Riesen: »Du bist ein so großer Kerl und kannst den Baum nicht einmal tragen.«

Sie gingen zusammen weiter, und als sie an einem Kirschbaum vorbeikamen, faßte der Riese die Krone des Baums, wo die zeitigsten Früchte hingen, bog sie herab, gab sie dem Schneider in die Hand und hieß ihn essen. Das Schneiderlein aber war viel zu schwach, um den Baum zu halten, und als der Riese losließ, fuhr der Baum in die Höhe, und der Schneider ward mit in die Luft geschnellt. Als er wieder ohne Schaden herabgefallen war, sprach der Riese: »Was ist das, hast du nicht Kraft, die schwache Gerte zu halten?« »An der Kraft fehlt es nicht«, antwortete das Schneiderlein, »meinst du, das wäre erwas für einen, der siebene mit einem Streich getroffen hat? Ich bin über den Baum gesprungen, weil die Jäger da unten in das Gebüsch schießen. Spring nach, wenn du's vermagst.« Der Riese machte den Versuch, konnte aber nicht über den Baum kommen, sondern blieb in den Ästen hängen, also daß das Schneiderlein auch hier die Oberhand behielt.

Der Riese sprach: »Wenn du ein so tapferer Kerl bist, so komm mit in unsere Höhle und übernachte bei uns.« Das Schneiderlein war bereit und folgte ihm. Als sie in der Höhle anlangten, saßen da noch andere Riesen beim Feuer, und jeder hatte ein gebratenes Schaf in der Hand und aß davon. Das Schneiderlein sah sich um und dachte: »Es ist doch hier viel weitläuftiger als in meiner Werkstatt.« Der Riese wies ihm ein Bett an und sagte, er sollte sich hineinlegen und ausschlafen. Dem Schneiderlein war aber das Bett zu groß, er legte sich nicht hinein, sondern kroch in eine Ecke. Als es Mitternacht war und der Riese meinte, das Schneiderlein läge in tiefem Schlafe, so stand er auf, nahm eine große Eisenstange und schlug das Bett mit einem Schlag durch und meinte, er hätte dem Grashüpfer den Garaus gemacht. Mit dem frühsten Morgen gingen die Riesen in den Wald und hatten das Schneiderlein ganz vergessen, da kam es auf einmal ganz lustig und verwegen dahergeschritten. Die Riesen erschraken, fürchteten, es schlüge sie alle tot, und liefen in einer Hast fort.

the tailor sat down on a bough, and the giant, who was unable to look back, had to carry off the whole tree and the little tailor to boot. In the back the tailor was quite merry and cheerful, and whistled the song "Three tailors rode out of the city gate," as if carrying the tree were child's play. After the giant had dragged the heavy load some distance, he couldn't go on, and he shouted: "Listen, I've got to drop the tree." The tailor jumped off nimbly, embraced the tree with both arms, as if he'd been carrying it, and said to the giant: "A big fellow like you, and you can't even carry the tree!"

They journeyed on together, and when they came to a cherry tree, the giant seized the top of the tree, where the ripest fruit was hanging, bent it down, placed it in the tailor's hand, and told him to eat. But the little tailor was much too weak to hold onto the tree, and when the giant let it go, the tree sprang up again, and the tailor was catapulted into the air along with it. When he had landed unharmed, the giant said: "What's this? Don't you have the strength to hold onto a thin twig like that?" "It isn't lack of strength," the little tailor replied; "do you think that that would give trouble to someone who took out seven at one blow? I leaped over the tree because the hunters down there are shooting into the shrubbery. You make the same jump if you can!" The giant tried, but couldn't get over the tree; he got caught in the boughs, so that this time, too, the little tailor had the upper hand.

The giant said: "If you're such a brave fellow, come with me to our cave and spend the night with us." The little tailor was willing, and followed him. When they reached the cave, other giants were sitting by the fire there; each of them had a roast sheep in his hand and was eating it. The little tailor looked around and thought: "There's really much more space here than in my workshop." The giant showed him a bed and told him to lie down on it and sleep his fill. But the bed was too big for the little tailor; he didn't lie down on it, but crept into a corner. When it was midnight, and the giant thought the little tailor was fast asleep, he got up, took a big crowbar, and demolished the bed with one blow, thinking he had put an end to that grasshopper. Very early in the morning the giants went into the forest; they had thoroughly forgotten about the little tailor when he suddenly came striding by, quite merry and impudent. The giants were frightened, and fearing he would kill them all, they ran away hurriedly.

Das Schneiderlein zog weiter, immer seiner spitzen Nase nach. Nachdem es lange gewandert war, kam es in den Hof eines königlichen Palastes, und da es Müdigkeit empfand, so legte es sich ins Gras und schlief ein. Während es da lag, kamen die Leute, betrachteten es von allen Seiten und lasen auf dem Gürtel: Siebene auf einen Streich. »Ach«, sprachen sie, »was will der große Kriegsheld hier mitten im Frieden? Das muß ein mächtiger Herr sein.« Sie gingen und meldeten es dem König und meinten, wenn Krieg ausbrechen sollte, wäre das ein wichtiger und nützlicher Mann, den man um keinen Preis fortlassen dürfte. Dem König gefiel der Rat, und er schickte einen von seinen Hofleuten an das Schneiderlein ab, der sollte ihm, wenn es aufgewacht wäre, Krigesdienste anbieten. Der Abgesandte blieb bei dem Schläfer stehen, wartete, bis er seine Glieder streckte und die Augen aufschlug, und brachte dann seinen Antrag vor. »Eben deshalb bin ich hierhergekommen«, antwortete er, »ich bin bereit, in des Königs Dienste zu treten.« Also ward er ehrenvoll empfangen und ihm eine besondere Wohnung angewiesen.

Die Kriegsleute aber waren dem Schneiderlein aufgesessen und wünschten, es wäre tausend Meilen weit weg. »Was soll daraus werden?« sprachen sie untereinander. »Wenn wir Zank mit ihm kriegen und er haut zu, so fallen auf jeden Streich siebene. Da kann unsereiner nicht bestehen.« Also faßten sie einen Entschluß, begaben sich allesamt zum König und baten um ihren Abschied. »Wir sind nicht gemacht«, sprachen sie, »neben einem Mann auszuhalten, der siebene auf einen Streich schlägt.« Der König war traurig, daß er um des einen willen alle seine treuen Diener verlieren sollte, wünschte, daß seine Augen ihn nie gesehen hätten, und wäre ihn gerne wieder losgewesen. Aber er getrauete sich nicht, ihm den Abschied zu geben, weil er fürchtete, er möchte ihn samt seinem Volke totschlagen und sich auf den königlichen Thron setzen. Er sann lange hin und her, endlich fand er einen Rat. Er schickte zu dem Schneiderlein und ließ ihm sagen, weil er ein so großer Kriegsheld wäre, so wollte er ihm ein Anerbieten machen. In einem Walde seines Landes hausten zwei Riesen, die mit Rauben, Morden, Sengen und Brennen großen Schaden stifteten: niemand dürfte sich ihnen nahen, ohne sich in Lebensgefahr zu setzen. Wenn er diese beiden Riesen überwände und tötete, so wollte er ihm seine einzige Tochter zur Gemahlin geben und das halbe Königreich zur Ehesteuer: auch sollten hundert Reiter mitziehen und ihm Beistand leisten. »Das wäre so etwas für einen Mann, wie du bist«, dachte das Schneiderlein, »eine schöne Königstochter und ein halbes Königreich wird einem nicht alle Tage

The little tailor traveled on, constantly following his pointy nose. After walking a long way, he arrived at the courtyard of a royal palace; and since he was tired, he lay down on the grass and fell asleep. While he lay there, people came, observed him from every angle, and read on his belt: "Seven at one blow!" "Ah," they said, "what is this great war hero doing here in peacetime? He must be a mighty lord." They went and reported this to the king; their belief was that, if war should break out, he would be an important and useful man, who should by no means be allowed to depart. The king approved of their advice, and he dispatched one of his courtiers to the little tailor to offer him a military position when he woke up. The envoy remained with the sleeper, waited till he stretched his arms and legs and opened his eyes, and then made his proposal. "That's exactly why I came here," he replied; "I'm willing to enter the king's service." And so he was given an honorable reception and special lodgings were assigned to him.

But the military men were hostile to the little tailor and wished him a thousand miles off. "How will this turn out?" they said to one another. "If we quarrel with him and he strikes us, seven will fall at each blow. Ordinary men like us couldn't withstand him." So they reached a decision, went all together to the king, and requested their discharge. "It isn't in us," they said, "to hold out against a man who kills seven at one blow." The king was unhappy about losing all his faithful servants for the sake of one man, and he wished he had never set eyes on him; he would have liked to be rid of him. But he didn't dare discharge him, because he was afraid the stranger might kill him and all his subjects and place himself on the royal throne. For a long time his thoughts ran in all directions, and finally he hit upon a ruse. He sent to the little tailor and had him told that, since he was such a great war hero, he had a proposal to make to him. In a certain forest in his country there lived two giants who were causing great damage by robbing, killing, scorching, and burning: no one could get near them without putting his life in peril. If he were to conquer and kill those two giants, he would give him his only daughter as a wife, with half the kingdom as dowry; also, a hundred cavalrymen would go along to assist him. "That would be a good deal for a man like you," thought the little tailor; "the offer of a beautiful princess and half a kingdom doesn't come along every day." "Oh, yes," was

angeboten.« »O ja«, gab er zur Antwort, »die Riesen will ich schon bändigen und habe die hundert Reiter dabei nicht nötig: wer siebene auf einen Streich trifft, braucht sich vor zweien nicht zu fürchten.«

Das Schneiderlein zog aus, und die hundert Reiter folgten ihm. Als er zu dem Rand des Waldes kam, sprach er zu seinen Begleitern: »Bleibt hier nur halten, ich will schon allein mit den Riesen fertig werden.« Dann sprang er in den Wald hinein und schaute sich rechts und links um. Über ein Weilchen erblickte er beide Riesen: sie lagen unter einem Baume und schliefen und schnarchten dabei, daß sich die Äste auf und nieder bogen. Das Schneiderlein, nicht faul, las beide Taschen voll Steine und stieg damit auf den Baum. Als es in der Mitte war, rutschte es auf einem Ast, bis es gerade über die Schläfer zu sitzen kam, und ließ dem einen Riesen einen Stein nach dem andern auf die Brust fallen. Der Riese spürte lange nichts, doch endlich wachte er auf, stieß seinen Gesellen an und sprach: »Was schlägst du mich?« »Du träumst«, sagte der andere, »ich schlage dich nicht.« Sie legten sich wieder zum Schlaf, da warf der Schneider auf den zweiten einen Stein herab. »Was soll das?« rief der andere. »Warum wirfst du mich?« »Ich werfe dich nicht«, antwortete der erste und brummte. Sie zankten sich eine Weile herum, doch weil sie müde waren, ließen sie's gut sein, und die Augen fielen ihnen wieder zu. Das Schneiderlein fing sein Spiel von neuem an, suchte den dicksten Stein aus und warf ihn dem ersten Riesen mit aller Gewalt auf die Brust. »Das ist zu arg!« schrie er, sprang wie ein Unsinniger auf und stieß seinen Gesellen wider den Baum, daß dieser zitterte. Der andere zahlte mit gleicher Münze, und sie gerieten in solche Wut, daß sie Bäume ausrissen, aufeinander losschlugen, so lang, bis sie endlich beide zugleich tot auf die Erde fielen. Nun sprang das Schneiderlein herab. »Ein Glück nur«, sprach es, »daß sie den Baum, auf dem ich saß, nicht ausgerissen haben, sonst hätte ich wie ein Eichhörnchen auf einen andern springen müssen; doch unsereiner ist flüchtig!« Es zog sein Schwert und versetzte jedem ein paar tüchtige Hiebe in die Brust, dann ging es hinaus zu den Reitern und sprach: »Die Arbeit ist getan, ich habe beiden den Garaus gemacht; aber hart ist es hergegangen, sie haben in der Not Bäume ausgerissen und sich gewehrt, doch das hilft alles nichts, wenn einer kommt wie ich, der siebene auf einen Streich schlägt.« »Seid Ihr denn nicht verwundet?« fragten die Reiter. »Das hat gute Wege«, antwortete der Schneider, »kein Haar haben sie mir gekrümmt.« Die Reiter wollten ihm keinen Glauben beimessen und ritten in den Wald

his reply, "I'll definitely subdue the giants, and I don't need the hundred cavalrymen to do it; a man who kills seven at one blow doesn't have to be afraid of two."

The little tailor set out, and the hundred cavalrymen followed him. When he reached the edge of the woods, he said to his escort: "Just halt here; I'll surely polish off the giants on my own." Then he dashed into the woods, looking to the right and to the left. After a while he caught sight of the two giants: they were lying under a tree asleep and snoring so hard that the boughs were dancing up and down. The little tailor, not at all lazy, filled both pockets with stones that he gathered, and climbed up the tree with them. When he was in the middle, he slid along a bough until he was sitting directly over the sleepers; then he dropped one stone after another onto the chest of one giant. For a long time the giant didn't feel a thing, but he finally woke up, gave his companion a poke, and said: "Why are you hitting me?" "You're dreaming," the other one said; "I'm not hitting you." They lay down to sleep again, and the tailor threw a stone down on the second giant. "What's the meaning of this?" the second giant cried. "Why are you throwing things at me?" "I'm not throwing things at you," the first one replied, grumbling. They quarreled for a while, but because they were tired, they made up, and their eyes shut again. The little tailor resumed his game, sought out the heaviest stone and threw it onto the first giant's chest with full force. "That's going too far!" the giant shouted; he jumped up like a madman and pushed his companion against the tree, making it tremble. The second giant repaid him in kind, and they worked themselves up into such a great fury that they uprooted trees and mauled each other until they finally fell down dead at the same moment. Now the little tailor jumped down. "It was lucky," he said, "that they didn't uproot the tree I was sitting on, or else I'd have had to leap onto another one like a squirrel; but men of my sort are springy!" He drew his sword and gave each one a few hefty cuts in the chest, then he went out to the cavalrymen and said: "The job is done, I've polished them both off; but it was tough going; in their distress they uprooted trees to defend themselves, but none of that does any good when someone like me comes along, who can kill seven at one blow." "Aren't you even wounded?" the cavalrymen asked. "Are you kidding?" the tailor replied; "they didn't harm a hair of my head." The cavalrymen refused to believe him and rode into the

hinein; da fanden sie die Riesen in ihrem Blute schwimmend, und ringsherum lagen die ausgerissenen Bäume.

Das Schneiderlein verlangte von dem König die versprochene Belohnung, den aber reute sein Versprechen, und er sann aufs neue, wie er sich den Helden vom Halse schaffen könnte. »Ehe du meine Tochter und das halbe Reich erhältst«, sprach er zu ihm, »mußt du noch eine Heldentat vollbringen. In dem Walde läuft ein Einhorn, das großen Schaden anrichtet, das mußt du erst einfangen.« »Vor einem Einhorne fürchte ich mich noch weniger als vor zwei Riesen; siebene auf einen Streich, das ist meine Sache.« Er nahm sich einen Strick und eine Axt mit, ging hinaus in den Wald und hieß abermals die, welche ihm zugeordnet waren, außen warten. Er brauchte nicht lange zu suchen, das Einhorn kam bald daher und sprang geradezu auf den Schneider los, als wollte es ihn ohne Umstände aufspießen. »Sachte, sachte«, sprach er, »so geschwind geht das nicht«, blieb stehen und wartete, bis das Tier ganz nahe war, dann sprang er behendiglich hinter den Baum. Das Einhorn rannte mit aller Kraft gegen den Baum und spießte sein Horn so fest in den Stamm, daß es nicht Kraft genug hatte, es wieder herauszuziehen, und so war es gefangen. »Jetzt hab ich das Vöglein«, sagte der Schneider, kam hinter dem Baum hervor, legte dem Einhorn den Strick erst um den Hals, dann hieb er mit der Axt das Horn aus dem Baum, und als alles in Ordnung war, führte er das Tier ab und brachte es dem König.

Der König wollte ihm den verheißenen Lohn noch nicht gewähren und machte eine dritte Forderung. Der Schneider sollte ihm vor der Hochzeit erst ein Wildschwein fangen, das in dem Wald großen Schaden tat; die Jäger sollten ihm Beistand leisten. »Gerne«, sprach der Schneider, »das ist ein Kinderspiel.« Die Jäger nahm er nicht mit in den Wald, und sie waren's wohl zufrieden, denn das Wildschwein hatte sie schon mehrmals so empfangen, daß sie keine Lust hatten, ihm nachzustellen. Als das Schwein den Schneider erblickte, lief es mit schäumendem Munde und wetzenden Zähnen auf ihn zu und wollte ihn zur Erde werfen; der flüchtige Held aber sprang in eine Kapelle, die in der Nähe war, und gleich oben zum Fenster in einem Satze wieder hinaus. Das Schwein war hinter ihm hergelaufen, er aber hüpfte außen herum und schlug die Türe hinter ihm zu; da war das wütende Tier gefangen, das viel zu schwer und unbehilflich war, um zu dem Fenster hinauszuspringen. Das Schneiderlein rief die Jäger herbei, die mußten den Gefangenen mit eigenen Augen sehen; der Held aber begab sich zum Könige, der nun, er mochte wollen oder nicht, sein Versprechen halten mußte und ihm seine Tochter und

forest; there they found the giants drenched in their own blood, while the uprooted trees were scattered all around.

The little tailor requested the promised reward from the king, who now regretted his promise and plotted once more how to get the hero off his hands. "Before you receive my daughter and half the kingdom," he said to him, "you must accomplish another heroic feat. In the forest a unicorn is running around and creating great havoc; first you must catch it." "I'm even less afraid of a unicorn than of two giants; seven at one blow, that's my speed." He took along a rope and an axe, went out into the forest, and once again ordered the men who had been assigned to him to wait outside the woods. He didn't have to search very long; the unicorn came by very soon and made a dash right at the tailor, as if it intended to skewer him without much to-do. "Easy, easy," he said, "things won't go as fast as all that"; he remained standing where he was and waited until the animal was very close; then he nimbly hopped behind the tree. The unicorn ran against the tree with all its might, ramming its horn so firmly into the trunk that it didn't have the strength to pull it out again; and so it was caught. "Now I've got the critter," said the tailor; he came out from behind the tree, first put the rope around the unicorn's neck, then chopped the horn loose from the tree with his axe; when everything was in order, he led the animal away and brought it to the king.

The king still refused to grant him the promised reward, and made a third demand. Before the wedding the tailor must first catch a wild boar that was creating great havoc in the forest; the huntsmen were to back him up. "Gladly," said the little tailor; "that's child's play." He didn't take the huntsmen along into the forest, and that suited them fine, because numerous times in the past the wild boar had given them such a reception that they had no desire to pursue it. When the boar caught sight of the tailor, it charged him with foaming mouth and gnashing tusks, intending to knock him down; but the agile hero dashed into a nearby chapel, and immediately jumped out the high window again at one bound. The boar had run in after him, but once outside the building, the tailor darted around it and slammed the door shut on the boar; then the raging beast was trapped, since it was much too heavy and clumsy to jump out the window. The little tailor called over the huntsmen so they could see the captive with their own eyes; and the hero made his way to the king, who now, whether he wanted to or not, had to keep his promise and

das halbe Königreich übergab. Hätte er gewußt, daß kein Kriegsheld, sondern ein Schneiderlein vor ihm stand, es wäre ihm noch mehr zu Herzen gegangen. Die Hochzeit ward also mit großer Pracht und kleiner Freude gehalten und aus einem Schneider ein König gemacht.

Nach einiger Zeit hörte die junge Königin in der Nacht, wie ihr Gemahl im Traume sprach: »Junge, mach mir den Wams und flick mir die Hosen, oder ich will dir die Elle über die Ohren schlagen.« Da merkte sie, in welcher Gasse der junge Herr geboren war, klagte am andern Morgen ihrem Vater ihr Leid und bat, er möchte ihr von dem Manne helfen, der nichts anders als ein Schneider wäre. Der König sprach ihr Trost zu und sagte: »Laß in der nächsten Nacht deine Schlafkammer offen, meine Diener sollen außen stehen und, wenn er eingeschlafen ist, hineingehen, ihn binden und auf ein Schiff tragen, das ihn in die weite Welt führt.« Die Frau war damit zufrieden, des Königs Waffenträger aber, der alles mit angehört hatte, war dem jungen Herrn gewogen und hinterbrachte ihm den ganzen Anschlag. »Dem Ding will ich einen Riegel vorschieben«, sagte das Schneiderlein. Abends legte es sich zu gewöhnlicher Zeit mit seiner Frau zu Bett; als sie glaubte, er sei eingeschlafen, stand sie auf, öffnete die Türe und legte sich wieder. Das Schneiderlein, das sich nur stellte, als wenn es schlief, fing an, mit heller Stimme zu rufen: »Junge, mach mir den Wams und flick mir die Hosen, oder ich will dir die Elle über die Ohren schlagen! Ich habe siebene mit einem Streich getroffen, zwei Riesen getötet, ein Einhorn fortgeführt und ein Wildschwein gefangen und sollte mich vor denen fürchten, die draußen vor der Kammer stehen!« Als diese den Schneider also sprechen hörten, überkam sie eine große Furcht, sie liefen, als wenn das wilde Heer hinter ihnen wäre, und keiner wollte sich mehr an ihn wagen. Also war und blieb das Schneiderlein sein Lebtag ein König.

Aschenputtel

Einem reichen Manne, dem wurde seine Frau krank, und als sie fühlte, daß ihr Ende herankam, rief sie ihr einziges Töchterlein zu sich ans Bett und sprach: »Liebes Kind, bleib fromm und gut, so wird

hand over his daughter and half the kingdom. Had he known that it wasn't a war hero but a little tailor that stood before him, he would have felt even worse about it. And so the wedding was celebrated with great splendor and little joy, and a tailor became a king.

One night some time afterward, the young queen heard her husband talking in his sleep: "Boy, finish that jerkin and mend those trousers, or you'll feel my ell measure on your ears!" Then she realized what alley her young lord was born in; the next day she lamented her woe to her father, asking him to rid her of that man, who was nothing but a tailor. The king comforted her, saying: "This coming night, leave your bedroom unlocked; my servants will be waiting just outside and, after he falls asleep, they'll go in, tie him up, and carry him onto a ship that will take him out into the wide world." The tailor's wife was satisfied with that, but the king's squire, who had overheard everything, liked the young husband and secretly reported the whole plot to him. "I'll take proper measures in this matter," the little tailor said. In the evening he went to bed with his wife at the usual time; when she thought he had fallen asleep, she got up, opened the door, and lay down again. The little tailor, who was only pretending to be asleep, began to cry out loud: "Boy, finish that jerkin and mend those trousers, or you'll feel my ell measure on your ears! I've demolished seven at one blow, killed two giants, led away a unicorn, and captured a wild boar, and should I be afraid of the men who are standing outside my bedroom?" When they heard the tailor say that, they were stricken with great fear and ran as if the Wild Hunt[4] was after them; none of them was willing to face him any longer. And so the little tailor was, and remained, a king all his life.

Ash-Wallower [Cinderella]

A rich man's wife fell ill, and when she felt her end drawing near, she called her little daughter, an only child, to her bedside and said: "Dear child, remain pious and good, and then God will

---

4. The terrifying stormy ride of the sky god and his retinue in Norse and Teutonic mythology.

dir der liebe Gott immer beistehen, und ich will vom Himmel auf dich herabblicken und will um dich sein.« Darauf tat sie die Augen zu und verschied. Das Mädchen ging jeden Tag hinaus zu dem Grabe der Mutter und weinte und blieb fromm und gut. Als der Winter kam, deckte der Schnee ein weißes Tüchlein auf das Grab, und als die Sonne im Frühjahr es wieder herabgezogen hatte, nahm sich der Mann eine andere Frau.

Die Frau hatte zwei Töchter mit ins Haus gebracht, die schön und weiß von Angesicht waren, aber garstig und schwarz von Herzen. Da ging eine schlimme Zeit für das arme Stiefkind an. »Soll die dumme Gans bei uns in der Stube sitzen!« sprachen sie. »Wer Brot essen will, muß es verdienen: hinaus mit der Küchenmagd.« Sie nahmen ihm seine schönen Kleider weg, zogen ihm einen grauen alten Kittel an und gaben ihm hölzerne Schuhe. »Seht einmal die stolze Prinzessin, wie sie geputzt ist!« riefen sie, lachten und führten es in die Küche. Da mußte es von Morgen bis Abend schwere Arbeit tun, früh vor Tag aufstehn, Wasser tragen, Feuer anmachen, kochen und waschen. Obendrein taten ihm die Schwestern alles ersinnliche Herzeleid an, verspotteten es und schütteten ihm die Erbsen und Linsen in die Asche, so daß es sitzen und sie wieder auslesen mußte. Abends, wenn es sich müde gearbeitet hatte, kam es in kein Bett, sondern mußte sich neben den Herd in die Asche legen. Und weil es darum immer staubig und schmutzig aussah, nannten sie es *Aschenputtel*.

Es trug sich zu, daß der Vater einmal in die Messe ziehen wollte, da fragte er die beiden Stieftöchter, was er ihnen mitbringen sollte. »Schöne Kleider«, sagte die eine, »Perlen und Edelsteine« die zweite. »Aber du, Aschenputtel«, sprach er, »was willst du haben?« »Vater, das erste Reis, das Euch auf Eurem Heimweg an den Hut stößt, das brecht für mich ab.« Er kaufte nun für die beiden Stiefschwestern schöne Kleider, Perlen und Edelsteine, und auf dem Rückweg, als er durch einen grünen Busch ritt, streifte ihn ein Haselreis und stieß ihm den Hut ab. Da brach er das Reis ab und nahm es mit. Als er nach Haus kam, gab er den Stieftöchtern, was sie sich gewünscht hatten, und dem Aschenputtel gab er das Reis von dem Haselbusch. Aschenputtel dankte ihm, ging zu seiner Mutter Grab und pflanzte das Reis darauf und weinte so sehr, daß die Tränen darauf niederfielen und es begossen. Es wuchs aber und ward ein schöner Baum. Aschenputtel ging alle Tage dreimal darunter, weinte und betete, und allemal kam ein weißes Vöglein auf den Baum, und wenn es einen Wunsch aussprach, so warf ihm das Vöglein herab, was es sich gewünscht hatte.

always stand by you, and I shall look down upon you from heaven and be at your side." Then she closed her eyes and passed away. The girl went out to her mother's grave every day and wept, and she remained pious and good. When winter came, the snow spread a white cloth over the grave, and when the spring sun had removed it again, the man married another woman.

This woman had brought two daughters into the household with her; they were beautiful and white of countenance, but nasty and black of heart. Then a bad time began for the poor stepchild. "Is that silly goose to sit in the parlor with us?" they said. "Whoever wants to eat bread has to earn it; out with the scullion!" They took away her beautiful clothes, dressed her in an old gray smock, and gave her wooden shoes. "Just look at the proud princess, how she's adorned!" they called; they laughed and led her to the kitchen. There she had to do heavy labor from morning to evening; she had to get up early before daybreak, bring in water, light the fire, cook, and do the laundry. On top of that, the sisters gave her every imaginable grief, mocking her and spilling her peas and lentils into the ashes so that she had to sit and gather them together again. In the evening, when she was tired from her labors, she had no bed to rest in, but had to lie down in the ashes next to the hearth. And because that always made her look dusty and grimy, they named her Ash-Wallower.

It came about that her father was once about to journey to the trade fair and asked his two stepdaughters what he should bring back for them. "Pretty dresses," said one. "Pearls and jewels," said the other. "And you, Ash-Wallower," he said, "what would you like?" "Father, the first sprig that brushes your hat on your way home: break that off for me." So for the two stepsisters he bought pretty dresses, pearls, and jewels, and on his return journey, while he was riding through green shrubbery, a hazel sprig brushed him and knocked off his hat. So he broke off the sprig and took it with him. When he got home, he gave his stepdaughters what they had asked for, and to Ash-Wallower he gave the sprig from the hazel bush. Ash-Wallower thanked him, went to her mother's grave, and planted the sprig on it, weeping so hard that her tears dropped down and watered it. It grew and became a beautiful tree. Ash-Wallower went under it three times every day, weeping and praying, and each time a little white bird alighted on the tree, and every time she expressed a wish the bird threw down what she had wished for.

Es begab sich aber, daß der König ein Fest anstellte, das drei Tage dauern sollte und wozu alle schönen Jungfrauen im Lande eingeladen wurden, damit sich sein Sohn eine Braut aussuchen möchte. Die zwei Stiefschwestern, als sie hörten, daß sie auch dabei erscheinen sollten, waren guter Dinge, riefen Aschenputtel und sprachen: »Kämm uns die Haare, bürste uns die Schuhe und mache uns die Schnallen fest, wir gehen zur Hochzeit auf des Königs Schloß.« Aschenputtel gehorchte, weinte aber, weil es auch gern zum Tanz mitgegangen wäre, und bat die Stiefmutter, sie möchte es ihm erlauben. »Du, Aschenputtel«, sprach sie, »bist voll Staub und Schmutz und willst zur Hochzeit? Du hast keine Kleider und Schuhe und willst tanzen!« Als es aber mit Bitten anhielt, sprach sie endlich: »Da habe ich dir eine Schüssel Linsen in die Asche geschüttet, wenn du die Linsen in zwei Stunden wieder ausgelesen hast, so sollst du mitgehen.« Das Mädchen ging durch die Hintertüre nach dem Garten und rief: »Ihr zahmen Täubchen, ihr Turteltäubchen, all ihr Vöglein unter dem Himmel, kommt und helft mir lesen,

>   die guten ins Töpfchen,
>   die schlechten ins Kröpfchen.«

Da kamen zum Küchenfenster zwei weiße Täubchen herein und danach die Turteltäubchen, und endlich schwirrten und schwärmten alle Vöglein unter dem Himmel herein und ließen sich um die Asche nieder. Und die Täubchen nickten mit den Köpfchen und fingen an pick, pick, pick, pick, und da fingen die übrigen auch an pick, pick, pick, pick und lasen alle guten Körnlein in die Schüssel. Kaum war eine Stunde herum, so waren sie schon fertig und flogen alle wieder hinaus. Da brachte das Mädchen die Schüssel der Stiefmutter, freute sich und glaubte, es dürfte nun mit auf die Hochzeit gehen. Aber sie sprach: »Nein, Aschenputtel, du hast keine Kleider und kannst nicht tanzen: du wirst nur ausgelacht.« Als es nun weinte, sprach sie: »Wenn du mir zwei Schüsseln voll Linsen in einer Stunde aus der Asche rein lesen kannst, so sollst du mitgehen«, und dachte: »Das kann es ja nimmermehr.« Als sie die zwei Schüsseln Linsen in die Asche geschüttet hatte, ging das Mädchen durch die Hintertüre nach dem Garten und rief: »Ihr zahmen Täubchen, ihr Turteltäubchen, all ihr Vöglein unter dem Himmel, kommt und helft mir lesen,

>   die guten ins Töpfchen,
>   die schlechten ins Kröpfchen.«

Da kamen zum Küchenfenster zwei weiße Täubchen herein und

Now, it came to pass that the king arranged a ball that would last three days; to it all the pretty maidens in the land were invited, so that his son could select a bride. When the two step-sisters heard that they were to attend also, they became cheerful; summoning Ash-Wallower, they said: "Comb our hair, brush our shoes, and fasten our buckles; we're going to the wedding at the king's palace." Ash-Wallower obeyed, but she wept because she would have liked to go along to the dance, and she asked her stepmother for permission to go. "You, Ash-Wallower," she said, "dusty and grimy as you are, you want to go to the wedding? You have no dresses or shoes, and you want to dance!" When the girl persisted in asking, her stepmother finally said: "Look: I've poured a plateful of lentils into the ashes; if you can sort out all the lentils in two hours, you can come along." The girl went into the garden through the back door and called: "You tame doves, you turtledoves, all you songbirds beneath the sky, come and help me sort out,

> the good ones for the pot,
> the bad ones for your crop."

Then two white doves came in by the kitchen window, and after them the turtledoves, and finally all the songbirds beneath the sky whirred and flocked inside and alighted around the ashes. And the doves nodded their little heads and began to peck, peck, peck, peck, and then the others also began to peck, peck, peck, peck, and they collected all the good lentils in the plate. Scarcely an hour had gone by before they were finished and all flew out again. Then the girl brought the plate to her stepmother, happy in the belief that she could now go along to the wedding. But the woman said: "No, Ash-Wallower, you have no dresses and you can't dance: you'll just be laughed at." When the girl started crying, she said: "If you can pick two plates of lentils cleanly out of the ashes in one hour, you can come along"; she thought to herself: "She can never do it." After she poured the two plates of lentils into the ashes, the girl went into the garden through the back door and called: "You tame doves, you turtledoves, all you songbirds beneath the sky, come and help me sort out,

> the good ones for the pot,
> the bad ones for your crop."

Then two white doves came in by the kitchen window, and after

danach die Turteltäubchen, und endlich schwirrten und schwärmten alle Vöglein unter dem Himmel herein und ließen sich um die Asche nieder. Und die Täubchen nickten mit ihren Köpfchen und fingen an pick, pick, pick, pick, und da fingen die übrigen auch an pick, pick, pick, pick und lasen alle guten Körner in die Schüsseln. Und eh eine halbe Stunde herum war, waren sie schon fertig und flogen alle wieder hinaus. Da trug das Mädchen die Schüsseln zu der Stiefmutter, freute sich und glaubte, nun dürfte es mit auf die Hochzeit gehen. Aber sie sprach: »Es hilft dir alles nichts: du kommst nicht mit, denn du hast keine Kleider und kannst nicht tanzen; wir müßten uns deiner schämen.« Darauf kehrte sie ihm den Rücken zu und eilte mit ihren zwei stolzen Töchtern fort.

Als nun niemand mehr daheim war, ging Aschenputtel zu seiner Mutter Grab unter den Haselbaum und rief:

> »Bäumchen, rüttel dich und schüttel dich,
> wirf Gold und Silber über mich.«

Da warf ihm der Vogel ein golden und silbern Kleid herunter und mit Seide und Silber ausgestickte Pantoffeln. In aller Eile zog es das Kleid an und ging zur Hochzeit. Seine Schwestern aber und die Stiefmutter kannten es nicht und meinten, es müßte eine fremde Königstochter sein, so schön sah es in dem goldenen Kleide aus. An Aschenputtel dachten sie gar nicht und dachten, es säße daheim im Schmutz und suchte die Linsen aus der Asche. Der Königssohn kam ihm entgegen, nahm es bei der Hand und tanzte mit ihm. Er wollte auch mit sonst niemand tanzen, also daß er ihm die Hand nicht losließ, und wenn ein anderer kam, es aufzufordern, sprach er: »Das ist meine Tänzerin.«

Es tanzte, bis es Abend war, da wollte es nach Haus gehen. Der Königssohn aber sprach: »Ich gehe mit und begleite dich«, denn er wollte sehen, wem das schöne Mädchen angehörte. Sie entwischte ihm aber und sprang in das Taubenhaus. Nun wartete der Königssohn, bis der Vater kam, und sagte ihm, das fremde Mädchen wär' in das Taubenhaus gesprungen. Der Alte dachte: »Sollte es Aschenputtel sein«, und sie mußten ihm Axt und Hacken bringen, damit er das Taubenhaus entzweischlagen konnte; aber es war niemand darin. Und als sie ins Haus kamen, lag Aschenputtel in seinen schmutzigen Kleidern in der Asche, und ein trübes Öllämpchen brannte im Schornstein; denn Aschenputtel war geschwind aus dem Taubenhaus hinten herabgesprungen und war zu dem Haselbäumchen gelaufen: da hatte es die schönen Kleider abgezogen und aufs Grab gelegt, und

them the turtledoves, and finally all the songbirds beneath the sky whirred and flocked inside and alighted around the ashes. And the doves nodded their little heads and began to peck, peck, peck, peck, and then the others also began to peck, peck, peck, peck, and they collected all the good lentils in the plate. And before a half hour had passed, they were finished and all flew out again. Then the girl brought the plate to her stepmother, happy in the belief that she could now go along to the wedding. But the woman said: "None of this does you any good: you're not coming along, because you have no dresses and you can't dance; we would be ashamed of you." Then she turned her back on her and hastened away with her two proud daughters.

When no one else was left at home, Ash-Wallower went to her mother's grave under the hazel tree and called:

> "Shake and shudder, little tree;
> drop gold and silver onto me."

Then the bird threw down a gold and silver gown and slippers embroidered with silk and silver. She hastily put on the gown and went to the wedding. Her sisters and stepmother didn't know her, but thought she must be a foreign princess, she looked so beautiful in her golden gown. They had no idea it was Ash-Wallower, who they imagined was sitting in the dirt at home picking the lentils out of the ashes. The prince came up to her, took her by the hand, and danced with her. He refused to dance with anyone else, so that he never released her hand; whenever another man came to invite her to dance, he said: "This lady is my partner."

She danced until evening, then she wanted to go home. But the prince said: "I'll come along and escort you," because he wanted to see whom the beautiful girl was related to. But she escaped him and dashed into the dovecote. Now the prince waited until her father came, then told him that the unknown girl had dashed into the dovecote. The old man thought: "Could it be Ash-Wallower?" And people were ordered to fetch him an axe and a pick, so he could demolish the dovecote; but there was nobody inside. And when they entered the house, Ash-Wallower was lying in the ashes in her dirty clothes, and a dim little oil lamp was burning in the hearth; because Ash-Wallower had swiftly jumped down from the back of the dovecote and had run to the little hazel tree: there she had removed the beautiful clothes and placed them on the

der Vogel hatte sie wieder weggenommen, und dann hatte es sich in seinem grauen Kittelchen in die Küche zur Asche gesetzt.

Am andern Tag, als das Fest von neuem anhub und die Eltern und Stiefschwestern wieder fort waren, ging Aschenputtel zu dem Haselbaum und sprach:

>»Bäumchen, rüttel dich und schüttel dich,
wirf Gold und Silber über mich.«

Da warf der Vogel ein noch viel stolzeres Kleid herab als am vorigen Tag. Und als es mit diesem Kleide auf der Hochzeit erschien, erstaunte jedermann über seine Schönheit. Der Königssohn aber hatte gewartet, bis es kam, nahm es gleich bei der Hand und tanzte nur allein mit ihm. Wenn die andern kamen und es aufforderten, sprach er: »Das ist meine Tänzerin.« Als es nun Abend war, wollte es fort, und der Königssohn ging ihm nach und wollte sehen, in welches Haus es ging: aber es sprang ihm fort und in den Garten hinter dem Haus. Darin stand ein schöner großer Baum, an dem die herrlichsten Birnen hingen, es kletterte so behend wie ein Eichhörnchen zwischen die Äste, und der Königssohn wußte nicht, wo es hingekommen war. Er wartete aber, bis der Vater kam, und sprach zu ihm: »Das fremde Mädchen ist mir entwischt, und ich glaube, es ist auf den Birnbaum gesprungen.« Der Vater dachte: »Sollte es Aschenputtel sein«, ließ sich die Axt holen und hieb den Baum um, aber es war niemand darauf. Und als sie in die Küche kamen, lag Aschenputtel da in der Asche, wie sonst auch, denn es war auf der andern Seite vom Baum herabgesprungen, hatte dem Vogel auf dem Haselbäumchen die schönen Kleider wieder gebracht und sein graues Kittelchen angezogen.

Am dritten Tag, als die Eltern und Schwestern fort waren, ging Aschenputtel wieder zu seiner Mutter Grab und sprach zu dem Bäumchen:

>»Bäumchen, rüttel dich und schüttel dich,
wirf Gold und Silber über mich.«

Nun warf ihm der Vogel ein Kleid herab, das war so prächtig und glänzend, wie es noch keins gehabt hatte, und die Pantoffeln waren ganz golden. Als es in dem Kleid zu der Hochzeit kam, wußten sie alle nicht, was sie vor Verwunderung sagen sollten. Der Königssohn tanzte ganz allein mit ihm, und wenn es einer aufforderte, sprach er: »Das ist meine Tänzerin.«

Als es nun Abend war, wollte Aschenputtel fort, und der

grave, and the bird had taken them away again; then, in her little gray smock, she had sat down on the ashes in the kitchen.

The next day, when the ball resumed and her parents and stepsisters were gone again, Ash-Wallower went to the hazel tree and said:

> "Shake and shudder, little tree;
> drop gold and silver onto me."

Then the bird threw down a gown much more magnificent than on the previous day. And when she appeared at the wedding in that gown, everyone was amazed at her beauty. The prince had awaited her arrival, and immediately he took her hand and danced with nobody but her. When other men came to invite her to dance, he said: "This lady is my partner." When evening came, she wanted to leave, and the prince followed her, trying to see what house she went into: but she dashed away from him and into the garden behind her house. In it there stood a tall, beautiful tree on which the most splendid pears were hanging; she climbed up among the boughs as nimbly as a squirrel, and the prince didn't know what had become of her. But he waited until her father came, and he said to him: "The unknown girl has escaped me, and I believe she has clambered up the pear tree." Her father thought: "Could it be Ash-Wallower?" He sent for his axe and chopped down the tree, but there was nobody in it. And when they entered the kitchen, Ash-Wallower was lying there in the ashes as usual, because she had jumped down on the other side of the tree, brought the beautiful clothes back to the bird on the little hazel tree, and put on her little gray smock.

On the third day, when her parents and sisters had left, Ash-Wallower once more went to her mother's grave and said to the little tree:

> "Shake and shudder, little tree;
> drop gold and silver onto me."

Now the bird threw down a gown that was more splendid and gleaming than either of the others, and the slippers were all of gold. When she arrived at the wedding in that gown, everyone was speechless with astonishment. The prince danced with her alone, and when another man asked to cut in, he said: "This lady is my partner."

Now, when evening came, Ash-Wallower wanted to leave, and

Königssohn wollte es begleiten, aber es entsprang ihm so geschwind,
daß er nicht folgen konnte. Der Königssohn hatte aber eine List gebraucht und hatte die ganze Treppe mit Pech bestreichen lassen: da
war, als es hinabsprang, der linke Pantoffel des Mädchens hängengeblieben. Der Königssohn hob ihn auf, und er war klein und zierlich
und ganz golden. Am nächsten Morgen ging er damit zu dem Mann
und sagte zu ihm:»Keine andere soll meine Gemahlin werden als die,
an deren Fuß dieser goldene Schuh paßt.« Da freuten sich die beiden
Schwestern, denn sie hatten schöne Füße. Die Älteste ging mit dem
Schuh in die Kammer und wollte ihn anprobieren, und die Mutter
stand dabei. Aber sie konnte mit der großen Zehe nicht hineinkom-
men, und der Schuh war ihr zu klein, da reichte ihr die Mutter ein
Messer und sprach:»Hau die Zehe ab: wann du Königin bist, so
brauchst du nicht mehr zu Fuß zu gehen.« Das Mädchen hieb die
Zehe ab, zwängte den Fuß in den Schuh, verbiß den Schmerz und
ging heraus zum Königssohn. Da nahm er sie als seine Braut aufs
Pferd und ritt mit ihr fort. Sie mußten aber an dem Grabe vorbei, da
saßen die zwei Täubchen auf dem Haselbäumchen und riefen:

>»Rucke di guck, rucke di guck,
>Blut ist im Schuck (Schuh):
>der Schuck ist zu klein,
>die rechte Braut sitzt noch daheim.«

Da blickte er auf ihren Fuß und sah, wie das Blut herausquoll. Er
wendete sein Pferd um, brachte die falsche Braut wieder nach Haus
und sagte, das wäre nicht die rechte, die andere Schwester sollte den
Schuh anziehen. Da ging diese in die Kammer und kam mit den
Zehen glücklich in den Schuh, aber die Ferse war zu groß. Da reichte
ihr die Mutter ein Messer und sprach:»Hau ein Stück von der Ferse
ab: wann du Königin bist, brauchst du nicht mehr zu Fuß zu gehen.«
Das Mädchen hieb ein Stück von der Ferse ab, zwängte den Fuß in
den Schuh, verbiß den Schmerz und ging heraus zum Königssohn. Da
nahm er sie als seine Braut aufs Pferd und ritt mit ihr fort. Als sie an
dem Haselbäumchen vorbeikamen, saßen die zwei Täubchen darauf
und riefen:

>»Rucke di guck, rucke di guck,
>Blut ist im Schuck:
>der Schuck ist zu klein,
>die rechte Braut sitzt noch daheim.«

Er blickte nieder auf ihren Fuß und sah, wie das Blut aus dem

the prince wanted to escort her, but she ran away from him so swiftly that he was unable to follow. But the prince had devised a ruse and had had the whole staircase smeared with pitch; and so, when the girl dashed away, her left slipper had gotten stuck. The prince picked it up, and it was small and dainty and all of gold. The next morning he took it to the father and said to him: "No other woman shall be my wife but the one whose foot this golden shoe fits." That made the two sisters happy, because they had beautiful feet. The elder went to her bedroom with the shoe and wanted to try it on, while her mother stood by. But she couldn't get her big toe into it—the shoe was too small for her—and her mother handed her a knife, saying: "Cut off the toe: when you're queen, you won't need to walk anymore." The girl cut off her toe, forced her foot into the shoe, suppressed her pain, and went out to the prince. Then he lifted her onto his horse, as his bride, and rode away with her. But they had to pass the grave, where the two doves were sitting on the little hazel tree calling:

"Look, look, look; coo, coo, coo;
there's blood in the shoe:
the shoe's too tight;
the real bride's still home, out of sight."

Then he looked at her foot and saw the blood oozing out of it. He turned his horse around, brought the false bride back home, and said she was the wrong woman; the second sister was to put on the shoe. Then she went to her bedroom and got her toes into the shoe successfully, but her heel was too big. Then her mother handed her a knife, saying: "Cut off a piece of your heel: when you're queen, you won't need to walk anymore." The girl cut off a piece of her heel, forced her foot into the shoe, suppressed her pain, and went out to the prince. Then he lifted her onto his horse, as his bride, and rode away with her. When they passed by the little hazel tree, the two doves were sitting on it and calling:

"Look, look, look; coo, coo, coo;
there's blood in the shoe:
the shoe's too tight;
the real bride's still home, out of sight."

He looked down at her foot and saw the blood oozing from

Schuh quoll und an den weißen Strümpfen ganz rot heraufgestiegen war. Da wendete er sein Pferd und brachte die falsche Braut wieder nach Haus. »Das ist auch nicht die rechte«, sprach er, »habt Ihr keine andere Tochter?« »Nein«, sagte der Mann, »nur von meiner verstorbenen Frau ist noch ein kleines verbuttetes Aschenputtel da: das kann unmöglich die Braut sein.« Der Königssohn sprach, er sollte es heraufschicken, die Mutter aber antwortete: »Ach nein, das ist viel zu schmutzig, das darf sich nicht sehen lassen.« Er wollte es aber durchaus haben, und Aschenputtel mußte gerufen werden. Da wusch es sich erst Hände und Angesicht rein, ging dann hin und neigte sich vor dem Königssohn, der ihm den goldenen Schuh reichte. Dann setzte es sich auf einen Schemel, zog den Fuß aus dem schweren Holzschuh und steckte ihn in den Pantoffel, der war wie angegossen. Und als es sich in die Höhe richtete und der König ihm ins Gesicht sah, so erkannte er das schöne Mädchen, das mit ihm getanzt hatte, und rief: »Das ist die rechte Braut!« Die Stiefmutter und die beiden Schwestern erschraken und wurden bleich vor Ärger: er aber nahm Aschenputtel aufs Pferd und ritt mit ihm fort. Als sie an dem Haselbäumchen vorbeikamen, riefen die zwei weißen Täubchen:

>»Rucke di guck, rucke di guck,
>kein Blut im Schuck:
>der Schuck ist nicht zu klein,
>die rechte Braut, die führt er heim.«

Und als sie das gerufen hatten, kamen sie beide herabgeflogen und setzten sich dem Aschenputtel auf die Schultern, eine rechts, die andere links, und blieben da sitzen.

Als die Hochzeit mit dem Königssohn sollte gehalten werden, kamen die falschen Schwestern, wollten sich einschmeicheln und teil an seinem Glück nehmen. Als die Brautleute nun zur Kirche gingen, war die Älteste zur rechten, die Jüngste zur linken Seite: da pickten die Tauben einer jeden das eine Auge aus. Hernach, als sie herausgingen, war die Älteste zur linken und die Jüngste zur rechten: da pickten die Tauben einer jeden das andere Auge aus. Und waren sie also für ihre Bosheit und Falschheit mit Blindheit auf ihr Lebtag gestraft.

the shoe and spreading upward, staining her white stockings all red. Then he turned his horse and brought the false bride back home again. "She's the wrong woman, too," he said; "have you no other daughter?" "No," the man of the house said; "there's just a little, unsightly sloven that my late wife bore to me: she can't possibly be the bride." The prince ordered him to send her upstairs, but her stepmother replied: "Oh, no, she's much too dirty, she mustn't let people see her." But he insisted on seeing her, and they had to summon Ash-Wallower. First she washed her hands and face clean, then she came and curtseyed to the prince, who handed her the golden shoe. Then she sat down on a stool, drew her foot out of the heavy wooden clog, and put it into the slipper, which fitted her perfectly. And when she stood up erect and the prince looked her in the eyes, he recognized the beautiful girl who had danced with him, and called: "This is the true bride!" Her stepmother and two sisters were alarmed and turned pale with vexation: but he lifted Ash-Wallower onto his horse and rode away with her. When they passed by the little hazel tree, the two white doves called:

> "Look, look, look; coo, coo, coo;
> no blood in the shoe:
> the shoe's not too small;
> the real bride's riding to the prince's hall."

And after saying that, they both flew down and alighted on Ash-Wallower's shoulders, one on the right and the other on the left, and they remained there.

When her wedding with the prince was to be celebrated, her deceitful sisters came, trying to ingratiate themselves and gain a share of her good fortune. Now, as the bridal party was going to the church, the elder sister was at the right, the younger at the left; then the doves pecked out one of each girl's eyes. After the ceremony, when the people came out, the elder sister was at the left and the younger at the right: then the doves pecked out each one's remaining eye. And so, because of their malice and falseness they were punished with blindness for the rest of their life.

Frau Holle

Eine Witwe hatte zwei Töchter, davon war die eine schön und fleißig,
die andere häßlich und faul. Sie hatte aber die häßliche und faule,
weil sie ihre rechte Tochter war, viel lieber, und die andere mußte alle
Arbeit tun und der Aschenputtel im Hause sein. Das arme Mädchen
mußte sich täglich auf die große Straße bei einem Brunnen setzen
und mußte so viel spinnen, daß ihm das Blut aus den Fingern sprang.
Nun trug es sich zu, daß die Spule einmal ganz blutig war, da bückte
es sich damit in den Brunnen und wollte sie abwaschen; sie sprang
ihm aber aus der Hand und fiel hinab. Es weinte, lief zur Stiefmutter
und erzählte ihr das Unglück. Sie schalt es aber so heftig und war so
unbarmherzig, daß sie sprach: »Hast du die Spule hinunterfallen
lassen, so hol sie auch wieder herauf.« Da ging das Mädchen zu dem
Brunnen zurück und wußte nicht, was es anfangen sollte; und in
seiner Herzensangst sprang es in den Brunnen hinein, um die Spule
zu holen. Es verlor die Besinnung, und als es erwachte und wieder zu
sich selber kam, war es auf einer schönen Wiese, wo die Sonne schien
und vieltausend Blumen standen. Auf dieser Wiese ging es fort und
kam zu einem Backofen, der war voller Brot; das Brot aber rief: »Ach,
zieh mich raus, zieh mich raus, sonst verbrenn ich: ich bin schon
längst ausgebacken.« Da trat es herzu und holte mit dem Brot-
schieber alles nacheinander heraus. Danach ging es weiter und kam
zu einem Baum, der hing voll Äpfel, und rief ihm zu: »Ach, schüttel
mich, schüttel mich, wir Äpfel sind alle miteinander reif.« Da schüttelte es den Baum, daß die Äpfel fielen, als regneten sie, und schüttelte, bis keiner mehr oben war; und als es alle in einen Haufen
zusammengelegt hatte, ging es wieder weiter. Endlich kam es zu
einem kleinen Haus, daraus guckte eine alte Frau, weil sie aber so
große Zähne hatte, ward ihm angst, und es wollte fortlaufen. Die alte
Frau aber rief ihm nach: »Was fürchtest du dich, liebes Kind? Bleib
bei mir, wenn du alle Arbeit im Hause ordentlich tun willst, so soll
dir's gut gehn. Du mußt nur achtgeben, daß du mein Bett gut machst
und es fleißig aufschüttelst, daß die Federn fliegen, dann schneit es in
der Welt*; ich bin die Frau Holle.« Weil die Alte ihm so gut zusprach,
so faßte sich das Mädchen ein Herz, willigte ein und begab sich in
ihren Dienst. Es besorgte auch alles nach ihrer Zufriedenheit und
schüttelte ihr das Bett immer gewaltig, auf daß die Federn wie

---

*Darum sagt man in Hessen, wenn es schneit, die Frau Holle macht ihr Bett.

Mother Holle

A widow had two daughters, one of whom was beautiful and diligent, the other ugly and lazy. But because the ugly, lazy one was
her own daughter, she loved her much more, and the other one
had to do all the work and be the household drudge. Every day
the poor girl had to go out onto the highway and sit by a well, and
spin so much that the blood spurted from her fingers. Now it
came about that the reel was once all bloody, so she bent over the
well with it, intending to wash it off; but it flew out of her hand
and fell in. She wept, ran to her stepmother, and told her of her
misfortune. But she scolded her so roughly and was so unmerci-
ful that she said: "If you've dropped the reel, bring it back up
again." Then the girl returned to the well, but didn't know how to
go about it; and in her despair she jumped into the well to retrieve
the reel. She lost consciousness, and when she awoke and came to
herself again, she was on a beautiful meadow, where the sun
shone and many thousands of flowers grew. She continued walking on this meadow and reached an oven that was full of bread;
and the bread called: "Oh, pull me out, pull me out, or else I'll get
burned to a crisp; for some time now I've been fully baked." Then
the girl went over and pulled out each loaf with the shovel, one
after the other. Then she continued on her way and reached a tree
that was full of apples and called to her: "Oh, shake me, shake me,
every one of us apples is ripe." Then she shook the tree, so that
the apples fell down in a thick shower, and she went on shaking it
until no more apples were left on it; and after stacking them all up
in a pile, she went her way. Finally she reached a little house, out
of which an old lady was looking; and because the woman had
such big teeth, she got scared and wanted to run away. But the old
lady called after her: "What are you afraid of, dear child? Stay with
me; if you're willing to do all the housework properly, you'll be
well cared for. Only, you must be sure to make my bed just right
and to shake out the quilts hard, so that the feathers fly; then it
snows on Earth;° I'm Mother Holle." Because the old lady spoke
to her so kindly, the girl took heart, consented, and entered her
service. And she tended to everything to the woman's satisfaction,
and always shook out her featherbed with great strength, so that

---

°That's why people in Hessia say, when it snows, that Mother Holle is making her bed. [Footnote in original text]

Schneeflocken umherflogen; dafür hatte es auch ein gut Leben bei
ihr, kein böses Wort und alle Tage Gesottenes und Gebratenes. Nun
war es eine Zeitlang bei der Frau Holle, da ward es traurig und wußte
anfangs selbst nicht, was ihm fehlte, endlich merkte es, daß es
Heimweh war; ob es ihm hier gleich vieltausendmal besser ging als zu
Haus, so hatte es doch ein Verlangen dahin. Endlich sagte es zu ihr:
»Ich habe den Jammer nach Haus kriegt, und wenn es mir auch noch
so gut hier unten geht, so kann ich doch nicht länger bleiben, ich muß
wieder hinauf zu den Meinigen.« Die Frau Holle sagte: »Es gefällt
mir, daß du wieder nach Haus verlangst, und weil du mir so treu gedient hast, so will ich dich selbst wieder hinaufbringen.« Sie nahm es
darauf bei der Hand und führte es vor ein großes Tor. Das Tor ward
aufgetan, und wie das Mädchen gerade darunterstand, fiel ein
gewaltiger Goldregen, und alles Gold blieb an ihm hängen, so daß es
über und über davon bedeckt war. »Das sollst du haben, weil du so
fleißig gewesen bist«, sprach die Frau Holle und gab ihm auch die
Spule wieder, die ihm in den Brunnen gefallen war. Darauf ward das
Tor verschlossen, und das Mädchen befand sich oben auf der Welt,
nicht weit von seiner Mutter Haus; und als es in den Hof kam, saß der
Hahn auf dem Brunnen und rief:

> »Kikeriki,
> unsere goldene Jungfrau ist wieder hie.«

Da ging es hinein zu seiner Mutter, und weil es so mit Gold bedeckt
ankam, ward es von ihr und der Schwester gut aufgenommen.

Das Mädchen erzählte alles, was ihm begegnet war, und als die
Mutter hörte, wie es zu dem großen Reichtum gekommen war,
wollte sie der andern, häßlichen und faulen Tochter gerne dasselbe
Glück verschaffen. Sie mußte sich an den Brunnen setzen und spinnen; und damit ihre Spule blutig ward, stach sie sich in die Finger
und stieß sich die Hand in die Dornhecke. Dann warf sie die Spule
in den Brunnen und sprang selber hinein. Sie kam, wie die andere,
auf die schöne Wiese und ging auf demselben Pfade weiter. Als sie
zu dem Backofen gelangte, schrie das Brot wieder: »Ach, zieh mich
raus, zieh mich raus, sonst verbrenn ich, ich bin schon längst ausgebacken.« Die Faule aber antwortete: »Da hätt ich Lust, mich
schmutzig zu machen«, und ging fort. Bald kam sie zu dem
Apfelbaum, der rief: »Ach, schüttel mich, schüttel mich, wir Äpfel
sind alle miteinander reif.« Sie antwortete aber: »Du kommst mir
recht, es könnte mir einer auf den Kopf fallen«, und ging damit
weiter. Als sie vor der Frau Holle Haus kam, fürchtete sie sich nicht,

the feathers flew about like snowflakes; in return, her life with her was a pleasant one: no hard words, and boiled and roasted food every day. After remaining with Mother Holle for some time, she became sad, and at first she herself didn't know what was wrong with her; finally she realized that she was homesick; even though she was many thousands of times better off there than at home, she still felt an urge to go back. Finally she said to the woman: "I've become homesick, and even though I'm so well off down here, I can't stay any longer, I must go back up to my own people." Mother Holle said: "I'm glad you want to go back home, and because you have served me so faithfully, I'll take you back up myself." Then she took her by the hand and led her to a lofty gate. The gate was opened, and when the girl was standing directly under it, a heavy shower of gold fell, and all the gold stuck to her, so that she was entirely covered with it. "That's for you because you've been so industrious," said Mother Holle, who also gave her back the reel that had fallen into the well. Then the gate was closed, and the girl found herself back up on Earth, not far from her mother's house; and when she came into the yard, the rooster was sitting on the well calling:

> "Cock-a-doodle-doo,
> our golden girl is here anew."

Then she went in to her mother, and because she arrived all covered with gold, she was welcomed kindly by her and by her sister.

The girl told them everything that had befallen her, and when her mother heard how she had become so rich, she wanted to achieve the same good fortune for her other daughter, the ugly, lazy one. This girl was now sent to sit at the well and spin; to make her reel bloody, she pricked her finger and thrust her hand into the thorny hedge. Then she threw the reel in the well and jumped in herself. Like the other girl, she arrived on the beautiful meadow and walked along the same path. When she reached the oven, the bread called once more: "Oh, pull me out, pull me out, or else I'll get burned to a crisp; for some time now I've been fully baked." But the lazy girl answered: "I'd really enjoy getting myself filthy!" And she went her way. Soon she reached the apple tree, which called: "Oh, shake me, shake me, every one of us apples is ripe." But she answered: "That's what you think! One of them might fall on my head." And she left. When she reached Mother Holle's house, she wasn't afraid, because she had already

weil sie von ihren großen Zähnen schon gehört hatte, und verdingte sich gleich zu ihr. Am ersten Tag tat sie sich Gewalt an, war fleißig und folgte der Frau Holle, wenn sie ihr etwas sagte, denn sie dachte an das viele Gold, das sie ihr schenken würde; am zweiten Tag aber fing sie schon an zu faulenzen, am dritten noch mehr, da wollte sie morgens gar nicht aufstehen. Sie machte auch der Frau Holle das Bett nicht, wie sich's gebührte, und schüttelte es nicht, daß die Federn aufflogen. Das ward die Frau Holle bald müde und sagte ihr den Dienst auf. Die Faule war das wohl zufrieden und meinte, nun würde der Goldregen kommen; die Frau Holle führte sie auch zu dem Tor, als sie aber darunterstand, ward statt des Goldes ein großer Kessel voll Pech ausgeschüttet. »Das ist zur Belohnung deiner Dienste«, sagte die Frau Holle und schloß das Tor zu. Da kam die Faule heim, aber sie war ganz mit Pech bedeckt, und der Hahn auf dem Brunnen, als er sie sah, rief:

> »Kikeriki,
> unsere schmutzige Jungfrau ist wieder hie.«

Das Pech aber blieb fest an ihr hängen und wollte, solange sie lebte, nicht abgehen.

Rotkäppchen

Es war einmal eine kleine süße Dirne, die hatte jedermann lieb, der sie nur ansah, am allerliebsten aber ihre Großmutter, die wußte gar nicht, was sie alles dem Kinde geben sollte. Einmal schenkte sie ihm ein Käppchen von rotem Sammet, und weil ihm das so wohl stand und es nichts anders mehr tragen wollte, hieß es nur das Rotkäppchen. Eines Tages sprach seine Mutter zu ihm: »Komm, Rotkäppchen, da hast du ein Stück Kuchen und eine Flasche Wein, bring das der Großmutter hinaus; sie ist krank und schwach und wird sich daran laben. Mach dich auf, bevor es heiß wird, und wenn du hinauskommst, so geh hübsch sittsam und lauf nicht vom Weg ab, sonst fällst du und zerbrichst das Glas, und die Großmutter hat nichts. Und wenn du in ihre Stube kommst, so vergiß nicht, guten Morgen zu sagen, und guck nicht erst in alle Ecken herum.«

»Ich will schon alles gut machen«, sagte Rotkäppchen zur Mutter und gab ihr die Hand darauf. Die Großmutter aber wohnte draußen im Wald, eine halbe Stunde vom Dorf. Wie nun Rotkäppchen in den

heard about her big teeth, and she immediately entered her service. On the first day she forced herself to be diligent and obey Mother Holle whenever she gave her orders, because her mind was on all the gold she would give her; but on the second day she already began to be idle; on the third day, even more so: she absolutely refused to get out of bed in the morning. Nor did she make Mother Holle's bed the correct way; she didn't shake it so the feathers flew. Mother Holle was soon tired of this, and discharged her. The lazy girl was contented, thinking that the shower of gold was now at hand; Mother Holle even led her to the gate, but when she was standing under it, instead of the gold a big kettle full of pitch was poured out over her. "This is the pay for your services," said Mother Holle, and shut the gate. Then the lazy girl came home, but she was entirely covered with pitch, and when the rooster on the well saw her, it called:

> "Cock-a-doodle-doo,
> our dirty girl is here anew."

And the pitch stuck to her; it wouldn't come off as long as she lived.

Little Red Hood [Little Red Riding Hood]

Once there was a sweet little girl who was loved by everyone who saw her, but most of all by her grandmother, who was never tired of giving the child gifts. Once she gave her a hood made of red velvet, and because it was so becoming to her and she wouldn't wear anything else on her head, she was simply called Little Red Hood. One day her mother said to her: "Come, Little Red Hood, here is a piece of cake and a bottle of wine; bring it over to your grandmother; she's sick and weak, and this will refresh her. Start out before the sun gets hot, and when you're outdoors, behave yourself and don't run off the path, or else you'll fall and break the glass, and your grandmother won't have anything. And when you go inside her cottage, don't forget to say good morning right away, and not stare into every corner first."

"I'll do everything properly," Little Red Hood said to her mother, and gave her her hand as a pledge. But her grandmother lived out in the forest, a half hour's walk from the village. Now,

Wald kam, begegnete ihm der Wolf. Rotkäppchen aber wußte nicht,
was das für ein böses Tier war, und fürchtete sich nicht vor ihm.
»Guten Tag, Rotkäppchen«, sprach er. »Schönen Dank, Wolf.« »Wo
hinaus so früh, Rotkäppchen?« »Zur Großmutter.« »Was trägst du
unter der Schürze?« »Kuchen und Wein: gestern haben wir
gebacken, da soll sich die kranke und schwache Großmutter etwas
zugut tun und sich damit stärken.« »Rotkäppchen, wo wohnt deine
Großmutter?« »Noch eine gute Viertelstunde weiter im Wald, unter
den drei großen Eichbäumen, da steht ihr Haus, unten sind die
Nußhecken, das wirst du ja wissen«, sagte Rotkäppchen. Der Wolf
dachte bei sich: »Das junge zarte Ding, das ist ein fetter Bissen, der
wird noch besser schmecken als die Alte: du mußt es listig anfangen,
damit du beide erschnappst.« Da ging er ein Weilchen neben
Rotkäppchen her, dann sprach er: »Rotkäppchen, sieh einmal die
schönen Blumen, die ringsumher stehen, warum guckst du dich
nicht um? Ich glaube, du hörst gar nicht, wie die Vöglein so lieblich
singen? Du gehst ja für dich hin, als wenn du zur Schule gingst, und
ist so lustig haußen in dem Wald.«

Rotkäppchen schlug die Augen auf, und als es sah, wie die
Sonnenstrahlen durch die Bäume hin und her tanzten und alles
voll schöner Blumen stand, dachte es: »Wenn ich der Großmutter
einen frischen Strauß mitbringe, der wird ihr auch Freude
machen; es ist so früh am Tag, daß ich doch zu rechter Zeit
ankomme«, lief vom Wege ab in den Wald hinein und suchte
Blumen. Und wenn es eine gebrochen hatte, meinte es, weiter hinaus stände eine schönere, und lief darnach, und geriet immer
tiefer in den Wald hinein. Der Wolf aber ging geradeswegs nach
dem Haus der Großmutter und klopfte an die Türe. »Wer ist
draußen?« »Rotkäppchen, das bringt Kuchen und Wein, mach
auf.« »Drück nur auf die Klinke«, rief die Großmutter, »ich bin zu
schwach und kann nicht aufstehen.« Der Wolf drückte auf die
Klinke, die Türe sprang auf, und er ging, ohne ein Wort zu
sprechen, gerade zum Bett der Großmutter und verschluckte sie.
Dann tat er ihre Kleider an, setzte ihre Haube auf, legte sich in ihr
Bett und zog die Vorhänge vor.

Rotkäppchen aber war nach den Blumen herumgelaufen, und als
es so viel zusammen hatte, daß es keine mehr tragen konnte, fiel ihm
die Großmutter wieder ein, und es machte sich auf den Weg zu ihr.
Es wunderte sich, daß die Türe aufstand, und wie es in die Stube trat,
so kam es ihm so seltsam darin vor, daß es dachte: »Ei, du mein Gott,
wie ängstlich wird mir's heute zumut, und bin sonst so gerne bei der

when Little Red Hood entered the forest, she was met by the wolf. Little Red Hood didn't know what a vicious animal he was, and she wasn't afraid of him. "Good day, Little Red Hood," he said. "Thank you, wolf." "Where to so early, Little Red Hood?" "To my grandmother's." "What are you carrying under your apron?" "Cake and wine: yesterday we baked, and my sick, weak grandmother is to enjoy some of it and get her strength back." "Little Red Hood, where does your grandmother live?" "Another good quarter-hour's walk deeper in the woods, under the three big oak trees, that's where her house is; below it are the nut hedges, as you surely know," said Little Red Hood. The wolf thought to himself: "This young, tender creature is a plump morsel, and she'll taste even better than the old lady: you've got to proceed by guile, so you can get hold of both of them." So he walked alongside Little Red Hood for a while, then said: "Little Red Hood, just see the beautiful flowers that are growing all around here; why don't you look around at them? I don't believe you even hear how sweetly the birds are singing. You're walking along in a beeline as if you were on the way to school, and it's so jolly out here in the woods."

Little Red Hood opened her eyes wide, and when she saw how the sunbeams were dancing to and fro among the trees and the whole area was full of beautiful flowers, she thought: "If I bring Grandmother a fresh bouquet, that will make her happy, too; it's so early in the day that I'll still get there in plenty of time." She ran off the path and into the woods, looking for flowers. And every time she picked one, she thought that an even prettier one was growing farther off, and she ran in that direction, getting deeper and deeper into the woods. But the wolf went straight to her grandmother's house and knocked at the door. "Who's there?" "It's Little Red Hood, bringing cake and wine; let me in." "Just press down on the latch," the grandmother called; "I'm too weak and can't get up." The wolf pressed the latch, the door flew open, and, without saying a word, he went straight to the grandmother's bed and gulped her down. Then he put on her clothes, put her nightcap on his head, lay down on her bed, and pulled the bed curtains shut.

But Little Red Hood had been running after the flowers, and after collecting so many that she couldn't carry any more, she remembered her grandmother again, and she set out for her house. She was surprised to find the door open, and when she stepped inside, it felt so odd to her there that she thought: "Oh, heavens, how nervous I feel today, though I usually so enjoy being at

Großmutter!« Es rief »Guten Morgen«, bekam aber keine Antwort. Darauf ging es zum Bett und zog die Vorhänge zurück: da lag die Großmutter und hatte die Haube tief ins Gesicht gesetzt und sah so wunderlich aus. »Ei, Großmutter, was hast du für große Ohren!« »Daß ich dich besser hören kann.« »Ei, Großmutter, was hast du für große Augen!« »Daß ich dich besser sehen kann.« »Ei, Großmutter, was hast du für große Hände!« »Daß ich dich besser packen kann.« »Aber, Großmutter, was hast du für ein entsetzlich großes Maul!« »Daß ich dich besser fressen kann.« Kaum hatte der Wolf das gesagt, so tat er einen Satz aus dem Bette und verschlang das arme Rotkäppchen.

Wie der Wolf sein Gelüsten gestillt hatte, legte er sich wieder ins Bett, schlief ein und fing an, überlaut zu schnarchen. Der Jäger ging eben an dem Haus vorbei und dachte: »Wie die alte Frau schnarcht, du mußt doch sehen, ob ihr etwas fehlt.« Da trat er in die Stube, und wie er vor das Bette kam, so sah er, daß der Wolf darin lag. »Finde ich dich hier, du alter Sünder«, sagte er, »ich habe dich lange gesucht.« Nun wollte er seine Büchse anlegen, da fiel ihm ein, der Wolf könnte die Großmutter gefressen haben und sie wäre noch zu retten: schoß nicht, sondern nahm eine Schere und fing an, dem schlafenden Wolf den Bauch aufzuschneiden. Wie er ein paar Schnitte getan hatte, da sah er das rote Käppchen leuchten, und noch ein paar Schnitte, da sprang das Mädchen heraus und rief: »Ach, wie war ich erschrocken, wie war's so dunkel in dem Wolf seinem Leib!« Und dann kam die alte Großmutter auch noch lebendig heraus und konnte kaum atmen. Rotkäppchen aber holte geschwind große Steine, damit füllten sie dem Wolf den Leib, und wie er aufwachte, wollte er fortspringen, aber die Steine waren so schwer, daß er gleich niedersank und sich totfiel.

Da waren alle drei vergnügt; der Jäger zog dem Wolf den Pelz ab und ging damit heim, die Großmutter aß den Kuchen und trank den Wein, den Rotkäppchen gebracht hatte, und erholte sich wieder, Rotkäppchen aber dachte: »Du willst dein Lebtag nicht wieder allein vom Wege ab in den Wald laufen, wenn dir's die Mutter verboten hat.«

✿

Es wird auch erzählt, daß einmal, als Rotkäppchen der alten Großmutter wieder Gebackenes brachte, ein anderer Wolf ihm zugesprochen und es vom Wege habe ableiten wollen. Rotkäppchen aber hütete sich und ging gerade fort seines Wegs und sagte der Großmutter, daß es dem Wolf begegnet wäre, der ihm guten Tag

grandmother's!" She called good morning, but got no answer. Then she went over to the bed and drew back the curtains: there lay her grandmother, whose nightcap was pulled down over her face, and who looked most peculiar. "Oh, grandmother, what big ears you have!" "The better to hear you with." "Oh, grandmother, what big eyes you have!" "The better to see you with." "Oh, grandmother, what big hands you have!" "The better to hold you with." "But, grandmother, what a horribly big mouth you have!" "The better to eat you with." Scarcely had the wolf said that when he bounded out of the bed and swallowed poor Little Red Hood.

After the wolf had sated his appetite, he went back to bed, fell asleep, and began to snore extremely loudly. The gamekeeper, who was just passing the house, thought: "How the old lady is snoring! You must see whether anything is wrong with her." So he entered the cottage, and when he came up to the bed, he saw the wolf lying on it. "So I find you here, you old reprobate," he said; "I've been looking for you for a long time." Now he wanted to level his gun, but it occurred to him that the wolf might have eaten the grandmother and she might still be saved: he didn't shoot, but he got a pair of scissors and began cutting open the sleeping wolf's belly. After a couple of snips, he saw the little red hood shining, and a few snips later, the girl jumped out, calling: "Oh, how frightened I was! How dark it was in the wolf's body!" And then her old grandmother came out, also still alive though she could hardly breathe. But Little Red Hood quickly gathered big stones, with which they filled the wolf's body; and when he awoke, he wanted to dash away, but the stones were so heavy that he immediately collapsed and fell dead.

Then all three were happy: the gamekeeper skinned the wolf and went home with its pelt; the grandmother ate the cake and drank the wine that Little Red Hood had brought her, and she recovered her strength. But Little Red Hood thought: "As long as you live, you'll never again run off the path into the woods when mother has told you not to."

✿

Some people also tell that once, when Little Red Hood was again bringing pastry to her old grandmother, another wolf spoke to her and tried to lead her off the path. But Little Red Hood was on the alert and went straight along her way; she told her grandmother that she had met the wolf, who had bidden her good day,

gewünscht, aber so bös aus den Augen geguckt hätte: »Wenn's nicht
auf offner Straße gewesen wäre, er hätte mich gefressen.« »Komm«,
sagte die Großmutter, »wir wollen die Türe verschließen, daß er
nicht herein kann.« Bald darnach klopfte der Wolf an und rief:
»Mach auf, Großmutter, ich bin das Rotkäppchen, ich bring dir
Gebackenes.« Sie schwiegen aber still und machten die Türe nicht
auf: da schlich der Graukopf etlichemal um das Haus, sprang
endlich aufs Dach und wollte warten, bis Rotkäppchen abends nach
Haus ginge, dann wollte er ihm nachschleichen und wollt's in der
Dunkelheit fressen. Aber die Großmutter merkte, was er im Sinn
hatte. Nun stand vor dem Haus ein großer Steintrog, da sprach sie
zu dem Kind: »Nimm den Eimer, Rotkäppchen, gestern hab ich
Würste gekocht, da trag das Wasser, worin sie gekocht sind, in den
Trog.« Rotkäppchen trug so lange, bis der große, große Trog ganz
voll war. Da stieg der Geruch von den Würsten dem Wolf in die
Nase, er schnupperte und guckte hinab, endlich machte er den Hals
so lang, daß er sich nicht mehr halten konnte und anfing zu
rutschen: so rutschte er vom Dach herab, gerade in den großen Trog
hinein, und ertrank. Rotkäppchen aber ging fröhlich nach Haus,
und tat ihm niemand etwas zuleid.

Die Bremer Stadtmusikanten

Es hatte ein Mann einen Esel, der schon lange Jahre die Säcke unverdrossen zur Mühle getragen hatte, dessen Kräfte aber nun zu
Ende gingen, so daß er zur Arbeit immer untauglicher ward. Da
dachte der Herr daran, ihn aus dem Futter zu schaffen, aber der Esel
merkte, daß kein guter Wind wehte, lief fort und machte sich auf den
Weg nach Bremen: dort, meinte er, könnte er ja Stadtmusikant werden. Als er ein Weilchen fortgegangen war, fand er einen Jagdhund
auf dem Wege liegen, der jappte wie einer, der sich müde gelaufen
hat. »Nun, was jappst du so, Packan?« fragte der Esel. »Ach«, sagte
der Hund, »weil ich alt bin und jeden Tag schwächer werde, auch auf
der Jagd nicht mehr fort kann, hat mich mein Herr wollen totschlagen, da hab ich Reißaus genommen; aber womit soll ich nun mein
Brot verdienen?« »Weißt du was«, sprach der Esel, »ich gehe nach
Bremen und werde dort Stadtmusikant, geh mit und laß dich auch bei
der Musik annehmen. Ich spiele die Laute, und du schlägst die
Pauken.« Der Hund war's zufrieden, und sie gingen weiter. Es

but who had had an evil look in his eyes: "If it hadn't been on the open road, he would have eaten me." "Come," said her grandmother, "we'll lock the door so he can't get in." Shortly afterward, the wolf knocked at the door and called: "Let me in, grandmother, I'm Little Red Hood and I've brought you some pastry." But they kept silent and didn't open the door: then Grayhead crept around the house a few times, finally leapt onto the roof, and decided to wait until Little Red Hood went home in the evening; he intended to slink after her then and eat her up in the dark. But her grandmother sensed what he had in mind. Now, in front of the house there was a big stone trough; she said to the child: "Take the bucket, Little Red Hood; I cooked sausages yesterday; carry the water they were boiled in out to the trough, and empty it there." Little Red Hood made repeated trips with the water until the big, big trough was completely filled. Then the smell of the sausage floated up to the wolf's nostrils; he sniffed and looked down; finally he stretched out his neck so far that he couldn't hold on anymore and began to slide down: and so he slid off the roof right into the big trough, where he drowned. And Little Red Hood went happily home, and no one did her any harm.

The Bremen Town Musicians

A man had a donkey which for many years had tirelessly carried his sacks of grain to the mill, but whose strength was now giving out, so that the animal was increasingly incapable of doing his job. Then his master considered getting rid of him to save on his feed, but the donkey realized an ill wind was blowing; he ran away and headed for Bremen: there, he thought, he could become a town musician. After proceeding for a while, he found a hunting hound lying on the road, panting like someone worn out with running. "Now, why are you panting like that, Grabber?" the donkey asked. "Ah," said the dog, "because I'm old and getting weaker every day, so I can't go out to hunt anymore, my master wanted to kill me, and I bolted; but how am I to earn my bread now?" "You know what?" said the donkey; "I'm going to Bremen to become a town musician there; come along and get a job with the band, too. I'll play the lute, and you beat the kettledrums." The dog agreed, and they proceeded. Before very long, there was

dauerte nicht lange, so saß da eine Katze an dem Weg und machte ein Gesicht wie drei Tage Regenwetter. »Nun, was ist dir in die Quere gekommen, alter Bartputzer?« sprach der Esel. »Wer kann da lustig sein, wenn's einem an den Kragen geht«, antwortete die Katze, »weil ich nun zu Jahren komme, meine Zähne stumpf werden und ich lieber hinter dem Ofen sitze und spinne als nach Mäusen herumjage, hat mich meine Frau ersäufen wollen; ich habe mich zwar noch fortgemacht, aber nun ist guter Rat teuer: wo soll ich hin?« »Geh mit uns nach Bremen, du verstehst dich doch auf die Nachtmusik, da kannst du ein Stadtmusikant werden.« Die Katze hielt das für gut und ging mit. Darauf kamen die drei Landesflüchtigen an einem Hof vorbei, da saß auf dem Tor der Haushahn und schrie aus Leibeskräften. »Du schreist einem durch Mark und Bein«, sprach der Esel, »was hast du vor?« »Da hab ich gut Wetter prophezeit«, sprach der Hahn, »weil unserer lieben Frauen Tag ist, wo sie dem Christkindlein die Hemdchen gewaschen hat und sie trocknen will; aber weil morgen zum Sonntag Gäste kommen, so hat die Hausfrau doch kein Erbarmen und hat der Köchin gesagt, sie wollte mich morgen in der Suppe essen, und da soll ich mir heut abend den Kopf abschneiden lassen. Nun schrei ich aus vollem Hals, solang ich noch kann.« »Ei was, du Rotkopf«, sagte der Esel, »zieh lieber mit uns fort, wir gehen nach Bremen, etwas Besseres als den Tod findest du überall; du hast eine gute Stimme, und wenn wir zusammen musizieren, so muß es eine Art haben.« Der Hahn ließ sich den Vorschlag gefallen, und sie gingen alle viere zusammen fort.

Sie konnten aber die Stadt Bremen in einem Tag nicht erreichen und kamen abends in einen Wald, wo sie übernachten wollten. Der Esel und der Hund legten sich unter einen großen Baum, die Katze und der Hahn machten sich in die Äste, der Hahn aber flog bis in die Spitze, wo es am sichersten für ihn war. Ehe er einschlief, sah er sich noch einmal nach allen vier Winden um, da däuchte ihn, er sähe in der Ferne ein Fünkchen brennen, und rief seinen Gesellen zu, es müßte nicht gar weit ein Haus sein, denn es scheine ein Licht. Sprach der Esel: »So müssen wir uns aufmachen und noch hingehen, denn hier ist die Herberge schlecht.« Der Hund meinte, ein paar Knochen und etwas Fleisch dran täten ihm auch gut. Also machten sie sich auf den Weg nach der Gegend, wo das Licht war, und sahen es bald heller schimmern, und es ward immer größer, bis sie vor ein hell erleuchtetes Räuberhaus kamen. Der Esel, als der größte, näherte sich dem Fenster und schaute hinein. »Was siehst du, Grauschimmel?« fragte der Hahn. »Was ich sehe?« antwortete der

a cat sitting by the road with an expression like three days of rainy weather. "Now, what's gone wrong for you, old whisker-preener?" said the donkey. "Who can be merry when he's getting it in the neck?" the cat replied; "because I'm along in years, because my teeth are becoming blunt, and I'd rather sit behind the stove and purr than chase around after mice, my mistress wanted to drown me; yes, I got away in time, but now I'm in a quandary: where to go?" "Come with us to Bremen; after all, you have experience as a nighttime serenader, you can become a town musician." The cat thought it was a good idea, and went along. Then the three who were fleeing their country passed by a barnyard, and on the gate sat the rooster of the house crowing with all his might. "Your crowing is so loud it goes right through me," said the donkey; "what are you up to?" "I was predicting good weather," said the rooster, "because it's a feast day of the Blessed Virgin, when she has washed the Christ Child's little shirts and wants to dry them; but because guests are coming for Sunday dinner tomorrow, my mistress has no pity, and she told the cook she wanted me to be in the soup tomorrow, and so I'm to have my head cut off tonight. Now I'm crowing as hard as possible while I still can." "Say there, Redcomb," said the donkey, "instead of that, join us on our journey; we're going to Bremen; you'll find something better than death wherever you go; you have a good voice, and if we make music together, it will surely be delectable." The rooster approved of the proposal, and all four proceeded together.

But they couldn't reach the town of Bremen in one day, and in the evening they entered a forest, where they intended to spend the night. The donkey and the dog lay down under a tall tree, the cat and the rooster went up into the boughs; but the rooster flew all the way to the top, where it was safest for him. Before he fell asleep, he looked around once more in all directions, and he imagined he saw a point of light shining in the distance; so he called to his companions, reporting that there must be a house not far away, because a light was burning. The donkey said: "In that case, we must set out and go there, because our lodgings here are bad." The dog thought that a couple of bones with some meat on them would do him some good, too. So they set out toward the area where the light was, and soon saw it gleam more brightly; it got bigger all the time until they stood before a brightly illuminated den of thieves. The donkey, being the biggest of them, approached the window and looked in. "What

Esel. »Einen gedeckten Tisch mit schönem Essen und Trinken, und Räuber sitzen daran und lassen's sich wohl sein.« »Das wäre was für uns«, sprach der Hahn. »Ja, ja, ach, wären wir da!« sagte der Esel. Da ratschlagten die Tiere, wie sie es anfangen müßten, um die Räuber hinauszujagen, und fanden endlich ein Mittel. Der Esel mußte sich mit den Vorderfüßen auf das Fenster stellen, der Hund auf des Esels Rücken springen, die Katze auf den Hund klettern, und endlich flog der Hahn hinauf und setzte sich der Katze auf den Kopf. Wie das geschehen war, fingen sie auf ein Zeichen insgesamt an, ihre Musik zu machen: der Esel schrie, der Hund bellte, die Katze miaute, und der Hahn krähte; dann stürzten sie durch das Fenster in die Stube hinein, daß die Scheiben klirrten. Die Räuber fuhren bei dem entsetzlichen Geschrei in die Höhe, meinten nicht anders, als ein Gespenst käme herein, und flohen in größter Furcht in den Wald hinaus. Nun setzten sich die vier Gesellen an den Tisch, nahmen mit dem vorlieb, was übriggeblieben war, und aßen, als wenn sie vier Wochen hungern sollten.

Wie die vier Spielleute fertig waren, löschten sie das Licht aus und suchten sich eine Schlafstätte, jeder nach seiner Natur und Bequemlichkeit. Der Esel legte sich auf den Mist, der Hund hinter die Türe, die Katze auf den Herd bei die warme Asche, und der Hahn setzte sich auf den Hahnenbalken; und weil sie müde waren von ihrem langen Weg, schliefen sie auch bald ein. Als Mitternacht vorbei war und die Räuber von weitem sahen, daß kein Licht mehr im Haus brannte, auch alles ruhig schien, sprach der Hauptmann: »Wir hätten uns doch nicht sollen ins Bockshorn jagen lassen«, und hieß einen hingehen und das Haus untersuchen. Der Abgeschickte fand alles still, ging in die Küche, ein Licht anzuzünden, und weil er die glühenden, feurigen Augen der Katze für lebendige Kohlen ansah, hielt er ein Schwefelhölzchen daran, daß es Feuer fangen sollte. Aber die Katze verstand keinen Spaß, sprang ihm ins Gesicht, spie und kratzte. Da erschrak er gewaltig, lief und wollte zur Hintertüre hinaus, aber der Hund, der da lag, sprang auf und biß ihn ins Bein; und als er über den Hof an dem Miste vorbeirannte, gab ihm der Esel noch einen tüchtigen Schlag mit dem Hinterfuß; der Hahn aber, der vom Lärmen aus dem Schlaf geweckt und munter geworden war, rief vom Balken herab: »Kikeriki!« Da lief der Räuber, was er konnte, zu seinem Hauptmann zurück und sprach: »Ach, in dem Haus sitzt eine greuliche Hexe, die hat mich angehaucht und mit ihren langen Fingern mir das Gesicht zerkratzt; und vor der Türe steht ein Mann mit einem Messer, der hat mich ins Bein gestochen; und auf dem Hof

do you see, Old Gray?" asked the rooster. "What I see?" answered the donkey. "A laid table with fine food and drink, and
robbers sitting at it enjoying themselves." "We could use some of
that," said the rooster. "Yes, yes; oh, if we were only in there!" said
the donkey. Then the animals held council on what they needed
to do to chase out the robbers; and they finally found a way. The
donkey placed his forefeet against the window, the dog jumped
onto the donkey's back, the cat climbed onto the dog, and, as a
finish, the rooster flew up and perched on the cat's head. When
that was done, at a signal they all began to perform their music:
the donkey brayed, the dog barked, the cat meowed, and the
rooster crowed; then they dived inside through the window, making the panes rattle. At that horrible outcry the robbers jumped
out of their seats, thinking that a ghost had definitely broken in;
and in the greatest fear they fled out into the forest. Now the four
companions sat down at the table, making do with the leftovers,
and ate as if they wouldn't eat again for a month.

When the four minstrels were done, they put out the light and
looked for a place to sleep, each one in accordance with his nature
and comfort. The donkey lay down on the dungheap, the dog behind the door, the cat on the hearth by the warm ashes; and the
rooster perched on the highest beam, the "rooster beam." Because
they were weary from their long walk, they soon fell asleep. When
midnight had passed, and the robbers saw from a distance that no
light was burning in the house anymore, and all seemed calm, their
chief said: "After all, we shouldn't have let anyone throw a scare
into us"; and he ordered one man to go over and search the house.
The man so delegated found everything quiet; he went into the
kitchen to put on a light, and, because he took the cat's glowing,
blazing eyes for hot embers, he held a match to them so it would
catch on fire. But the cat wasn't in a joking mood; she leaped at his
face, spitting and scratching. That gave him an awful fright; as he
ran, he wanted to leave by the back door, but the dog, who was
lying there, jumped up and bit him in the leg; and when he ran past
the dungheap on his way across the yard, the donkey gave him a
solid kick with one hind leg; while the rooster, who had been awakened by the noise and was now fully alert, called down from the
beam: "Cock-a-doodle-doo!" Then the robber ran as fast as he
could back to his chief, and said: "Oh, there's a horrible witch in
the house; she blew in my face and scratched it with her long fingers; and outside the door there's a man with a knife who stabbed

liegt ein schwarzes Ungetüm, das hat mit einer Holzkeule auf mich losgeschlagen; und oben auf dem Dache, da sitzt der Richter, der rief: ›Bringt mir den Schelm her.‹ Da machte ich, daß ich fortkam.« Von nun an getrauten sich die Räuber nicht weiter in das Haus, den vier Bremer Musikanten gefiel's aber so wohl darin, daß sie nicht wieder heraus wollten. Und der das zuletzt erzählt hat, dem ist der Mund noch warm.

Tischchendeckdich, Goldesel und Knüppel aus dem Sack

Vorzeiten war ein Schneider, der drei Söhne hatte und nur eine einzige Ziege. Aber die Ziege, weil sie alle zusammen mit ihrer Milch ernährte, mußte ihr gutes Futter haben und täglich hinaus auf die Weide geführt werden. Die Söhne taten das auch nach der Reihe. Einmal brachte sie der älteste auf den Kirchhof, wo die schönsten Kräuter standen, ließ sie da fressen und herumspringen. Abends, als es Zeit war heimzugehen, fragte er: »Ziege, bist du satt?« Die Ziege antwortete:

> »Ich bin so satt,
> ich mag kein Blatt: meh! meh!«

»So komm nach Haus«, sprach der Junge, faßte sie am Strickchen, führte sie in den Stall und band sie fest. »Nun«, sagte der alte Schneider, »hat die Ziege ihr gehöriges Futter?« »Oh«, antwortete der Sohn, »die ist so satt, sie mag kein Blatt.« Der Vater aber wollte sich selbst überzeugen, ging hinab in den Stall, streichelte das liebe Tier und fragte: »Ziege, bist du auch satt?« Die Ziege antwortete:

> »Wovon sollt ich satt sein?
> Ich sprang nur über Gräbelein
> und fand kein einzig Blättelein: meh! meh!«

»Was muß ich hören!« rief der Schneider, lief hinauf und sprach zu dem Jungen: »Ei, du Lügner, sagst, die Ziege wäre satt, und hast sie hungern lassen?« Und in seinem Zorne nahm er die Elle von der Wand und jagte ihn mit Schlägen hinaus.

Am andern Tag war die Reihe am zweiten Sohn, der suchte an der Gartenhecke einen Platz aus, wo lauter gute Kräuter standen, und die

me in the leg; and in the yard there's a black monster that let fly at me with a wooden cudgel; and up on the roof the judge sits, and he shouted: 'Bring that criminal over here!' So I beat it out of there!" From then on the robbers no longer dared venture into the house; but the four Bremen musicians liked it there so much that they never wanted to leave. And the person who told this story last still has his lips warm with talking.

Table-Set-Yourself, Gold-Donkey, and Cudgel-Out-of-the-Sack

Long ago there lived a tailor who had three sons and just a single goat. But because the goat nourished them all with her milk, she had to have good feed and had to be led out to pasture daily. And the sons did this, taking turns. One day, the eldest took her to the churchyard, where the finest grasses grew, allowing her to eat and caper about there. In the evening, when it was time to go home, he asked: "Goat, are you full?" The goat replied:

> "I feel so stuffed,
> no more grass, not a tuft! Bleat, bleat!"

"Then, come home," the boy said, grasped her cord leash, led her to her pen, and tied her up. "Now," said the old tailor, "did the goat get the feed she needed?" "Oh," his son replied, "she's so stuffed, she doesn't want a tuft." But his father wanted personal assurance of this; he went down to the pen, stroked his dear animal, and asked: "Goat, are you really full?" The goat replied:

> "How can I be full, alas?
> Over graves I had to pass,
> and didn't find one blade of grass! Bleat, bleat!"

"What's this I hear?" shouted the tailor; he ran up and said to the boy: "Oh, you liar, you say the goat got full, and you let her starve?" And in his wrath he took his ell measure down from the wall and drove him out with blows.

The next day, it was the second son's turn; he located a spot by the garden hedge that had nothing but good grasses, and the goat

Ziege fraß sie rein ab. Abends, als er heim wollte, fragte er: »Ziege, bist du satt?« Die Ziege antwortete:

>»Ich bin so satt,
> ich mag kein Blatt: meh! meh!«

»So komm nach Haus«, sprach der Junge, zog sie heim und band sie im Stalle fest. »Nun«, sagte der alte Schneider, »hat die Ziege ihr gehöriges Futter?« »Oh«, antwortete der Sohn, »die ist so satt, sie mag kein Blatt.« Der Schneider wollte sich darauf nicht verlassen, ging hinab in den Stall und fragte: »Ziege, bist du auch satt?« Die Ziege antwortete:

> »Wovon sollt ich satt sein?
> Ich sprang nur über Gräbelein
> und fand kein einzig Blättelein: meh! meh!«

»Der gottlose Bösewicht!« schrie der Schneider. »So ein frommes Tier hungern zu lassen!« Lief hinauf und schlug mit der Elle den Jungen zur Haustüre hinaus.

Die Reihe kam jetzt an den dritten Sohn, der wollte seine Sache gut machen, suchte Buschwerk mit dem schönsten Laube aus und ließ die Ziege daran fressen. Abends, als er heim wollte, fragte er: »Ziege, bist du auch satt?« Die Ziege antwortete:

> »Ich bin so satt,
> ich mag kein Blatt: meh! meh!«

»So komm nach Haus«, sagte der Junge, führte sie in den Stall und band sie fest. »Nun«, sagte der alte Schneider, »hat die Ziege ihr gehöriges Futter?« »Oh«, antwortete der Sohn, »die ist so satt, sie mag kein Blatt.« Der Schneider traute nicht, ging hinab und fragte: »Ziege, bist du auch satt?« Das boshafte Tier antwortete:

> »Wovon sollt ich satt sein?
> Ich sprang nur über Gräbelein
> und fand kein einzig Blättelein: meh! meh!«

»O die Lügenbrut!« rief der Schneider. »Einer so gottlos und pflichtvergessen wie der andere! Ihr sollt mich nicht länger zum Narren haben!« Und vor Zorn ganz außer sich, sprang er hinauf und gerbte dem armen Jungen mit der Elle den Rücken so gewaltig, daß er zum Haus hinaussprang.

Der alte Schneider war nun mit seiner Ziege allein. Am andern Morgen ging er hinab in den Stall, liebkoste die Ziege und sprach:

ate them down to the ground. In the evening, when he wanted to go home, he asked: "Goat, are you full?" The goat replied:

> "I feel so stuffed,
> no more grass, not a tuft! Bleat, bleat!"

"Then, come home," said the boy, who drew her home and tied her up in the pen. "Now," said the old tailor, "did the goat get the feed she needed?" "Oh," his son replied, "she's so stuffed, she doesn't want a tuft." The tailor was unwilling to rely on that statement; he went down to the pen and asked: "Goat, are you really full?" The goat replied:

> "How can I be full, alas?
> Over graves I had to pass,
> and didn't find one blade of grass! Bleat, bleat!"

"That's wicked villain!" the tailor shouted. "To let such a devoted animal go hungry!" He ran up and drove the boy out the door of the house with his ell measure.

Now it was the turn of the third son, who wanted to do a good job; he located shrubbery with the tenderest foliage and set the goat to browse there. In the evening, when he wanted to go home, he asked: "Goat, are you really full?" The goat replied:

> "I feel so stuffed,
> no more grass, not a tuft! Bleat, bleat!"

"Then, come home," said the boy, who led her into the pen and tied her up. "Now," said the old tailor, "did the goat get the feed she needed?" "Oh," his son replied, "she's so stuffed, she doesn't want a tuft." The tailor didn't trust him, but went down and asked: "Goat, are you really full?" The malicious animal replied:

> "How can I be full, alas?
> Over graves I had to pass,
> and didn't find one blade of grass! Bleat, bleat!"

"Such a pack of liars!" the tailor shouted. "All equally wicked and undutiful! You're not going to pull the wool over my eyes anymore!" And, beside himself with rage, he dashed up to the house and tanned the poor boy's back with the ell measure so violently that he darted out of the house.

Now the old tailor was alone with his goat. The next morning he went down to the pen, caressed the goat, and said: "Come,

»Komm, mein liebes Tierlein, ich will dich selbst zur Weide führen.«
Er nahm sie am Strick und brachte sie zu grünen Hecken und unter
Schafrippe und was sonst die Ziegen gerne fressen. »Da kannst du
dich einmal nach Herzenslust sättigen«, sprach er zu ihr und ließ sie
weiden bis zum Abend. Da fragte er: »Ziege, bist du satt?« Sie
antwortete:

>»Ich bin so satt,
> ich mag kein Blatt: meh! meh!«

»So komm nach Haus«, sagte der Schneider, führte sie in den Stall
und band sie fest. Als er wegging, kehrte er sich noch einmal um und
sagte: »Nun bist du doch einmal satt!« Aber die Ziege machte es ihm
nicht besser und rief:

> »Wovon sollt ich satt sein?
> Ich sprang nur über Gräbelein
> und fand kein einzig Blättelein: meh! meh!«

Als der Schneider das hörte, stutzte er und sah wohl, daß er seine drei
Söhne ohne Ursache verstoßen hatte. »Wart«, rief er, »du un-
dankbares Geschöpf, dich fortzujagen ist noch zu wenig, ich will dich
zeichnen, daß du dich unter ehrbaren Schneidern nicht mehr darfst
sehen lassen.« In einer Hast sprang er hinauf, holte sein Bartmesser,
seifte der Ziege den Kopf ein und schor sie so glatt wie seine flache
Hand. Und weil die Elle zu ehrenvoll gewesen wäre, holte er die
Peitsche und versetzte ihr solche Hiebe, daß sie in gewaltigen
Sprüngen davonlief.

Der Schneider, als er so ganz einsam in seinem Hause saß, verfiel
in große Traurigkeit und hätte seine Söhne gerne wieder gehabt, aber
niemand wußte, wo sie hingeraten waren. Der älteste war zu einem
Schreiner in die Lehre gegangen, da lernte er fleißig und unverdrossen, und als seine Zeit herum war, daß er wandern sollte,
schenkte ihm der Meister ein Tischchen, das gar kein besonderes
Ansehen hatte und von gewöhnlichem Holz war; aber es hatte eine
gute Eigenschaft. Wenn man es hinstellte und sprach: »Tischchen,
deck dich«, so war das gute Tischchen auf einmal mit einem saubern
Tüchlein bedeckt und stand da ein Teller und Messer und Gabel
daneben und Schüsseln mit Gesottenem und Gebratenem, soviel
Platz hatten, und ein großes Glas mit rotem Wein leuchtete, daß
einem das Herz lachte. Der junge Gesell dachte: »Damit hast du
genug für dein Lebtag«, zog guter Dinge in der Welt umher und
bekümmerte sich gar nicht darum, ob ein Wirtshaus gut oder schlecht

my dear little beastie, I myself will take you out to pasture." He led her by the rope and brought her to green hedges, and into patches of yarrow and all the things goats like to eat. "Here you can finally fill up to your heart's content," he said to her, letting her browse till evening. Then he asked: "Goat, are you full?" She replied:

> "I feel so stuffed,
> no more grass, not a tuft! Bleat, bleat!"

"Then, come home," said the tailor, who led her into the pen and tied her up. As he was walking away, he turned around once more and said: "Now you're finally full, I'm sure!" But the goat didn't treat him any better; she called:

> "How can I be full, alas?
> Over graves I had to pass,
> and didn't find one blade of grass! Bleat, bleat!"

When the tailor heard that, he gave a start and realized that he had driven away his three sons for no good reason. "Wait," he cried, "you ungrateful creature; to chase you away isn't enough; I'll put a mark on you so you won't dare show your face to respectable tailors!" He swiftly ran up to the house, fetched his razor, lathered the goat's head, and shaved her so smooth as the palm of his hand. And because the ell measure would have been too honorable for her, he fetched a whip and treated her to such lashes that she ran away in mighty bounds.

When the tailor found himself so all alone in his house, he fell prey to great melancholy and would gladly have had his sons back, but nobody knew what had become of them. The eldest had apprenticed himself to a cabinetmaker, from whom he learned industriously and tirelessly; when his time came to be an itinerant journeyman, his master presented him with a little table that didn't look like anything in particular and was made of a common kind of wood; but it had one good property. When someone put it down and said, "Table, set yourself," the kindly table was suddenly spread with a clean little tablecloth, and on it stood a plate, with knife and fork next to it, and platters of boiled and roasted food, as much as would fit on it; and a big glass of red wine sparkled there, so as to make anyone glad at heart. The young journeyman thought: "With this you're set for life"; he cheerfully traveled everywhere, never worrying about whether any inn was good or

und ob etwas darin zu finden war oder nicht. Wenn es ihm gefiel, so kehrte er gar nicht ein, sondern im Felde, im Wald, auf einer Wiese, wo er Lust hatte, nahm er sein Tischchen vom Rücken, stellte es vor sich und sprach:»Deck dich«, so war alles da, was sein Herz begehrte. Endlich kam es ihm in den Sinn, er wollte zu seinem Vater zurückkehren, sein Zorn würde sich gelegt haben, und mit dem Tischchendeckdich würde er ihn gerne wieder aufnehmen. Es trug sich zu, daß er auf dem Heimweg abends in ein Wirtshaus kam, das mit Gästen angefüllt war; sie hießen ihn willkommen und luden ihn ein, sich zu ihnen zu setzen und mit ihnen zu essen, sonst würde er schwerlich noch etwas bekommen.»Nein«, antwortete der Schreiner, »die paar Bissen will ich euch nicht vor dem Munde nehmen, lieber sollt ihr meine Gäste sein.« Sie lachten und meinten, er triebe seinen Spaß mit ihnen. Er aber stellte sein hölzernes Tischchen mitten in die Stube und sprach:»Tischchen, deck dich.« Augenblicklich war es mit Speisen besetzt, so gut, wie sie der Wirt nicht hätte herbeischaffen können und wovon der Geruch den Gästen lieblich in die Nase stieg. »Zugegriffen, liebe Freunde«, sprach der Schreiner, und die Gäste, als sie sahen, wie es gemeint war, ließen sich nicht zweimal bitten, rückten heran, zogen ihre Messer und griffen tapfer zu. Und was sie am meisten verwunderte, wenn eine Schüssel leer geworden war, so stellte sich gleich von selbst eine volle an ihren Platz. Der Wirt stand in einer Ecke und sah dem Dinge zu; er wußte gar nicht, was er sagen sollte, dachte aber:»Einen solchen Koch könntest du in deiner Wirtschaft wohl brauchen.« Der Schreiner und seine Gesellschaft waren lustig bis in die späte Nacht, endlich legten sie sich schlafen, und der junge Geselle ging auch zu Bett und stellte sein Wünschtischchen an die Wand. Dem Wirte aber ließen seine Gedanken keine Ruhe, es fiel ihm ein, daß in seiner Rumpelkammer ein altes Tischchen stände, das geradeso aussähe; das holte er ganz sachte herbei und vertauschte es mit dem Wünschtischchen. Am andern Morgen zahlte der Schreiner sein Schlafgeld, packte sein Tischchen auf, dachte gar nicht daran, daß er ein falsches hätte, und ging seiner Wege. Zu Mittag kam er bei seinem Vater an, der ihn mit großer Freude empfing.»Nun, mein lieber Sohn, was hast du gelernt?« sagte er zu ihm.»Vater, ich bin ein Schreiner geworden.«»Ein gutes Handwerk«, erwiderte der Alte,»aber was hast du von deiner Wanderschaft mitgebracht?«»Vater, das Beste, was ich mitgebracht habe, ist das Tischchen.« Der Schneider betrachtete es von allen Seiten und sagte:»Daran hast du kein Meisterstück gemacht, das ist ein altes und schlechtes Tischchen.«»Aber es ist ein Tischchendeck-

bad, or was well provided with food or not. When he felt like it, he didn't go into one, but, instead, on a field, in the woods, on a meadow, wherever he wanted, he took his little table off his back, put it down in front of him, and said, "Set yourself," and everything his heart desired was there. Finally it occurred to him to go back home to his father, whose anger would have cooled by then; he'd gladly welcome him back with the table-set-yourself. It came about that, on his way home in the evening, he arrived at an inn that was filled with guests; they welcomed him and invited him to sit down and dine with them, or else he'd have great difficulty finding anything to eat. "No," the cabinetmaker replied, "I won't take those few morsels out of your mouth; instead, you shall be *my* guests." They laughed, thinking he was having fun with them. But he placed his little wooden table in the middle of the room and said: "Table, set yourself." In a moment it was loaded with food more delicious than any the innkeeper could have provided; the aroma tickled the guests' noses pleasantly. "Help yourselves, dear friends," the cabinetmaker said, and when the guests saw the real situation, they didn't wait to be asked twice, but moved closer, took out their knives, and fell to with a will. But what astonished them the most was that, whenever a platter was emptied, a full one immediately appeared in its place. The innkeeper stood in a corner watching the event; he didn't know what to say, but he was thinking: "You could use a cook like that in your establishment." The cabinetmaker and his party made merry till late into the night; finally they went to bed, and the young journeyman also went to bed, placing his little wish-fulfilling table against the wall. But the innkeeper's thoughts gave him no rest; he remembered that in his storage room there was an old table that looked exactly the same; he brought it out very quietly and exchanged it for the wish-fulfilling table. The next morning, the cabinetmaker paid for his room, placed his table on his back, never imagining it wasn't the real one, and went his way. At noon he reached home, where his father welcomed him with great joy. "Now, my dear son, what trade have you learned?" he asked him. "Father, I've become a cabinetmaker." "A good trade," the old man responded; "but what have you brought back from your travels?" "Father, the best thing I've brought back is this little table." The tailor studied it from every angle, and said: "In this you haven't produced a masterpiece, it's a simple old table." "But it's a table-set-yourself," his son replied; "when I put it down and tell it to set itself, immediately

dich«, antwortete der Sohn, »wenn ich es hinstelle und sage ihm, es sollte sich decken, so stehen gleich die schönsten Gerichte darauf und ein Wein dabei, der das Herz erfreut. Ladet nur alle Verwandte und Freunde ein, die sollen sich einmal laben und erquicken, denn das Tischchen macht sie alle satt.« Als die Gesellschaft beisammen war, stellte er sein Tischchen mitten in die Stube und sprach: »Tischchen, deck dich.« Aber das Tischchen regte sich nicht und blieb so leer wie ein anderer Tisch, der die Sprache nicht versteht. Da merkte der arme Geselle, daß ihm das Tischchen vertauscht war, und schämte sich, daß er wie ein Lügner dastand. Die Verwandten aber lachten ihn aus und mußten ungetrunken und ungegessen wieder heimwandern. Der Vater holte seine Lappen wieder herbei und schneiderte fort, der Sohn aber ging bei einem Meister in die Arbeit.

Der zweite Sohn war zu einem Müller gekommen und bei ihm in die Lehre gegangen. Als er seine Jahre herum hatte, sprach der Meister: »Weil du dich so wohl gehalten hast, so schenke ich dir einen Esel von einer besondern Art, er zieht nicht am Wagen und trägt auch keine Säcke.« »Wozu ist er denn nütze?« fragte der junge Geselle. »Er speit Gold«, antwortete der Müller, »wenn du ihn auf ein Tuch stellst und sprichst ›Bricklebrit‹, so speit dir das gute Tier Goldstücke aus, hinten und vorn.« »Das ist eine schöne Sache«, sprach der Geselle, dankte dem Meister und zog in die Welt. Wenn er Gold nötig hatte, brauchte er nur zu seinem Esel »Bricklebrit« zu sagen, so regnete es Goldstücke, und er hatte weiter keine Mühe, als sie von der Erde aufzuheben. Wo er hinkam, war ihm das Beste gut genug, und je teurer, je lieber, denn er hatte immer einen vollen Beutel. Als er sich eine Zeitlang in der Welt umgesehen hatte, dachte er: »Du mußt deinen Vater aufsuchen, wenn du mit dem Goldesel kommst, so wird er seinen Zorn vergessen und dich gut aufnehmen.« Es trug sich zu, daß er in dasselbe Wirtshaus geriet, in welchem seinem Bruder das Tischchen vertauscht war. Er führte seinen Esel an der Hand, und der Wirt wollte ihm das Tier abnehmen und anbinden, der junge Geselle aber sprach: »Gebt Euch keine Mühe, meinen Grauschimmel führe ich selbst in den Stall und binde ihn auch selbst an, denn ich muß wissen, wo er steht.« Dem Wirt kam das wunderlich vor, und er meinte, einer, der seinen Esel selbst besorgen müßte, hätte nicht viel zu verzehren; als aber der Fremde in die Tasche griff, zwei Goldstücke herausholte und sagte, er sollte nur etwas Gutes für ihn einkaufen, so machte er große Augen, lief und suchte das Beste, das er auftreiben konnte. Nach der Mahlzeit fragte der Gast, was er schuldig wäre, der Wirt wollte

the tastiest dishes are standing on it, along with a wine that warms the cockles of your heart. Just invite all our relatives and friends to have a wonderful feast, because the table will fill all of them up." When the company was assembled, he put his little table down in the middle of the room and said: "Table, set yourself." But the table didn't budge and remained as empty as any other table that doesn't understand what you're saying to it. Then the poor journeyman realized that the tables had been switched on him, and was ashamed at appearing to be a liar. His relatives had a good laugh at his expense, and had to go home without food and drink. His father brought out his odds and ends of cloth again, and went back to his tailor's trade, while his son went to work for a master artisan.

The second son had come to a miller and had apprenticed himself there. When his years of apprenticeship were over, his master said: "Because you've conducted yourself so well, I'm giving you a donkey of a special breed; he doesn't pull a cart or carry sacks of grain." "What's he good for, then?" asked the young journeyman. "He spits gold," the miller replied; "when you place him over a cloth and say 'Bricklebrit,' the good beast spits out gold pieces for you, in front and in back." "That's something really nice," saidi the journeyman; he thanked his master, and set out on his travels. Whenever he needed money, all he had to do was say "Bricklebrit" to his donkey, and it rained gold pieces. The only effort he had to make was to pick them up off the ground. Wherever he arrived, the best was none too good for him, and the dearer things were, the better, because his purse was always full. After examining the ways of the world for a time, he thought to himself: "You must go home to your father; when you arrive with the gold-donkey, he'll forget his anger and welcome you in." It came about that he found himself in the same inn in which his brother's little table had been replaced by another. He led over his donkey on foot, and the innkeeper wanted to take the animal and tie it up, but the young journeyman said: "Don't take the trouble; I'll lead my gray donkey into the stable myself, and I'll tie him up myself, because I have to know where he's located." This puzzled the innkeeper, and he imagined that someone who had to take care of his donkey himself couldn't have much to spend; but when the stranger reached into his pocket, brought out two gold pieces, and said that the innkeeper should buy some very good provisions for him, his eyes bulged out, and he hastened to procure the best things he could hunt up. After the meal his guest asked how

die doppelte Kreide nicht sparen und sagte, noch ein paar Goldstücke müßte er zulegen. Der Geselle griff in die Tasche, aber sein Gold war eben zu Ende. »Wartet einen Augenblick, Herr Wirt«, sprach er, »ich will nur gehen und Gold holen«; nahm aber das Tischtuch mit. Der Wirt wußte nicht, was das heißen sollte, war neugierig, schlich ihm nach, und da der Gast die Stalltüre zuriegelte, so guckte er durch ein Astloch. Der Fremde breitete unter dem Esel das Tuch aus, rief »Bricklebrit«, und augenblicklich fing das Tier an, Gold zu speien von hinten und vorn, daß es ordentlich auf die Erde herabregnete. »Ei der tausend«, sagte der Wirt, »da sind die Dukaten bald geprägt! So ein Geldbeutel ist nicht übel!« Der Gast bezahlte seine Zeche und legte sich schlafen, der Wirt aber schlich in der Nacht herab in den Stall, führte den Münzmeister weg und band einen andern Esel an seine Stelle. Den folgenden Morgen in der Frühe zog der Geselle mit seinem Esel ab und meinte, er hätte seinen Goldesel. Mittags kam er bei seinem Vater an, der sich freute, als er ihn wiedersah, und ihn gerne aufnahm. »Was ist aus dir geworden, mein Sohn?« fragte der Alte. »Ein Müller, lieber Vater«, antwortete er. »Was hast du von deiner Wanderschaft mitgebracht?« »Weiter nichts als einen Esel.« »Esel gibt's hier genug«, sagte der Vater, »da wäre mir doch eine gute Ziege lieber gewesen.« »Ja«, antwortete der Sohn, »aber es ist kein gemeiner Esel, sondern ein Goldesel: wenn ich sage ›Bricklebrit‹, so speit Euch das gute Tier ein ganzes Tuch voll Goldstücke. Laßt nur alle Verwandte herbeirufen, ich mache sie alle zu reichen Leuten.« »Das laß ich mir gefallen«, sagte der Schneider, »dann brauch ich mich mit der Nadel nicht weiter zu quälen«, sprang selbst fort und rief die Verwandten herbei. Sobald sie beisammen waren, hieß sie der Müller Platz machen, breitete sein Tuch aus und brachte den Esel in die Stube. »Jetzt gebt acht«, sagte er und rief »Bricklebrit«, aber es waren keine Goldstücke, was herabfiel, und es zeigte sich, daß das Tier nichts von der Kunst verstand, denn es bringt's nicht jeder Esel so weit. Da machte der arme Müller ein langes Gesicht, sah, daß er betrogen war, und bat die Verwandten um Verzeihung, die so arm heimgingen, als sie gekommen waren. Es blieb nichts übrig, der Alte mußte wieder nach der Nadel greifen und der Junge sich bei einem Müller verdingen.

Der dritte Bruder war zu einem Drechsler in die Lehre gegangen, und weil es ein kunstreiches Handwerk ist, mußte er am längsten lernen. Seine Brüder aber meldeten ihm in einem Briefe, wie schlimm es ihnen ergangen wäre und wie sie der Wirt noch am letzten Abende

much he owed; the innkeeper had no qualms about chalking up double the proper amount, and said that the young man had to add another couple of gold pieces. The journeyman reached into his pocket, but his gold had just run out. "Wait a moment, innkeeper," he said, "I'll just go get some money"; and he took along the tablecloth. The innkeeper didn't know what was going on, and out of curiosity he sneaked after him; when his guest bolted the stable door, he peeped in through a knothole. The stranger spread the cloth under the donkey and called out "Bricklebrit," and at once the animal began to spit out money from front and back, so that there was a literal shower of it onto the ground. "Well, I'll be," said the innkeeper, "the ducats are ready-minted! A purse like that isn't bad!" The guest paid his bill and went to bed, but the innkeeper went stealthily down to the stable at night, led away the director of the mint, and tied another donkey in his place. Early the next morning, the journeyman departed with the donkey, thinking he had his gold-donkey. At noon he reached home, and his father was glad to see him again and gave him a hearty welcome. "What have you become, son?" the old man asked. "A miller, father dear," he replied. "What have you brought back from your travels?" "Nothing but a donkey." "There are plenty of donkeys here," his father said; "I would have preferred a good goat." "Yes," his son replied, "but it's no ordinary donkey, it's a gold-donkey: whenever I say 'Bricklebrit,' the good animal spits out a whole sheetful of gold pieces. Just have all our relatives summoned here, and I'll make each one of them rich." "That sounds good to me," said the tailor; "then I won't need to plague myself with my needle anymore"; he personally dashed out and summoned his relatives. As soon as they were all assembled, the miller bade them give him some room; he spread out his cloth and led the donkey into the room. "Now pay attention," he said, and called "Bricklebrit," but what came down was not gold pieces, and it was evident that the animal didn't know its business at all: because not every donkey becomes so accomplished! Then the poor miller pulled a long face, realized that he had been cheated, and asked forgiveness of his relatives, who went home as poor as they had come. There was nothing else for it: the old man had to reach for his needle again, and the young man had to hire himself out to a miller.

The third brother had become apprentice to a turner, and because that's a complicated trade, his apprenticeship was the longest. But his brothers informed him in a letter how badly things had gone with them, and how, on the last evening before their homecoming,

um ihre schönen Wünschdinge gebracht hätte. Als der Drechsler nun ausgelernt hatte und wandern sollte, so schenkte ihm sein Meister, weil er sich so wohl gehalten, einen Sack und sagte: »Es liegt ein Knüppel darin.« »Den Sack kann ich umhängen, und er kann mir gute Dienste leisten, aber was soll der Knüppel darin? Der macht ihn nur schwer.« »Das will ich dir sagen«, antwortete der Meister, »hat dir jemand etwas zuleid getan, so sprich nur ›Knüppel, aus dem Sack‹, so springt dir der Knüppel heraus unter die Leute und tanzt ihnen so lustig auf dem Rücken herum, daß sie sich acht Tage lang nicht regen und bewegen können; und eher läßt er nicht ab, als bis du sagst ›Knüppel, in den Sack‹.« Der Gesell dankte ihm, hing den Sack um, und wenn ihm jemand zu nahe kam und auf den Leib wollte, so sprach er: »Knüppel, aus dem Sack«, alsbald sprang der Knüppel heraus und klopfte einem nach dem andern den Rock oder Wams gleich auf dem Rücken aus und wartete nicht erst, bis er ihn ausgezogen hatte; und das ging so geschwind, daß eh sich's einer versah, die Reihe schon an ihm war. Der junge Drechsler langte zur Abendzeit in dem Wirtshaus an, wo seine Brüder waren betrogen worden. Er legte seinen Ranzen vor sich auf den Tisch und fing an zu erzählen, was er alles Merkwürdiges in der Welt gesehen habe. »Ja«, sagte er, »man findet wohl ein Tischchendeckdich, einen Goldesel und dergleichen: lauter gute Dinge, die ich nicht verachte, aber das ist alles nichts gegen den Schatz, den ich mir erworben habe und mit mir da in meinem Sack führe.« Der Wirt spitzte die Ohren: »Was in aller Welt mag das sein?« dachte er. »Der Sack ist wohl mit lauter Edelsteinen angefüllt; den sollte ich billig auch noch haben, denn aller guten Dinge sind drei.« Als Schlafenszeit war, streckte sich der Gast auf die Bank und legte seinen Sack als Kopfkissen unter. Der Wirt, als er meinte, der Gast läge in tiefem Schlaf, ging herbei, rückte und zog ganz sachte und vorsichtig an dem Sack, ob er ihn vielleicht wegziehen und einen andern unterlegen könnte. Der Drechsler aber hatte schon lange darauf gewartet, wie nun der Wirt eben einen herzhaften Ruck tun wollte, rief er: »Knüppel, aus dem Sack.« Alsbald fuhr das Knüppelchen heraus, dem Wirt auf den Leib und rieb ihm die Nähte, daß es eine Art hatte. Der Wirt schrie zum Erbarmen, aber je lauter er schrie, desto kräftiger schlug der Knüppel ihm den Takt dazu auf dem Rücken, bis er endlich erschöpft zur Erde fiel. Da sprach der Drechsler: »Wo du das Tischchendeckdich und den Goldesel nicht wieder herausgibst, so soll der Tanz von neuem angehen.« »Ach nein«, rief der Wirt ganz kleinlaut, »ich gebe alles gerne wieder heraus, laßt nur den verwünschten Kobold wieder in den Sack

the innkeeper had deprived them of their lovely wish-fulfilling possessions. Now, when the turner's apprenticeship was over and he
was about to begin his travels, his master gave him a sack because
he had behaved so well; he said: "There's a cudgel in it." "I can sling
the sack over my shoulder, and it can come in handy for me, but
why the cudgel inside? It just makes it heavy." "I'll tell you why," his
master replied; "if anyone has done you any wrong, just say 'Cudgel,
out of the sack' and the cudgel will leap out among the people and
do such a merry dance on their backs that they won't be able to
move or stir for a week; and it won't stop till you say 'Cudgel, back
in the sack.'" The journeyman thanked him and slung the sack over
his shoulder; and whenever anyone became menacing and seemed
about to attack him, he said "Cudgel, out of the sack" and the cudgel immediately leaped out and beat the dust out of the jacket or
doublet of one man after another—while the clothes were still on
their backs, without waiting for them to take them off! And it happened so rapidly that before any man expected, it was already his
turn. In the evening the young turner reached the inn where his
brothers had been cheated. He placed his knapsack on the table in
front of him and began to tell about all the strange things he had
seen on his travels. "Yes," he said, "people do come across a table-
set-yourself, a gold-donkey, and the like: quite good things, which I
don't belittle, but none of them is anything compared to the treasure I've acquired and is right here in my sack." The innkeeper
pricked up his ears. "What in the world can it be?" he thought. "The
sack is probably filled with nothing but jewels; it's only right for me
to have that, too, because all good things come in threes." At bedtime, the guest stretched out on the bench, placing his sack under
his head as a pillow. When the innkeeper thought his guest was fast
asleep, he went over and tugged and pulled at the sack very gently
and carefully, trying to yank it out and substitute another one for it.
But the turner had long been waiting for the right moment; now,
when the innkeeper was just about to give a hefty tug, he cried:
"Cudgel, out of the sack." The little cudgel immediately flew out
and attacked the innkeeper, giving him a drubbing that was a joy to
behold. The innkeeper screamed bloody murder, but the louder he
yelled, the harder the cudgel beat time on his back to his music,
until he finally fell to the floor in exhaustion. Then the turner said:
"If you don't hand over the table-set-yourself and the gold-donkey,
the dance will start all over again." "Oh, no," called the innkeeper
humbly and apologetically, "I'll gladly hand everything back; just

kriechen.« Da sprach der Geselle: »Ich will Gnade für Recht ergehen lassen, aber hüte dich vor Schaden!« Dann rief er: »Knüppel, in den Sack!«, und ließ ihn ruhen.

Der Drechsler zog am andern Morgen mit dem Tischchendeckdich und dem Goldesel heim zu seinem Vater. Der Schneider freute sich, als er ihn wiedersah, und fragte auch ihn, was er in der Fremde gelernt hätte. »Lieber Vater«, antwortete er, »ich bin ein Drechsler geworden.« »Ein kunstreiches Handwerk«, sagte der Vater, »was hast du von der Wanderschaft mitgebracht?« »Ein kostbares Stück, lieber Vater«, antwortete der Sohn, »einen Knüppel in dem Sack.« »Was!« rief der Vater. »Einen Knüppel! Das ist der Mühe wert! Den kannst du dir von jedem Baume abhauen.« »Aber einen solchen nicht, lieber Vater: sage ich ›Knüppel, aus dem Sack‹, so springt der Knüppel heraus und macht mit dem, der es nicht gut mit mir meint, einen schlimmen Tanz und läßt nicht eher nach, als bis er auf der Erde liegt und um gut Wetter bittet. Seht Ihr, mit diesem Knüppel habe ich das Tischchendeckdich und den Goldesel wieder herbeigeschafft, die der diebische Wirt meinen Brüdern abgenommen hatte. Jetzt laßt sie beide rufen und ladet alle Verwandten ein, ich will sie speisen und tränken und will ihnen die Taschen noch mit Gold füllen.« Der alte Schneider wollte nicht recht trauen, brachte aber doch die Verwandten zusammen. Da deckte der Drechsler ein Tuch in die Stube, führte den Goldesel herein und sagte zu seinem Bruder: »Nun, lieber Bruder, sprich mit ihm.« Der Müller sagte: »Bricklebrit«, und augenblicklich sprangen die Goldstücke auf das Tuch herab, als käme ein Platzregen, und der Esel hörte nicht eher auf, als bis alle so viel hatten, daß sie nicht mehr tragen konnten. (Ich sehe dir's an, du wärst auch gerne dabei gewesen.) Dann holte der Drechsler das Tischchen und sagte: »Lieber Bruder, nun sprich mit ihm.« Und kaum hatte der Schreiner »Tischchen, deck dich« gesagt, so war es gedeckt und mit den schönsten Schüsseln reichlich besetzt. Da ward eine Mahlzeit gehalten, wie der gute Schneider noch keine in seinem Hause erlebt hatte, und die ganze Verwandtschaft blieb beisammen bis in die Nacht, und waren alle lustig und vergnügt. Der Schneider verschloß Nadel und Zwirn, Elle und Bügeleisen in einen Schrank und lebte mit seinen drei Söhnen in Freude und Herrlichkeit.

Wo ist aber die Ziege hingekommen, die schuld war, daß der Schneider seine drei Söhne fortjagte? Das will ich dir sagen. Sie schämte sich, daß sie einen kahlen Kopf hatte, lief in eine Fuchshöhle und verkroch sich hinein. Als der Fuchs nach Haus kam, funkelten ihm ein paar große Augen aus der Dunkelheit entgegen, daß er

make that damned goblin crawl back into the sack." Then the journeyman said: "I'll show you mercy, but watch out for trouble!" Then he called "Cudgel, back in the sack," and gave him a rest.

The next morning the turner went home to his father with the table-set-yourself and the gold-donkey. The tailor was happy to see him again, and asked him, as well, what trade he had learned in foreign parts. "Father dear," he replied, "I've become a turner." "A very accomplished trade," his father said; "what have you brought back from your travels?" "A precious item, father dear," his son replied, "a cudgel in a sack." "What!" his father cried. "A cudgel! Very worthwhile! You can cut one from any tree." "But not one like this, father dear: if I say 'Cudgel, out of the sack,' the cudgel jumps out and does a wicked dance on anyone who has evil intentions against me; and it doesn't stop till he's lying on the ground begging for a let-up. Look: with this cudgel I've got back the table-set-yourself and the gold-donkey that the thievish innkeeper took away from my brothers. Now have them both summoned and invite all our relatives; I'll give them food and drink, and on top of that I'll fill their pockets with gold." The old tailor was unwilling to believe it, but he did assemble his relatives. Then the turner spread out a cloth on the floor of the room, led in the gold-donkey, and said to his brother: "Now, brother dear, talk to him." The miller said "Bricklebrit" and immediately gold pieces rained down onto the cloth, as if from a cloudburst, and the donkey didn't stop until everyone had so much, they couldn't carry it anymore. (I can see by your expression that you wouldn't have minded being there.) Then the turner brought the little table and said: "Brother dear, now talk to it." And scarcely had the cabinetmaker said "Table, set yourself" when it was set and abundantly covered with the finest platters. Then they enjoyed a meal like no other the good tailor had ever experienced in his house, and all the relatives stayed together until nighttime, all of them merry and contented. The tailor locked away his needle and thread, ell measure, and flatiron in a cupboard, and he and his three sons lived in joy and splendor.

But what happened to the goat that was responsible for the tailor's chasing away his three sons? I'll tell you. She was ashamed of having a bald head; she ran into a fox's burrow and crept out of sight. When the fox came home, two big eyes were gleaming at him out of the dark, so that he got frightened and

erschrak und wieder zurücklief. Der Bär begegnete ihm, und da der Fuchs ganz verstört aussah, so sprach er: »Was ist dir, Bruder Fuchs, was machst du für ein Gesicht?« »Ach«, antwortete der Rote, »ein grimmig Tier sitzt in meiner Höhle und hat mich mit feurigen Augen angeglotzt.« »Das wollen wir bald austreiben«, sprach der Bär, ging mit zu der Höhle und schaute hinein; als er aber die feurigen Augen erblickte, wandelte ihn ebenfalls Furcht an: er wollte mit dem grimmigen Tiere nichts zu tun haben und nahm Reißaus. Die Biene begegnete ihm, und da sie merkte, daß es ihm in seiner Haut nicht wohl zumute war, sprach sie: »Bär, du machst ja ein gewaltig verdrießlich Gesicht, wo ist deine Lustigkeit geblieben?« »Du hast gut reden«, antwortete der Bär, »es sitzt ein grimmiges Tier mit Glotzaugen in dem Hause des Roten, und wir können es nicht herausjagen.« Die Biene sprach: »Du dauerst mich, Bär, ich bin ein armes schwaches Geschöpf, das ihr im Wege nicht anguckt, aber ich glaube doch, daß ich euch helfen kann.« Sie flog in die Fuchshöhle, setzte sich der Ziege auf den glatten geschorenen Kopf und stach sie so gewaltig, daß sie aufsprang, »meh! meh!« schrie und wie toll in die Welt hineinlief; und weiß niemand auf diese Stunde, wo sie hingelaufen ist.

Daumesdick

Es war ein armer Bauersmann, der saß abends beim Herd und schürte das Feuer, und die Frau saß und spann. Da sprach er: »Wie ist's so traurig, daß wir keine Kinder haben! Es ist so still bei uns, und in den andern Häusern ist's so laut und lustig.« »Ja«, antwortete die Frau und seufzte, »wenn's nur ein einziges wäre, und wenn's auch ganz klein wäre, nur daumensgroß, so wollt ich schon zufrieden sein; wir hätten's doch von Herzen lieb.« Nun geschah es, daß die Frau kränklich ward und nach sieben Monaten ein Kind gebar, das zwar an allen Gliedern vollkommen, aber nicht länger als ein Daumen war. Da sprachen sie: »Es ist, wie wir es gewünscht haben, und es soll unser liebes Kind sein«, und nannten es nach seiner Gestalt *Daumesdick*. Sie ließen's nicht an Nahrung fehlen, aber das Kind ward nicht größer, sondern blieb, wie es in der ersten Stunde gewesen war; doch schaute es verständig aus den Augen und zeigte sich bald als ein kluges und behendes Ding, dem alles glückte, was es anfing.

Der Bauer machte sich eines Tages fertig, in den Wald zu gehen und Holz zu fällen, da sprach er so vor sich hin: »Nun wollt ich, daß

ran away. The bear met him, and since the fox looked quite per-
turbed, he said: "What's wrong, Brother Fox, why have you got
that look on your face?" "Oh," Red answered, "a vicious animal
is sitting in my lair, and it glared at me with blazing eyes." "We'll
soon drive it out," said the bear, and accompanied him to his
burrow and looked in; but when he saw the blazing eyes, he, too,
was overcome with fear: he wanted to have nothing to do with
that vicious animal, and he lit out. The bee met him, and when
she noticed that his disposition was soured, she said: "Bear,
you're pulling an awfully long face; what's happened to all your
jolliness?" "It's all right for you to talk," the bear replied; "a vicious animal with glaring eyes is sitting in Red's house, and we
can't drive it out." The bee said: "I feel sorry for you, bear; I'm a
poor, weak creature that you two don't even look at when you
pass by, but all the same I believe I can help you." She flew to
the fox's burrow, alighted on the goat's smoothly shaved head,
and stung her so hard that she leaped up, cried "Bleat, bleat!"
and ran outdoors as if mad; and to this day no one knows where
she ran to.

Big-as-a-Thumb [Tom Thumb]

There was a poor farmer who was sitting by his hearth in the
evening, stirring the fire, while his wife sat spinning. Then he
said: "How sad it is that we have no children! It's so quiet at our
place, and in the other houses it's so bustling and jolly." "Yes," his
wife replied with a sigh, "even if there was just one, and even if
it was very small, only as big as a thumb, I'd be contented; we'd
love it dearly, anyway." Now it came about that the woman became pregnant and, seven months later, gave birth to a child that
was physically perfect but no taller than a thumb. Then they
said: "It's just as we wished, and it will be our dear child"; and,
because of the boy's size, they named him Big-as-a-Thumb. The
child was well provided with nourishment, but grew no bigger,
remaining the same size as at birth; yet, the look in his eyes was
intelligent, and he soon proved to be a clever, handy boy who
was successful in everything he undertook.

One day the farmer made ready to go into the forest to chop
down trees, and he said to himself: "Now I wish there were

einer da wäre, der mir den Wagen nachbrächte.« »O Vater«, rief
Daumesdick, »den Wagen will ich schon bringen, verlaßt Euch drauf,
er soll zur bestimmten Zeit im Walde sein.« Da lachte der Mann und
sprach: »Wie sollte das zugehen, du bist viel zu klein, um das Pferd
mit dem Zügel zu leiten.« »Das tut nichts, Vater, wenn nur die
Mutter anspannen will, ich setze mich dem Pferd ins Ohr und rufe
ihm zu, wie es gehen soll.« »Nun«, antwortete der Vater, »einmal
wollen wir's versuchen.« Als die Stunde kam, spannte die Mutter an
und setzte Daumesdick ins Ohr des Pferdes, und dann rief der
Kleine, wie das Pferd gehen sollte: »Jüh und joh! Hott und har!« Da
ging es ganz ordentlich, als wie bei einem Meister, und der Wagen
fuhr den rechten Weg nach dem Walde. Es trug sich zu, als er eben
um eine Ecke bog und der Kleine »Har, har!« rief, daß zwei fremde
Männer daherkamen. »Mein«, sprach der eine, »was ist das? Da fährt
ein Wagen, und ein Fuhrmann ruft dem Pferde zu und ist doch nicht
zu sehen.« »Das geht nicht mit rechten Dingen zu«, sagte der andere,
»wir wollen dem Karren folgen und sehen, wo er anhält.« Der Wagen
aber fuhr vollends in den Wald hinein und richtig zu dem Platze, wo
das Holz gehauen ward. Als Daumesdick seinen Vater erblickte, rief
er ihm zu: »Siehst du, Vater, da bin ich mit dem Wagen, nun hol mich
herunter.« Der Vater faßte das Pferd mit der linken und holte mit der
rechten sein Söhnlein aus dem Ohr, das sich ganz lustig auf einen
Strohhalm niedersetzte. Als die beiden fremden Männer den
Daumesdick erblickten, wußten sie nicht, was sie vor Verwunderung
sagen sollten. Da nahm der eine den andern beiseit und sprach:
»Hör, der kleine Kerl könnte unser Glück machen, wenn wir ihn in
einer großen Stadt vor Geld sehen ließen: wir wollen ihn kaufen.« Sie
gingen zu dem Bauer und sprachen: »Verkauft uns den kleinen
Mann, er soll's gut bei uns haben.« »Nein«, antwortete der Vater, »es
ist mein Herzblatt und ist mir für alles Gold in der Welt nicht feil.«
Daumesdick aber, als er von dem Handel gehört, war an den
Rockfalten seines Vaters hinaufgekrochen, stellte sich ihm auf die
Schulter und wisperte ihm ins Ohr: »Vater, gib mich nur hin, ich will
schon wieder zurückkommen.« Da gab ihn der Vater für ein schönes
Stück Geld den beiden Männern hin. »Wo willst du sitzen?«
sprachen sie zu ihm. »Ach, setzt mich nur auf den Rand von eurem
Hut, da kann ich auf und ab spazieren und die Gegend betrachten,
und falle doch nicht herunter.« Sie taten ihm den Willen, und als
Daumesdick Abschied von seinem Vater genommen hatte, machten
sie sich mit ihm fort. So gingen sie, bis es dämmerig ward, da sprach
der Kleine: »Hebt mich einmal herunter, es ist nötig.« »Bleib nur

someone to bring the cart after me." "Oh, father," Big-as-a-Thumb called, "I'll bring the wagon, rely on it, it'll be in the forest at the proper time." Then the man laughed and said: "How could that be done? You're much too small to lead the horse with the reins." "That makes no difference, father; if mother will just harness him, I'll sit down in the horse's ear and instruct him which way to go." "Well," his father replied, "let's try it once." When the time came, Big-as-a-Thumb's mother harnessed the horse and put Big-as-a-Thumb in its ear; then the little fellow shouted out the directions: "Right! Left! Gee! Haw!" Things went perfectly smoothly, as with a master driver, and the cart took the correct path to the woods. It so happened that, just as it was taking a curve and the little fellow was calling "Haw, haw!" two unfamiliar men came by. "Say," said one of them, "what's this? A cart is driving, and a carter is calling to the horse, but he's nowhere to be seen." "There's something eerie about this," said the other; "let's follow the cart and see where it stops." But the cart drove all the way into the woods and to the very place where the trees were being felled. When Big-as-a-Thumb caught sight of his father, he shouted to him: "See, father? Here I am with the cart; now take me down." His father grasped the horse with his left hand and, with his right, took his little son out of its ear; the boy sat down on a straw in great merriment. When the two strangers caught sight of Big-as-a-Thumb, they were speechless with astonishment. Then one of them took the other over to one side and said: "Listen, that little chap could make our fortune if we exhibited him for money in a big town: let's buy him." They went to the farmer and said: "Sell us the little man; he'll have a good life with us." "No," the father replied, "he's the apple of my eye, and I wouldn't sell him for all the gold in the world." But after Big-as-a-Thumb heard the negotiations, he crawled up his father's jacket pleats; taking a stand on his shoulder, he whispered in his ear: "Father, let them have me, I'll surely come back." Then his father sold him to the two men for a substantial amount of money. "Where do you want to sit?" they asked him. "Oh, just put me on the brim of your hat; there I can walk back and forth and look at the scenery, and I won't fall off." They granted his request, and after Big-as-a-Thumb had said good-bye to his father, they set out with him. They were walking that way until dusk; then the little fellow said: "Please put me down; I've got to go." "Just stay up there," said the man on whose head he was sitting;

droben«, sprach der Mann, auf dessen Kopf er saß, »ich will mir
nichts draus machen, die Vögel lassen mir auch manchmal was drauf-
fallen.« »Nein«, sprach Daumesdick, »ich weiß auch, was sich schickt:
hebt mich nur geschwind herab.« Der Mann nahm den Hut ab und
setzte den Kleinen auf einen Acker am Weg, da sprang und kroch er
ein wenig zwischen den Schollen hin und her, dann schlüpfte er
plötzlich in ein Mausloch, das er sich ausgesucht hatte. »Guten
Abend, ihr Herren, geht nur ohne mich heim«, rief er ihnen zu und
lachte sie aus. Sie liefen herbei und stachen mit Stöcken in das
Mausloch, aber das war vergebliche Mühe: Daumesdick kroch
immer weiter zurück, und da es bald ganz dunkel ward, so mußten
sie mit Ärger und mit leerem Beutel wieder heimwandern.

Als Daumesdick merkte, daß sie fort waren, kroch er aus dem unterirdischen Gang wieder hervor. »Es ist auf dem Acker in der
Finsternis so gefährlich gehen«, sprach er, »wie leicht bricht einer
Hals und Bein!« Zum Glück stieß er an ein leeres Schneckenhaus.
»Gottlob«, sagte er, »da kann ich die Nacht sicher zubringen«, und
setzte sich hinein. Nicht lang, als er eben einschlafen wollte, so hörte
er zwei Männer vorübergehen, davon sprach der eine: »Wie wir's nur
anfangen, um dem reichen Pfarrer sein Geld und sein Silber zu
holen?« »Das könnt ich dir sagen«, rief Daumesdick dazwischen.
»Was war das?« sprach der eine Dieb erschrocken. »Ich hörte jemand
sprechen.« Sie blieben stehen und horchten, da sprach Daumesdick
wieder: »Nehmt mich mit, so will ich euch helfen.« »Wo bist du
denn?« »Sucht nur auf der Erde und merkt, wo die Stimme her-
kommt«, antwortete er. Da fanden ihn endlich die Diebe und hoben
ihn in die Höhe. »Du kleiner Wicht, was willst du uns helfen!«
sprachen sie. »Seht«, antwortete er, »ich krieche zwischen den
Eisenstäben in die Kammer des Pfarrers und reiche euch heraus, was
ihr haben wollt.« »Wohlan«, sagten sie, »wir wollen sehen, was du
kannst.« Als sie bei dem Pfarrhaus kamen, kroch Daumesdick in die
Kammer, schrie aber gleich aus Leibeskräften: »Wollt ihr alles haben,
was hier ist?« Die Diebe erschraken und sagten: »So sprich doch leise,
damit niemand aufwacht.« Aber Daumesdick tat, als hätte er sie nicht
verstanden, und schrie von neuem: »Was wollt ihr? Wollt ihr alles
haben, was hier ist?« Das hörte die Köchin, die in der Stube daran
schlief, richtete sich im Bette auf und horchte. Die Diebe aber waren
vor Schrecken ein Stück Wegs zurückgelaufen, endlich faßten sie
wieder Mut und dachten: »Der kleine Kerl will uns necken.« Sie
kamen zurück und flüsterten ihm zu: »Nun mach Ernst und reich uns
etwas heraus.« Da schrie Daumesdick noch einmal, so laut er konnte:

"I won't pay it any mind; plenty of times the birds drop some-thing on me." "No," said Big-as-a-Thumb, "I know perfectly well what's proper; please put me down right this minute." The man took off his hat and set the little fellow down in a field alongside the path; then he leapt away, crept a little distance here and there among the sods, and suddenly slipped into a mouse hole that he had been looking for. "Good evening, gentlemen; go home with-out me!" he called to them, making fun of them. They ran over and jabbed into the mouse hole with sticks, but it was wasted ef-fort: Big-as-a-Thumb crept deeper and deeper in, and since it soon got completely dark outside, they were compelled to wend their way home again heavy with vexation and light of purse.

When Big-as-a-Thumb was sure they had gone, he crept out of the underground passage. "Walking on the field in the dark is so dangerous," he said; "in no time you could break a leg or your neck!" Fortunately he came upon an empty snail shell. "Thank heaven," he said, "in this I can spend the night in safety"; and he entered it. Before long, just as he was about to fall asleep, he heard two men walking by, one of whom was saying: "How shall we go about laying our hands on the rich parson's money and silverware?" "I could tell you that," Big-as-a-Thumb loudly interrupted. "What was that?" said one of the thieves, frightened. "I heard somebody talking." They stood still and listened; then Big-as-a-Thumb spoke again: "Take me along, and I'll help you." "Where are you?" "Just look on the ground and find where my voice is coming from," he replied. Then the thieves finally found him and lifted him up. "Little runt, how can you help us?" they said. "Look," he replied, "I'll creep between the window bars into the parson's room and I'll hand you out whatever you want." "Fine," they said, "we'll see what you can do." When they got to the parsonage, Big-as-a-Thumb crept into the room, but immediately yelled with all his might: "Do you want everything that's in here?" The thieves were alarmed, and said: "Talk softly, can't you, so no one wakes up!" But Big-as-a-Thumb acted as if he hadn't understood them, and yelled again: "What do you want? Do you want everything that's in here?" That was heard by the cook, who slept in the adjacent room; she sat up in bed and listened. But the thieves, in their fright, had run off a little distance; finally they took heart again, thinking: "The lit-tle chap wants to tease us." They came back and whispered to him: "Now be serious and hand something out to us." Then Big-as-a-Thumb yelled once more, as loud as he could: "Yes, I'll give you

»Ich will euch ja alles geben, reicht nur die Hände herein.« Das hörte
die horchende Magd ganz deutlich, sprang aus dem Bett und
stolperte zur Tür herein. Die Diebe liefen fort und rannten, als wäre
der wilde Jäger hinter ihnen; die Magd aber, als sie nichts bemerken
konnte, ging, ein Licht anzuzünden. Wie sie damit herbeikam,
machte sich Daumesdick, ohne daß er gesehen wurde, hinaus in die
Scheune; die Magd aber, nachdem sie alle Winkel durchgesucht und
nichts gefunden hatte, legte sich endlich wieder zu Bett und glaubte,
sie hätte mit offenen Augen und Ohren doch nur geträumt.

    Daumesdick war in den Heuhälmchen herumgeklettert und hatte
einen schönen Platz zum Schlafen gefunden: da wollte er sich ausruhen, bis es Tag wäre, und dann zu seinen Eltern wieder heimgehen.
Aber er mußte andere Dinge erfahren! Ja, es gibt viel Trübsal und Not
auf der Welt! Die Magd stieg, als der Tag graute, schon aus dem Bett,
um das Vieh zu füttern. Ihr erster Gang war in die Scheune, wo sie
einen Arm voll Heu packte, und gerade dasjenige, worin der arme
Daumesdick lag und schlief. Er schlief aber so fest, daß er nichts
gewahr ward und nicht eher aufwachte, als bis er in dem Maul der Kuh
war, die ihn mit dem Heu aufgerafft hatte. »Ach Gott«, rief er, »wie bin
ich in die Walkmühle geraten!«, merkte aber bald, wo er war. Da hieß
es aufpassen, daß er nicht zwischen die Zähne kam und zermalmt ward,
und hernach mußte er doch mit in den Magen hinabrutschen. »In dem
Stübchen sind die Fenster vergessen«, sprach er, »und scheint keine
Sonne hinein; ein Licht wird auch nicht gebracht.« Überhaupt gefiel
ihm das Quartier schlecht, und was das schlimmste war, es kam immer
mehr neues Heu zur Türe hinein, und der Platz ward immer enger. Da
rief er endlich in der Angst, so laut er konnte: »Bringt mir kein frisch
Futter mehr, bringt mir kein frisch Futter mehr.« Die Magd melkte
gerade die Kuh, und als sie sprechen hörte, ohne jemand zu sehen, und
es dieselbe Stimme war, die sie auch in der Nacht gehört hatte, erschrak
sie so, daß sie von ihrem Stühlchen herabglitschte und die Milch ver-
schüttete. Sie lief in der größten Hast zu ihrem Herrn und rief: »Ach
Gott, Herr Pfarrer, die Kuh hat geredet.« »Du bist verrückt«,
antwortete der Pfarrer, ging aber doch selbst in den Stall und wollte
nachsehen, was es da gäbe. Kaum aber hatte er den Fuß hineingesetzt,
so rief Daumesdick aufs neue: »Bringt mir kein frisch Futter mehr,
bringt mir kein frisch Futter mehr.« Da erschrak der Pfarrer selbst,
meinte, es wäre ein böser Geist in die Kuh gefahren, und hieß sie töten.
Sie ward geschlachtet, der Magen aber, worin Daumesdick steckte, auf

everything; just stick your hands in." The listening maid heard that distinctly; she jumped out of bed and stumbled into the room. The thieves lit out, running as if the Wild Huntsman[5] was after them; as for the maid, when she didn't notice anything unusual, she went to light a candle. When she returned with it, Big-as-a-Thumb, without being seen, made his way out to the barn; after the maid had searched every corner, finding nothing, she finally went back to bed, thinking she had merely been dreaming, after all, with open eyes and ears.

Big-as-a-Thumb had climbed around amid the wisps of hay and had found a fine place for sleeping: he intended to get a good rest there until daylight, and then return home to his parents. But other things were in store for him! Yes, there's plenty of grief and distress in the world! As day was breaking, the maid got out of bed to feed the livestock. Her first trip was to the barn, where she seized an armful of hay from the very area where poor Big-as-a-Thumb was lying asleep. But he was sleeping so soundly that he didn't notice a thing, and didn't wake up until he was in the mouth of the cow, which had snatched him up along with the hay. "Oh, God," he shouted, "how did I get into the fulling mill?" But he soon realized where he was. He had to take care not to fall between the teeth and get crushed; after that, he still had no choice but to slide along down into the cow's stomach. "They forgot to put windows in this parlor," he said, "and no sunshine gets in; nobody's coming with a candle, either." All in all, he was displeased with his quarters and, worst of all, fresh hay was constantly coming in through the door, and space was getting scarcer and scarcer. So, in his anguish, he finally shouted, as loud as he could: "Don't bring me any more fodder! Don't bring me any more fodder!" At that moment the maid was milking the cow, and when she heard someone talking, but couldn't see anyone—and it was the same voice that she had heard during the night, besides— she got so scared that she slid off her stool and spilled the milk. In the greatest haste she ran to her master, crying: "Oh, God! Parson, the cow spoke." "You're crazy," the parson replied, but he did go to the stable in person, intending to see what was going on. Scarcely had he set foot inside when Big-as-a-Thumb shouted again: "Don't bring me any more fodder! Don't bring me any more fodder!" Then the parson himself got scared, thinking that an evil spirit had entered the cow; and he ordered the animal killed. It was slaughtered, and

5. See footnote 4, at the end of "The Brave Little Tailor" (page 77).

den Mist geworfen. Daumesdick hatte große Mühe, sich hindurchzuarbeiten, doch brachte er's so weit, daß er Platz bekam, aber als er eben sein Haupt herausstrecken wollte, kam ein neues Unglück. Ein hungriger Wolf lief heran und verschlang den ganzen Magen mit einem Schluck. Daumesdick verlor den Mut nicht. »Vielleicht«, dachte er, »läßt der Wolf mit sich reden«, und rief ihm aus dem Wanste zu: »Lieber Wolf, ich weiß dir einen herrlichen Fraß.« »Wo ist der zu holen?« sprach der Wolf. »In dem und dem Haus, da mußt du durch die Gosse hineinkriechen und wirst Kuchen, Speck und Wurst finden, soviel du essen willst«, und beschrieb ihm genau seines Vaters Haus. Der Wolf ließ sich das nicht zweimal sagen, drängte sich in der Nacht zur Gosse hinein und fraß in der Vorratskammer nach Herzenslust. Als er sich gesättigt hatte, wollte er wieder fort, aber er war so dick geworden, daß er denselben Weg nicht wieder hinaus konnte. Darauf hatte Daumesdick gerechnet und fing nun an, in dem Leib des Wolfs einen gewaltigen Lärmen zu machen, tobte und schrie, was er konnte. »Willst du stille sein«, sprach der Wolf, »du weckst die Leute auf.« »Ei was«, antwortete der Kleine, »du hast dich satt gefressen, ich will mich auch lustig machen«, und fing von neuem an, aus allen Kräften zu schreien. Davon erwachte endlich sein Vater und seine Mutter, liefen an die Kammer und schauten durch die Spalte hinein. Wie sie sahen, daß ein Wolf darin hauste, liefen sie davon, und der Mann holte die Axt und die Frau die Sense. »Bleib dahinten«, sprach der Mann, als sie in die Kammer traten, »wenn ich ihm einen Schlag gegeben habe und er davon noch nicht tot ist, so mußt du auf ihn einhauen und ihm den Leib zerschneiden.« Da hörte Daumesdick die Stimme seines Vaters und rief: »Lieber Vater, ich bin hier, ich stecke im Leibe des Wolfs.« Sprach der Vater voll Freuden: »Gottlob, unser liebes Kind hat sich wieder gefunden«, und hieß die Frau die Sense wegtun, damit Daumesdick nicht beschädigt würde. Danach holte er aus und schlug dem Wolf einen Schlag auf den Kopf, daß er tot niederstürzte, dann suchten sie Messer und Schere, schnitten ihm den Leib auf und zogen den Kleinen wieder hervor. »Ach«, sprach der Vater, »was haben wir für Sorge um dich ausgestanden!« »Ja, Vater, ich bin viel in der Welt herumgekommen; gottlob, daß ich wieder frische Luft schöpfe!« »Wo bist du denn all gewesen?« »Ach, Vater, ich war in einem Mauseloch, in einer Kuh Bauch und in eines Wolfes Wanst; nun bleib ich bei euch.« »Und wir verkaufen dich um alle Reichtümer der Welt nicht wieder«, sprachen die Eltern, herzten und küßten ihren lieben Daumesdick. Sie gaben ihm zu essen und trinken und ließen ihm neue Kleider machen, denn die seinigen waren ihm auf der Reise verdorben.

its stomach, in which Big-as-a-Thumb was located, was thrown onto the dungheap. Big-as-a-Thumb had a terrible time working his way out, but he finally managed to make enough space to get out. But just as he was about to stick his head out, a new misfortune arrived. A hungry wolf ran over and swallowed the whole stomach in one gulp. Big-as-a-Thumb didn't lose heart. He thought: "Maybe the wolf will listen to reason"; and he called to him out of his paunch: "Dear wolf, I know where you can find a wonderful meal." "Where can I get it?" asked the wolf. "In a house I know of; you just have to creep in through the drainpipe, and you'll find as much cake, bacon, and sausage as you can eat"; and he gave him an exact description of his father's house. The wolf didn't have to be told twice; in the night he squeezed into the drainpipe and ate to his heart's content in the pantry. When he was full, he wanted to go back out, but he had become so fat that he couldn't get out again the same way. Big-as-a-Thumb had counted on that, and from inside the wolf's body he now started to make a horrendous noise, ranting and yelling as loud as he could. "Will you be quiet?!" said the wolf; "you'll awaken the people." "Come on, now," the little fellow replied, "you've eaten till you're full; I want to have a little fun, too"; and he started again to yell with all his might. This finally awakened his father and mother, who ran to the pantry and looked in through the door crack. When they saw a wolf inside, they ran away, the man fetching an axe and his wife a scythe. "Stay behind me," the man said as they entered the pantry; "if he's not dead yet after I give him a blow, you've got to light into him and cut his body open." Then Big-as-a-Thumb heard his father's voice and called: "Father dear, I'm here, I'm in the wolf's body." His father said, full of joy: "Thank heaven, our dear child has made his way back!" He ordered his wife to put away the scythe, to avoid injuring Big-as-a-Thumb. Then he swung and landed a blow on the wolf's head that killed it instantly; next, they fetched a knife and scissors, cut open the wolf's body, and pulled the little fellow out again. "Oh," his father said, "how worried we were about you!" "Yes, father, I've had many adventures out in the world; thank heaven, I can breathe fresh air again!" "Where were you?" "Oh, father, I was in a mouse hole, in a cow's stomach, and in a wolf's paunch; now I'm going to stay with you." "And we won't sell you again for all the riches in the world," his parents said, as they hugged and kissed their beloved Big-as-a-Thumb. They gave him food and drink and had new clothes made for him because his old ones had gotten ruined in his travels.

Die sechs Schwäne

Es jagte einmal ein König in einem großen Wald und jagte einem
Wild so eifrig nach, daß ihm niemand von seinen Leuten folgen konnte. Als der Abend herankam, hielt er still und blickte um sich, da sah
er, daß er sich verirrt hatte. Er suchte einen Ausgang, konnte aber
keinen finden. Da sah er eine alte Frau mit wackelndem Kopfe, die
auf ihn zukam; das war aber eine Hexe. »Liebe Frau«, sprach er zu
ihr, »könnt Ihr mir nicht den Weg durch den Wald zeigen?« »O ja,
Herr König«, antwortete sie, »das kann ich wohl, aber es ist eine
Bedingung dabei, wenn Ihr die nicht erfüllt, so kommt Ihr nimmermehr aus dem Wald und müßt darin Hungers sterben.« »Was ist das
für eine Bedingung?« fragte der König. »Ich habe eine Tochter«, sagte
die Alte, »die so schön ist, wie Ihr eine auf der Welt finden könnt, und
wohl verdient, Eure Gemahlin zu werden, wollt Ihr die zur Frau
Königin machen, so zeige ich Euch den Weg aus dem Walde.« Der
König in der Angst seines Herzens willigte ein, und die Alte führte ihn
zu ihrem Häuschen, wo ihre Tochter beim Feuer saß. Sie empfing
den König, als wenn sie ihn erwartet hätte, und er sah wohl, daß sie
sehr schön war, aber sie gefiel ihm doch nicht, und er konnte sie ohne
heimliches Grausen nicht ansehen. Nachdem er das Mädchen zu sich
aufs Pferd gehoben hatte, zeigte ihm die Alte den Weg, und der
König gelangte wieder in sein königliches Schloß, wo die Hochzeit
gefeiert wurde.

Der König war schon einmal verheiratet gewesen und hatte von
seiner ersten Gemahlin sieben Kinder, sechs Knaben und ein
Mädchen, die er über alles auf der Welt liebte. Weil er nun fürchtete,
die Stiefmutter möchte sie nicht gut behandeln und ihnen gar ein
Leid antun, so brachte er sie in ein einsames Schloß, das mitten in
einem Walde stand. Es lag so verborgen und der Weg war so schwer
zu finden, daß er ihn selbst nicht gefunden hätte, wenn ihm nicht eine
weise Frau ein Knäuel Garn von wunderbarer Eigenschaft geschenkt
hätte; wenn er das vor sich hinwarf, so wickelte es sich von selbst los
und zeigte ihm den Weg. Der König ging aber so oft hinaus zu seinen
lieben Kindern, daß der Königin seine Abwesenheit auffiel; sie ward
neugierig und wollte wissen, was er draußen ganz allein in dem Walde
zu schaffen habe. Sie gab seinen Dienern viel Geld, und die verrieten
ihr das Geheimnis und sagten ihr auch von dem Knäuel, das allein
den Weg zeigen könnte. Nun hatte sie keine Ruhe, bis sie herausge-
bracht hatte, wo der König das Knäuel aufbewahrte, und dann

The Six Swans

A king was once hunting in a great forest, pursuing a roe deer so zealously that none of his attendants was able to follow him. When evening came, he halted and looked all around; then he realized he was lost. He sought a way out but couldn't find any. Then he saw an old woman, with shaking head, coming toward him; but she was a witch. "Dear lady," he said to her, "can you show me the way out of the woods?" "Oh, yes, your majesty," she replied, "I certainly can, but there's a condition attached; if you don't meet it, you'll never get out of the forest and you'll starve here." "What is the condition?" the king asked. "I have a daughter," the old woman said, "who is so beautiful that there's none other like her in the world, and she certainly deserves to be your wife; if you agree to make her your queen, I'll show you the way out of the woods." In his anguish of heart the king consented, and the old woman led him to her little house, where her daughter was sitting by the fire. She welcomed the king as if she had been expecting him, and he saw that she was indeed very beautiful, but all the same he didn't like her and he couldn't look at her without feeling a secret dread. After he had lifted the girl onto his horse behind him, the old woman showed him the way, and the king arrived back at the royal palace, where the wedding was celebrated.

The king had already been married once before, and had seven children by his first wife, six boys and a girl; he loved them better than anything else in the world. Because he now feared that their stepmother might mistreat them and even do them some injury, he brought them to a solitary mansion that stood in the center of a forest. It was so secluded, and the path to it so hard to find, that he himself wouldn't have found it if a wise-woman hadn't made him a gift of a ball of yarn that had magic powers; when he threw it in front of him, it unrolled by itself and showed him the way. But the king went out to see his beloved children so often that the queen noticed his absence; she became curious and wanted to know what business he had all alone out in the woods. She gave a large amount of money to his servants, who betrayed his secret to her, also telling her about the yarn, which was the only thing that could show the way. Now she couldn't rest until she discovered where the king kept the yarn; then she made little shirts of white

machte sie kleine weißseidene Hemdchen, und da sie von ihrer
Mutter die Hexenkünste gelernt hatte, so nähete sie einen Zauber
hinein. Und als der König einmal auf die Jagd geritten war, nahm sie
die Hemdchen und ging in den Wald, und das Knäuel zeigte ihr den
Weg. Die Kinder, die aus der Ferne jemand kommen sahen, meinten,
ihr lieber Vater käme zu ihnen, und sprangen ihm voll Freude entgegen. Da warf sie über ein jedes eins von den Hemdchen, und wie das
ihren Leib berührt hatte, verwandelten sie sich in Schwäne und flogen über den Wald hinweg. Die Königin ging ganz vergnügt nach
Haus und glaubte ihre Stiefkinder los zu sein, aber das Mädchen war
ihr mit den Brüdern nicht entgegengelaufen, und sie wußte nichts
von ihm. Anderntags kam der König und wollte seine Kinder be-
suchen, er fand aber niemand als das Mädchen. »Wo sind deine
Brüder?« fragte der König. »Ach, lieber Vater«, antwortete es, »die
sind fort und haben mich allein zurückgelassen«, und erzählte ihm,
daß es aus seinem Fensterlein mit angesehen habe, wie seine Brüder
als Schwäne über den Wald weggeflogen wären, und zeigte ihm die
Federn, die sie in dem Hof hatten fallen lassen und die es aufgelesen
hatte. Der König trauerte, aber er dachte nicht, daß die Königin die
böse Tat vollbracht hätte, und weil er fürchtete, das Mädchen würde
ihm auch geraubt, so wollte er es mit fortnehmen. Aber es hatte Angst
vor der Stiefmutter und bat den König, daß es nur noch diese Nacht
im Waldschloß bleiben dürfte.

Das arme Mädchen dachte: »Meines Bleibens ist nicht länger hier,
ich will gehen und meine Brüder suchen.« Und als die Nacht kam,
entfloh es und ging gerade in den Wald hinein. Es ging die ganze
Nacht durch und auch den andern Tag in einem fort, bis es vor
Müdigkeit nicht weiter konnte. Da sah es eine Wildhütte, stieg hinauf
und fand eine Stube mit sechs kleinen Betten, aber es getraute nicht,
sich in eins zu legen, sondern kroch unter eins, legte sich auf den
harten Boden und wollte die Nacht da zubringen. Als aber die Sonne
bald untergehen wollte, hörte es ein Rauschen und sah, daß sechs
Schwäne zum Fenster hereingeflogen kamen. Sie setzten sich auf den
Boden und bliesen einander an und bliesen sich alle Federn ab, und
ihre Schwanenhaut streifte sich ab wie ein Hemd. Da sah sie das
Mädchen an und erkannte ihre Brüder, freute sich und kroch unter
dem Bett hervor. Die Brüder waren nicht weniger erfreut, als sie ihr
Schwesterchen erblickten, aber ihre Freude war von kurzer Dauer.
»Hier kann deines Bleibens nicht sein«, sprachen sie zu ihm, »das ist
eine Herberge für Räuber, wenn die heimkommen und finden dich,
so ermorden sie dich.« »Könnt ihr mich denn nicht beschützen?«

silk and, since she had learned witchcraft from her mother, she sewed a spell into them. And when the king rode out hunting one day, she took the little shirts and entered the forest, and the yarn showed her the way. The children, seeing someone coming in the distance, thought their dear father was visiting them, and dashed out to meet him, full of joy. Then she threw one of the little shirts over each one of them, and the moment the shirts touched their bodies, they were turned into swans and flew away over the woods. Fully satisfied, the queen returned home, believing she was rid of her stepchildren, but the girl hadn't run out to greet her along with her brothers, and the queen knew nothing about the girl. The next day the king came, intending to visit his children, and found no one but the girl. "Where are your brothers?" the king asked. "Oh, father dear," she replied, "they're gone and they've left me all alone here"; and she told him that she had watched from her little window how her brothers had flown away over the forest in the shape of swans, and she showed him the feathers which they had dropped into the courtyard and which she had gathered up. The king was sad, but he didn't think that the queen had done that evil deed; and because he was afraid that the girl would be stolen from him, too, he wanted to take her along with him. But she was afraid of her stepmother and begged the king to let her stay in the forest mansion just for that night.

The poor girl thought to herself: "I can't stay here any longer; I want to go and look for my brothers." And when night came, she escaped, heading straight into the woods. She walked all night and the next day as well until she was so tired she couldn't go on. Then she saw a rustic cabin, climbed the front stairs, and found a room with six little beds; but she didn't dare lie down on them; instead, she crept under one and lay down on the hard floor, intending to spend the night there. But when the sun was close to setting, she heard a fluttering and saw six swans fly in through the window. They alighted on the floor and blew on one another, blowing off all their feathers, and their swan skins slipped off like a shirt. Then the girl looked at them and recognized her brothers; in her happiness she crept out from under the bed. Her brothers were no less joyful at catching sight of their young sister, but their joy was of brief duration. "You can't stay here," they said to her; "it's a den of thieves, and if they come home and find you, they'll murder you." "Can't you protect me?" their sister asked. "No," they replied,

fragte das Schwesterchen. »Nein«, antworteten sie, »denn wir können nur eine Viertelstunde lang jeden Abend unsere Schwanenhaut ablegen und haben in dieser Zeit unsere menschliche Gestalt, aber dann werden wir wieder in Schwäne verwandelt.« Das Schwesterchen weinte und sagte: »Könnt ihr denn nicht erlöst werden?« »Ach nein«, antworteten sie, »die Bedingungen sind zu schwer. Du darfst sechs Jahre lang nicht sprechen und nicht lachen und mußt in der Zeit sechs Hemdchen für uns aus Sternenblumen zusammennähen. Kommt ein einziges Wort aus deinem Munde, so ist alle Arbeit verloren.« Und als die Brüder das gesprochen hatten, war die Viertelstunde herum, und sie flogen als Schwäne wieder zum Fenster hinaus.

Das Mädchen aber faßte den festen Entschluß, seine Brüder zu erlösen, und wenn es auch sein Leben kostete. Es verließ die Wildhütte, ging mitten in den Wald und setzte sich auf einen Baum und brachte da die Nacht zu. Am andern Morgen ging es aus, sammelte Sternblumen und fing an zu nähen. Reden konnte es mit niemand, und zum Lachen hatte es keine Lust: es saß da und sah nur auf seine Arbeit. Als es schon lange Zeit da zugebracht hatte, geschah es, daß der König des Landes in dem Wald jagte und seine Jäger zu dem Baum kamen, auf welchem das Mädchen saß. Sie riefen es an und sagten: »Wer bist du?« Es gab aber keine Antwort. »Komm herab zu uns«, sagten sie, »wir wollen dir nichts zuleid tun.« Es schüttelte bloß mit dem Kopf. Als sie es weiter mit Fragen bedrängten, so warf es ihnen seine goldene Halskette herab und dachte sie damit zufriedenzustellen. Sie ließen aber nicht ab, da warf es ihnen seinen Gürtel herab, und als auch dies nicht half, seine Strumpfbänder, und nach und nach alles, was es anhatte und entbehren konnte, so daß es nichts mehr als sein Hemdlein behielt. Die Jäger ließen sich aber damit nicht abweisen, stiegen auf den Baum, hoben das Mädchen herab und führten es vor den König. Der König fragte: »Wer bist du? Was machst du auf dem Baum?« Aber es antwortete nicht. Er fragte es in allen Sprachen, die er wußte, aber es blieb stumm wie ein Fisch. Weil es aber so schön war, so ward des Königs Herz gerührt, und er faßte eine große Liebe zu ihm. Er tat ihm seinen Mantel um, nahm es vor sich aufs Pferd und brachte es in sein Schloß. Da ließ er ihm reiche Kleider antun, und es strahlte in seiner Schönheit wie der helle Tag, aber es war kein Wort aus ihm herauszubringen. Er setzte es bei Tisch an seine Seite, und seine bescheidenen Mienen und seine Sittsamkeit gefielen ihm so sehr, daß er sprach: »Diese begehre ich zu heiraten und keine andere auf der Welt«, und nach einigen Tagen vermählte er sich mit ihr.

"because we can strip off our swan skins and go about as human beings for only fifteen minutes every evening; then we turn back into swans again." Their sister wept and said: "Can't you be delivered from the spell?" "Oh, no," they replied, "the necessary conditions are too hard to meet. For six years, sister, you mustn't speak, and during that time you must sew us six little shirts out of asters. If just one word comes out of your mouth, all the work will have been wasted." And when the brothers had said that, the fifteen minutes were up, and they flew out the window again as swans.

But the girl made a firm decision to deliver her brothers, even if it cost her her life. She left the cabin, walked deep into the woods, sat down on a tree bough, and spent the night there. The next morning she went out, picked asters, and began sewing. She couldn't talk to anyone, and she didn't feel like laughing: she sat there with her eyes glued to her work. After she had spent quite some time there, it came about that the king of the country was hunting in the forest and his huntsmen came to the tree in which the girl was sitting. They called to her, saying: "Who are you?" But she made no reply. "Come down to us," they said, "we won't harm you." She merely shook her head. When they besieged her with more questions, she threw her golden necklace down to them, thinking she'd pacify them that way. But they didn't let up, so she threw down her belt, and when even that did no good, her garters, and gradually everything she had on and could get along without, until she kept nothing more than her little shift. But the hunters wouldn't be put off that way; they climbed the tree, brought the girl down, and led her to the king. The king said: "Who are you? What were you doing in the tree?" But she didn't answer. He asked her in every language that he knew, but she remained mute as a fish. But because she was so beautiful, the king's heart was touched, and he conceived a great love for her. He placed his cloak around her, sat her in front of him on his horse, and brought her to his palace. There he had her dressed in rich garments, and she beamed in her beauty like the bright sunshine, but no one could get a word out of her. He placed her beside him at the table, and her modest ways and good behavior pleased him so much that he said: "This woman I desire to wed, and none other in the world"; and a few days later he married her.

Der König aber hatte eine böse Mutter, die war unzufrieden mit dieser Heirat und sprach schlecht von der jungen Königin. »Wer weiß, wo die Dirne her ist«, sagte sie, »die nicht reden kann; sie ist eines Königs nicht würdig.« Über ein Jahr, als die Königin das erste Kind zur Welt brachte, nahm es ihr die Alte weg und bestrich ihr im Schlafe den Mund mit Blut. Da ging sie zum König und klagte sie an, sie wäre eine Menschenfresserin. Der König wollte es nicht glauben und litt nicht, daß man ihr ein Leid antat. Sie saß aber beständig und nähete an den Hemden und achtete auf nichts anderes. Das nächstemal, als sie wieder einen schönen Knaben gebar, übte die falsche Schwiegermutter denselben Betrug aus, aber der König konnte sich nicht entschließen, ihren Reden Glauben beizumessen. Er sprach: »Sie ist zu fromm und gut, als daß sie so etwas tun könnte, wäre sie nicht stumm und könnte sie sich verteidigen, so würde ihre Unschuld an den Tag kommen.« Als aber das drittemal die Alte das neugeborne Kind raubte und die Königin anklagte, die kein Wort zu ihrer Verteidigung vorbrachte, so konnte der König nicht anders, er mußte sie dem Gericht übergeben, und das verurteilte sie, den Tod durchs Feuer zu erleiden.

Als der Tag herankam, wo das Urteil sollte vollzogen werden, da war zugleich der letzte Tag von den sechs Jahren herum, in welchen sie nicht sprechen und nicht lachen durfte, und sie hatte ihre lieben Brüder aus der Macht des Zaubers befreit. Die sechs Hemden waren fertig geworden, nur daß an dem letzten der linke Ärmel noch fehlte. Als sie nun zum Scheiterhaufen geführt wurde, legte sie die Hemden auf ihren Arm, und als sie oben stand und das Feuer eben sollte angezündet werden, so schaute sie sich um, da kamen sechs Schwäne durch die Luft dahergezogen. Da sah sie, daß ihre Erlösung nahte, und ihr Herz regte sich in Freude. Die Schwäne rauschten zu ihr her und senkten sich herab, so daß sie ihnen die Hemden überwerfen konnte; und wie sie davon berührt wurden, fielen die Schwanenhäute ab, und ihre Brüder standen leibhaftig vor ihr und waren frisch und schön; nur dem jüngsten fehlte der linke Arm, und er hatte dafür einen Schwanenflügel am Rücken. Sie herzten und küßten sich, und die Königin ging zu dem Könige, der ganz bestürzt war, und fing an zu reden und sagte: »Liebster Gemahl, nun darf ich sprechen und dir offenbaren, daß ich unschuldig bin und fälschlich angeklagt«, und erzählte ihm von dem Betrug der Alten, die ihre drei Kinder weggenommen und verborgen hätte. Da wurden sie zu großer

But the king had a wicked mother who was dissatisfied with this marriage and spoke ill of the young queen. "Who knows where the peasant girl comes from?" she said; "she can't even talk; she isn't worthy of a king." A year later, when the queen gave birth to her first child, the old woman took it away from her and smeared her mouth with blood while she was sleeping. Then she went to the king to accuse her of being a cannibal. The king refused to believe it and wouldn't allow any harm to be done to her. But she steadfastly sat sewing the shirts and paid no mind to anything else. The next time, after she became the mother of a lovely boy, her treacherous mother-in-law played the same trick, but the king couldn't bring himself to lend credence to her report. He said: "She's too decent and kind to do a thing like that; if she could speak and defend herself, her innocence would be made public." But after the old woman had stolen the third newborn child, making an accusation against the queen, who uttered not a word in her own defense, the king had no other choice but to hand her over for trial, and she was sentenced to suffer death by burning.

When the day came on which the sentence was to be carried out, it was the same day that concluded the six years during which she couldn't speak or laugh; and she had delivered her beloved brothers from the power of the spell. She had completed the six shirts; only the left sleeve was still missing on the last one. Now, when she was led to the pyre, she placed the shirts over her arm, and when she was standing atop it and the fire was just about to be lit, she looked behind her, and there were six swans approaching through the air. Then she saw that her[6] deliverance was near, and her heart jumped for joy. The swans fluttered over to her and alighted so that she could throw the shirts over them; and the moment they were touched by them, their swan skins fell off, and her brothers were standing before her in their own bodies, looking energetic and handsome; only, the youngest one was missing his left arm: instead, he had a swan's wing on his back. They hugged and kissed, and the queen went to the king, who was completely astounded; beginning to speak, she said: "Dearest husband, now I may speak and inform you that I am innocent and wrongly accused"; and she told him about the deceitful ways of the old woman, who had taken away her three children and hidden them.

---

6. Possibly: "their."

Freude des Königs herbeigeholt, und die böse Schwiegermutter
wurde zur Strafe auf den Scheiterhaufen gebunden und zu Asche verbrannt. Der König aber und die Königin mit ihren sechs Brüdern
lebten lange Jahre in Glück und Frieden.

Dornröschen

Vorzeiten war ein König und eine Königin, die sprachen jeden Tag:
»Ach, wenn wir doch ein Kind hätten!«, und kriegten immer keins. Da
trug sich zu, als die Königin einmal im Bade saß, daß ein Frosch aus
dem Wasser ans Land kroch und zu ihr sprach: »Dein Wunsch wird
erfüllt werden, ehe ein Jahr vergeht, wirst du eine Tochter zur Welt
bringen.« Was der Frosch gesagt hatte, das geschah, und die Königin
gebar ein Mädchen, das war so schön, daß der König vor Freude sich
nicht zu lassen wußte und ein großes Fest anstellte. Er ladete nicht
bloß seine Verwandte, Freunde und Bekannte, sondern auch die
weisen Frauen dazu ein, damit sie dem Kind hold und gewogen
wären. Es waren ihrer dreizehn in seinem Reiche, weil er aber nur
zwölf goldene Teller hatte, von welchen sie essen sollten, so mußte
eine von ihnen daheim bleiben. Das Fest ward mit aller Pracht
gefeiert, und als es zu Ende war, beschenkten die weisen Frauen das
Kind mit ihren Wundergaben: die eine mit Tugend, die andere mit
Schönheit, die dritte mit Reichtum, und so mit allem, was auf der
Welt zu wünschen ist. Als elfe ihre Sprüche eben getan hatten, trat
plötzlich die dreizehnte herein. Sie wollte sich dafür rächen, daß sie
nicht eingeladen war, und ohne jemand zu grüßen oder nur anzusehen, rief sie mit lauter Stimme: »Die Königstochter soll sich in ihrem
funfzehnten Jahr an einer Spindel stechen und tot hinfallen.« Und
ohne ein Wort weiter zu sprechen, kehrte sie sich um und verließ den
Saal. Alle waren erschrocken, da trat die zwölfte hervor, die ihren
Wunsch noch übrig hatte, und weil sie den bösen Spruch nicht
aufheben, sondern nur ihn mildern konnte, so sagte sie: »Es soll aber
kein Tod sein, sondern ein hundertjähriger tiefer Schlaf, in welchen
die Königstochter fällt.«

Der König, der sein liebes Kind vor dem Unglück gern bewahren
wollte, ließ den Befehl ausgehen, daß alle Spindeln im ganzen
Königreiche sollten verbrannt werden. An dem Mädchen aber wurden die Gaben der weisen Frauen sämtlich erfüllt, denn es war so
schön, sittsam, freundlich und verständig, daß es jedermann, der es

Then, to the king's great joy, they were brought out of concealment; as a punishment, the wicked mother-in-law was tied to the
stake and burnt to ashes. But the king and queen and her six
brothers lived a long life in happiness and peace.

Little Briar Rose [Sleeping Beauty]

In days of old there lived a king and queen who said every day:
"Oh, if we only had a child!" But they never had one. Then it so
happened, when the queen was once sitting in her bath, that a
frog crept out of the water onto dry land and said to her: "Your
wish will be granted; before a year is over, you will give birth to
a daughter." What the frog predicted came to pass, and the
queen bore a girl who was so beautiful that the king was beside
himself with joy and gave a large party. He invited not merely his
relatives, friends, and acquaintances, but also the wise-women,
so that they would be favorably inclined toward the child. There
were thirteen of them in his kingdom, but because he had only
twelve golden plates for them to eat off, one of them had to stay
home. The feast was celebrated with great splendor, and when
it was over, the wise-women gave wondrous gifts to the child:
one of them gave virtue; the second, beauty; the third, wealth;
and so on, until the girl was endowed with everything desirable
in life. Right after the eleventh wise-woman had spoken her
charm, the thirteenth suddenly burst in. She wanted to take revenge for not being invited, and without greeting or even looking at anyone, she called out loudly: "In her fifteenth year the
princess shall prick herself on a spindle and shall fall down
dead." And, without saying another word, she turned on her
heel and left the hall. Everyone was alarmed, but then the
twelfth wise-woman stepped forward; she had yet to express her
wish, and because she couldn't undo the evil charm but only
soften it, she said: "The princess shall not die, but shall fall into
a deep sleep that lasts a hundred years."

The king, who dearly wanted to protect his beloved child from
that misfortune, issued a command that all the spindles in the
whole kingdom were to be burned. But all the gifts made to the
girl by the wise-women came into effect, for she was so beautiful, well-behaved, friendly, and intelligent that everyone who

ansah, liebhaben mußte. Es geschah, daß an dem Tage, wo es gerade
funfzehn Jahr alt ward, der König und die Königin nicht zu Haus
waren und das Mädchen ganz allein im Schloß zurückblieb. Da ging
es allerorten herum, besah Stuben und Kammern, wie es Lust hatte,
und kam endlich auch an einen alten Turm. Es stieg die enge
Wendeltreppe hinauf und gelangte zu einer kleinen Türe. In dem
Schloß steckte ein verrosteter Schlüssel, und als es umdrehte, sprang
die Türe auf, und saß da in einem kleinen Stübchen eine alte Frau mit
einer Spindel und spann emsig ihren Flachs. »Guten Tag, du altes
Mütterchen«, sprach die Königstochter, »was machst du da?« »Ich
spinne«, sagte die Alte und nickte mit dem Kopf. »Was ist das für ein
Ding, das so lustig herumspringt?« sprach das Mädchen, nahm die
Spindel und wollte auch spinnen. Kaum hatte sie aber die Spindel
angerührt, so ging der Zauberspruch in Erfüllung, und sie stach sich
damit in den Finger.

In dem Augenblick aber, wo sie den Stich empfand, fiel sie auf das
Bett nieder, das da stand, und lag in einem tiefen Schlaf. Und dieser
Schlaf verbreitete sich über das ganze Schloß: der König und die
Königin, die eben heimgekommen waren und in den Saal getreten
waren, fingen an einzuschlafen, und der ganze Hofstaat mit ihnen. Da
schliefen auch die Pferde im Stall, die Hunde im Hofe, die Tauben
auf dem Dache, die Fliegen an der Wand, ja, das Feuer, das auf dem
Herde flackerte, ward still und schlief ein, und der Braten hörte auf
zu brutzeln, und der Koch, der den Küchenjungen, weil er etwas
versehen hatte, in den Haaren ziehen wollte, ließ ihn los und schlief.
Und der Wind legte sich, und auf den Bäumen vor dem Schloß regte
sich kein Blättchen mehr.

Rings um das Schloß aber begann eine Dornenhecke zu wachsen,
die jedes Jahr höher ward und endlich das ganze Schloß umzog und
darüber hinaus wuchs, daß gar nichts mehr davon zu sehen war, selbst
nicht die Fahne auf dem Dach. Es ging aber die Sage in dem Land von
dem schönen schlafenden Dornröschen, denn so ward die Königstochter genannt, also daß von Zeit zu Zeit Königssöhne kamen und
durch die Hecke in das Schloß dringen wollten. Es war ihnen aber
nicht möglich, denn die Dornen, als hätten sie Hände, hielten fest
zusammen, und die Jünglinge blieben darin hängen, konnten sich
nicht wieder losmachen und starben eines jämmerlichen Todes. Nach
langen, langen Jahren kam wieder einmal ein Königssohn in das Land
und hörte, wie ein alter Mann von der Dornenhecke erzählte, es sollte
ein Schloß dahinter stehen, in welchem eine wunderschöne Königstochter, Dornröschen genannt, schon seit hundert Jahren schliefe,

saw her had to love her. It came about that, on the day when she turned fifteen, the king and queen weren't home and the girl was left all alone in the palace. So she walked around all over, inspecting the rooms and chambers just as she pleased, until she finally came to an ancient tower. She climbed the narrow spiral staircase and found herself in front of a small door. A rusty key was in the lock, and when she turned it, the door flew open, and there in a tiny room sat an old lady with a spindle, diligently spinning her flax. "Good day, you sweet old lady," said the princess, "what's that you're doing?" "I'm spinning," said the old woman, nodding her head. "What sort of thing is it that's dancing about so merrily?" asked the girl; she took the spindle and wanted to do some spinning herself. But scarcely had she touched the spindle when the magic charm took effect, and she pricked her finger with it.

And at the very moment that she felt the smart, she dropped onto the bed that was in the room and was already fast asleep. And that sleep spread through the whole palace: the king and queen, who had just arrived home and had entered the great hall, began to doze off, and all the courtiers with them. Then the horses in the stable were also asleep, as well as the dogs in the courtyard, the pigeons on the roof, and the flies on the wall; yes, even the fire that was flickering on the hearth became still and fell asleep, and the roast stopped sizzling, and the cook, who was just about to pull the kitchen boy's hair because he had neglected something, let him go and went to sleep. And the wind died down, and on the trees in front of the palace not a leaf was stirring anymore.

And all around the palace a thorn hedge began to grow, becoming taller every year until it finally encircled the whole palace and grew out beyond it, so that nothing more could be seen of it, not even the banner on the roof. But a legend passed throughout the land about the beautiful sleeping Little Briar Rose (for that was the name of the princess), so that from time to time princes came and tried to make their way through the hedge to the palace. But they couldn't do it because the thorns clung together closely, as if they had hands, and the young men were left hanging there; they couldn't get loose again and died a miserable death. Many, many years later, a prince entered the land once more and heard an old man telling a story about the thorn hedge: there was said to be a palace behind it, in which a miraculously beautiful princess named Little Briar Rose had

und mit ihr schliefe der König und die Königin und der ganze Hofstaat. Er wußte auch von seinem Großvater, daß schon viele Königssöhne gekommen wären und versucht hätten, durch die Dornenhecke zu dringen, aber sie wären darin hängengeblieben und eines
traurigen Todes gestorben. Da sprach der Jüngling: »Ich fürchte mich
nicht, ich will hinaus und das schöne Dornröschen sehen.« Der gute
Alte mochte ihm abraten, wie er wollte, er hörte nicht auf seine
Worte.

Nun waren aber gerade die hundert Jahre verflossen, und der Tag
war gekommen, wo Dornröschen wieder erwachen sollte. Als der
Königssohn sich der Dornenhecke näherte, waren es lauter große
schöne Blumen, die taten sich von selbst auseinander und ließen ihn
unbeschädigt hindurch, und hinter ihm taten sie sich wieder als eine
Hecke zusammen. Im Schloßhof sah er die Pferde und scheckigen
Jagdhunde liegen und schlafen, auf dem Dache saßen die Tauben und
hatten das Köpfchen unter den Flügel gesteckt. Und als er ins Haus
kam, schliefen die Fliegen an der Wand, der Koch in der Küche hielt
noch die Hand, als wollte er den Jungen anpacken, und die Magd saß
vor dem schwarzen Huhn, das sollte gerupft werden. Da ging er
weiter und sah im Saale den ganzen Hofstaat liegen und schlafen, und
oben bei dem Throne lag der König und die Königin. Da ging er noch
weiter, und alles war so still, daß einer seinen Atem hören konnte, und
endlich kam er zu dem Turm und öffnete die Türe zu der kleinen
Stube, in welcher Dornröschen schlief. Da lag es und war so schön,
daß er die Augen nicht abwenden konnte, und er bückte sich und gab
ihm einen Kuß. Wie er es mit dem Kuß berührt hatte, schlug Dornröschen die Augen auf, erwachte und blickte ihn ganz freundlich an.
Da gingen zie zusammen herab, und der König erwachte und die
Königin und der ganze Hofstaat und sahen einander mit großen
Augen an. Und die Pferde im Hof standen auf und rüttelten sich; die
Jagdhunde sprangen und wedelten; die Tauben auf dem Dache zogen
das Köpfchen unterm Flügel hervor, sahen umher und flogen ins
Feld; die Fliegen an den Wänden krochen weiter; das Feuer in der
Küche erhob sich, flackerte und kochte das Essen; der Braten fing
wieder an zu brutzeln; und der Koch gab dem Jungen eine Ohrfeige,
daß er schrie; und die Magd rupfte das Huhn fertig. Und da wurde
die Hochzeit das Königssohns mit dem Dornröschen in aller Pracht
gefeiert, und sie lebten vergnügt bis an ihr Ende.

been sleeping for a hundred years now; and, along with her, the king and queen and all the courtiers were sleeping. He had also heard from his grandfather that many princes had already come and attempted to penetrate the thorn hedge, but had remained hanging in it and had died an unhappy death. Then the young man said: "I'm not afraid; I'll go there and see beautiful Little Briar Rose." The king old man tried and tried to dissuade him, but the prince wouldn't listen to him.

But now the hundred years were just over, and the day had come on which Little Briar Rose was to wake up again. When the prince approached the thorn hedge, it was nothing but big, beautiful flowers that separated of their own will and let him through unharmed, closing again behind him like a hedge. In the palace yard he saw the horses and the spotted hunting hounds lying in slumber; on the roof sat the pigeons with their heads tucked under their wings. And when he entered the building, the flies were asleep on the wall, the cook in the kitchen still held out his hand as if about to seize the boy, and the maid was sitting in front of the black chicken that had to be plucked. Then he walked on, and in the great hall he saw all the courtiers lying asleep, and up near the throne lay the king and queen. Then he walked further still, and everything was so quiet that you could hear your own breathing; finally, he reached the tower and opened the door to the small room in which Little Briar Rose was sleeping. There she lay, and she was so beautiful that he couldn't take his eyes off her; he leaned over and gave her a kiss. The moment he touched her with his kiss, Little Briar Rose opened her eyes, awoke, and gave him a most friendly glance. Then they went downstairs together, and the king awoke, as did the queen and all the courtiers; and they looked at one another with staring eyes. And the horses in the courtyard stood up and shook themselves; the hunting hounds jumped and wagged their tails; the pigeons on the roof drew their heads out from under their wings, looked around, and flew into the countryside; the flies on the wall went on crawling; the fire in the kitchen flared up, flickered, and cooked the food; the roast began sizzling again; and the cook boxed the boy's ear so hard that he yelled; and the maid finished plucking the chicken. And then the wedding of the prince and Little Briar Rose was celebrated with great splendor, and they lived happily for the rest of their days.

Sneewittchen

Es war einmal mitten im Winter, und die Schneeflocken fielen wie
Federn vom Himmel herab, da saß eine Königin an einem Fenster,
das einen Rahmen von schwarzem Ebenholz hatte, und nähte. Und
wie sie so nähte und nach dem Schnee aufblickte, stach sie sich mit
der Nadel in den Finger, und es fielen drei Tropfen Blut in den
Schnee. Und weil das Rote im weißen Schnee so schön aussah, dachte
sie bei sich: »Hätt ich ein Kind so weiß wie Schnee, so rot wie Blut
und so schwarz wie das Holz an dem Rahmen.« Bald darauf bekam sie
ein Töchterlein, das war so weiß wie Schnee, so rot wie Blut und so
schwarzhaarig wie Ebenholz, und ward darum das Sneewittchen
(Schneeweißchen) genannt. Und wie das Kind geboren war, starb die
Königin.

Über ein Jahr nahm sich der König eine andere Gemahlin. Es war
eine schöne Frau, aber sie war stolz und übermütig und konnte nicht
leiden, daß sie an Schönheit von jemand sollte übertroffen werden.
Sie hatte einen wunderbaren Spiegel, wenn sie vor den trat und sich
darin beschaute, sprach sie:

>»Spieglein, Spieglein an der Wand,
>wer ist die schönste im ganzen Land?«

So antwortete der Spiegel:

>»Frau Königin, Ihr seid die schönste im Land.«

Da war sie zufrieden, denn sie wußte, daß der Spiegel die Wahrheit
sagte.

Sneewittchen aber wuchs heran und wurde immer schöner, und als
es sieben Jahr alt war, war es so schön wie der klare Tag und schöner
als die Königin selbst. Als diese einmal ihren Spiegel fragte:

>»Spieglein, Spieglein an der Wand,
>wer ist die schönste im ganzen Land?«,

so antwortete er:

>»Frau Königin, Ihr seid die schönste hier,
>aber Sneewittchen ist tausendmal schöner als Ihr.«

Da erschrak die Königin und ward gelb und grün vor Neid. Von
Stund an, wenn sie Sneewittchen erblickte, kehrte sich ihr das Herz
im Leibe herum, so haßte sie das Mädchen. Und der Neid und
Hochmut wuchsen wie ein Unkraut in ihrem Herzen immer höher,

Snow White

Once, in midwinter, while the snowflakes were falling from the sky like feathers, a queen was sitting and sewing by a window that had a frame of black ebony. And as she was sewing, she looked up at the snow and pricked her finger with the needle; and three drops of blood fell onto the snow. And because the red looked so pretty against the white snow, she thought to herself: "I wish I had a child as white as snow, as red as blood, and as black as the wood of the frame." Shortly thereafter she had a daughter who was as white as snow and as red as blood, with hair as black as ebony, and who was thus called Snow White. And when the child was born, the queen died.

A year later the king took another wife. She was a beautiful woman, but she was proud and haughty and couldn't bear to be surpassed in beauty by anyone. She had a miraculous mirror; whenever she stepped in front of it and looked at her reflection in it, she'd say:

> "Little mirror hanging there,
> in all the country who's most fair?"

And the mirror would reply:

> "Queen, you're the fairest in the country."

That satisfied her, because she knew that the mirror always told the truth.

But Snow White grew up, becoming more beautiful all the time, and when she was seven years old she was as beautiful as the bright daylight and more beautiful than the queen herself. Once when the queen asked her mirror:

> "Little mirror hanging there,
> in all the country who's most fair?"

it answered:

> "Queen, you're the fairest where you are,
> but Snow White is more beautiful by far."

Then the queen grew alarmed and turned yellow and green with envy. From then on, whenever she caught sight of Snow White, her heart twisted inside her, so greatly did she hate the girl. And envy and pridefulness, like weeds, grew taller and taller

daß sie Tag und Nacht keine Ruhe mehr hatte. Da rief sie einen Jäger und sprach: »Bring das Kind hinaus in den Wald, ich will's nicht mehr vor meinen Augen sehen. Du sollst es töten und mir Lunge und Leber zum Wahrzeichen mitbringen.« Der Jäger gehorchte und führte es hinaus, und als er den Hirschfänger gezogen hatte und Sneewittchens unschuldiges Herz durchbohren wollte, fing es an zu weinen und sprach: »Ach, lieber Jäger, laß mir mein Leben; ich will in den wilden Wald laufen und nimmermehr wieder heimkommen.« Und weil es so schön war, hatte der Jäger Mitleiden und sprach: »So lauf hin, du armes Kind.« »Die wilden Tiere werden dich bald gefressen haben«, dachte er, und doch war's ihm, als wär ein Stein von seinem Herzen gewälzt, weil er es nicht zu töten brauchte. Und als gerade ein junger Frischling dahergesprungen kam, stach er ihn ab, nahm Lunge und Leber heraus und brachte sie als Wahrzeichen der Königin mit. Der Koch mußte sie in Salz kochen, und das boshafte Weib aß sie auf und meinte, sie hätte Sneewittchens Lunge und Leber gegessen.

Nun war das arme Kind in dem großen Wald mutterselig allein, und ward ihm so angst, daß es alle Blätter an den Bäumen ansah und nicht wußte, wie es sich helfen sollte. Da fing es an zu laufen und lief über die spitzen Steine und durch die Dornen, und die wilden Tiere sprangen an ihm vorbei, aber sie taten ihm nichts. Es lief, solange nur die Füße noch fort konnten, bis es bald Abend werden wollte, da sah es ein kleines Häuschen und ging hinein, sich zu ruhen. In dem Häuschen war alles klein, aber so zierlich und reinlich, daß es nicht zu sagen ist. Da stand ein weiß gedecktes Tischlein mit sieben kleinen Tellern, jedes Tellerlein mit seinem Löffelein, ferner sieben Messerlein und Gäblein und sieben Becherlein. An der Wand waren sieben Bettlein nebeneinander aufgestellt und schneeweiße Laken darübergedeckt. Sneewittchen, weil es so hungrig und durstig war, aß von jedem Tellerlein ein wenig Gemüs und Brot und trank aus jedem Becherlein einen Tropfen Wein; denn es wollte nicht einem allein alles wegnehmen. Hernach, weil es so müde war, legte es sich in ein Bettchen, aber keins paßte; das eine war zu lang, das andere zu kurz, bis endlich das siebente recht war: und darin blieb es liegen, befahl sich Gott und schlief ein.

Als es ganz dunkel geworden war, kamen die Herren von dem Häuslein, das waren die sieben Zwerge, die in den Bergen nach Erz hackten und gruben. Sie zündeten ihre sieben Lichtlein an, und wie es nun hell im Häuslein ward, sahen sie, daß jemand darin gewesen war, denn es stand nicht alles so in der Ordnung, wie sie es verlassen

in her heart, so that she no longer had peace by day or night. Therefore she summoned a huntsman and said: "Take the child out to the woods; I don't want to see her in front of me anymore. You are to kill her and bring back her lungs and liver to me as proof." The huntsman obeyed and led the girl into the forest, but after he drew his dagger with the intention of piercing Snow White's innocent heart, she started to weep, saying: "Oh, dear huntsman, let me live; I shall run into the wild forest and never come home again." And because she was so beautiful, the huntsman felt compassion and said: "All right, run away, you poor child." He thought to himself: "The wild animals will soon eat you"; nevertheless he felt as if a stone had rolled off his heart because he didn't need to kill her. And when a young wild boar happened to dash by, he stabbed it, removed its lungs and liver, and brought them to the queen as proof. The cook was ordered to boil them in salty water, and the malicious woman ate them up, thinking she had eaten Snow White's lungs and liver.

Now the poor child was all alone in the great forest, and she was in such anguish that she looked at every leaf on every tree, and didn't know what to do next. Then she started to run, and she ran over sharp stones and through thorns, and the wild animals darted past her, but did her no harm. She ran as long as her legs could carry her, until it was nearly evening, when she saw a little cottage and went in to rest. Everything in the cottage was small, but more dainty and clean than words can tell. There was a little table with a white tablecloth and seven little plates, each plate with its little spoon, in addition to seven little knives and forks and seven little goblets. Seven little beds were placed against the wall in a row; they were covered with snowy white sheets. Because Snow White was so hungry and thirsty, she ate a bit of vegetables and bread from each little plate and drank a drop of wine from each little goblet; you see, she didn't want to take everything away from one person. After that, because she was so tired, she lay down on one of the little beds; but none of them suited her: the first was too long, the second too short, until finally the seventh was just right; there she remained lying, commended herself to God, and fell asleep.

When it was completely dark, the owners of the cottage arrived; they were the seven dwarfs who hewed and dug for ore in the mountains. They lit their seven little candles, and now that there was light in the cottage, they saw that someone had been there, because not everything was in order as they had left it.

hatten. Der erste sprach: »Wer hat auf meinem Stühlchen gesessen?«
Der zweite: »Wer hat von meinem Tellerchen gegessen?« Der dritte:
»Wer hat von meinem Brötchen genommen?« Der vierte: »Wer hat
von meinem Gemüschen gegessen?« Der fünfte: »Wer hat mit
meinem Gäbelchen gestochen?« Der sechste: »Wer hat mit meinem
Messerchen geschnitten?« Der siebente: »Wer hat aus meinem
Becherlein getrunken?« Dann sah sich der erste um und sah, daß auf
seinem Bett eine kleine Dälle war, da sprach er: »Wer hat in mein
Bettchen getreten?« Die andern kamen gelaufen und riefen: »In
meinem hat auch jemand gelegen.« Der siebente aber, als er in sein
Bett sah, erblickte Sneewittchen, das lag darin und schlief. Nun rief
er die andern, die kamen herbeigelaufen und schrien vor Verwunderung, holten ihre sieben Lichtlein und beleuchteten Sneewittchen.
»Ei, du mein Gott! Ei, du mein Gott!« riefen sie. »Was ist das Kind so
schön!« Und hatten so große Freude, daß sie es nicht aufweckten,
sondern im Bettlein fortschlafen ließen. Der siebente Zwerg aber
schlief bei seinen Gesellen, bei jedem eine Stunde, da war die Nacht
herum.

Als es Morgen war, erwachte Sneewittchen, und wie es die sieben
Zwerge sah, erschrak es. Sie waren aber freundlich und fragten: »Wie
heißt du?« »Ich heiße Sneewittchen«, antwortete es. »Wie bist du in
unser Haus gekommen?« sprachen weiter die Zwerge. Da erzählte es
ihnen, daß seine Stiefmutter es hätte wollen umbringen lassen, der
Jäger hätte ihm aber das Leben geschenkt, und da wär es gelaufen
den ganzen Tag, bis es endlich ihr Häuslein gefunden hätte. Die
Zwerge sprachen: »Willst du unsern Haushalt versehen, kochen, betten, waschen, nähen und stricken, und willst du alles ordentlich und
reinlich halten, so kannst du bei uns bleiben, und es soll dir an nichts
fehlen.« »Ja«, sagte Sneewittchen, »von Herzen gern«, und blieb bei
ihnen. Es hielt ihnen das Haus in Ordnung; morgens gingen sie in die
Berge und suchten Erz und Gold, abends kamen sie wieder, und da
mußte ihr Essen bereit sein. Den Tag über war das Mädchen allein,
da warnten es die guten Zwerglein und sprachen: »Hüte dich vor
deiner Stiefmutter, die wird bald wissen, daß du hier bist; laß ja niemand herein.«

Die Königin aber, nachdem sie Sneewittchens Lunge und Leber
glaubte gegessen zu haben, dachte nicht anders, als sie wäre wieder
die erste und allerschönste, trat vor ihren Spiegel und sprach:

»Spieglein, Spieglein an der Wand,
wer ist die schönste im ganzen Land?«

The first one said: "Who sat on my little chair?" The second: "Who ate off my little plate?" The third: "Who took some of my little loaf?" The fourth: "Who ate some of my little vegetables?" The fifth: "Who jabbed with my little fork?" The sixth: "Who cut with my little knife?" The seventh: "Who drank out of my little goblet?" Then the first one looked around and, seeing that there was a slight depression on his bed, he said: "Who got into my little bed?" The others ran over and cried: "Someone's been lying on mine, too." But when the seventh looked at his bed, he caught sight of Snow White, who was lying there asleep. Now he summoned the others, who came running over and shouted with amazement, fetched their seven little candles, and threw their light on Snow White. "Oh, my heavens! Oh, my heavens!" they cried. "How beautiful the child is!" And they were so happy that they didn't wake her, but let her go on sleeping on the little bed. The seventh dwarf slept with his companions, an hour with each, and then the night was over.

When it was morning, Snow White woke up, and when she saw the seven dwarfs, she got frightened. But they were friendly, and asked her: "What's your name?" "My name is Snow White," she replied. "How did you happen to come to our house?" the dwarfs asked next. Then she told them that her stepmother had tried to have her killed, but the huntsman had spared her life, and she had then run all day long until she had finally found their cottage. The dwarfs said: "If you're willing to manage our housekeeping, cook, make beds, do laundry, sew, and knit, and if you're willing to keep everything orderly and clean, you can stay with us and you'll lack for nothing." "Yes," said Snow White, "with all my heart"; and she remained with them. She kept their house in order; every morning they went to the mountains in search of ore and gold; in the evening they returned, and then their food had to be ready. All day long the girl was alone, so the kind little dwarfs warned her, saying: "Watch out for your stepmother; she'll soon find out that you're here; don't let anyone in."

But after the queen thought she had eaten Snow White's lungs and liver, she was sure that she was once again the first and the most beautiful; she stepped in front of her mirror and said:

> "Little mirror hanging there,
> in all the country who's most fair?"

Da antwortete der Spiegel:

> »Frau Königin, Ihr seid die schönste hier,
> aber Sneewittchen über den Bergen
> bei den sieben Zwergen
> ist noch tausendmal schöner als Ihr.«

Da erschrak sie, denn sie wußte, daß der Spiegel keine Unwahrheit sprach, und merkte, daß der Jäger sie betrogen hatte und Sneewittchen noch am Leben war. Und da sann und sann sie aufs neue, wie sie es umbringen wollte; denn solange sie nicht die schönste war im ganzen Land, ließ ihr der Neid keine Ruhe. Und als sie sich endlich etwas ausgedacht hatte, färbte sie sich das Gesicht und kleidete sich wie eine alte Krämerin, und war ganz unkenntlich. In dieser Gestalt ging sie über die sieben Berge zu den sieben Zwergen, klopfte an die Türe und rief: »Schöne Ware feil! feil!« Sneewittchen guckte zum Fenster heraus und rief: »Guten Tag, liebe Frau, was habt Ihr zu verkaufen?« »Gute Ware, schöne Ware«, antwortete sie, »Schnürriemen von allen Farben«, und holte einen hervor, der aus bunter Seide geflochten war. »Die ehrliche Frau kann ich hereinlassen«, dachte Sneewittchen, riegelte die Türe auf und kaufte sich den hübschen Schnürriemen. »Kind«, sprach die Alte, »wie du aussiehst! Komm, ich will dich einmal ordentlich schnüren.« Sneewittchen hatte kein Arg, stellte sich vor sie und ließ sich mit dem neuen Schnürriemen schnüren; aber die Alte schnürte geschwind und schnürte so fest, daß dem Sneewittchen der Atem verging und es für tot hinfiel. »Nun bist du die schönste gewesen«, sprach sie und eilte hinaus.

Nicht lange darauf, zur Abendzeit, kamen die sieben Zwerge nach Haus, aber wie erschraken sie, als sie ihr liebes Sneewittchen auf der Erde liegen sahen; und es regte und bewegte sich nicht, als wäre es tot. Sie hoben es in die Höhe, und weil sie sahen, daß es zu fest geschnürt war, schnitten sie den Schnürriemen entzwei: da fing es an, ein wenig zu atmen, und ward nach und nach wieder lebendig. Als die Zwerge hörten, was geschehen war, sprachen sie: »Die alte Krämerfrau war niemand als die gottlose Königin: hüte dich und laß keinen Menschen herein, wenn wir nicht bei dir sind.«

Das böse Weib aber, als es nach Haus gekommen war, ging vor den Spiegel und fragte:

> »Spieglein, Spieglein an der Wand,
> wer ist die schönste im ganzen Land?«

And the mirror replied:

> "Queen, you're the fairest where you are,
> but Snow White, who the hills did roam
> and now lives in the seven dwarfs' home,
> is more beautiful than you by far."

Then she became alarmed because she knew that the mirror never told a lie, and she realized that the huntsman had deceived her, and Snow White was still alive. Then she planned and planned again how to go about killing her: for, as long as she wasn't the most beautiful woman in the whole country, her envy gave her no rest. And when she had finally devised a scheme, she dyed her face and put on the garb of an old peddler, so that she was quite unrecognizable. In that guise she crossed the seven mountains and arrived at the home of the seven dwarfs; knocking at the door, she called: "Beautiful things for sale! For sale!" Snow White looked out the window and called: "Good day, dear lady, what do you have to sell?" "Nice things, pretty things," she replied, "bodice laces of all colors"; and she pulled out one that was braided of colorful silk. "I can let this honest woman in," thought Snow White; she unbarred the door and bought the pretty lace. "Child," said the old woman, "how you look! Come here, I'll tie the lace for you properly." Snow White, who had no suspicions, stood in front of her and let herself be laced up with the new lace; but the old woman laced her quickly, and so tightly that Snow White lost her breath and fell down as if dead. "Now you *were* the most fair," the woman said, and hastened to depart.

Not long afterward, toward evening, the seven dwarfs came home, and how alarmed they were to find their beloved Snow White lying on the floor! She didn't stir or budge, and she seemed to be dead. They lifted her up, and because they saw that she was laced too tightly, they cut the lace in two; then she began to draw a few breaths, and gradually came to life again. When the dwarfs heard what had happened, they said: "The old peddler woman was none other than the wicked queen; be careful, and let no one in when we're not with you."

But when the evil woman got home, she went to her mirror and asked:

> "Little mirror hanging there,
> in all the country who's most fair?"

Da antwortete er wie sonst:

>»Frau Königin, Ihr seid die schönste hier,
aber Sneewittchen über den Bergen
bei den sieben Zwergen
ist noch tausendmal schöner als Ihr.«

Als sie das hörte, lief ihr alles Blut zum Herzen, so erschrak sie, denn sie sah wohl, daß Sneewittchen wieder lebendig geworden war. »Nun aber«, sprach sie, »will ich etwas aussinnen, das dich zugrunde richten soll«, und mit Hexenkünsten, die sie verstand, machte sie einen giftigen Kamm. Dann verkleidete sie sich und nahm die Gestalt eines andern alten Weibes an. So ging sie hin über die sieben Berge zu den sieben Zwergen, klopfte an die Türe und rief: »Gute Ware feil! feil!« Sneewittchen schaute heraus und sprach: »Geht nur weiter, ich darf niemand hereinlassen.« »Das Ansehen wird dir doch erlaubt sein«, sprach die Alte, zog den giftigen Kamm heraus und hielt ihn in die Höhe. Da gefiel er dem Kinde so gut, daß es sich betören ließ und die Türe öffnete. Als sie des Kaufs einig waren, sprach die Alte: »Nun will ich dich einmal ordentlich kämmen.« Das arme Sneewittchen dachte an nichts und ließ die Alte gewähren, aber kaum hatte sie den Kamm in die Haare gesteckt, als das Gift darin wirkte und das Mädchen ohne Besinnung niederfiel. »Du Ausbund von Schönheit«, sprach das boshafte Weib, »jetzt ist's um dich geschehen«, und ging fort. Zum Glück aber war es bald Abend, wo die sieben Zwerglein nach Haus kamen. Als sie Sneewittchen wie tot auf der Erde liegen sahen, hatten sie gleich die Stiefmutter in Verdacht, suchten nach und fanden den giftigen Kamm, und kaum hatten sie ihn herausgezogen, so kam Sneewittchen wieder zu sich und erzählte, was vorgegangen war. Da warnten sie es noch einmal, auf seiner Hut zu sein und niemand die Türe zu öffnen.

Die Königin stellte sich daheim vor den Spiegel und sprach:

>»Spieglein, Spieglein an der Wand,
wer ist die schönste im ganzen Land?«

Da antwortete er wie sonst:

>»Frau Königin, Ihr seid die schönste hier,
aber Sneewittchen über den Bergen
bei den sieben Zwergen
ist noch tausendmal schöner als Ihr.«

Then it answered as before:

> "Queen, you're the fairest where you are,
> but Snow White, who the hills did roam
> and now lives in the seven dwarfs' home,
> is more beautiful than you by far."

When she heard that, all her blood flowed to her heart, she was so alarmed, because she realized that Snow White had come to life again. "But now," she said, "I'll devise something that will totally destroy you"; and with the witch's arts that she understood, she made a poisoned comb. Next, she disguised herself, taking the form of a different old woman. Then she crossed the seven mountains and arrived at the home of the seven dwarfs; knocking at the door, she called: "Beautiful things for sale! For sale!" Snow White looked out and said: "Go your way, I'm not allowed to let anyone in." "You're surely permitted to look at things," the old woman said, as she pulled out the poisoned comb and held it up. The child liked it so much that she let herself be fooled, and she opened the door. When they had come to terms over the sale, the old woman said: "Now I'll give you a proper combing." Poor Snow White didn't imagine anything was wrong and let the woman have her way, but scarcely had she thrust the comb into her hair when the poison in it took effect and the girl fell down unconscious. "You paragon of beauty," said the malicious woman, "it's all up with you now"; and she left. But fortunately it wasn't long until evening, when the seven dwarfs came home. When they saw Snow White lying on the floor dead, they immediately suspected her stepmother; they made a search and discovered the poisoned comb, and scarcely had they drawn it out when Snow White came to, and told them what had occurred. Then they warned her again to be on her guard and not to open the door to anybody.

Back home, the queen stood before her mirror and said:

> "Little mirror hanging there,
> in all the country who's most fair?"

Then it replied as previously:

> "Queen, you're the fairest where you are,
> but Snow White, who the hills did roam
> and now lives in the seven dwarfs' home,
> is more beautiful than you by far."

Als sie den Spiegel so reden hörte, zitterte und bebte sie vor Zorn. »Sneewittchen soll sterben«, rief sie, »und wenn es mein eignes Leben kostet.« Darauf ging sie in eine ganz verborgene einsame Kammer, wo niemand hinkam, und machte da einen giftigen, giftigen Apfel. Äußerlich sah er schön aus, weiß mit roten Backen, daß jeder, der ihn erblickte, Lust danach bekam, aber wer ein Stückchen davon aß, der mußte sterben. Als der Apfel fertig war, färbte sie sich das Gesicht und verkleidete sich in eine Bauersfrau, und so ging sie über die sieben Berge zu den sieben Zwergen. Sie klopfte an, Sneewittchen streckte den Kopf zum Fenster heraus und sprach: »Ich darf keinen Menschen einlassen, die sieben Zwerge haben mir's verboten.« »Mir auch recht«, antwortete die Bäurin, »meine Äpfel will ich schon loswerden. Da, einen will ich dir schenken.« »Nein«, sprach Sneewittchen, »ich darf nichts annehmen.« »Fürchtest du dich vor Gift?« sprach die Alte. »Siehst du, da schneide ich den Apfel in zwei Teile; den roten Backen iß du, den weißen will ich essen.« Der Apfel war aber so künstlich gemacht, daß der rote Backen allein vergiftet war. Sneewittchen lusterte den schönen Apfel an, und als es sah, daß die Bäurin davon aß, so konnte es nicht länger widerstehen, streckte die Hand hinaus und nahm die giftige Hälfte. Kaum aber hatte es einen Bissen davon im Mund, so fiel es tot zur Erde nieder. Da betrachtete es die Königin mit grausigen Blicken und lachte überlaut und sprach: »Weiß wie Schnee, rot wie Blut, schwarz wie Ebenholz! Diesmal können dich die Zwerge nicht wieder erwecken.« Und als sie daheim den Spiegel befragte:

> »Spieglein, Spieglein an der Wand,
> wer ist die schönste im ganzen Land?«,

so antwortete er endlich:

> »Frau Königin, Ihr seid die schönste im Land.«

Da hatte ihr neidisches Herz Ruhe, so gut ein neidisches Herz Ruhe haben kann.

Die Zwerglein, wie sie abends nach Haus kamen, fanden Sneewittchen auf der Erde liegen, und es ging kein Atem mehr aus seinem Mund, und es war tot. Sie hoben es auf, suchten, ob sie was Giftiges fänden, schnürten es auf, kämmten ihm die Haare, wuschen es mit Wasser und Wein, aber es half alles nichts; das liebe Kind war tot und blieb tot. Sie legten es auf eine Bahre und setzten sich alle siebene daran und beweinten es, und weinten drei Tage lang. Da

When she heard the mirror say that, she shivered and shook
with anger. "Snow White shall die," she called, "even if it costs my
own life." Then she went to a totally secluded, solitary chamber
that no one ever visited; there she made a poisonous, poisonous
apple. It looked beautiful on the outside, white with red cheeks,
so that everyone who caught sight of it got an appetite for it, but
whoever ate even a little piece of it, was doomed to die. When
the apple was ready, she dyed her face and disguised herself as a
farmer's wife; then she crossed the seven mountains and arrived
at the home of the seven dwarfs. She knocked; Snow White put
her head out the window and said: "I'm not allowed to let anyone
in; the seven dwarfs have forbidden me to do it." "That's all the
same to me," the farmer's wife replied, "I'll get my apples off my
hands, anyway. Here, let me make you a present of one." "No,"
said Snow White, "I'm not allowed to accept anything." "Are you
afraid of poison?" the old woman said. "Watch, I'm cutting the
apple in two; you eat the red cheek, I'll eat the white one." But
the apple was so craftily made that only the red cheek was poisoned. Snow White had a craving for the pretty apple, and when
she saw the farmer's wife eating some of it, she was no longer able
to resist; she stretched out her hand and took the poisoned half.
But scarcely did she have a morsel of it in her mouth when she
fell to the floor dead. Then the queen studied her with a fearful
gaze, laughed very loud, and said: "White as snow, red as blood,
black as ebony! This time the dwarfs can't wake you up again."
And back home, when she asked the mirror:

> "Little mirror hanging there,
> in all the country who's most fair?"

it finally answered:

> "Queen, you're the fairest in the country."

Then her envious heart was at peace, to the extent that an envious heart can be at peace.

When the dwarfs came home in the evening, they found Snow
White lying on the floor; no breath was issuing from her lips anymore, and she was dead. They lifted her up, searched for any
poisoned object, undid her laces, combed her hair, washed her
with water and wine, but nothing did any good; the beloved
child was definitely dead. They placed her on a bier, and all
seven of them sat down beside it and wept for her; they wept

wollten sie es begraben, aber es sah noch so frisch aus wie ein lebender Mensch und hatte noch seine schönen roten Backen. Sie sprachen: »Das können wir nicht in die schwarze Erde versenken«, und ließen einen durchsichtigen Sarg von Glas machen, daß man es von allen Seiten sehen konnte, legten es hinein und schrieben mit goldenen Buchstaben seinen Namen darauf, und daß es eine Königstochter wäre. Dann setzten sie den Sarg hinaus auf den Berg, und einer von ihnen blieb immer dabei und bewachte ihn. Und die Tiere kamen auch und beweinten Sneewittchen, erst eine Eule, dann ein Rabe, zuletzt ein Täubchen.

Nun lag Sneewittchen lange, lange Zeit in dem Sarg und verweste nicht, sondern sah aus, als wenn es schliefe, denn es war noch so weiß als Schnee, so rot als Blut und so schwarzhaarig wie Ebenholz. Es geschah aber, daß ein Königssohn in den Wald geriet und zu dem Zwergenhaus kam, da zu übernachten. Er sah auf dem Berg den Sarg, und das schöne Sneewittchen darin, und las, was mit goldenen Buchstaben darauf geschrieben war. Da sprach er zu den Zwergen: »Laßt mir den Sarg, ich will euch geben, was ihr dafür haben wollt.« Aber die Zwerge antworteten: »Wir geben ihn nicht um alles Gold in der Welt.« Da sprach er: »So schenkt mir ihn, denn ich kann nicht leben, ohne Sneewittchen zu sehen, ich will es ehren und hochachten wie mein Liebstes.« Wie er so sprach, empfanden die guten Zwerglein Mitleiden mit ihm und gaben ihm den Sarg. Der Königssohn ließ ihn nun von seinen Dienern auf den Schultern forttragen. Da geschah es, daß sie über einen Strauch stolperten, und von dem Schüttern fuhr der giftige Apfelgrütz, den Sneewittchen abgebissen hatte, aus dem Hals. Und nicht lange, so öffnete es die Augen, hob den Deckel vom Sarg in die Höhe und richtete sich auf, und war wieder lebendig. »Ach Gott, wo bin ich?« rief es. Der Königssohn sagte voll Freude: »Du bist bei mir«, und erzählte, was sich zugetragen hatte, und sprach: »Ich habe dich lieber als alles auf der Welt; komm mit mir in meines Vaters Schloß, du sollst meine Gemahlin werden.« Da war ihm Sneewittchen gut und ging mit ihm, und ihre Hochzeit ward mit großer Pracht und Herrlichkeit angeordnet.

Zu dem Fest wurde aber auch Sneewittchens gottlose Stiefmutter eingeladen. Wie sie sich nun mit schönen Kleidern angetan hatte, trat sie vor den Spiegel und sprach:

> »Spieglein, Spieglein an der Wand,
> wer ist die schönste im ganzen Land?«

Der Spiegel antwortete:

three days long. Then they wanted to bury her, but she still looked as healthy as a living person and still had lovely red cheeks. They said: "We can't lower someone like this into the black earth," and they had a coffin of transparent glass made, in which she could be seen from all sides; they placed her in it and wrote her name on it in gold letters, stating that she was a princess. Then they placed the coffin outside on the mountain, and one of them was always with it, guarding it. And the wild creatures came, too, and wept for Snow White, first an owl, then a raven, and finally a dove.

Now Snow White lay in the coffin for a long, long time; she didn't decompose, but looked as if she were asleep, for she was still as white as snow and as red as blood, with hair as black as ebony. But it came to pass that a prince entered the forest and arrived at the dwarfs' house, hoping to spend the night there. On the mountain he saw the coffin, with lovely Snow White in it, and read what was written on it in gold letters. Then he said to the dwarfs: "Let me have the coffin; I'll give you whatever you want for it." But the dwarfs replied: "We won't give it up for all the gold in the world." Then he said: "In that case, make me a present of it, because I can't live without looking at Snow White; I will honor and revere her like my dearest treasure." When he said that, the kind dwarfs felt compassion for him and gave him the coffin. Now the prince had his servants bear it away on their shoulders. Then they happened to trip over a bush, and that jolt made the piece of poisonous apple that Snow White had bitten off fly out of her throat. Before long, she opened her eyes, lifted up the lid of the coffin, and sat up; she was alive again. "Oh, Lord, where am I?" she cried. Overjoyed, the prince said: "You're with me," and he told her what had happened, saying: "I love you more than anything else in the world; come with me to my father's palace; you shall be my wife." Then Snow White felt affection for him, and she went with him, and their wedding was arranged with great splendor and pomp.

And even Snow White's wicked stepmother was invited to the feast. After putting on beautiful clothes, she stepped in front of the mirror and said:

> "Little mirror hanging there,
> in all the country who's most fair?"

The mirror replied:

»Frau Königin, Ihr seid die schönste hier,
aber die junge Königin ist tausendmal schöner als Ihr.«

Da stieß das böse Weib einen Fluch aus, und ward ihr so angst, so
angst, daß sie sich nicht zu lassen wußte. Sie wollte zuerst gar nicht
auf die Hochzeit kommen; doch ließ es ihr keine Ruhe, sie mußte fort
und die junge Königin sehen. Und wie sie hineintrat, erkannte sie
Sneewittchen, und vor Angst und Schrecken stand sie da und konnte
sich nicht regen. Aber es waren schon eiserne Pantoffeln über
Kohlenfeuer gestellt und wurden mit Zangen hereingetragen und vor
sie hingestellt. Da mußte sie in die rotglühenden Schuhe treten und
so lange tanzen, bis sie tot zur Erde fiel.

Rumpelstilzchen

Es war einmal ein Müller, der war arm, aber er hatte eine schöne
Tochter. Nun traf es sich, daß er mit dem König zu sprechen kam, und
um sich ein Ansehen zu geben, sagte er zu ihm: »Ich habe eine
Tochter, die kann Stroh zu Gold spinnen.« Der König sprach zum
Müller: »Das ist eine Kunst, die mir wohl gefällt, wenn deine Tochter
so geschickt ist, wie du sagst, so bring sie morgen in mein Schloß, da
will ich sie auf die Probe stellen.« Als nun das Mädchen zu ihm gebracht ward, führte er es in eine Kammer, die ganz voll Stroh lag, gab
ihr Rad und Haspel und sprach: »Jetzt mache dich an die Arbeit, und
wenn du diese Nacht durch bis morgen früh dieses Stroh nicht zu
Gold versponnen hast, so mußt du sterben.« Darauf schloß er die
Kammer selbst zu, und sie blieb allein darin.

Da saß nun die arme Müllerstochter und wußte um ihr Leben
keinen Rat: sie verstand gar nichts davon, wie man Stroh zu Gold
spinnen konnte, und ihre Angst ward immer größer, daß sie endlich
zu weinen anfing. Da ging auf einmal die Türe auf und trat ein kleines
Männchen herein und sprach: »Guten Abend, Jungfer Müllerin,
warum weint Sie so sehr?« »Ach«, antwortete das Mädchen, »ich soll
Stroh zu Gold spinnen und verstehe das nicht.« Sprach das Männchen: »Was gibst du mir, wenn ich dir's spinne?« »Mein Halsband«,
sagte das Mädchen. Das Männchen nahm das Halsband, setzte sich
vor das Rädchen, und schnurr, schnurr, schnurr, dreimal gezogen, war
die Spule voll. Dann steckte es eine andere auf, und schnurr, schnurr,
schnurr, dreimal gezogen, war auch die zweite voll; und so ging's fort

"Queen, you're the fairest where you are,
     but the young queen is more beautiful by far."

Then the evil woman uttered a curse and became so ill at ease, so ill at ease, that she was beside herself. At first she had no desire to attend the wedding; but she had no peace, she had to go and take a look at the young queen. And as she entered, she recognized Snow White, and out of fear and fright she stood there unable to move. But iron slippers had already been placed over coal flames; now they were carried in with tongs and set down in front of her. Then she was forced to put her feet into the red-hot shoes and keep on dancing until she fell to the floor dead.

Rumpelstiltskin

Once there was a miller who was poor but had a beautiful daughter. Now it came about that he got into conversation with the king, and, in order to make himself look good, he said to him: "I have a daughter who can spin straw into gold." The king said to the miller: "That's a talent I really admire; if your daughter is as skillful as you say, bring her to my palace tomorrow and I'll put her to the test." Well, when the girl was brought to him, he led her to a room that was completely filled with straw, gave her a spinning wheel and a reel, and said: "Now get to work; you have till tomorrow morning; if you don't finish spinning this straw into gold tonight, you must die." Then he locked the door to the room with his own hands, and she was left alone in it.

Well, there sat the poor miller's daughter; for the life of her, she had no idea what to do: she was totally ignorant of the art of spinning straw into gold, and her anxiety steadily increased, so that she finally started to cry. Then the door suddenly opened and a little gnome came in and said: "Good evening, miller's daughter, why are you crying so hard?" "Oh," the girl replied, "I'm supposed to spin straw into gold, and I don't know how." The little man said: "What will you give me if I spin it for you?" "My necklace," the girl said. The little man took the necklace, sat down at the wheel, and hum, hum, hum, three pulls and the reel was full. Then he put another one on, and hum, hum, hum, three pulls and the second one was full, too; and so it went on till

bis zum Morgen, da war alles Stroh versponnen, und alle Spulen
waren voll Gold. Bei Sonnenaufgang kam schon der König, und als er
das Gold erblickte, erstaunte er und freute sich, aber sein Herz ward
nur noch goldgieriger. Er ließ die Müllerstochter in eine andere
Kammer voll Stroh bringen, die noch viel größer war, und befahl ihr,
das auch in einer Nacht zu spinnen, wenn ihr das Leben lieb wäre.
Das Mädchen wußte sich nicht zu helfen und weinte, da ging abermals die Türe auf, und das kleine Männchen erschien und sprach:
»Was gibst du mir, wenn ich dir das Stroh zu Gold spinne?« »Meinen
Ring von dem Finger«, antwortete das Mädchen. Das Männchen
nahm den Ring, fing wieder an zu schnurren mit dem Rade und hatte
bis zum Morgen alles Stroh zu glänzendem Gold gesponnen. Der
König freute sich über die Maßen bei dem Anblick, war aber noch
immer nicht Goldes satt, sondern ließ die Müllerstochter in eine noch
größere Kammer voll Stroh bringen und sprach: »Die mußt du noch
in dieser Nacht verspinnen: gelingt dir's aber, so sollst du meine
Gemahlin werden.« »Wenn's auch eine Müllerstochter ist«, dachte er,
»eine reichere Frau finde ich in der ganzen Welt nicht.« Als das
Mädchen allein war, kam das Männlein zum drittenmal wieder und
sprach: »Was gibst du mir, wenn ich dir noch diesmal das Stroh
spinne?« »Ich habe nichts mehr, das ich geben könnte«, antwortete
das Mädchen. »So versprich mir, wenn du Königin wirst, dein erstes
Kind.« »Wer weiß, wie das noch geht«, dachte die Müllerstochter und
wußte sich auch in der Not nicht anders zu helfen; sie versprach also
dem Männchen, was es verlangte, und das Männchen spann dafür
noch einmal das Stroh zu Gold. Und als am Morgen der König kam
und alles fand, wie er gewünscht hatte, so hielt er Hochzeit mit ihr,
und die schöne Müllerstochter ward eine Königin.

Über ein Jahr brachte sie ein schönes Kind zur Welt und dachte gar
nicht mehr an das Männchen: da trat es plötzlich in ihre Kammer und
sprach: »Nun gib mir, was du versprochen hast.« Die Königin erschrak
und bot dem Männchen alle Reichtümer des Königreichs an, wenn es
ihr das Kind lassen wollte: aber das Männchen sprach: »Nein, etwas
Lebendes ist mir lieber als alle Schätze der Welt.« Da fing die Königin
so an zu jammern und zu weinen, daß das Männchen Mitleiden mit
ihr hatte: »Drei Tage will ich dir Zeit lassen«, sprach er, »wenn du bis
dahin meinen Namen weißt, so sollst du dein Kind behalten.«

Nun besann sich die Königin die ganze Nacht über auf alle Namen,
die sie jemals gehört hatte, und schickte einen Boten über Land, der
sollte sich erkundigen weit und breit, was es sonst noch für Namen
gäbe. Als am andern Tag das Männchen kam, fing sie an mit Kaspar,

morning, when all the straw was spun and all the reels were full of gold. At sunrise the king was already there; when he caught sight of the gold, he was both astonished and happy, but his heart became even greedier for gold. He had the miller's daughter taken to another straw-filled room that was much bigger, and he ordered her to spin all this straw, too, in one night if she valued her life. The girl didn't know how to go about it, and she was weeping, when the door opened again and the little gnome appeared, saying: "What will you give me if I spin the straw into gold for you?" "The ring on my finger," the girl replied. The little man took the ring, started making the wheel hum again, and when morning came he had spun all the straw into shining gold. The king was exceedingly overjoyed at the sight, but he was not yet sated with gold; rather, he had the miller's daughter taken to an even larger room filled with straw, and he said: "You must spin this tonight; if you succeed, you shall be my wife." He thought to himself: "Even if she's only a miller's daughter, I won't find a wealthier woman in the whole world." When the girl was alone, the little man came for the third time and said: "What will you give me if I spin the straw for you this time, too?" "I have nothing left to give," the girl replied. "Then promise me your first child when you become queen." "Who knows how it will all turn out?" the miller's daughter thought to herself; and, besides, in her distress she didn't know what else to do; and so she promised the little man what he asked for, and in return the little man once more spun the straw into gold. When the king arrived in the morning and found everything as he had wished, he married her and the beautiful miller's daughter became a queen.

A year later she gave birth to a lovely child, and no longer remembered the little man; then he suddenly entered her bedroom and said: "Now give me what you promised." The queen was alarmed and offered the little man all the riches of the kingdom if he would only let her keep her child; but the little man said: "No, a living thing is dearer to me than all the treasures in the world." Then the queen began to lament and weep so bitterly that the little man felt sorry for her: "I give you three days' time," he said; "if you find out my name by then, you can keep your child."

Now the queen spent the whole night recalling all the names she had ever heard; and she sent out a scout to inquire near and far into any other names that might exist. When the little man came the next day, she began with Gaspar, Melchior, and Balthasar,

Melchior, Balzer und sagte alle Namen, die sie wußte, nach der Reihe
her, aber bei jedem sprach das Männlein:»So heiß ich nicht.« Den
zweiten Tag ließ sie in der Nachbarschaft herumfragen, wie die Leute
da genannt würden, und sagte dem Männlein die ungewöhnlichsten
und seltsamsten Namen vor:»Heißt du vielleicht Rippenbiest oder
Hammelswade oder Schnürbein?« Aber es antwortete immer:»So
heiß ich nicht.« Den dritten Tag kam der Bote wieder zurück und
erzählte:»Neue Namen habe ich keinen einzigen finden können, aber
wie ich an einen hohen Berg um die Waldecke kam, wo Fuchs und
Has sich gute Nacht sagen, so sah ich da ein kleines Haus, und vor
dem Haus brannte ein Feuer, und um das Feuer sprang ein gar zu
lächerliches Männchen, hüpfte auf einem Bein und schrie:

> ›Heute back ich, morgen brau ich,
> übermorgen hol ich der Königin ihr Kind;
> ach, wie gut ist, daß niemand weiß,
> daß ich Rumpelstilzchen heiß!‹«

Da könnt ihr denken, wie die Königin froh war, als sie den Namen
hörte, und als bald hernach das Männlein hereintrat und fragte:
»Nun, Frau Königin, wie heiß ich?«, fragte sie erst:»Heißest du
Kunz?«»Nein«.»Heißest du Heinz?«»Nein.«»Heißt du etwa
Rumpelstilzchen?«

»Das hat dir der Teufel gesagt, das hat dir der Teufel gesagt«,
schrie das Männlein und stieß mit dem rechten Fuß vor Zorn so tief
in die Erde, daß es bis an den Leib hineinfuhr, dann packte es in
seiner Wut den linken Fuß mit beiden Händen und riß sich selbst
mitten entzwei.

Der goldene Vogel

Es war vorzeiten ein König, der hatte einen schönen Lustgarten hinter seinem Schloß, darin stand ein Baum, der goldene Äpfel trug. Als
die Äpfel reiften, wurden sie gezählt, aber gleich den nächsten
Morgen fehlte einer. Das ward dem König gemeldet, und er befahl,
daß alle Nächte unter dem Baume Wache sollte gehalten werden.
Der König hatte drei Söhne, davon schickte er den ältesten bei ein-
brechender Nacht in den Garten; wie es aber Mitternacht war, konnte er sich des Schlafes nicht erwehren, und am nächsten Morgen

then mentioned all the names she knew one by one, but each time the little man said: "That's not what I'm called." The next day she asked around among her neighbors what the local people were called, and she recited the most unusual and odd names to the little man: "Are you perhaps named Ribbeast, Muttonshank, or Laceleg?" But he replied each time: "That's not what I'm called." On the third day the scout returned and reported: "I haven't been able to discover any new names, but as I reached a high mountain, turning around the corner of the forest, where the fox and the hare say good night to each other, I saw a little house, and in front of the house a fire was burning, and around the fire a really ridiculous little man was jumping, hopping on one foot and yelling:

> 'Today I bake, tomorrow brew;
> day after that, fetch the queen's child;
> how glad I am that folks don't know
> by the name of Rumpelstiltskin I go!'"

You can imagine how happy the queen was when she heard the name; and when the little man came in shortly afterward and asked: "Now, queen, what's my name?," she first asked: "Is your name Kunz?" "No." "Is your name Heinz?" "No." "Could your name possibly be Rumpelstiltskin?"

"It was the devil who told you that! It was the devil who told you that!" the little man shouted; and in his anger he stamped his right foot, driving it so deep in the ground that he sank in up to his waist; then in his frenzy he seized his left foot in both hands and tore himself apart down the middle.

The Golden Bird

In olden days there lived a king who had beautiful pleasure grounds in back of his palace; in them was a tree that bore golden apples. When the apples grew ripe, they were counted, but on the very next morning one was missing. This was reported to the king, who ordered a watch to be kept below the tree every night. The king had three sons, the eldest of whom he sent into the garden as night was falling; but when midnight came, he couldn't help but fall asleep, and the next morning another apple was missing. On

fehlte wieder ein Apfel. In der folgenden Nacht mußte der zweite
Sohn wachen, aber dem erging es nicht besser: als es zwölf Uhr
geschlagen hatte, schlief er ein, und morgens fehlte ein Apfel. Jetzt
kam die Reihe zu wachen an den dritten Sohn, der war auch bereit,
aber der König traute ihm nicht viel zu und meinte, er würde noch
weniger ausrichten als seine Brüder; endlich aber gestattete er es
doch. Der Jüngling legte sich also unter den Baum, wachte und ließ
den Schlaf nicht Herr werden. Als es zwölf schlug, so rauschte etwas
durch die Luft, und er sah im Mondschein einen Vogel daherfliegen,
dessen Gefieder ganz von Gold glänzte. Der Vogel ließ sich auf dem
Baume nieder und hatte eben einen Apfel abgepickt, als der Jüngling
einen Pfeil nach ihm abschoß. Der Vogel entflog, aber der Pfeil hatte
sein Gefieder getroffen, und eine seiner goldenen Federn fiel herab.
Der Jüngling hob sie auf, brachte sie am andern Morgen dem König
und erzählte ihm, was er in der Nacht gesehen hatte. Der König ver-
sammelte seinen Rat, und jedermann erklärte, eine Feder wie diese
sei mehr wert als das gesamte Königreich. »Ist die Feder so kostbar«,
erklärte der König, »so hilft mir auch die eine nichts, sondern ich will
und muß den ganzen Vogel haben.«

Der älteste Sohn machte sich auf den Weg, verließ sich auf seine
Klugheit und meinte den goldenen Vogel schon zu finden. Wie er
eine Strecke gegangen war, sah er an dem Rande eines Waldes einen
Fuchs sitzen, legte seine Flinte an und zielte auf ihn. Der Fuchs rief:
»Schieß mich nicht, ich will dir dafür einen guten Rat geben. Du bist
auf dem Weg nach dem goldenen Vogel und wirst heut abend in ein
Dorf kommen, wo zwei Wirtshäuser einander gegenüberstehen. Eins
ist hell erleuchtet, und es geht darin lustig her: da kehr aber nicht ein,
sondern geh ins andere, wenn es dich auch schlecht ansieht.« »Wie
kann mir wohl so ein albernes Tier einen vernünftigen Rat erteilen!«
dachte der Königssohn und drückte los, aber er fehlte den Fuchs, der
den Schwanz streckte und schnell in den Wald lief. Darauf setzte er
seinen Weg fort und kam abends in das Dorf, wo die beiden Wirtshäuser standen: in dem einen ward gesungen und gesprungen, das andere hatte ein armseliges, betrübtes Ansehen. »Ich wäre wohl ein
Narr«, dachte er, »wenn ich in das lumpige Wirtshaus ginge und das
schöne liegenließ.« Also ging er in das lustige ein, lebte da in Saus und
Braus und vergaß den Vogel, seinen Vater und alle guten Lehren.

Als eine Zeit verstrichen und der älteste Sohn immer und immer
nicht nach Haus gekommen war, so machte sich der zweite auf den
Weg und wollte den goldenen Vogel suchen. Wie dem ältesten begegnete ihm der Fuchs und gab ihm den guten Rat, den er nicht achtete.

the following night the second son had to stand guard, but he had no better luck: when the clock struck twelve, he fell asleep and in the morning an apple was missing. Now it was the third son's turn to be vigilant, and he was ready and willing, but the king didn't have much confidence in him and thought he'd be of even less use than his brothers; finally, however, he gave him permission to go. And so the young man lay down under the tree, stayed awake, and didn't let sleep overpower him. At the stroke of twelve, there was a whirring in the air, and in the moonlight he saw flying toward him a bird whose plumage was all shiny with gold. The bird alighted on the tree and had just detached an apple with its beak when the young man shot an arrow at it. The bird flew away, but the arrow had hit its plumage, and one of its golden feathers flew down. The young man picked it up, brought it to the king the next morning, and told him what he had seen at night. The king convened his council, and everyone declared that a feather like that was more valuable than the entire kingdom. "If the feather is that precious," the king stated, "I have no use for just one; I want, and must have, the whole bird."

The eldest son set out, relying on his shrewdness, and certain that he'd soon find the golden bird. After he had proceeded some distance, he saw a fox sitting by the edge of a forest; he leveled his gun and took aim at it. The fox called: "Don't shoot me, and in return I'll give you some good advice. You're on your way to the golden bird, and this evening you'll arrive in a village where there are two inns opposite each other. One is brightly lit, and the people in it are merry; don't go into that one, but into the other, even if you don't like the looks of it." "How can such a foolish animal possibly give me sensible advice?" the prince thought, and he pulled the trigger; but he missed the fox, who stretched out his tail and quickly ran into the woods. Then the prince resumed his journey, and in the evening he reached the village with the two inns: in one of them there was singing and dancing, whereas the other one looked poverty-stricken and dreary. "I'd surely be a fool," he thought, "to go to the rundown inn and pass the nice one by." So he entered the merry one, where he lived a wild life and forgot all about the bird, his father, and every good principle.

After some time had gone by and the eldest son still hadn't come home, the second one set out in search of the golden bird. Like his elder brother, he met the fox, who gave him the same good advice; but he didn't heed it. He arrived at the two inns; his

Er kam zu den beiden Wirtshäusern, wo sein Bruder am Fenster des einen stand, aus dem der Jubel erschallte, und ihn anrief. Er konnte nicht widerstehen, ging hinein und lebte nur seinen Lüsten.

Wiederum verstrich eine Zeit, da wollte der jüngste Königssohn ausziehen und sein Heil versuchen, der Vater aber wollte es nicht zulassen. »Es ist vergeblich«, sprach er, »der wird den goldenen Vogel noch weniger finden als seine Brüder, und wenn ihm ein Unglück zustößt, so weiß er sich nicht zu helfen; es fehlt ihm am Besten.« Doch endlich, wie keine Ruhe mehr da war, ließ er ihn ziehen. Vor dem Walde saß wieder der Fuchs, bat um sein Leben und erteilte den guten Rat. Der Jüngling war gutmütig und sagte: »Sei ruhig, Füchslein, ich tue dir nichts zuleid.« »Es soll dich nicht gereuen«, antwortete der Fuchs, »und damit du schneller fortkommst, so steig hinten auf meinen Schwanz.« Und kaum hat er sich aufgesetzt, so fing der Fuchs an zu laufen, und da ging's über Stock und Stein, daß die Haare im Winde pfiffen. Als sie zu dem Dorfe kamen, stieg der Jüngling ab, befolgte den guten Rat und kehrte, ohne sich umzusehen, in das geringe Wirtshaus ein, wo er ruhig übernachtete. Am andern Morgen, wie er auf das Feld kam, saß da schon der Fuchs und sagte: »Ich will dir weiter sagen, was du zu tun hast. Geh du immer geradeaus, endlich wirst du an ein Schloß kommen, vor dem eine ganze Schar Soldaten liegt, aber kümmre dich nicht darum, denn sie werden alle schlafen und schnarchen; geh mittendurch und geradeswegs in das Schloß hinein, und geh durch alle Stuben, zuletzt wirst du in eine Kammer kommen, wo ein goldener Vogel in einem hölzernen Käfig hängt. Nebenan steht ein leerer Goldkäfig zum Prunk, aber hüte dich, daß du den Vogel nicht aus seinem schlechten Käfig herausnimmst und in den prächtigen tust, sonst möchte es dir schlimm ergehen.« Nach diesen Worten streckte der Fuchs wieder seinen Schwanz aus, und der Königssohn setzte sich auf; da ging's über Stock und Stein, daß die Haare im Winde pfiffen. Als er bei dem Schloß angelangt war, fand er alles so, wie der Fuchs gesagt hatte. Der Königssohn kam in die Kammer, wo der goldene Vogel in einem hölzernen Käfig saß, und ein goldener stand daneben; die drei goldenen Äpfel aber lagen in der Stube umher. Da dachte er, es wäre lächerlich, wenn er den schönen Vogel in dem gemeinen und häßlichen Käfig lassen wollte, öffnete die Türe, packte ihn und setzte ihn in den goldenen. In dem Augenblick aber tat der Vogel einen durchdringenden Schrei. Die Soldaten erwachten, stürzten herein und führten ihn ins Gefängnis. Den andern Morgen wurde er vor ein Gericht gestellt und, da er alles bekannte, zum Tode verurteilt. Doch sagte der

brother was standing at the window of the one from which a joyous noise was issuing, and called to him. He couldn't resist, went in, and lived only for his pleasures.

Another while went by, and then the youngest son wanted to set out and test his luck, but his father wouldn't allow it. "It's no use," he said; "he's even less likely to find the golden bird than his brothers were, and if he meets with a misfortune, he'll be helpless; he's not too bright." But finally, when the lad gave him no peace, he let him go. Once again the fox was sitting just outside the forest; he pleaded for his life and offered the good advice. The young man was good-natured and said: "Be calm, little fox, I won't hurt you." "You won't be sorry," the fox replied, "and, in order to travel more quickly, climb onto my tail." No sooner had the youth sat down on it than the fox began to run; they dashed over stocks and stones, the lad's hair whistling in the wind. When they reached the village, the young man got off, followed the good advice, and, without looking around, entered the humble inn, where he spent the night peacefully. When he stepped out into the countryside the following morning, the fox was already sitting there, and said: "I'll give you further instructions on what to do. Keep going straight ahead; eventually you'll reach a palace in front of which a whole troop of soldiers will be lying; but don't worry about them, because they'll all be sleeping and snoring; pass right among them and directly into the palace, and go through all the rooms; you'll finally reach a chamber in which a golden bird is hanging in a wooden cage. Right next to it there's an empty golden cage just for show, but take care not to remove the bird from its plain cage and put it in the flashy one, or else things may go badly with you." After saying this, the fox extended his tail again, and the prince sat down on it; then they dashed over stocks and stones, the lad's hair whistling in the wind. When he reached the palace, he found that everything was as the fox had described. The prince entered the chamber in which the golden bird sat in a wooden cage, with a golden one beside it; and the three golden apples were lying here and there in the room. Then he thought it would be ridiculous to let the beautiful bird remain in the cheap, ugly cage; he opened the door, seized it, and put it in the golden one. But at that moment the bird uttered a piercing cry. The soldiers awoke, dashed in, and led him off to jail. The next morning he was brought before the court and, since he confessed to everything, he was

König, er wollte ihm unter einer Bedingung das Leben schenken, wenn er ihm nämlich das goldene Pferd brächte, welches noch schneller liefe als der Wind, und dann sollte er obendrein zur Belohnung den goldenen Vogel erhalten.

Der Königssohn machte sich auf den Weg, seufzte aber und war traurig, denn wo sollte er das goldene Pferd finden? Da sah er auf einmal seinen alten Freund, den Fuchs, an dem Wege sitzen. »Siehst du«, sprach der Fuchs, »so ist es gekommen, weil du mir nicht gehört hast. Doch sei gutes Mutes, ich will mich deiner annehmen und dir sagen, wie du zu dem goldenen Pferd gelangst. Du mußt geradesweges fortgehen, so wirst du zu einem Schloß kommen, wo das Pferd im Stalle steht. Vor dem Stall werden die Stallknechte liegen, aber sie werden schlafen und schnarchen, und du kannst geruhig das goldene Pferd herausführen. Aber eins mußt du in acht nehmen, leg ihm den schlechten Sattel von Holz und Leder auf und ja nicht den goldenen, der dabeihängt, sonst wird es dir schlimm ergehen.« Dann streckte der Fuchs seinen Schwanz aus, der Königssohn setzte sich auf, und es ging fort über Stock und Stein, daß die Haare im Winde pfiffen. Alles traf so ein, wie der Fuchs gesagt hatte, er kam in den Stall, wo das goldene Pferd stand; als er ihm aber den schlechten Sattel auflegen wollte, so dachte er: »Ein so schönes Tier wird verschändet, wenn ich ihm nicht den guten Sattel auflege, der ihm gebührt.« Kaum aber berührte der goldene Sattel das Pferd, so fing es an, laut zu wiehern. Die Stallknechte erwachten, ergriffen den Jüngling und warfen ihn ins Gefängnis. Am andern Morgen wurde er vom Gerichte zum Tode verurteilt, doch versprach ihm der König, das Leben zu schenken und dazu das goldene Pferd, wenn er die schöne Königstochter vom goldenen Schlosse herbeischaffen könnte.

Mit schwerem Herzen machte sich der Jüngling auf den Weg, doch zu seinem Glücke fand er bald den treuen Fuchs. »Ich sollte dich nur deinem Unglück überlassen«, sagte der Fuchs, »aber ich habe Mitleiden mit dir und will dir noch einmal aus deiner Not helfen. Dein Weg führt dich gerade zu dem goldenen Schlosse: abends wirst du anlangen und nachts, wenn alles still ist, dann geht die schöne Königstochter ins Badehaus, um da zu baden. Und wenn sie hineingeht, so spring auf sie zu und gib ihr einen Kuß, dann folgt sie dir, und du kannst sie mit dir fortführen: nur dulde nicht, daß sie vorher von ihren Eltern Abschied nimmt, sonst kann es dir schlimm ergehen.« Dann streckte der Fuchs seinen Schwanz, der Königssohn setzte sich auf, und so ging es über Stock und Stein, daß die Haare im Winde pfiffen. Als er beim goldenen Schloß ankam, war es so, wie der

sentenced to death. But the king said he would spare his life on one condition: if he brought him the golden horse that ran even more swiftly than the wind; if he did that, he would receive the golden bird as a reward, besides.

The prince set out, but sighing and sadly, for where was he to find the golden horse? Then he suddenly saw his old friend, the fox, sitting by the roadside. "See?" said the fox; "it turned out this way because you didn't listen to me. But buck up, I'll look after you, and I'll tell you how to get to the golden horse. You must continue going straight ahead, and you'll reach a palace where the horse is in the stable. In front of the stable the grooms will be lying, but they'll be sleeping and snoring, and you can lead out the golden horse without fretting. But you must be careful of one thing: put the simple wood-and-leather saddle on it, and not the golden one that's hanging next to it, or else things will go badly for you." Then the fox extended his tail, the prince sat down on it, and they dashed over stocks and stones, the lad's hair whistling in the wind. Everything was just as the fox had said; he arrived at the stable in which the golden horse was kept; but as he was about to put the plain saddle on it, he thought: "A beautiful beast like this one will be dishonored if I don't fit it out with the good saddle that it deserves." But scarcely had the golden saddle touched the horse when it began neighing loudly. The grooms awoke, seized the young man, and threw him in jail. The next morning he was tried and sentenced to death, but the king promised to spare his life and make him a present of the golden horse if he could bring him the beautiful princess from the golden palace.

Heavy at heart, the young man set out, but, to his good fortune, he soon found the faithful fox. "I really ought to abandon you to your bad luck," the fox said, "but I feel sorry for you, and I'm willing to help you out of your trouble again. Your path will lead you straight to the golden palace: you'll get there in the evening, and at night, when all is quiet, the beautiful princess will go to the bathhouse to bathe. When she enters it, run over to her and give her a kiss; then she'll follow you, and you can lead her away with you: only, don't allow her to say good-bye to her parents first, or else things can go badly for you." Then the fox extended his tail, the prince sat down on it, and they dashed over stocks and stones, the lad's hair whistling in the wind. When he arrived at the golden palace, it was just as the fox had

Fuchs gesagt hatte. Er wartete bis um Mitternacht, als alles in tiefem Schlaf lag und die schöne Jungfrau ins Badehaus ging, da sprang er hervor und gab ihr einen Kuß. Sie sagte, sie wollte gerne mit ihm gehen, bat ihn aber flehentlich und mit Tränen, er möchte ihr erlauben, vorher von ihren Eltern Abschied zu nehmen. Er widerstand anfänglich ihren Bitten, als sie aber immer mehr weinte und ihm zu Fuß fiel, so gab er endlich nach. Kaum aber war die Jungfrau zu dem Bette ihres Vaters getreten, so wachte er und alle anderen, die im Schloß waren, auf, und der Jüngling ward festgehalten und ins Gefängnis gesetzt.

Am andern Morgen sprach der König zu ihm: »Dein Leben ist verwirkt, und du kannst bloß Gnade finden, wenn du den Berg abträgst, der vor meinen Fenstern liegt und über welchen ich nicht hinaussehen kann, und das mußt du binnen acht Tagen zustande bringen. Gelingt dir das, so sollst du meine Tochter zur Belohnung haben.« Der Königssohn fing an, grub und schaufelte, ohne abzulassen, als er aber nach sieben Tagen sah, wie wenig er ausgerichtet hatte und alle seine Arbeit so gut wie nichts war, so fiel er in große Traurigkeit und gab alle Hoffnung auf. Am Abend des siebenten Tags aber erschien der Fuchs und sagte: »Du verdienst nicht, daß ich mich deiner annehme, aber geh nur hin und lege dich schlafen, ich will die Arbeit für dich tun.« Am andern Morgen, als er erwachte und zum Fenster hinaussah, so war der Berg verschwunden. Der Jüngling eilte voll Freude zum König und meldete ihm, daß die Bedingung erfüllt wäre, und der König mochte wollen oder nicht, er mußte Wort halten und ihm seine Tochter geben.

Nun zogen die beiden zusammen fort, und es währte nicht lange, so kam der treue Fuchs zu ihnen. »Das Beste hast du zwar«, sagte er, »aber zu der Jungfrau aus dem goldenen Schloß gehört auch das goldene Pferd.« »Wie soll ich das bekommen?« fragte der Jüngling. »Das will ich dir sagen«, antwortete der Fuchs, »zuerst bring dem Könige, der dich nach dem goldenen Schlosse geschickt hat, die schöne Jungfrau. Da wird unerhörte Freude sein, sie werden dir das goldene Pferd gerne geben und werden dir's vorführen. Setz dich alsbald auf und reiche allen zum Abschied die Hand herab, zuletzt der schönen Jungfrau, und wenn du sie gefaßt hast, so zieh sie mit einem Schwung hinauf und jage davon: und niemand ist imstande, dich einzuholen, denn das Pferd läuft schneller als der Wind.«

Alles wurde glücklich vollbracht, und der Königssohn führte die schöne Jungfrau auf dem goldenen Pferde fort. Der Fuchs blieb nicht

described. He waited till midnight, when everyone was fast asleep, and the beautiful maiden went to the bathhouse; then he jumped out of hiding and gave her a kiss. She said she would gladly go with him, but she begged him with tears and sobs to allow her to say good-bye to her parents before leaving. At first he resisted her tears, but when she cried harder and harder, and knelt down before him, he finally gave in. But scarcely had the maiden walked over to her father's bed when he and everyone else in the palace woke up, and the young man was arrested and put in jail.

The following morning, the king said to him: "You have forfeited your life, and the only way you can find mercy is to remove the mountain that's in front of my windows, obstructing my view; and you must complete the task within eight days. If you're successful, you shall have my daughter as a reward." The prince began; he dug and shoveled without letup; but after seven days, when he saw how little he had accomplished, all his work amounting to almost nothing, he became despondent and gave up all hope. On the evening of the seventh day, however, the fox appeared and said: "You don't deserve my taking you in hand, but just go lie down and sleep; I'll do the work for you." The next morning when he awoke and looked out the window, the mountain had disappeared. Overjoyed, the young man hastened to the king and reported that he had met his terms; and, whether he wanted to or not, the king had to keep his word and give him his daughter.

Now the two set out together, and before very long the faithful fox came to them. "Yes, you now have the best thing of all, but the golden horse belongs with the maiden from the golden palace." "How am I to acquire it?" the young man asked. "I'll tell you," replied the fox; "first, take the beautiful maiden to the king who sent you to the golden palace. They'll be deliriously happy, and they'll gladly give you the golden horse and will lead it out to you. Mount it immediately and, as you take your leave, give your hand to everyone, leaving the beautiful maiden for last; once you've got hold of her, pull her up with one tug and ride away fast: no one will be able to overtake you because the horse runs more swiftly than the wind."

All this was successfully accomplished, and the prince led the beautiful maiden away on the golden horse. The fox didn't

zurück und sprach zu dem Jüngling: »Jetzt will ich dir auch zu dem goldenen Vogel verhelfen. Wenn du nahe bei dem Schlosse bist, wo sich der Vogel befindet, so laß die Jungfrau absitzen, und ich will sie in meine Obhut nehmen. Dann reit mit dem goldenen Pferd in den Schloßhof: bei dem Anblick wird große Freude sein, und sie werden dir den goldenen Vogel herausbringen. Wie du den Käfig in der Hand hast, so jage zu uns zurück und hole dir die Jungfrau wieder ab.« Als der Anschlag geglückt war und der Königssohn mit seinen Schätzen heimreiten wollte, so sagte der Fuchs: »Nun sollst du mich für meinen Beistand belohnen.« »Was verlangst du dafür?« fragte der Jüngling. »Wenn wir dort in den Wald kommen, so schieß mich tot und hau mir Kopf und Pfoten ab.« »Das wäre eine schöne Dankbarkeit«, sagte der Königssohn, »das kann ich dir unmöglich gewähren.« Sprach der Fuchs: »Wenn du es nicht tun willst, so muß ich dich verlassen; ehe ich aber fortgehe, will ich dir noch einen guten Rat geben. Vor zwei Stücken hüte dich, kauf kein Galgenfleisch und setze dich an keinen Brunnenrand.« Damit lief er in den Wald.

Der Jüngling dachte: »Das ist ein wunderliches Tier, das seltsame Grillen hat. Wer wird Galgenfleisch kaufen! Und die Lust, mich an einen Brunnenrand zu setzen, ist mir noch niemals gekommen.« Er ritt mit der schönen Jungfrau weiter, und sein Weg führte ihn wieder durch das Dorf, in welchem seine beiden Brüder geblieben waren. Da war großer Auflauf und Lärmen, und als er fragte, was da vor wäre, hieß es, es sollten zwei Leute aufgehängt werden. Als er näher hinzukam, sah er, daß es seine Brüder waren, die allerhand schlimme Streiche verübt und all ihr Gut vertan hatten. Er fragte, ob sie nicht könnten freigemacht werden. »Wenn Ihr für sie bezahlen wollt«, antworteten die Leute, »aber was wollt Ihr an die schlechten Menschen Euer Geld hängen und sie loskaufen.« Er besann sich aber nicht, zahlte für sie, und als sie freigegeben waren, so setzten sie die Reise gemeinschaftlich fort.

Sie kamen in den Wald, wo ihnen der Fuchs zuerst begegnet war, und da es darin kühl und lieblich war und die Sonne heiß brannte, so sagten die beiden Brüder: »Laßt uns hier an dem Brunnen ein wenig ausruhen, essen und trinken.« Er willigte ein, und während des Gesprächs vergaß er sich, setzte sich an den Brunnenrand und versah sich nichts Arges. Aber die beiden Brüder warfen ihn rückwärts in den Brunnen, nahmen die Jungfrau, das Pferd und den Vogel und zogen heim zu ihrem Vater. »Da bringen wir nicht bloß den goldenen

remain behind; he said to the young man: "Now I'll also help you get the golden bird. When you're close to the palace where the bird is kept, let the maiden dismount, and I'll keep watch over her. Then ride the golden horse into the palace courtyard: at the sight of it everyone will be very happy, and they'll bring out the golden bird for you. As soon as you have the cage in your hand, dash back to us and fetch the maiden again." When the plan had worked out well, and the prince was about to ride home with his treasures, the fox said: "Now you must reward me for my assistance." "What do you want for it?" the young man asked. "When we reach the forest there, shoot me and cut off my head and paws." "That would really be showing my gratitude!" said the prince; "I can't possibly grant that request." The fox said: "If you won't do it, I must leave you; but before I go, I'll give you one more piece of advice. Be on your guard against two things: don't buy any gallows bait, and don't sit down on the rim of any well." Having said that, he ran into the forest.

The young man thought: "He's a peculiar animal, with odd fancies. Who's going to buy gallows bait? And the urge to sit down on the rim of a well is one that's never come over me yet." He continued riding with the beautiful maiden, and his path took him once more through the village in which his two brothers had remained. A big, noisy crowd was gathered there, and when he asked what was going on, he was told that two people were to be hanged. When he got closer, he saw that they were his brothers, who had committed all sorts of offenses, and had lost all their possessions. He asked whether there was any way to release them. "If you're willing to pay what they owe," the people replied, "but why would you want to throw out your money to ransom such good-for-nothings?" Yet, he didn't hesitate for a moment; he paid their debts, and when they were released, they all continued their journey together.

They arrived at the forest where the fox had first met them, and since it was cool and refreshing there on that hot, sunny day, the two brothers said: "Let's rest a little by the well, and have something to eat and drink." He agreed, and during their conversation he forgot what he had been told; he sat down on the rim of the well, suspecting nothing wrong. But his two brothers threw him backwards into the well, took the maiden, the horse, and the bird, and headed home to their father. "We're not only

Vogel«, sagten sie, »wir haben auch das goldene Pferd und die Jungfrau von dem goldenen Schlosse erbeutet.« Da war große Freude, aber das Pferd, das fraß nicht, der Vogel, der pfiff nicht, und die Jungfrau, die saß und weinte.

Der jüngste Bruder war aber nicht umgekommen. Der Brunnen war zum Glück trocken, und er fiel auf weiches Moos, ohne Schaden zu nehmen, konnte aber nicht wieder heraus. Auch in dieser Not verließ ihn der treue Fuchs nicht, kam zu ihm herabgesprungen und schalt ihn, daß er seinen Rat vergessen hätte. »Ich kann's aber doch nicht lassen«, sagte er, »ich will dir wieder an das Tageslicht helfen.« Er sagte ihm, er sollte seinen Schwanz anpacken und sich fest daran halten, und zog ihn dann in die Höhe. »Noch bist du nicht aus aller Gefahr«, sagte der Fuchs, »deine Brüder waren deines Todes nicht gewiß und haben den Wald mit Wächtern umstellt, die sollen dich töten, wenn du dich sehen ließest.« Da saß ein armer Mann am Weg, mit dem vertauschte der Jüngling die Kleider und gelangte auf diese Weise an des Königs Hof. Niemand erkannte ihn, aber der Vogel fing an zu pfeifen, das Pferd fing an zu fressen, und die schöne Jungfrau hörte Weinens auf. Der König fragte verwundert: »Was hat das zu bedeuten?« Da sprach die Jungfrau: »Ich weiß es nicht, aber ich war so traurig, und nun bin ich so fröhlich. Es ist mir, als wäre mein rechter Bräutigam gekommen.« Sie erzählte ihm alles, was geschehen war, obgleich die andern Brüder ihr den Tod angedroht hatten, wenn sie etwas verraten würde. Der König hieß alle Leute vor sich bringen, die in seinem Schloß waren, da kam auch der Jüngling als ein armer Mann in seinen Lumpenkleidern, aber die Jungfrau erkannte ihn gleich und fiel ihm um den Hals. Die gottlosen Brüder wurden ergriffen und hingerichtet, er aber ward mit der schönen Jungfrau vermählt und zum Erben des Königs bestimmt.

Aber wie ist es dem armen Fuchs ergangen? Lange danach ging der Königssohn einmal wieder in den Wald, da begegnete ihm der Fuchs und sagte: »Du hast nun alles, was du dir wünschen kannst, aber mit meinem Unglück will es kein Ende nehmen, und es steht doch in deiner Macht, mich zu erlösen«, und abermals bat er flehentlich, er möchte ihn totschießen und ihm Kopf und Pfoten abhauen. Also tat er's, und kaum war es geschehen, so verwandelte sich der Fuchs in einen Menschen und war niemand anders als der Bruder der schönen Königstochter, der endlich von dem Zauber, der auf ihm lag, erlöst war. Und nun fehlte nichts mehr zu ihrem Glück, solange sie lebten.

bringing the golden bird," they said, "we've also captured the golden horse and the maiden from the golden palace." The people were overjoyed, but the horse wouldn't eat, the bird wouldn't whistle, and the maiden sat and wept.

The youngest brother hadn't been killed, however. Luckily, the well was dry and he fell onto soft moss and was unharmed; but he couldn't get out. In this emergency, too, the faithful fox didn't abandon him; he came dashing by, and scolded him for forgetting his advice. "But I can't just let things go," he said; "I'll help you up to the daylight again." He told him to grab his tail and hold onto it tight; then he pulled him up. "You're not completely out of danger yet," said the fox; "your brothers weren't sure you were dead, and they've posted guards all around the forest with orders to kill you if you show your face." A poor man was sitting by the road; the young man exchanged clothes with him, and in that fashion he reached the king's court. No one recognized him, but the bird began to whistle, the horse began to eat, and the beautiful maiden ceased weeping. The king asked in astonishment: "What does this mean?" Then the maiden said: "I don't know, but I was so sad, and now I'm so happy. I feel as if my true bridegroom had come." She told him everything that had occurred, even though the other brothers had threatened her with death if she revealed anything. The king had everyone in his palace brought before him; the youth came, too, as a poor man in his ragged clothes, but the maiden recognized him at once and hugged him. The wicked brothers were seized and executed, whereas the youth was married to the maiden and was named the king's heir.

But what became of the poor fox? A long time afterward, the prince entered the forest again; there he met the fox, who said: "You now have everything you could wish for, but there's no end in sight for my unhappiness, even though you have the power to deliver me"; and once again he begged him tearfully to shoot him and cut off his head and paws. So he did it, and scarcely was it done when the fox turned into a man, who was none other than the beautiful princess's brother, finally released from the spell he had been under. And now nothing else was needed to make them all happy for the rest of their lives.

Allerleirauh

Es war einmal ein König, der hatte eine Frau mit goldenen Haaren, und sie war so schön, daß sich ihresgleichen nicht mehr auf Erden fand. Es geschah, daß sie krank lag, und als sie fühlte, daß sie bald sterben würde, rief sie den König und sprach:»Wenn du nach meinem Tode dich wieder vermählen willst, so nimm keine, die nicht ebenso schön ist, als ich bin, und die nicht solche goldene Haare hat, wie ich habe; das mußt du mir versprechen.« Nachdem es ihr der König versprochen hatte, tat sie die Augen zu und starb.

Der König war lange Zeit nicht zu trösten und dachte nicht daran, eine zweite Frau zu nehmen. Endlich sprachen seine Räte:»Es geht nicht anders, der König muß sich wieder vermählen, damit wir eine Königin haben.« Nun wurden Boten weit und breit umhergeschickt, eine Braut zu suchen, die an Schönheit der verstorbenen Königin ganz gleich käme. Es war aber keine in der ganzen Welt zu finden, und wenn man sie auch gefunden hätte, so war doch keine da, die solche goldene Haare gehabt hätte. Also kamen die Boten unverrichteter Sache wieder heim.

Nun hatte der König eine Tochter, die war geradeso schön wie ihre verstorbene Mutter, und hatte auch solche goldene Haare. Als sie herangewachsen war, sah sie der König einmal an und sah, daß sie in allem seiner verstorbenen Gemahlin ähnlich war, und fühlte plötzlich eine heftige Liebe zu ihr. Da sprach er zu seinen Räten:»Ich will meine Tochter heiraten, denn sie ist das Ebenbild meiner verstorbenen Frau, und sonst kann ich doch keine Braut finden, die ihr gleicht.« Als die Räte das hörten, erschraken sie und sprachen:»Gott hat verboten, daß der Vater seine Tochter heirate, aus der Sünde kann nichts Gutes entspringen, und das Reich wird mit ins Verderben gezogen.« Die Tochter erschrak noch mehr, als sie den Entschluß ihres Vaters vernahm, hoffte aber, ihn von seinem Vorhaben noch abzubringen. Da sagte sie zu ihm:»Eh ich Euren Wunsch erfülle, muß ich erst drei Kleider haben, eins so golden wie die Sonne, eins so silbern wie der Mond und eins so glänzend wie die Sterne; ferner verlange ich einen Mantel, von tausenderlei Pelz und Rauhwerk zusammengesetzt, und ein jedes Tier in Euerm Reich muß ein Stück von seiner Haut dazugeben.« Sie dachte aber:»Das anzuschaffen ist ganz unmöglich, und ich bringe damit meinen Vater von seinen bösen Gedanken ab.« Der König ließ aber nicht ab, und die geschicktesten Jungfrauen in seinem Reiche mußten die drei Kleider weben, eins so

All-Kinds-of-Fur [Catskin; Cap o' Rushes]

There was once a king who had a wife with golden hair, and she was so beautiful that there was no one else like her in the world. It came about that she fell ill, and when she felt that she would soon die, she sent for the king and said: "If you ever marry again after my death, don't take any woman who isn't exactly as beautiful as I am and doesn't have hair as golden as mine; you must promise me that." After she had received that promise from the king, she closed her eyes and died.

For some time the king was not to be consoled, and had no thought of taking another wife. Finally the members of his council said: "Nothing else will do; the king must marry again, so that we have a queen." Now messengers were sent out far and wide to seek a bride who would equal the late queen in beauty. But none was to be found in the whole world, and even if one had been found, she wouldn't have had the same golden hair. And so the messengers returned home, their mission unaccomplished.

Now, the king had a daughter who was just as beautiful as her late mother, and also had the same golden hair. Once, when she grew up, the king looked at her and saw that she was similar to his late wife in every way, and he suddenly conceived a violent love for her. Then he said to his council: "I want to marry my daughter, for she's the image of my late wife; otherwise, I'll never find a bride who resembles her." When the members of the council heard that, they were alarmed and said: "God has forbidden fathers to marry their daughters; nothing good can come of sin, and the kingdom will become involved in your family's ruin." His daughter was even more alarmed when she learned of her father's decision, but she hoped she could still talk him out of his plan. So she said to him: "Before I grant your wish, I must have three gowns, one as golden as the sun, one as silvery as the moon, and one as bright as the stars; in addition I demand a cloak sewn together from a thousand different pelts and furs, and every animal in your kingdom must contribute a piece of its hide." She thought: "It's totally impossible to procure all that, and in this way I'll make my father give up his wicked ideas." But the king persisted, and the most skillful maidens in his kingdom were compelled to weave the three gowns, one as golden as the sun, one as

golden wie die Sonne, eins so silbern wie der Mond und eins so glänzend wie die Sterne; und seine Jäger mußten alle Tiere im ganzen Reiche auffangen und ihnen ein Stück von ihrer Haut abziehen; daraus ward ein Mantel von tausenderlei Rauhwerk gemacht. Endlich, als alles fertig war, ließ der König den Mantel herbeiholen, breitete ihn vor ihr aus und sprach:»Morgen soll die Hochzeit sein.«

Als nun die Königstochter sah, daß keine Hoffnung mehr war, ihres Vaters Herz umzuwenden, so faßte sie den Entschluß, zu entfliehen. In der Nacht, während alles schlief, stand sie auf und nahm von ihren Kostbarkeiten dreierlei, einen goldenen Ring, ein goldenes Spinnrädchen und ein goldenes Haspelchen; die drei Kleider von Sonne, Mond und Sternen tat sie in eine Nußschale, zog den Mantel von allerlei Rauhwerk an und machte sich Gesicht und Hände mit Ruß schwarz. Dann befahl sie sich Gott und ging fort, und ging die ganze Nacht, bis sie in einen großen Wald kam. Und weil sie müde war, setzte sie sich in einen hohlen Baum und schlief ein.

Die Sonne ging auf, und sie schlief fort und schlief noch immer, als es schon hoher Tag war. Da trug es sich zu, daß der König, dem dieser Wald gehörte, darin jagte. Als seine Hunde zu dem Baum kamen, schnupperten sie, liefen ringsherum und bellten. Sprach der König zu den Jägern:»Seht doch, was dort für ein Wild sich versteckt hat.« Die Jäger folgten dem Befehl, und als sie wiederkamen, sprachen sie:»In dem hohlen Baum liegt ein wunderliches Tier, wie wir noch niemals eins gesehen haben: an seiner Haut ist tausenderlei Pelz; es liegt aber und schläft.« Sprach der König:»Seht zu, ob ihr's lebendig fangen könnt, dann bindet's auf den Wagen und nehmt's mit.« Als die Jäger das Mädchen anfaßten, erwachte es voll Schrecken und rief ihnen zu:»Ich bin ein armes Kind, von Vater und Mutter verlassen, erbarmt euch mein und nehmt mich mit.« Da sprachen sie:»*Allerleirauh*, du bist gut für die Küche, komm nur mit, da kannst du die Asche zusammenkehren.« Also setzten sie es auf den Wagen und fuhren heim in das königliche Schloß. Dort wiesen sie ihm ein Ställchen an unter der Treppe, wo kein Tageslicht hinkam, und sagten:»Rauhtierchen, da kannst du wohnen und schlafen.« Dann ward es in die Küche geschickt, da trug es Holz und Wasser, schürte das Feuer, rupfte das Federvieh, belas das Gemüs, kehrte die Asche und tat alle schlechte Arbeit.

Da lebte Allerleirauh lange Zeit recht armselig. Ach, du schöne Königstochter, wie soll's mit dir noch werden! Es geschah aber einmal, daß ein Fest im Schloß gefeiert ward, da sprach sie zum Koch:»Darf ich ein wenig hinaufgehen und zusehen? Ich will mich außen

silvery as the moon, and one as bright as the stars; and his huntsmen were compelled to catch all the animals in the whole kingdom and strip off a piece of their hide; from these pieces was
made a cloak of a thousand kinds of fur. Finally, when everything
was ready, the king sent for the cloak, spread it out in front of her,
and said: "The wedding is tomorrow."

When the princess now saw that there was no more hope of
changing her father's decision, she resolved to run away. At
night, while everyone was asleep, she got up and took three objects from among her treasures, a gold ring, a miniature gold
spinning wheel, and a miniature gold spinning reel; the three
gowns of sun, moon, and stars she placed inside a nutshell; she
put on the cloak of all kinds of fur, and blackened her face and
hands with soot. Then she commended herself to God and departed, walking all night until she came to a great forest. And because she was tired, she sat down in a hollow tree and fell asleep.

The sun rose, but she slept on, and she was still asleep when it
was already broad daylight. Then it came to pass that the king to
whom that forest belonged went hunting in it. When his hounds
reached that tree, they sniffed and ran around it, barking. The
king said to his huntsmen: "Go see what sort of game animal is
hiding there." The huntsmen obeyed his orders, and said upon
their return: "A peculiar animal is lying in the hollow tree, of a
type we've never seen before: there are a thousand different kinds
of fur on its hide; and it's lying there sleeping." The king said: "See
whether you can capture it alive; if so, tie it to the wagon and bring
it along." When the huntsmen seized the girl, she woke up in a
fright and shouted to them: "I'm a poor child, forsaken by my father and mother; have pity on me and take me along." Then they
said: "All-Kinds-of-Fur, you belong in the kitchen; come along,
and you can sweep together the ashes." And so they put her in the
wagon and drove home to the royal palace. There they assigned
her a tiny cubbyhole under the staircase, where no daylight pen-
etrated, and they said: "Little Furry Animal, you can live and
sleep here." Then she was sent to the kitchen, where she carried
firewood and water, stirred the fire, plucked the poultry, cleaned
the vegetables, swept the ashes, and did all the dirty work.

There All-Kinds-of-Fur lived in great poverty for a long time.
Oh, you beautiful princess, what's to become of you? But it once
came to pass that a party was being given in the palace, and she
said to the cook: "May I go upstairs and watch for a while? I'll

vor die Türe stellen.« Antwortete der Koch: »Ja, geh nur hin, aber in einer halben Stunde mußt du wieder hier sein und die Asche zusammentragen.« Da nahm sie ihr Öllämpchen, ging in ihr Ställchen, zog den Pelzrock aus und wusch sich den Ruß von dem Gesicht und den Händen ab, so daß ihre volle Schönheit wieder an den Tag kam. Dann machte sie die Nuß auf und holte ihr Kleid hervor, das wie die Sonne glänzte. Und wie das geschehen war, ging sie hinauf zum Fest, und alle traten ihr aus dem Weg, denn niemand kannte sie, und meinten nicht anders, als daß es eine Königstochter wäre. Der König aber kam ihr entgegen, reichte ihr die Hand und tanzte mit ihr und dachte in seinem Herzen: »So schön haben meine Augen noch keine gesehen.« Als der Tanz zu Ende war, verneigte sie sich, und wie sich der König umsah, war sie verschwunden, und niemand wußte wohin. Die Wächter, die vor dem Schlosse standen, wurden gerufen und ausgefragt, aber niemand hatte sie erblickt.

Sie war aber in ihr Ställchen gelaufen, hatte geschwind ihr Kleid ausgezogen, Gesicht und Hände schwarz gemacht und den Pelzmantel umgetan und war wieder Allerleirauh. Als sie nun in die Küche kam und an ihre Arbeit gehen und die Asche zusammenkehren wollte, sprach der Koch: »Laß das gut sein bis morgen und koche mir da die Suppe für den König, ich will auch einmal ein bißchen oben zugucken; aber laß mir kein Haar hineinfallen, sonst kriegst du in Zukunft nichts mehr zu essen.« Da ging der Koch fort, und Allerleirauh kochte die Suppe für den König und kochte eine Brotsuppe, so gut es konnte, und wie sie fertig war, holte es in dem Ställchen seinen goldenen Ring und legte ihn in die Schüssel, in welche die Suppe angerichtet ward. Als der Tanz zu Ende war, ließ sich der König die Suppe bringen und aß sie, und sie schmeckte ihm so gut, daß er meinte, niemals eine bessere Suppe gegessen zu haben. Wie er aber auf den Grund kam, sah er da einen goldenen Ring liegen und konnte nicht begreifen, wie er dahin geraten war. Da befahl er, der Koch sollte vor ihn kommen. Der Koch erschrak, wie er den Befehl hörte, und sprach zu Allerleirauh: »Gewiß hast du ein Haar in die Suppe fallen lassen; wenn's wahr ist, so kriegst du Schläge.« Als er vor den König kam, fragte dieser, wer die Suppe gekocht hätte. Antwortete der Koch: »Ich habe sie gekocht.« Der König aber sprach: »Das ist nicht wahr, denn sie war auf andere Art und viel besser gekocht als sonst.« Antwortete er: »Ich muß es gestehen, daß ich sie nicht gekocht habe, sondern das Rauhtierchen.« Sprach der König: »Geh und laß es heraufkommen.«

Als Allerleirauh kam, fragte der König: »Wer bist du?« »Ich bin ein

stand outside the door." The cook replied: "Yes, go right ahead, but you must be back here in half an hour to sweep together the ashes." Then she took her oil lamp, entered her cubbyhole, took off the fur cloak, and washed the soot off her face and hands, so that her full beauty was once again displayed. Next, she opened the nut and took out the gown that shone like the sun. After doing that, she went upstairs to the party, and everyone stepped back to let her pass, because no one recognized her, and they were sure that she was a princess. But the king came to meet her, gave her his hand, and danced with her, thinking to himself: "My eyes have never beheld a woman this beautiful." When the dance was over, she made a curtsey, and when the king looked around she had disappeared, no one knew where. The guards standing in front of the palace were summoned and questioned, but none of them had caught sight of her.

She had run to her cubbyhole, had speedily taken off her gown, had blackened her face and hands, and had put on the fur cloak; she was once again All-Kinds-of-Fur. When she now returned to the kitchen, intending to do her work and sweep together the ashes, the cook said: "Let things be until tomorrow; instead, cook the soup for the king; I want to have a little look around upstairs, too; but make sure no hair falls into it, or in the future you won't get any more to eat." Then the cook left, and All-Kinds-of-Fur cooked the soup for the king, making the best bread soup she knew how to make; and when it was ready, she got her gold ring out of her cubbyhole and placed it in the bowl in which the soup was served. When the dance was over, the king sent for the soup and ate it; he found it so delicious that he thought he had never eaten a better soup. But when he reached the bottom of the bowl, he saw a gold ring there, and he couldn't understand how it had gotten there. Then he ordered the cook to appear before him. The cook was frightened when he heard the command, and said to All-Kinds-of-Fur: "I'm sure you let a hair fall into the soup; if it's true, you'll be beaten." When he arrived before the king, the king asked who had cooked the soup. The cook replied: "I cooked it." And the king said: "That's not so, because it was cooked in a different way, and much better than usual." He replied: "I must confess that I didn't cook it myself; Little Furry Animal did." The king said: "Go and have her come up."

When All-Kinds-of-Fur arrived, the king asked her: "Who are

armes Kind, das keinen Vater und Mutter mehr hat.« Fragte er
weiter: »Wozu bist du in meinem Schloß?« Antwortete es: »Ich bin zu
nichts gut, als daß mir die Stiefeln um den Kopf geworfen werden.«
Fragte er weiter: »Wo hast du den Ring her, der in der Suppe war?«
Antwortete es: »Von dem Ring weiß ich nichts.« Also konnte der
König nichts erfahren und mußte es wieder fortschicken.

Über eine Zeit war wieder ein Fest, da bat Allerleirauh den Koch
wie vorigesmal um Erlaubnis, zusehen zu dürfen. Antwortete er: »Ja,
aber komm in einer halben Stunde wieder und koch dem König die
Brotsuppe, die er so gerne ißt.« Da lief es in sein Ställchen, wusch sich
geschwind und nahm aus der Nuß das Kleid, das so silbern war wie
der Mond, und tat es an. Da ging sie hinauf und glich einer Königstochter; und der König trat ihr entgegen und freute sich, daß er sie
wiedersah, und weil eben der Tanz anhub, so tanzten sie zusammen.
Als aber der Tanz zu Ende war, verschwand sie wieder so schnell, daß
der König nicht bemerken konnte, wo sie hinging. Sie sprang aber in
ihr Ställchen und machte sich wieder zum Rauhtierchen und ging in
die Küche, die Brotsuppe zu kochen. Als der Koch oben war, holte es
das goldene Spinnrad und tat es in die Schüssel, so daß die Suppe
darüber angerichtet wurde. Danach ward sie dem König gebracht,
der aß sie, und sie schmeckte ihm so gut wie das vorigemal, und ließ
den Koch kommen, der mußte auch diesmal gestehen, daß Allerleirauh die Suppe gekocht hätte. Allerleirauh kam da wieder vor den
König, aber sie antwortete, daß sie nur dazu da wäre, daß ihr die
Stiefeln an den Kopf geworfen würden und daß sie von dem goldenen
Spinnrädchen gar nichts wüßte.

Als der König zum drittenmal ein Fest anstellte, da ging es nicht
anders als die vorigemale. Der Koch sprach zwar: »Du bist eine
Hexe, Rauhtierchen, und tust immer etwas in die Suppe, davon sie
so gut wird und dem König besser schmeckt, als was ich koche«;
doch weil es so bat, so ließ er es auf die bestimmte Zeit hingehen.
Nun zog es ein Kleid an, das wie die Sterne glänzte, und trat damit
in den Saal. Der König tanzte wieder mit der schönen Jungfrau
und meinte, daß sie noch niemals so schön gewesen wäre. Und
während er tanzte, steckte er ihr, ohne daß sie es merkte, einen
goldenen Ring an den Finger, und hatte befohlen, daß der Tanz
recht lang währen sollte. Wie er zu Ende war, wollte er sie an den
Händen festhalten, aber sie riß sich los und sprang so geschwind
unter die Leute, daß sie vor seinen Augen verschwand. Sie lief,
was sie konnte, in ihr Ställchen unter der Treppe, weil sie aber zu
lange und über eine halbe Stunde geblieben war, so konnte sie das

you?" "I'm a poor child who no longer has any father or mother."
He then asked: "For what purpose are you in my palace?" "The
only thing I'm good for is to have boots thrown at my head." He
then asked: "Where did you get the ring that was in the soup?"
She replied: "I don't know anything about a ring." And so the king
was unable to learn anything, and he had to send her away again.

Some time later there was another party, and All-Kinds-of-Fur
asked the cook, like the last time, for permission to watch. He
replied: "Yes, but come back in half an hour and cook bread soup
for the king, he likes it so much." Then she ran to her cubbyhole,
washed herself quickly, took out of the nut the gown that was as silvery as the moon, and put it on. Then she went upstairs, looking
like a princess, and the king came to meet her, happy to see her
again; and because the dance was just beginning, they danced together. But when the dance was over, once again she vanished so
quickly that the king was unable to observe where she went. She
dashed to her cubbyhole, turned herself into the little furry animal
again, and went to the kitchen to cook the bread soup. While the
cook was upstairs, she fetched the miniature gold spinning wheel
and placed it in the bowl, so that the soup was poured in over it.
Then it was brought to the king, who ate it; he liked it as much as
the previous time, and sent for the cook, who was compelled to
admit, this time, too, that All-Kinds-of-Fur had cooked the soup.
So All-Kinds-of-Fur appeared before the king again, but replied
that all she was good for was to have boots thrown at her head, and
that she knew nothing at all about the little gold spinning wheel.

When the king gave a party for the third time, things went exactly as they previously had. To be sure, the cook said: "You're a
witch, Little Furry Animal, and you always put something in the
soup to make it taste so good, and the king likes it better than
what I cook"; but because she begged so hard, he let her go upstairs with a deadline for returning. Now she put on the gown
that was as bright as the stars, and she entered the ballroom with
it. Again the king danced with the beautiful maiden, thinking she
had never looked so lovely before. And while he was dancing,
without her knowledge he placed a gold ring on her finger; he
had given orders to make that dance a very long one. When it was
over, he tried to hold her hands tightly, but she tore herself away
and dashed through the midst of the guests so rapidly that she
disappeared before his eyes. She ran as fast as she could to her
cubbyhole beneath the stairs, but because she had remained

schöne Kleid nicht ausziehen, sondern warf nur den Mantel von
Pelz darüber, und in der Eile machte sie sich auch nicht ganz
rußig, sondern ein Finger blieb weiß. Allerleirauh lief nun in die
Küche, kochte dem König die Brotsuppe und legte, wie der Koch
fort war, den goldenen Haspel hinein. Der König, als er den
Haspel auf dem Grunde fand, ließ Allerleirauh rufen; da erblickte
er den weißen Finger und sah den Ring, den er im Tanze ihr
angesteckt hatte. Da ergriff er sie an der Hand und hielt sie fest,
und als sie sich losmachen und fortspringen wollte, tat sich der
Pelzmantel ein wenig auf, und das Sternenkleid schimmerte hervor. Der König faßte den Mantel und riß ihn ab. Da kamen die
goldenen Haare hervor, und sie stand da in voller Pracht und
konnte sich nicht länger verbergen. Und als sie Ruß und Asche aus
ihrem Gesicht gewischt hatte, da war sie schöner, als man noch jemand auf Erden gesehen hat. Der König aber sprach: »Du bist
meine liebe Braut, und wir scheiden nimmermehr voneinander.«
Darauf ward die Hochzeit gefeiert, und sie lebten vergnügt bis an
ihren Tod.

Sechse kommen durch die ganze Welt

Es war einmal ein Mann, der verstand allerlei Künste; er diente im
Krieg und hielt sich brav und tapfer, aber als der Krieg zu Ende war,
bekam er den Abschied und drei Heller Zehrgeld auf den Weg.
»Wart«, sprach er, »das laß ich mir nicht gefallen, finde ich die
rechten Leute, so soll mir der König noch die Schätze des ganzen
Landes herausgeben.« Da ging er voll Zorn in den Wald und sah
einen darin stehen, der hatte sechs Bäume ausgerupft, als wären's
Kornhalme. Sprach er zu ihm: »Willst du mein Diener sein und mit
mir ziehen?« »Ja«, antwortete er, »aber erst will ich meiner Mutter
das Wellchen Holz heimbringen«, und nahm einen von den Bäumen
und wickelte ihn um die fünf andern, hob die Welle auf die Schulter
und trug sie fort. Dann kam er wieder und ging mit seinem Herrn,
der sprach: »Wir zwei sollten wohl durch die ganze Welt kommen.«
Und als sie ein Weilchen gegangen waren, fanden sie einen Jäger, der
lag auf den Knien, hatte die Büchse angelegt und zielte. Sprach der
Herr zu ihm: »Jäger, was willst du schießen?« Er antwortete: »Zwei
Meilen von hier sitzt eine Fliege auf dem Ast eines Eichbaums, der
will ich das linke Auge herausschießen.« »O geh mit mir«, sprach der

away too long, more than a half hour, she didn't have time to take off the beautiful gown, and she merely threw the fur cloak on top of it; and in her haste she didn't cover herself completely with soot, but left one finger white. Now All-Kinds-of-Fur ran into the kitchen, cooked the king's bread soup, and, once the cook was gone, placed the gold reel in it. When the king found the gold reel at the bottom of his bowl, he sent for All-Kinds-of-Fur; then he caught sight of her white finger and saw the ring he had slipped on her finger during the dance. Now he seized her hand and held it fast; when she tried to free herself and run away, her fur cloak opened slightly and the starry gown gleamed forth. The king seized her cloak and pulled it off. Then her golden hair was revealed, and she stood there in her full splendor, unable to conceal herself any longer. And when she had washed the soot and ashes off her face, she was more beautiful than any other woman yet seen on earth. And the king said: "You are my beloved bride, and we shall never part again." Then their wedding was celebrated, and they lived in contentment until they died.

Six Men Make Their Way in Life

There was once a man who was an expert in all sorts of skills; he served in the war, behaving loyally and bravely, and when the war was over he received his discharge and three pennies for his expenses on the way home. "Just wait," he said, "I won't put up with this; if I find the right associates, the king will some day hand over to me the treasures of the whole country." In his rage he entered the forest and saw standing there a man who had pulled up six trees as if they were stalks of grain. He said to him: "Would you like to be my servant and go wherever I go?" "Yes," he replied, "but first I want to bring this little bundle of firewood home to my mother"; and he took one of the trees and wrapped it around the other five, lifted the bundle onto his shoulder, and carried it away. Then he returned and set out with his master, who said: "The two of us surely ought to make our way in life." And after they had walked a short while, they came upon a hunter who was kneeling; he had leveled his rifle and was taking aim. The master said to him: "Hunter, what are you going to shoot at?" He replied: "Two miles from here a fly is sitting on the twig of an oak tree; I want to shoot out its left eye."

Mann, »wenn wir drei zusammen sind, sollten wir wohl durch die ganze Welt kommen.« Der Jäger war bereit und ging mit ihm, und sie kamen zu sieben Windmühlen, deren Flügel trieben ganz hastig herum, und ging doch links und rechts kein Wind und bewegte sich kein Blättchen. Da sprach der Mann: »Ich weiß nicht, was die Windmühlen treibt, es regt sich ja kein Lüftchen«, und ging mit seinen Dienern weiter, und als sie zwei Meilen fortgegangen waren, sahen sie einen auf einem Baum sitzen, der hielt das eine Nasenloch zu und blies aus dem andern. »Mein, was treibst du da oben?« fragte der Mann. Er antwortete: »Zwei Meilen von hier stehen sieben Windmühlen, seht, die blase ich an, daß sie laufen.« »O geh mit mir«, sprach der Mann, »wenn wir vier zusammen sind, sollten wir wohl durch die ganze Welt kommen.« Da stieg der Bläser herab und ging mit, und über eine Zeit sahen sie einen, der stand da auf einem Bein und hatte das andere abgeschnallt und neben sich gelegt. Da sprach der Herr: »Du hast dir's ja bequem gemacht zum Ausruhen.« »Ich bin ein Laufer«, antwortete er, »und damit ich nicht gar zu schnell springe, habe ich mir das eine Bein abgeschnallt; wenn ich mit zwei Beinen laufe, so geht's geschwinder, als ein Vogel fliegt.« »O geh mit mir, wenn wir fünf zusammen sind, sollten wir wohl durch die ganze Welt kommen.« Da ging er mit, und gar nicht lang, so begegneten sie einem, der hatte ein Hütchen auf, hatte es aber ganz auf dem einen Ohr sitzen. Da sprach der Herr zu ihm: »Manierlich, manierlich! Häng deinen Hut doch nicht auf ein Ohr, du siehst ja aus wie ein Hans Narr.« »Ich darf's nicht tun«, sprach der andere, »denn setz ich meinen Hut gerad, so kommt ein gewaltiger Frost, und die Vögel unter dem Himmel erfrieren und fallen tot zur Erde.« »O geh mit mir«, sprach der Herr, »wenn wir sechs zusammen sind, sollten wir wohl durch die ganze Welt kommen.«

Nun gingen die sechse in eine Stadt, wo der König hatte bekanntmachen lassen, wer mit seiner Tochter in die Wette laufen wollte und den Sieg davontrüge, der sollte ihr Gemahl werden; wer aber verlöre, müßte auch seinen Kopf hergeben. Da meldete sich der Mann und sprach: »Ich will aber meinen Diener für mich laufen lassen.« Der König antwortete: »Dann mußt du auch noch dessen Leben zum Pfand setzen, also daß sein und dein Kopf für den Sieg haften.« Als das verabredet und festgemacht war, schnallte der Mann dem Laufer das andere Bein an und sprach zu ihm: »Nun sei hurtig und hilf, daß wir siegen.« Es war aber bestimmt, daß wer am ersten Wasser aus einem weit abgelegenen Brunnen brächte, der sollte Sieger sein. Nun bekam der Laufer einen Krug, und die Königstochter auch einen, und

"Oh, come with me," the man said; "if the three of us stick together, we surely ought to make our way in life." The hunter was willing and went along, and they came to seven windmills, whose arms were turning quite rapidly, although no wind was blowing either to the left or right of it and not a leaf was stirring on the trees. Then the man said: "I don't know what's making the windmills turn; not even a breeze is blowing"; and he proceeded onward with his servants; and when they had walked two miles, they saw a man sitting in a tree, holding one of his nostrils closed and blowing out of the other. "Say, what are you doing up there?" asked the man. He replied: "Two miles from here there are seven windmills; you see, I'm blowing at them and making them work." "Oh, come with me," said the man; "if the four of us stick together, we surely ought to make our way in life." Then the blower climbed down and went along; and after a while they saw a man standing on one leg; he had unbuckled the other one and had set it down beside him. Then the master said: "You've made it cozy for yourself to take a rest." "I'm a runner," he answered, "and to keep from darting much too fast, I've unbuckled one of my legs; when I run on two legs, it's faster than a bird flies." "Oh, come with me; if the five of us stick together, we surely ought to make our way in life." He joined them, and before very long they met a man who was wearing a little hat, which was all pulled down over one ear. Then the master said to him: "What etiquette, what etiquette! Don't go around with your hat hanging from one ear; you look like a court jester." "I mustn't do what you say," the other man replied, "because if I put my hat on straight, it will cause a terrible frost, and the birds in the air will freeze and fall to the ground dead." "Oh, come with me," said the master; "if the six of us stick together, we surely ought to make our way in life."

Now the six of them came to a town where the king had proclaimed that any man who was willing to enter a foot race with his daughter, and could win, was to be her husband; but whoever lost had to surrender his head. Then the man announced his candidacy and said: "But I wish to have my servant run in my place." The king replied: "In that case you must pledge his life as well, so that both his head and yours are riding on your victory." When that was agreed upon and confirmed, the master buckled on the runner's other leg and said to him: "Now be speedy and help us win." The rules stated that whoever was the first to bring water from an extremely distant well would be the winner. Now the runner received a pitcher, and so did the princess, and they started

sie fingen zu gleicher Zeit zu laufen an; aber in einem Augenblick, als
die Königstochter erst eine kleine Strecke fort war, konnte den Laufer
schon kein Zuschauer mehr sehen, und es war nicht anders, als wäre
der Wind vorbeigesaust. In kurzer Zeit langte er bei dem Brunnen an,
schöpfte den Krug voll Wasser und kehrte wieder um. Mitten aber auf
dem Heimweg überkam ihn eine Müdigkeit, da setzte er den Krug
hin, legte sich nieder und schlief ein. Er hatte aber einen Pferdeschädel, der da auf der Erde lag, zum Kopfkissen gemacht, damit er
hart läge und bald wieder erwachte. Indessen war die Königstochter,
die auch gut laufen konnte, so gut es ein gewöhnlicher Mensch ver-
mag, bei dem Brunnen angelangt und eilte mit ihrem Krug voll
Wasser zurück; und als sie den Laufer da liegen und schlafen sah, war
sie froh und sprach: »Der Feind ist in meine Hände gegeben«, leerte
seinen Krug aus und sprang weiter. Nun wär alles verloren gewesen,
wenn nicht zu gutem Glück der Jäger mit seinen scharfen Augen oben
auf dem Schloß gestanden und alles mit angesehen hätte. Da sprach
er: »Die Königstochter soll doch gegen uns nicht aufkommen«, lud
seine Büchse und schoß so geschickt, daß er dem Laufer den
Pferdeschädel unter dem Kopf wegschoß, ohne ihm wehzutun. Da
erwachte der Laufer, sprang in die Höhe und sah, daß sein Krug leer
und die Königstochter schon weit voraus war. Aber er verlor den Mut
nicht, lief mit dem Krug wieder zum Brunnen zurück, schöpfte aufs
neue Wasser und war noch zehn Minuten eher als die Königstochter
daheim. »Seht Ihr«, sprach er, »jetzt hab ich erst die Beine aufge-
hoben, vorher war's gar kein Laufen zu nennen.«

Den König aber kränkte es, und seine Tochter noch mehr, daß sie
so ein gemeiner, abgedankter Soldat davontragen sollte; sie
ratschlagten miteinander, wie sie ihn samt seinen Gesellen loswürden.
Da sprach der König zu ihr: »Ich habe ein Mittel gefunden, laß dir
nicht bang sein, sie sollen nicht wieder heimkommen.« Und sprach zu
ihnen: »Ihr sollt euch nun zusammen lustig machen, essen und
trinken«, und führte sie zu einer Stube, die hatte einen Boden von
Eisen, und die Türen waren auch von Eisen, und die Fenster waren
mit eisernen Stäben verwahrt. In der Stube war eine Tafel, mit
köstlichen Speisen besetzt, da sprach der König zu ihnen: »Geht
hinein und laßt's euch wohl sein.« Und wie sie darinnen waren, ließ er
die Türe verschließen und verriegeln. Dann ließ er den Koch kommen und befahl ihm, ein Feuer so lang unter die Stube zu machen,
bis das Eisen glühend würde. Das tat der Koch, und es fing an und
ward den sechsen in der Stube, während sie an der Tafel saßen, ganz
warm, und sie meinten, das käme vom Essen; als aber die Hitze

running at the same time; but in a moment, while the princess had covered only a short distance, none of the spectators could see the runner anymore, and it was exactly as if the wind had roared by. In almost no time he reached the well, filled his pitcher with water, and turned back. But when halfway back he was overcome by weariness; he put down the pitcher, lay down, and fell asleep. He had made a pillow of a horse's skull that he found on the ground there, so that he'd be lying on a hard object and would wake up soon. Meanwhile the princess, who was also a good runner, and ran as well as an ordinary person can, had reached the well and was hastening back with her water-filled pitcher; when she saw the runner lying asleep there, she was glad, and said: "The enemy has fallen into my hands"; she emptied his pitcher and ran on. Now all would have been lost if the hunter, with his keen eyesight, hadn't fortunately been standing upstairs in the palace watching everything that was going on. Saying: "The princess mustn't prevail against us," he loaded his rifle and made such a skillful shot that he knocked the horse's skull out from under the runner's head without doing him any harm. Then the runner awoke, jumped up, and saw that his pitcher was empty, and the princess far ahead of him. But he didn't lose heart; he ran back to the well with the pitcher, drew water again, and was back at the starting point ten minutes sooner than the princess, in spite of everything. "You see," he said, "I just now started to pick up my feet; before that, you couldn't really call it running."

But the king was vexed, and his daughter even more so, at the thought of a common discharged soldier winning her hand; they took counsel together as to how to get rid of him and his companions. Then the king said to her: "I've thought of a way; don't be afraid, they won't be back here." And he said to them: "Now all of you should make merry, eat, and drink"; and he led them to a room that had an iron floor; the doors were also of iron, and the windows were protected by iron bars. In the room there was a table laden with delicious food; the king said to them: "Go in and enjoy yourselves." And once they were inside, he had the door locked and bolted. Then he sent for the cook and ordered him to make a fire under the room until the iron was red-hot. The cook obeyed, and the fire began to burn; and while the six of them were in the room seated at the table, they got very warm, and thought it was because they were eating; when the heat continued to increase, however, and they wanted to leave, but found

immer größer ward und sie hinaus wollten, Türe und Fenster aber verschlossen fanden, da merkten sie, daß der König Böses im Sinne gehabt hatte und sie ersticken wollte. »Es soll ihm aber nicht gelingen«, sprach der mit dem Hütchen, »ich will einen Frost kommen lassen, vor dem sich das Feuer schämen und verkriechen soll.« Da setzte er sein Hütchen gerade, und alsobald fiel ein Frost, daß alle Hitze verschwand und die Speisen auf den Schüsseln anfingen zu frieren. Als nun ein paar Stunden herum waren und der König glaubte, sie wären in der Hitze verschmachtet, ließ er die Türe öffnen und wollte selbst nach ihnen sehen. Aber wie die Türe aufging, standen sie alle sechse da, frisch und gesund, und sagten, es wäre ihnen lieb, daß sie heraus könnten, sich zu wärmen, denn bei der großen Kälte in der Stube frören die Speisen an den Schüsseln fest. Da ging der König voll Zorn hinab zu dem Koch, schalt ihn und fragte, warum er nicht getan hätte, was ihm wäre befohlen worden. Der Koch aber antwortete: »Es ist Glut genug da, seht nur selbst.« Da sah der König, daß ein gewaltiges Feuer unter der Eisenstube brannte, und merkte, daß er den sechsen auf diese Weise nichts anhaben könnte.

Nun sann der König aufs neue, wie er der bösen Gäste loswürde, ließ den Meister kommen und sprach: »Willst du Gold nehmen und dein Recht auf meine Tochter aufgeben, so sollst du haben, soviel du willst.« »O ja, Herr König«, antwortete er, »gebt mir so viel, als mein Diener tragen kann, so verlange ich Eure Tochter nicht.« Das war der König zufrieden, und jener sprach weiter: »So will ich in vierzehn Tagen kommen und es holen.« Darauf rief er alle Schneider aus dem ganzen Reich herbei, die mußten vierzehn Tage lang sitzen und einen Sack nähen. Und als er fertig war, mußte der Starke, welcher Bäume ausrupfen konnte, den Sack auf die Schulter nehmen und mit ihm zu dem König gehen. Da sprach der König: »Was ist das für ein gewaltiger Kerl, der den hausgroßen Ballen Leinewand auf der Schulter trägt?« Erschrak und dachte: »Was wird der für Gold wegschleppen!« Da hieß er eine Tonne Gold herbringen, die mußten sechszehn der stärksten Männer tragen, aber der Starke packte sie mit einer Hand, steckte sie in den Sack und sprach: »Warum bringt ihr nicht gleich mehr, das deckt ja kaum den Boden.« Da ließ der König nach und nach seinen ganzen Schatz herbeitragen, den schob der Starke in den Sack hinein, und der Sack ward davon noch nicht zur Hälfte voll. »Schafft mehr herbei«, rief er, »die paar Brocken füllen nicht.« Da mußten noch siebentausend Wagen mit Gold in dem ganzen Reich zusammengefahren werden; die schob der Starke samt den vorgespannten Ochsen in seinen

the door and window locked, they realized that the king had had
evil in mind and wanted them to suffocate. "But he won't succeed," said the one with the little hat; "I'll bring on such a frost
that the fire will be put to shame by it and will creep away." Then
he put his hat on straight, and immediately a frost came, making
all the heat disappear, while the food on the platters began to
freeze. Well, after a couple of hours had gone by, and the king
thought they had perished in the heat, he had the door opened,
and wanted to see in person what had become of them. But when
the door opened, all six of them were standing there, perky and
healthy, saying they were glad they could come out and warm up,
because it was so cold in the room that the food was frozen fast
to the platters. Then the king went downstairs to the cook in a
rage, scolded him, and asked why he hadn't done what he had
been ordered to. But the cook replied: "There's plenty of fire
there; see for yourself." Then the king saw that a tremendous
blaze was burning under the iron room, and he realized that he
couldn't injure the six companions in that manner.

Now the king pondered again as to how to get rid of his trou-
blesome guests; he sent for the master and said: "If you're willing
to take gold and give up your right to my daughter, you can have
as much as you want." "Oh, yes, your majesty," he replied; "give
me as much as my servant can carry, and I won't ask for your
daughter." The king was satisfied with that, and the man continued: "So, then, I'll be back to get it in two weeks." Now he summoned all the tailors in the whole kingdom, and they had to sit
for two weeks sewing a sack. When it was ready, he ordered the
strong man, who was able to uproot trees, to put the sack on his
shoulder and go to the king with it. Then the king said: "What a
powerful fellow he is to be able to carry a bale of canvas as big as
a house on his shoulder!" He was alarmed and he thought: "All
the gold he'll tote away!" Next, the king ordered a barrel of gold
to be brought over; it took sixteen of his most powerful men to
carry it, but the strong man picked it up with one hand, put it in
the sack, and said: "Why don't you bring more right away? This
barely covers the bottom." Then the king gradually had his entire
treasury brought over; the strong man shoved it into the sack, but
the sack didn't become even half full. "Get more," he called;
"these few crumbs won't fill my sack." Then another seven thousand cartloads of gold had to be assembled throughout the kingdom; the strong man shoved them into his sack together with the

Sack. »Ich will's nicht lange besehen«, sprach er, »und nehmen, was
kommt, damit der Sack nur voll wird.« Wie alles darinstak, ging doch
noch viel hinein, da sprach er: »Ich will dem Ding nur ein Ende
machen, man bindet wohl einmal einen Sack zu, wenn er auch noch
nicht voll ist.« Dann huckte er ihn auf den Rücken und ging mit
seinen Gesellen fort.

Als der König nun sah, wie der einzige Mann des ganzen Landes
Reichtum forttrug, ward er zornig und ließ seine Reiterei aufsitzen,
die sollten den sechsen nachjagen und hatten Befehl, dem Starken
den Sack wieder abzunehmen. Zwei Regimenter holten sie bald ein
und riefen ihnen zu: »Ihr seid Gefangene, legt den Sack mit dem
Gold nieder oder ihr werdet zusammengehauen.« »Was sagt ihr?«
sprach der Bläser. »Wir wären Gefangene? Eher sollt ihr sämtlich in
der Luft herumtanzen«, hielt das eine Nasenloch zu und blies mit
dem andern die beiden Regimenter an, da fuhren sie auseinander
und in die blaue Luft über alle Berge weg, der eine hierhin, der andere dorthin. Ein Feldwebel rief um Gnade, er hätte neun Wunden
und wäre ein braver Kerl, der den Schimpf nicht verdiente. Da ließ
der Bläser ein wenig nach, so daß er ohne Schaden wieder herabkam,
dann sprach er zu ihm: »Nun geh heim zum König und sag, er sollte
nur noch mehr Reiterei schicken, ich wollte sie alle in die Luft
blasen.« Der König, als er den Bescheid vernahm, sprach: »Laßt die
Kerle gehen, die haben etwas an sich.« Da brachten die sechs den
Reichtum heim, teilten ihn unter sich und lebten vergnügt bis an ihr
Ende.

Hans im Glück

Hans hatte sieben Jahre bei seinem Herrn gedient, da sprach er zu
ihm: »Herr, meine Zeit ist herum, nun wollte ich gerne wieder heim
zu meiner Mutter, gebt mir meinen Lohn.« Der Herr antwortete:
»Du hast mir treu und ehrlich gedient, wie der Dienst war, so soll der
Lohn sein«, und gab ihm ein Stück Gold, das so groß als Hansens
Kopf war. Hans zog sein Tüchlein aus der Tasche, wickelte den
Klumpen hinein, setzte ihn auf die Schulter und machte sich auf den
Weg nach Haus. Wie er so dahinging und immer ein Bein vor das andere setzte, kam ihm ein Reiter in die Augen, der frisch und fröhlich
auf einem muntern Pferd vorbeitrabte. »Ach«, sprach Hans ganz laut,
»was ist das Reiten ein schönes Ding! Da sitzt einer wie auf einem

oxen that were harnessed to them. "I won't examine things too closely," he said; "I'll just take whatever comes, as long as the sack gets filled." When everything was inside, there was still plenty of room, and he said: "I just want to get this over with; after all, people sometimes tie up a sack even if it isn't full yet." Then he heaved it onto his back and left with his companions.

Now, when the king saw how that one man was carrying away the wealth of the whole country, he became furious and ordered his cavalry to mount; they were to pursue the six men, and had orders to recover the sack from the strong man. Two regiments soon caught up with them and called to them: "You're our prisoners; put the sack of gold down or you'll be cut to pieces!" "What's that you say?" the blower said. "That we're your prisoners? Before that happens, the whole bunch of you will be dancing around in the air"; he stopped up one nostril and blew out of the other at the two regiments; they were scattered and flew into the blue sky across all the mountains, one man here, another there. One sergeant begged for mercy, saying that he had received nine wounds in the line of duty, and was a respectable fellow who didn't deserve such a disgrace. So the blower eased up a little, allowing him to descend unharmed; then he said to him: "Now go home to the king and tell him to go on sending more cavalry; I want to blow them all into the air." When the king got that information, he said: "Let the fellows go, there's something weird about them." Then the six men brought the riches home, shared them, and lived in contentment for the rest of their lives.

Hans in Luck

Hans had served his master for seven years; now he said to him: "Master, my time of service is up; I'd like to go home to my mother now; give me my pay." His master replied: "You've served me faithfully and honestly; as your service was, so shall your pay be"; and he gave him a gold nugget that was as big as Hans's head. Hans pulled his handkerchief out of his pocket, wrapped the lump of gold in it, put it on his shoulder, and set out for home. As he was walking along, regularly setting one foot down in front of the other, he caught sight of a mounted man who was trotting by, hale and happy, on a frisky horse. "Oh," said Hans out loud, "how lovely it is to ride! You sit as if on a chair, you don't stub your toe

Stuhl, stößt sich an keinen Stein, spart die Schuh und kommt fort, er weiß nicht wie.« Der Reiter, der das gehört hatte, hielt an und rief: »Ei, Hans, warum laufst du auch zu Fuß?« »Ich muß ja wohl«, antwortete er, »da habe ich einen Klumpen heimzutragen: es ist zwar Gold, aber ich kann den Kopf dabei nicht geradhalten, auch drückt mir's auf die Schulter.« »Weißt du was«, sagte der Reiter, »wir wollen tauschen: ich gebe dir mein Pferd, und du gibst mir deinen Klumpen.« »Von Herzen gern«, sprach Hans, »aber ich sage Euch, Ihr müßt Euch damit schleppen.« Der Reiter stieg ab, nahm das Gold und half dem Hans hinauf, gab ihm die Zügel fest in die Hände und sprach: »Wenn's nun recht geschwind soll gehen, so mußt du mit der Zunge schnalzen und hopp, hopp rufen.«

Hans war seelenfroh, als er auf dem Pferde saß und so frank und frei dahinritt. Über ein Weilchen fiel's ihm ein, es sollte noch schneller gehen, und fing an, mit der Zunge zu schnalzen und hopp, hopp zu rufen. Das Pferd setzte sich in starken Trab, und ehe sich's Hans versah, war er abgeworfen und lag in einem Graben, der die Äcker von der Landstraße trennte. Das Pferd wäre auch durchgegangen, wenn es nicht ein Bauer aufgehalten hätte, der des Weges kam und eine Kuh vor sich hertrieb. Hans suchte seine Glieder zusammen und machte sich wieder auf die Beine. Er war aber verdrießlich und sprach zu dem Bauer: »Es ist ein schlechter Spaß, das Reiten, zumal wenn man auf so eine Mähre gerät wie diese, die stößt und einen herabwirft, daß man den Hals brechen kann; ich setze mich nun und nimmermehr wieder auf. Da lob ich mir Eure Kuh, da kann einer mit Gemächlichkeit hinterhergehen und hat obendrein seine Milch, Butter und Käse jeden Tag gewiß. Was gäb ich darum, wenn ich so eine Kuh hätte!« »Nun«, sprach der Bauer, »geschieht Euch so ein großer Gefallen, so will ich Euch wohl die Kuh für das Pferd vertauschen.« Hans willigte mit tausend Freuden ein; der Bauer schwang sich aufs Pferd und ritt eilig davon.

Hans trieb seine Kuh ruhig vor sich her und bedachte den glücklichen Handel. »Hab ich nur ein Stück Brot, und daran wird mir's doch nicht fehlen, so kann ich, sooft mir's beliebt, Butter und Käse dazu essen; hab ich Durst, so melk ich meine Kuh und trinke Milch. Herz, was verlangst du mehr?« Als er zu einem Wirtshaus kam, machte er halt, aß in der großen Freude alles, was er bei sich hatte, sein Mittags- und Abendbrot, rein auf und ließ sich für seine letzten paar Heller ein halbes Glas Bier einschenken. Dann trieb er seine Kuh weiter, immer nach dem Dorfe seiner Mutter zu. Die Hitze ward drückender, je näher der Mittag kam, und Hans befand sich in einer Heide, die wohl

on any stone, you save shoe leather, and you get where you want before you even know it." The horseman, who had heard this, halted and called: "Say, Hans, why are you going on foot yourself?" "I have to," he replied; "I've got a lump to carry home: it's gold, of course, but it doesn't allow me to hold my head up straight, and it presses on my shoulder." "You know what," said the horseman, "let's trade: I'll give you my horse, and you'll give me your lump." "With great pleasure," said Hans, "but I've got to warn you, it will make you drag yourself along." The horseman dismounted, took the gold, and helped Hans up; he placed the reins firmly in his hands and said: "When you want to go really fast, click with your tongue and yell 'Hop to it!'"

Hans was tickled pink when he sat on the horse and rode away so boldly and freely. After a while it occurred to him he could be going even faster, and he began to click with his tongue and yell "Hop to it!" The horse changed to a lively trot and, before Hans knew it, he had been thrown and was lying in the ditch that separated the fields from the highway. The horse would have bolted, too, if it hadn't been stopped by a farmer who was heading that way, driving a cow in front of him. Hans pulled himself together and stood up again. But he was annoyed, and he said to the farmer: "Riding is a bad joke, especially when you find yourself on a mare like this one, which bucks and throws you, so you're liable to break your neck; never ever will I ride a horse again. That's what I like about your cow; a person can walk after her at a comfortable pace, and, on top of that, he's sure of getting milk, butter, and cheese every day. What wouldn't I give to have a cow like that!" "Well," the farmer said, "if it will make you so happy, I'll trade my cow for your horse." Hans agreed with enormous joy; the farmer jumped onto the horse and rode away hastily.

Hans drove his cow in front of him peacefully, thinking over the good deal he had made. "If I only have a piece of bread, and I'm sure I'll never lack for that, then I can eat butter and cheese with it as often as I like; when I'm thirsty, I'll milk my cow and drink milk. What more can anyone ask for?" When he arrived at an inn, he paused in his journey; in his great joy he ate every last bit of food he had with him, both his lunch and his supper; and with his last few pennies he ordered half a glass of beer. Then he drove his cow onward, heading all the while for his mother's village. The heat was growing more oppressive, the nearer it was to midday, and Hans found himself on a heath that would probably take

noch eine Stunde dauerte. Da ward es ihm ganz heiß, so daß ihm vor
Durst die Zunge am Gaumen klebte. »Dem Ding ist zu helfen«,
dachte Hans, »jetzt will ich meine Kuh melken und mich an der Milch
laben.« Er band sie an einen dürren Baum, und da er keinen Eimer
hatte, so stellte er seine Ledermütze unter, aber wie er sich auch be-
mühte, es kam kein Tropfen Milch zum Vorschein. Und weil er sich
ungeschickt dabei anstellte, so gab ihm das ungeduldige Tier endlich
mit einem der Hinterfüße einen solchen Schlag vor den Kopf, daß er
zu Boden taumelte und eine Zeitlang sich gar nicht besinnen konnte,
wo er war. Glücklicherweise kam gerade ein Metzger des Weges, der
auf einem Schubkarren ein junges Schwein liegen hatte. »Was sind
das für Streiche!« rief er und half dem guten Hans auf. Hans erzählte,
was vorgefallen war. Der Metzger reichte ihm seine Flasche und
sprach: »Da trinkt einmal und erholt Euch. Die Kuh will wohl keine
Milch geben, das ist ein altes Tier, das höchstens noch zum Ziehen
taugt oder zum Schlachten.« »Ei, ei«, sprach Hans und strich sich die
Haare über den Kopf, »wer hätte das gedacht! Es ist freilich gut, wenn
man so ein Tier ins Haus abschlachten kann, was gibt's für Fleisch!
Aber ich mache mir aus dem Kuhfleisch nicht viel, es ist mir nicht
saftig genug. Ja, wer so ein junges Schwein hätte! Das schmeckt anders, dabei noch die Würste.« »Hört, Hans«, sprach da der Metzger,
»Euch zuliebe will ich tauschen und will Euch das Schwein für die
Kuh lassen.« »Gott lohn Euch Eure Freundschaft«, sprach Hans,
übergab ihm die Kuh, ließ sich das Schweinchen vom Karren losmachen und den Strick, woran es gebunden war, in die Hand geben.

Hans zog weiter und überdachte, wie ihm doch alles nach Wunsch
ginge, begegnete ihm je eine Verdrießlichkeit, so würde sie doch
gleich wiedergutgemacht. Es gesellte sich danach ein Bursch zu ihm,
der trug eine schöne weiße Gans unter dem Arm. Sie boten einander
die Zeit, und Hans fing an, von seinem Glück zu erzählen und wie er
immer so vorteilhaft getauscht hätte. Der Bursch erzählte ihm, daß
er die Gans zu einem Kindtaufschmaus brächte. »Hebt einmal«, fuhr
er fort und packte sie bei den Flügeln, »wie schwer sie ist, die ist aber
auch acht Wochen lang genudelt worden. Wer in den Braten beißt,
muß sich das Fett von beiden Seiten abwischen.« »Ja«, sprach Hans
und wog sie mit der einen Hand, »die hat ihr Gewicht, aber mein
Schwein ist auch keine Sau.« Indessen sah sich der Bursch nach allen
Seiten ganz bedenklich um, schüttelte auch wohl mit dem Kopf.

another hour to cross. He got very hot, so that his tongue was
sticking to the roof of his mouth with thirst. "There's a remedy for
this," Hans thought; "I'll milk my cow now, and refresh myself
with the milk." He tied her to a dead tree, and since he had no
pail, he put his leather cap under her, but try as he would, not a
drop of milk appeared. And because he was going about it clum-
sily, the impatient animal finally gave him such a kick in the head
with one hind leg that he reeled to the ground and for a while had
no recollection of where he was. Fortunately, just then a butcher
came along pushing a young pig in a wheelbarrow. "What kind of
games are these?" he called, and he helped good Hans get up.
Hans told him what had occurred. The butcher handed him his
bottle, saying: "Take a drink and get your strength back. This cow
probably will never give any milk; she's an old animal, and by now
is only good, at best, for pulling wagons or for slaughtering." "My,
my," said Hans, running his hand through his hair, "who would
have thought it? Of course, it's a good thing when you can slaughter such an animal at home; all the meat you get! But I don't care
very much for cow's meat, I don't find it juicy enough. Yes, if I had
a young pig like yours! Now there's a flavor for you, not to mention the sausages!" "Listen, Hans," the butcher then said, "as a
favor to you, I'll make a trade and leave you the pig in place of the
cow." "May God reward you for your friendship," said Hans; he
handed over the cow, had the young pig untied from the wheelbarrow, and took hold of the cord it was tied to.

   Hans moved on, reviewing in his mind the way everything was
going according to his wishes; whenever he experienced any vexation, it was set right again immediately. Later on, he was joined
by a youngster who was carrying a beautiful white goose under his
arm. They greeted each other, and Hans began telling about his
good luck and the series of advantageous exchanges he had made.
The youngster told him that he was taking the goose to a chris-
tening party. "Just lift it," he continued, grabbing it by the wings,
"and see how heavy it is; it's been fattened for eight weeks, that's
why. Whoever bites into it when it's roasted will have to wipe away
the fat from both sides of his mouth." "Yes," said Hans, weighing
it in one hand, "it's good and heavy, but my pig is nothing to
sneeze at, either."[7] Meanwhile the youngster was looking around

---

   7. It's impossible to translate the pun in the humorous German idiom (literally: "my pig is no sow").

»Hört«, fing er darauf an, »mit Eurem Schweine mag's nicht ganz
richtig sein. In dem Dorfe, durch das ich gekommen bin, ist eben
dem Schulzen eins aus dem Stall gestohlen worden. Ich fürchte, ich
fürchte, Ihr habt's da in der Hand. Sie haben Leute ausgeschickt,
und es wäre ein schlimmer Handel, wenn sie Euch mit dem Schwein
erwischten: das geringste ist, daß Ihr ins finstere Loch gesteckt
werdet.« Dem guten Hans ward bang: »Ach Gott«, sprach er, »helft
mir aus der Not, Ihr wißt hier herum bessern Bescheid, nehmt mein
Schwein da und laßt mir Eure Gans.« »Ich muß schon etwas aufs
Spiel setzen«, antwortete der Bursche, »aber ich will doch nicht
schuld sein, daß Ihr ins Unglück geratet.« Er nahm also das Seil in
die Hand und trieb das Schwein schnell auf einen Seitenweg fort; der
gute Hans aber ging, seiner Sorgen entledigt, mit der Gans unter
dem Arme der Heimat zu. »Wenn ich's recht überlege«, sprach er mit
sich selbst, »habe ich noch Vorteil bei dem Tausch: erstlich den guten
Braten, hernach die Menge von Fett, die herausträufeln wird, das
gibt Gänsefettbrot auf ein Vierteljahr; und endlich die schönen
weißen Federn, die laß ich mir in mein Kopfkissen stopfen, und
darauf will ich wohl ungewiegt einschlafen. Was wird meine Mutter
eine Freude haben!«

Als er durch das letzte Dorf gekommen war, stand da ein
Scherenschleifer mit seinem Karren, sein Rad schnurrte, und er sang
dazu:

> »Ich schleife die Schere und drehe geschwind
> und hänge mein Mäntelchen nach dem Wind.«

Hans blieb stehen und sah ihm zu; endlich redete er ihn an und sprach:
»Euch geht's wohl, weil Ihr so lustig bei Eurem Schleifen seid.« »Ja«,
antwortete der Scherenschleifer, »das Handwerk hat einen güldenen
Boden. Ein rechter Schleifer ist ein Mann, der, sooft er in die Tasche
greift, auch Geld darin findet. Aber wo habt Ihr die schöne Gans
gekauft?« »Die hab ich nicht gekauft, sondern für mein Schwein einge-
tauscht.« »Und das Schwein?« »Das hab ich für eine Kuh gekriegt.«
»Und die Kuh?« »Die hab ich für ein Pferd bekommen.« »Und das
Pferd?« »Dafür hab ich einen Klumpen Gold, so groß als mein Kopf,
gegeben.« »Und das Gold?« »Ei, das war mein Lohn für sieben Jahre
Dienst.« »Ihr habt Euch jederzeit zu helfen gewußt«, sprach der
Schleifer, »könnt Ihr's nun dahin bringen, daß Ihr das Geld in der Tasche
springen hört, wenn Ihr aufsteht, so habt Ihr Euer Glück gemacht.«
»Wie soll ich das anfangen?« sprach Hans. »Ihr müßt ein Schleifer wer-
den wie ich; dazu gehört eigentlich nichts als ein Wetzstein, das andere

in every direction with a most serious expression, and was shaking his head sadly. "Listen," he then began to say, "things may not be quite right with your pig. In the village that I walked through, one has just been stolen from the mayor's pen. I'm afraid, I'm afraid you've got it there in your hand. They've sent people out, and it would be bad for you if they caught you with the pig: at the very least, you'll be thrown into the black dungeon." Good Hans got frightened: "My heavens!" he said; "help me out of my distress; in these parts you know your way around better than I do; take my pig and leave me your goose." "I'd be taking a risk," the youngster replied, "but I don't want to be to blame for your getting into trouble." So he took the rope in his hand and quickly drove the pig off onto a side path, while good Hans, relieved of his worries, walked on homeward with the goose under his arm. "When I think it over carefully," he said to himself, "the trade is still to my advantage: first of all, the good roast, then all the fat that will trickle out of it, which will provide enough goose fat to smear onto bread slices for three months; and finally the beautiful white feathers that I'll have my pillow stuffed with, so I can fall asleep on it even without being rocked. How happy my mother will be!"

When he had crossed the last village, a scissors grinder was standing there with his cart; his wheel was humming, and he was singing to its accompaniment:

> "I turn my wheel, and the knife, I grind it,
> and I trim my sails to the wind as I find it."

Hans halted and watched him; finally he addressed him, saying: "You must be doing all right, because you're so jolly while you grind." "Yes," the scissors grinder replied, "this trade is very profitable. An honest-to-goodness scissors grinder is a man who finds money in his pocket every time he reaches in. But where did you buy that beautiful goose?" "I didn't buy it, I traded my pig for it." "And the pig?" "I got that for a cow." "And the cow?" "I received that for a horse." "And the horse?" "For that I gave a lump of gold as big as my head." "And the gold?" "Oh, that was my pay for seven years' service." "Each time you've managed to get ahead," said the scissors grinder; "if you can now do so well that you hear money jingling in your pocket every time you stand up, your happiness will be complete." "How do I do that?" asked Hans. "You must become a scissors grinder like me; all you actually need for it is a grindstone, the rest you can get anywhere.

findet sich schon von selbst. Da hab ich einen, der ist zwar ein wenig schadhaft, dafür sollt Ihr mir aber auch weiter nichts als Eure Gans geben; wollt Ihr das?« »Wie könnt Ihr noch fragen«, antwortete Hans, »ich werde ja zum glücklichsten Menschen auf Erden; habe ich Geld, sooft ich in die Tasche greife, was brauche ich da länger zu sorgen?« Reichte ihm die Gans hin und nahm den Wetzstein in Empfang. »Nun«, sprach der Schleifer und hob einen gewöhnlichen schweren Feldstein, der neben ihm lag, auf, »da habt Ihr noch einen tüchtigen Stein dazu, auf dem sich's gut schlagen läßt und Ihr Eure alten Nägel geradeklopfen könnt. Nehmt hin und hebt ihn ordentlich auf.«

Hans lud den Stein auf und ging mit vergnügtem Herzen weiter; seine Augen leuchteten vor Freude: »Ich muß in einer Glückshaut geboren sein«, rief er aus, »alles, was ich wünsche, trifft mir ein wie einem Sonntagskind.« Indessen, weil er seit Tagesanbruch auf den Beinen gewesen war, begann er müde zu werden; auch plagte ihn der Hunger, da er allen Vorrat auf einmal in der Freude über die erhandelte Kuh aufgezehrt hatte. Er konnte endlich nur mit Mühe weitergehen und mußte jeden Augenblick haltmachen; dabei drückten ihn die Steine ganz erbärmlich. Da konnte er sich des Gedankens nicht erwehren, wie gut es wäre, wenn er sie gerade jetzt nicht zu tragen brauchte. Wie eine Schnecke kam er zu einem Feldbrunnen geschlichen, wollte da ruhen und sich mit einem frischen Trunk laben; damit er aber die Steine im Niedersitzen nicht beschädigte, legte er sie bedächtig neben sich auf den Rand des Brunnens. Darauf setzte er sich nieder und wollte sich zum Trinken bücken, da versah er's, stieß ein klein wenig an, und beide Steine plumpten hinab. Hans, als er sie mit seinen Augen in die Tiefe hatte versinken sehen, sprang vor Freuden auf, kniete dann nieder und dankte Gott mit Tränen in den Augen, daß er ihm auch diese Gnade noch erwiesen und ihn auf eine so gute Art, und ohne daß er sich einen Vorwurf zu machen brauchte, von den schweren Steinen befreit hätte, die ihm allein noch hinderlich gewesen wären. »So glücklich wie ich«, rief er aus, »gibt es keinen Menschen unter der Sonne.« Mit leichtem Herzen und frei von aller Last sprang er nun fort, bis er daheim bei seiner Mutter war.

Die Gänsemagd

Es lebte einmal eine alte Königin, der war ihr Gemahl schon lange Jahre gestorben, und sie hatte eine schöne Tochter. Wie die erwuchs,

I have one here that's a little damaged, I admit, so all you need to give me for it is your goose; are you willing?" "How can you even ask?" Hans replied; "I'll be the luckiest person on earth; if I have money whenever I reach into my pocket, what more do I have to worry about?" He handed him the goose and received the grindstone. "Now," said the scissors grinder, picking up an ordinary heavy rock that was lying next to him, "here you have in addition a fine stone that's good to beat on when you're straightening out your old bent nails. Take it and guard it well."

Hans loaded the rock onto the grindstone and went his way with a contented heart; his eyes were beaming with joy: "I must have been born with a lucky caul," he exclaimed; "everything I wish for comes to me, as if I were a Sunday's child." Meanwhile, because he had been on his feet since daybreak, he began to feel tired; also, he was tormented by hunger, because in his joy over receiving the cow he had consumed all his provisions at one time. Finally he could only keep walking with difficulty, and he had to stop every minute; besides, the stones were weighing him down mercilessly. So he couldn't resist the thought of how good it would be if he didn't need to carry them right at the moment. Like a snail he crawled over to a well in a field, intending to rest there and refresh himself with a cool drink; but, in order not to damage the stones as he sat down, he placed them carefully at his side on the rim of the well. Then he sat down and was about to lean over to drink, when he became careless and shoved the stones ever so slightly, and both of them sank down. When Hans saw them disappear into the depths with his own eyes, he jumped up for joy, then knelt down and thanked God with tears in his eyes for showing him this mercy, too, and freeing him of the heavy stones, the only things that had still been hindering him, and for doing it in such a kind way, so that he had nothing to reproach himself for. "There's no one under the sun as lucky as I am!" he exclaimed. Light of heart and free of every burden, he now dashed onward until he was home with his mother.

The Goose Girl

There once lived an old queen whose husband had long been dead; she had a beautiful daughter. When the girl grew up, she

wurde sie weit über Feld an einen Königssohn versprochen. Als nun die Zeit kam, wo sie vermählt werden sollten und das Kind in das fremde Reich abreisen mußte, packte ihr die Alte gar viel köstliches Gerät und Geschmeide ein, Gold und Silber, Becher und Kleinode, kurz, alles, was nur zu einem königlichen Brautschatz gehörte, denn sie hatte ihr Kind von Herzen lieb. Auch gab sie ihr eine Kammerjungfer bei, welche mitreiten und die Braut in die Hände des Bräutigams überliefern sollte, und jede bekam ein Pferd zur Reise, aber das Pferd der Königstochter hieß *Falada* und konnte sprechen. Wie nun die Abschiedsstunde da war, begab sich die alte Mutter in ihre Schlafkammer, nahm ein Messerlein und schnitt damit in ihre Finger, daß sie bluteten; darauf hielt sie ein weißes Läppchen unter und ließ drei Tropfen Blut hineinfallen, gab sie der Tochter und sprach: »Liebes Kind, verwahre sie wohl, sie werden dir unterweges not tun.«

Also nahmen beide voneinander betrübten Abschied; das Läppchen steckte die Königstochter in ihren Busen vor sich, setzte sich aufs Pferd und zog nun fort zu ihrem Bräutigam. Da sie eine Stunde geritten waren, empfand sie heißen Durst und sprach zu ihrer Kammerjungfer: »Steig ab und schöpfe mir mit meinem Becher, den du für mich mitgenommen hast, Wasser aus dem Bache, ich möchte gern einmal trinken.« »Wenn Ihr Durst habt«, sprach die Kammerjungfer, »so steigt selber ab, legt Euch ans Wasser und trinkt, ich mag Eure Magd nicht sein.« Da stieg die Königstochter vor großem Durst herunter, neigte sich über das Wasser im Bach und trank und durfte nicht aus dem goldenen Becher trinken. Da sprach sie: »Ach Gott!« Da antworteten die drei Blutstropfen: »Wenn das deine Mutter wüßte, das Herz im Leibe tät ihr zerspringen.« Aber die Königsbraut war demütig, sagte nichts und stieg wieder zu Pferd. So ritten sie etliche Meilen weiter fort, aber der Tag war warm, die Sonne stach, und sie durstete bald von neuem. Da sie nun an einen Wasserfluß kamen, rief sie noch einmal ihrer Kammerjungfer: »Steig ab und gib mir aus meinem Goldbecher zu trinken«, denn sie hatte aller bösen Worte längst vergessen. Die Kammerjungfer sprach aber noch hochmütiger: »Wollt Ihr trinken, so trinkt allein, ich mag nicht Eure Magd sein.« Da stieg die Königstochter hernieder vor großem Durst, legte sich über das fließende Wasser, weinte und sprach: »Ach Gott!« Und die Blutstropfen antworteten wiederum: »Wenn das deine Mutter wüßte, das Herz im Leibe tät ihr zerspringen.« Und wie sie so trank und sich recht überlehnte, fiel ihr das Läppchen, worin die drei Tropfen waren, aus dem Busen und floß mit dem Wasser fort, ohne daß sie es in ihrer großen Angst merkte. Die Kammerjungfer hatte

was promised to a prince who lived far away. Now, when the time came for her to be married, and the girl had to leave home for that foreign kingdom, her old mother packed up a great many precious belongings and jewelry, gold and silver, goblets and gems—in short, everything befitting a royal trousseau—because she loved the girl dearly. She also sent along with her a lady's maid, who was to accompany her and hand her over to her bridegroom; each of them was given a horse for the journey; the princess's horse was named Falada, and he could speak. Well, when the time for parting was at hand, the old mother went to her bedroom, took a little knife and cut her fingers with it so they bled; then she held a little white cloth under them and let three drops of blood fall into it; giving them to her daughter, she said: "My dear child, keep them carefully, you'll have need of them on your journey."

And so the two of them made a sad leave-taking; the princess tucked the cloth into her bodice, mounted her horse, and set out to meet her bridegroom. After they had ridden for an hour, she felt very thirsty and said to her maid: "Dismount and, with my goblet that you brought along for me, draw water from that brook; I'd really like a drink." "If you're thirsty," the maid said, "dismount yourself, stretch out by the water, and drink; I don't want to be your servant." So, in her great thirst, the princess dismounted, leaned over the water in the brook, and drank; she wasn't allowed to drink from the golden goblet. Then she said: "Ah, God!" And the three drops of blood answered: "If your mother knew about this, her heart would burst within her." But the royal bride was humble; she said nothing and mounted her horse again. And so they rode onward several miles, but it was a warm day, the sun was strong, and soon she got thirsty again. Since they had now arrived at a river, she called to her maid again: "Dismount and give me a drink from my golden goblet"— because she had long since forgotten the former spiteful words. But the maid said, even more haughtily than before, "If you want to drink, arrange it on your own; I don't want to be your servant." So, in her great thirst, the princess dismounted, stretched out over the flowing water, wept, and said: "Ah, God!" And the drops of blood again answered: "If your mother knew about this, her heart would burst within her." And while she was drinking in that fashion, leaning very far over the water, the cloth that contained the three drops of blood fell out of her bodice and was carried away with the stream; in her great anguish, she

aber zugesehen und freute sich, daß sie Gewalt über die Braut bekäme: denn damit, daß diese die Blutstropfen verloren hatte, war sie schwach und machtlos geworden. Als sie nun wieder auf ihr Pferd steigen wollte, das da hieß Falada, sagte die Kammerfrau:»Auf Falada gehör ich, und auf meinen Gaul gehörst du«; und das mußte sie sich gefallen lassen. Dann befahl ihr die Kammerfrau mit harten Worten, die königlichen Kleider auszuziehen und ihre schlechten anzulegen, und endlich mußte sie sich unter freiem Himmel verschwören, daß sie am königlichen Hof keinem Menschen etwas davon sprechen wollte; und wenn sie diesen Eid nicht abgelegt hätte, wäre sie auf der Stelle umgebracht worden. Aber Falada sah das alles an und nahm's wohl in acht.

Die Kammerfrau stieg nun auf Falada und die wahre Braut auf das schlechte Roß, und so zogen sie weiter, bis sie endlich in dem königlichen Schloß eintrafen. Da war große Freude über ihre Ankunft, und der Königssohn sprang ihnen entgegen, hob die Kammerfrau vom Pferde und meinte, sie wäre seine Gemahlin; sie ward die Treppe hinaufgeführt, die wahre Königstochter aber mußte unten stehenbleiben. Da schaute der alte König am Fenster und sah sie im Hof halten und sah, wie sie fein war, zart und gar schön; ging alsbald hin ins königliche Gemach und fragte die Braut nach der, die sie bei sich hätte und da unten im Hofe stände und wer sie wäre. »Die hab ich mir unterwegs mitgenommen zur Gesellschaft; gebt der Magd was zu arbeiten, daß sie nicht müßig steht.« Aber der alte König hatte keine Arbeit für sie und wußte nichts, als daß er sagte: »Da hab ich so einen kleinen Jungen, der hütet die Gänse, dem mag sie helfen.« Der Junge hieß *Kürdchen* (Konrädchen), dem mußte die wahre Braut helfen Gänse hüten.

Bald aber sprach die falsche Braut zu dem jungen König: »Liebster Gemahl, ich bitte Euch, tut mir einen Gefallen.« Er antwortete: »Das will ich gerne tun.« »Nun, so laßt den Schinder rufen und da dem Pferde, worauf ich hergeritten bin, den Hals abhauen, weil es mich unterweges geärgert hat.« Eigentlich aber fürchtete sie, daß das Pferd sprechen möchte, wie sie mit der Königstochter umgegangen war. Nun war das so weit geraten, daß es geschehen und der treue Falada sterben sollte, da kam es auch der rechten Königstochter zu Ohr, und sie versprach dem Schinder heimlich ein Stück Geld, das sie ihm bezahlen wollte, wenn er ihr einen kleinen Dienst erwiese. In der Stadt war ein großes finsteres Tor, wo sie abends und morgens mit den Gänsen durch mußte, unter das finstere Tor möchte er dem Falada seinen Kopf hinnageln, daß sie ihn doch noch mehr als einmal

didn't notice it. But her maid had seen it happen, and she was glad to have acquired control over the bride, because by losing the drops of blood she had become weak and powerless. When she now wanted to remount her horse Falada, her maid said: "I belong on Falada, and you belong on my nag"; and the princess had to put up with it. Then her maid harshly ordered her to take off her royal garments and put on the maid's plain ones; and finally she had to swear beneath the open sky that she wouldn't tell a soul about all this at the royal court; if she hadn't taken that oath, she would have been killed on the spot. But Falada observed all this and kept it well in mind.

Now the maid mounted Falada, and the true bride mounted the inferior horse; and so they proceeded until they finally reached the royal palace. There was great rejoicing at their arrival, and the prince ran out to greet them; he lifted the maid from her horse, in the belief that she was his bride; she was led up the front stairs, while the real princess had to remain below. Then the old king looked out a window, saw her left alone in the courtyard, and saw how elegant, delicate, and really beautiful she was; he immediately went to the royal chamber and asked the bride about the woman she had along with her, who had remained down in the courtyard; he wanted to know who she was. "On the way here, I took her along for company; give the maid some work to do, so she doesn't stand around in idleness." But the old king had no work for her, and all that he could come up with was: "There's a little boy who tends the geese for me; she can be his assistant." The boy was called little Kurt (little Konrad), and the true bride had to help him tend the geese.

But before long the false bride said to the young king: "My dearest husband, please do me a favor." He replied: "I'd be glad to." "Please summon the horse flayer and have him cut off the head of the horse on which I rode here, because he irritated me on the journey." In reality she was afraid that the horse might tell how she had behaved to the princess. Now things had gone so far that it really was to occur—faithful Falada was to die—and the news reached the real princess, too; in secret she promised to pay the flayer a sum of money if he performed a slight service for her. In the town there was a big, dark gateway, through which she had to pass with her geese morning and evening; she asked him to nail Falada's head under that dark gateway, so that she could see him more than just once again. So, the flayer's helper

sehen könnte. Also versprach das der Schindersknecht zu tun, hieb den Kopf ab und nagelte ihn unter das finstere Tor fest.

Des Morgens früh, da sie und Kürdchen unterm Tor hinaustrieben, sprach sie im Vorbeigehen:

>O du Falada, da du hangest.«

Da antwortete der Kopf:

>O du Jungfer Königin, da du gangest,
wenn das deine Mutter wüßte,
ihr Herz tät ihr zerspringen.«

Da zog sie still weiter zur Stadt hinaus, und sie trieben die Gänse aufs Feld. Und wenn sie auf der Wiese angekommen war, saß sie nieder und machte ihre Haare auf, die waren eitel Gold, und Kürdchen sah sie und freute sich, wie sie glänzten, und wollte ihr ein paar ausraufen. Da sprach sie:

>Weh, weh, Windchen,
nimm Kürdchen sein Hütchen,
und laß 'n sich mit jagen,
bis ich mich geflochten und geschnatzt
und wieder aufgesatzt.«

Und da kam ein so starker Wind, daß er dem Kürdchen sein Hütchen wegwehte über alle Land, und es mußte ihm nachlaufen. Bis es wieder kam, war sie mit dem Kämmen und Aufsetzen fertig, und er konnte keine Haare kriegen. Da war Kürdchen bös und sprach nicht mit ihr; und so hüteten sie die Gänse, bis daß es Abend ward, dann gingen sie nach Haus.

Den andern Morgen, wie sie unter dem finstern Tor hinaustrieben, sprach die Jungfrau:

>O du Falada, da du hangest.«

Falada antwortete:

>O du Jungfer Königin, da du gangest,
wenn das deine Mutter wüßte,
das Herz tät ihr zerspringen.«

Und in dem Feld setzte sie sich wieder auf die Wiese und fing an, ihr Haar auszukämmen, und Kürdchen lief und wollte danach greifen, da sprach sie schnell:

promised to do that; he cut off the horse's head and nailed it underneath the dark gate.

Early in the morning, when she and little Kurt drove out the geese below the gate, she said as she went by:

> "O Falada, nailed there night and day!"

And the head answered:

> "O queen, as goose girl making your way,
> if your mother knew the worst,
> then her heart would simply burst."

Then in silence she proceeded farther out of town, and they drove the geese into the countryside. When they had reached the meadow, she sat down and unbound her hair, which was pure gold; little Kurt saw it and was delighted at the way it shone, and he wanted to pluck out a few hairs. Then she said:

> "Blow, blow, dear wind,
> bear off Kurt's little hat,
> and make him chase after it
> till I have, with all due care,
> braided and put up my hair."

Then such a strong wind arose that it blew off Kurt's little hat to a great distance, and he had to run after it. By the time he returned, she was through combing and arranging her hair, and he was unable to get any loose hairs. Then little Kurt got angry and wouldn't talk to her; and in that way they tended the geese until it was evening and they went home.

The next morning, when they were driving out the geese below the dark gate, the maiden said:

> "O Falada, nailed there night and day!"

Falada replied:

> "O queen, as goose girl making your way,
> if your mother knew the worst,
> then her heart would simply burst."

Outside town she sat down in the meadow again and began to comb out her hair; little Kurt ran over and wanted to grab it, and she said quickly:

»Weh, weh, Windchen,
nimm Kürdchen sein Hütchen,
und laß 'n sich mit jagen,
bis ich mich geflochten und geschnatzt
und wieder aufgesatzt.«

Da wehte der Wind und wehte ihm das Hütchen vom Kopf weit weg, daß Kürdchen nachlaufen mußte; und als es wiederkam, hatte sie längst ihr Haar zurecht, und es konnte keins davon erwischen; und so hüteten sie die Gänse, bis es Abend ward.

Abends aber, nachdem sie heimgekommen waren, ging Kürdchen vor den alten König und sagte: »Mit dem Mädchen will ich nicht länger Gänse hüten.« »Warum denn?« fragte der alte König. »Ei, das ärgert mich den ganzen Tag.« Da befahl ihm der alte König zu erzählen, wie's ihm denn mit ihr ginge. Da sagte Kürdchen: »Morgens, wenn wir unter dem finstern Tor mit der Herde durchkommen, so ist da ein Gaulskopf an der Wand, zu dem redet sie:

»Falada, da du hangest.«

Da antwortet der Kopf:

»O du Königsjungfer, da du gangest,
wenn das deine Mutter wüßte,
das Herz tät ihr zerspringen.«

Und so erzählte Kürdchen weiter, was auf der Gänsewiese geschähe und wie es da dem Hut im Winde nachlaufen müßte.

Der alte König befahl ihm, den nächsten Tag wieder hinauszutreiben, und er selbst, wie es Morgen war, setzte sich hinter das finstere Tor und hörte da, wie sie mit dem Haupt des Falada sprach; und dann ging er ihr auch nach in das Feld und barg sich in einem Busch auf der Wiese. Da sah er nun bald mit seinen eigenen Augen, wie die Gänsemagd und der Gänsejunge die Herde getrieben brachte und wie nach einer Weile sie sich setzte und ihre Haare losflocht, die strahlten von Glanz. Gleich sprach sie wieder:

»Weh, weh, Windchen,
faß Kürdchen sein Hütchen,
und laß 'n sich mit jagen,
bis daß ich mich geflochten und geschnatzt
und wieder aufgesatzt.«

Da kam ein Windstoß und fuhr mit Kürdchens Hut weg, daß es weit zu laufen hatte, und die Magd kämmte und flocht ihre Locken still fort, welches der alte König alles beobachtete. Darauf ging er

"Blow, blow, dear wind,
bear off Kurt's little hat,
and make him chase after it
till I have, with all due care,
braided and put up my hair."

Then the wind blew and blew his little hat off his head and far away, so that little Kurt had to run after it; when he got back, she had long finished doing her hair, and he was unable to snatch any of it; and in that way they tended the geese until evening.

But in the evening, after they got home, little Kurt went to the old king and said: "I don't want to tend geese anymore with that girl." "Why not?" asked the old king. "Oh, she irritates me all day long." Then the old king commanded him to tell what had happened to him in her company. And little Kurt said: "In the morning, when we pass below the dark gate with the flock, there's a nag's head on the wall, and she says to it:

'O Falada, nailed there night and day!'

Then the head answers:

'O queen, as goose girl making your way,
if your mother knew the worst,
then her heart would simply burst.'"

And so little Kurt continued to tell what happened at the goose pasture, and how he had to run after his hat there in the wind.

The old king commanded him to drive out the geese again the next day; and when morning came, he himself sat down behind the dark gate and listened to the girl's conversation with Falada's head; then he also followed her out of town and hid in a bush on the meadow. There he soon saw with his own eyes how the goose girl and the goose boy came up driving their flock, and how, after a while, she sat down and unbraided her hair, which radiated light. Immediately she said once more:

"Blow, blow, dear wind,
carry off Kurt's little hat,
and make him chase after it
till I have, with all due care,
braided and put up my hair."

Then there came a gust of wind and made off with little Kurt's hat, so that he had to run far away, while the girl continued to comb and braid her tresses quietly; the old king observed all

unbemerkt zurück, und als abends die Gänsemagd heimkam, rief er sie beiseite und fragte, warum sie dem allem so täte. »Das darf ich Euch nicht sagen, und darf auch keinem Menschen mein Leid klagen, denn so hab ich mich unter freiem Himmel verschworen, weil ich sonst um mein Leben gekommen wäre.« Er drang in sie und ließ ihr keinen Frieden, aber er konnte nichts aus ihr herausbringen. Da sprach er: »Wenn du mir nichts sagen willst, so klag dem Eisenofen da dein Leid«, und ging fort. Da kroch sie in den Eisenofen, fing an zu jammern und zu weinen, schüttete ihr Herz aus und sprach: »Da sitze ich nun, von aller Welt verlassen, und bin doch eine Königstochter, und eine falsche Kammerjungfer hat mich mit Gewalt dahin gebracht, daß ich meine königlichen Kleider habe ablegen müssen, und hat meinen Platz bei meinem Bräutigam eingenommen, und ich muß als Gänsemagd gemeine Dienste tun. Wenn das meine Mutter wüßte, das Herz im Leib tät ihr zerspringen.« Der alte König stand aber außen an der Ofenröhre, lauerte ihr zu und hörte, was sie sprach. Da kam er wieder herein und hieß sie aus dem Ofen gehen. Da wurden ihr königliche Kleider angetan, und es schien ein Wunder, wie sie so schön war. Der alte König rief seinen Sohn und offenbarte ihm, daß er die falsche Braut hätte: die wäre bloß ein Kammermädchen, die wahre aber stände hier, als die gewesene Gänsemagd. Der junge König war herzensfroh, als er ihre Schönheit und Tugend erblickte, und ein großes Mahl wurde angestellt, zu dem alle Leute und guten Freunde gebeten wurden. Obenan saß der Bräutigam, die Königstochter zur einen Seite und die Kammerjungfer zur andern, aber die Kammerjungfer war verblendet und erkannte jene nicht mehr in dem glänzenden Schmuck. Als sie nun gegessen und getrunken hatten und gutes Muts waren, gab der alte König der Kammerfrau ein Rätsel auf, was eine solche wert wäre, die den Herrn so und so betrogen hätte, erzählte damit den ganzen Verlauf und fragte: »Welches Urteils ist diese würdig?« Da sprach die falsche Braut: »Die ist nichts Besseres wert, als daß sie splitternackt ausgezogen und in ein Faß gesteckt wird, das inwendig mit spitzen Nägeln beschlagen ist; und zwei weiße Pferde müssen vorgespannt werden, die sie Gasse auf Gasse ab zu Tode schleifen.« »Das bist du«, sprach der alte König, »und hast dein eigen Urteil gefunden, und danach soll dir widerfahren.« Und als das Urteil vollzogen war, vermählte sich der junge König mit seiner rechten Gemahlin, und beide beherrschten ihr Reich in Frieden und Seligkeit.

this. Then he returned without being noticed, and in the evening, when the goose girl came home, he called her to one side and asked her why she did all that. "I'm not allowed to tell you, I'm not allowed to reveal my sorrows to anyone, because I took an oath under the open sky not to do so; you see, otherwise I would have lost my life." He insisted on her telling, and gave her no peace, but he couldn't get anything out of her. Then he said: "If you won't say anything to me, reveal your sorrow to the iron stove"; and he left. Then she crept into the iron stove, began to wail and weep, and poured out her heart, saying: "Now I sit here, forsaken by everyone, even though I'm a princess; a treacherous lady's maid forced me to take off my royal garments, and she took my place with my bridegroom, and I have to perform lowly chores as a goose girl. If my mother knew this, her heart would burst within her." But the old king was standing outside by the stovepipe, keeping watch on her and listening to what she said. After that, he came in again and ordered her to come out of the stove. Then she was dressed in royal garments, and her beauty seemed miraculous. The old king summoned his son and disclosed to him that his bride was not the right woman: she was merely a lady's maid; the true bride was standing there—the former goose girl. The young king was overjoyed when he saw her beauty and virtue, and a great banquet was prepared, to which all the courtiers and good friends of the family were invited. At the head of the table sat the bridegroom, with the princess on one side of him and the lady's maid on the other; but the lady's maid was dazzled, and no longer recognized the other woman in her radiant adornment. Now, after they had enjoyed their food and drink and all were cheerful, the old king asked a question of the lady's maid: what would a woman deserve who had deceived her lord and master in such and such a way; he narrated the whole course of events, then asked her: "What sentence should such a woman receive?" Then the substitute bride said: "She deserves nothing better than to be stripped stark naked and placed in a vat that is studded inside with sharp nails; two white horses should be hitched to it to drag her to death up and down the streets." "That woman is you," said the old king; "you have uttered your own sentence, and you shall be treated accordingly." And after the sentence was carried out, the young king married his proper bride, and the two of them governed their kingdom in peace and happiness.

Die zertanzten Schuhe

Es war einmal ein König, der hatte zwölf Töchter, eine immer schöner als die andere. Sie schliefen zusammen in einem Saal, wo ihre Betten nebeneinanderstanden, und abends, wenn sie darin lagen, schloß der König die Tür zu und verriegelte sie. Wenn er aber am Morgen die Türe aufschloß, so sah er, daß ihre Schuhe zertanzt waren, und niemand konnte herausbringen, wie das zugegangen war. Da ließ der König ausrufen, wer's könnte ausfindig machen, wo sie in der Nacht tanzten, der sollte sich eine davon zur Frau wählen und nach seinem Tod König sein; wer sich aber meldete und es nach drei Tagen und Nächten nicht herausbrächte, der hätte sein Leben verwirkt. Nicht lange, so meldete sich ein Königssohn und erbot sich, das Wagnis zu unternehmen. Er ward wohl aufgenommen und abends in ein Zimmer geführt, das an den Schlafsaal stieß. Sein Bett war da aufgeschlagen, und er sollte achthaben, wo sie hingingen und tanzten; und damit sie nichts heimlich treiben konnten oder zu einem andern Ort hinausgingen, war auch die Saaltüre offen gelassen. Dem Königssohn fiel's aber wie Blei auf die Augen, und er schlief ein, und als er am Morgen aufwachte, waren alle zwölfe zum Tanz gewesen, denn ihre Schuhe standen da und hatten Löcher in den Sohlen. Den zweiten und dritten Abend ging's nicht anders, und da ward ihm sein Haupt ohne Barmherzigkeit abgeschlagen. Es kamen hernach noch viele und meldeten sich zu dem Wagestück, sie mußten aber alle ihr Leben lassen. Nun trug sich's zu, daß ein armer Soldat, der eine Wunde hatte und nicht mehr dienen konnte, sich auf dem Weg nach der Stadt befand, wo der König wohnte. Da begegnete ihm eine alte Frau, die fragte ihn, wo er hin wollte. »Ich weiß selber nicht recht«, sprach er, und setzte im Scherz hinzu: »Ich hätte wohl Lust, ausfindig zu machen, wo die Königstöchter ihre Schuhe vertanzen, und darnach König zu werden.« »Das ist so schwer nicht«, sagte die Alte, »du mußt den Wein nicht trinken, der dir abends gebracht wird, und mußt tun, als wärst du fest eingeschlafen.« darauf gab sie ihm ein Mäntelchen und sprach: »Wenn du das umhängst, so bist du unsichtbar und kannst den zwölfen dann nachschleichen.« Wie der Soldat den guten Rat bekommen hatte, ward's Ernst bei ihm, so daß er ein Herz faßte, vor den König ging und sich als Freier meldete. Er ward so gut aufgenommen wie die andern auch, und wurden ihm königliche Kleider angetan. Abends zur Schlafenszeit ward er in das Vorzimmer geführt, und als er zu Bette gehen wollte, kam die äl-

The Danced-Out Shoes

There was once a king who had twelve daughters, each one more beautiful than the next. They used to sleep together in one large room where their beds were side by side; in the evening, when they were in bed, the king would lock the door and bolt it. But when he opened the door in the morning, he saw that their shoes were worn out with dancing, and no one was able to discover how that had happened. Then the king issued a proclamation: whoever could learn where they danced at night was to choose one of them for his wife and become king after he died; but anyone who applied for the task, and couldn't find out within the space of three days and nights, was to forfeit his life. Before long a prince applied and offered to undertake that risky task. He was warmly welcomed, and in the evening he was led to a room that adjoined the princesses's bedroom. A bed was prepared for him there, and he was to pay attention to where they went to dance; so that they couldn't do anything secretly or go out some other way, the door to their room was left unlocked, as well. But the prince's eyelids became as heavy as lead, and he fell asleep; when he awoke in the morning, all twelve had been dancing, because their shoes were there with holes in the bottoms. On the second and third evenings, things were just the same, and so his head was cut off without mercy. Afterwards, many more men came and applied for the perilous adventure, but all of them lost their lives. It now came about that a poor soldier, who had been wounded and was no longer fit for duty, was on the road to the town where the king lived. Then he met an old woman, who asked him where he was headed. "I myself don't rightly know," he said, and added jokingly: "I wouldn't mind finding out where the princesses wear out their shoes dancing, so I could become king later on." "That's not so difficult," said the old woman; "you must avoid drinking the wine that's brought to you in the evening, and you must pretend to be fast asleep." Then she gave him a short cape, saying: "Whenever you throw this over your shoulders, you will become invisible, and then you can sneak after the twelve girls." When the soldier received that good advice, he became serious about the matter; he plucked up his courage, appeared before the king, and declared himself a suitor. He was welcomed as hospitably as the rest, and he was dressed in royal garb. In the evening at bedtime he was taken to that anteroom, and when he was about to go to bed, the eldest princess came, bringing him a goblet of wine; but he had tied a sponge under his chin, and

teste und brachte ihm einen Becher Wein; aber er hatte sich einen Schwamm unter das Kinn gebunden, ließ den Wein da hineinlaufen und trank keinen Tropfen. Dann legte er sich nieder, und als er ein Weilchen gelegen hatte, fing er an zu schnarchen wie im tiefsten Schlaf. Das hörten die zwölf Königstöchter, lachten, und die älteste sprach: »Der hätte auch sein Leben sparen können.« Danach standen sie auf, öffneten Schränke, Kisten und Kasten und holten prächtige Kleider heraus; putzten sich vor den Spiegeln, sprangen herum und freuten sich auf den Tanz. Nur die jüngste sagte: »Ich weiß nicht, ihr freut euch, aber mir ist so wunderlich zumute: gewiß widerfährt uns ein Unglück.« »Du bist eine Schneegans«, sagte die älteste, »die sich immer fürchtet. Hast du vergessen, wieviel Königssöhne schon umsonst dagewesen sind? Dem Soldaten hätt ich nicht einmal brauchen einen Schlaftrunk zu geben, der Lümmel wäre doch nicht aufgewacht.« Wie sie alle fertig waren, sahen sie erst nach dem Soldaten, aber der hatte die Augen zugetan, rührte und regte sich nicht, und sie glaubten nun ganz sicher zu sein. Da ging die älteste an ihr Bett und klopfte daran; alsbald sank es in die Erde, und sie stiegen durch die Öffnung hinab, eine nach der andern, die älteste voran. Der Soldat, der alles mit angesehen hatte, zauderte nicht lange, hing sein Mäntelchen um und stieg hinter der jüngsten mit hinab. Mitten auf der Treppe trat er ihr ein wenig aufs Kleid, da erschrak sie und rief: »Was ist das? Wer hält mich am Kleid?« »Sei nicht so einfältig«, sagte die älteste, »du bist an einem Haken hängengeblieben.« Da gingen sie vollends hinab, und wie sie unten waren, standen sie in einem wunderprächtigen Baumgang, da waren alle Blätter von Silber und schimmerten und glänzten. Der Soldat dachte: »Du willst dir ein Wahrzeichen mitnehmen«, und brach einen Zweig davon ab: da fuhr ein gewaltiger Krach aus dem Baume. Die jüngste rief wieder: »Es ist nicht richtig, habt ihr den Knall gehört?« Die älteste aber sprach: »Das sind Freudenschüsse, weil wir unsere Prinzen bald erlöst haben.« Sie kamen darauf in einen Baumgang, wo alle Blätter von Gold, und endlich in einen dritten, wo sie klarer Demant waren; von beiden brach er einen Zweig ab, wobei es jedesmal krachte, daß die jüngste vor Schrecken zusammenfuhr: aber die älteste blieb dabei, es wären Freudenschüsse. Sie gingen weiter und kamen zu einem großen Wasser, darauf standen zwölf Schifflein, und in jedem Schifflein saß ein schöner Prinz, die hatten auf die zwölfe gewartet, und jeder nahm eine zu sich, der Soldat aber setzte sich mit der jüngsten ein. Da sprach der Prinz: »Ich weiß nicht, das Schiff ist heute viel schwerer,

he let the wine flow into it, while he didn't drink a drop. Then he lay down, and after lying there awhile, he began to snore as if fast asleep. The twelve princesses heard it and laughed, and the eldest said: "This one, too, could have been more careful with his life." Then they got up, opened wardrobes, trunks, and chests, and took splendid gowns out of them; they adorned themselves in front of the mirrors and skipped about, looking forward to the dance. Only, the youngest one said: "I don't know; you're looking forward to it, but I have such an odd feeling: I'm sure we're in for some misfortune." "You're a silly goose," her eldest sister said, "and you're always afraid. Have you forgotten how many princes have already been here for nothing? As for the soldier, I didn't even need to give him a sleeping potion; that roughneck wouldn't have woken up anyway." When all of them were ready, they first took a look at the soldier, but he had his eyes closed, and didn't stir or budge, and they now believed they had nothing to worry about. Then the eldest princess went to her bed and knocked on it; immediately it sank through the floor, and they walked down through the opening, one after the other, the eldest in front. The soldier, who had observed all of this, didn't hesitate long, but put on his cape and followed them down, walking right behind the youngest sister. Halfway down the stairs he stepped on her gown for an instant; she became alarmed and cried out: "What's this? Who's tugging me by my dress?" "Don't be such a simpleton," said her eldest sister, "you got caught on a hook." Then they reached the bottom of the stairs and, down there, they were on a stupendous avenue of trees where all the leaves were of silver, glittering and shining. The soldier said to himself: "You ought to take along a piece of evidence"; and he broke off a twig: then a tremendous noise issued from the tree. The youngest princess shouted again: "There's something wrong; didn't you hear that crack?" But her eldest sister said: "Those are volleys of rejoicing because we will soon have released our princes from their spell." After that, they came to an avenue of trees where all the leaves were of gold, and finally to a third, where they were diamonds of the purest water; he broke off a twig in each avenue, creating an awful noise each time, so that the youngest princess started in fear: but the eldest princess insisted that they were volleys of rejoicing. They went on and reached a broad river where twelve small boats were waiting; in each boat sat a handsome prince; the princes had been expecting the twelve girls, and now each one helped a princess into his boat, and the soldier sat down in the youngest princess's boat. Then her prince said: "I don't

und ich muß aus allen Kräften rudern, wenn ich es fortbringen soll.« »Wovon sollte das kommen«, sprach die jüngste, »als vom warmen Wetter, es ist mir auch so heiß zumut.« Jenseits des Wassers aber stand ein schönes, hellerleuchtetes Schloß, woraus eine lustige Musik erschallte von Pauken und Trompeten. Sie ruderten hinüber, traten ein, und jeder Prinz tanzte mit seiner Liebsten; der Soldat tanzte aber unsichtbar mit, und wenn eine einen Becher mit Wein hielt, so trank er ihn aus, daß er leer war, wenn sie ihn an den Mund brachte; und der jüngsten ward auch angst darüber, aber die älteste brachte sie immer zum Schweigen. Sie tanzten da bis drei Uhr am andern Morgen, wo alle Schuhe durchgetanzt waren und sie aufhören mußten. Die Prinzen fuhren sie über das Wasser wieder zurück, und der Soldat setzte sich diesmal vornenhin zur ältesten. Am Ufer nahmen sie von ihren Prinzen Abschied und versprachen, in der folgenden Nacht wiederzukommen. Als sie an der Treppe waren, lief der Soldat voraus und legte sich in sein Bett, und als die zwölf langsam und müde heraufgetrippelt kamen, schnarchte er schon wieder so laut, daß sie's alle hören konnten, und sie sprachen: »Vor dem sind wir sicher.« Da taten sie ihre schönen Kleider aus, brachten sie weg, stellten die zertanzten Schuhe unter das Bett und legten sich nieder. Am andern Morgen wollte der Soldat nichts sagen, sondern das wunderliche Wesen noch mit ansehen, und ging die zweite und die dritte Nacht wieder mit. Da war alles wie das erstemal, und sie tanzten jedesmal, bis die Schuhe entzwei waren. Das drittemal aber nahm er zum Wahrzeichen einen Becher mit. Als die Stunde gekommen war, wo er antworten sollte, steckte er die drei Zweige und den Becher zu sich und ging vor den König, die zwölfe aber standen hinter der Türe und horchten, was er sagen würde. Als der König die Frage tat: »Wo haben meine zwölf Töchter ihre Schuhe in der Nacht vertanzt?«, so antwortete er: »Mit zwölf Prinzen in einem unterirdischen Schloß«, berichtete, wie es zugegangen war, und holte die Wahrzeichen hervor. Da ließ der König seine Töchter kommen und fragte sie, ob der Soldat die Wahrheit gesagt hätte, und da sie sahen, daß sie verraten waren und Leugnen nichts half, so mußten sie alles eingestehen. Darauf fragte ihn der König, welche er zur Frau haben wollte. Er antwortete: »Ich bin nicht mehr jung, so gebt mir die älteste.« Da ward noch an selbigem Tage die Hochzeit gehalten und ihm das Reich nach des Königs Tode versprochen. Aber die Prinzen wurden auf so viel Tage wieder verwünscht, als sie Nächte mit den zwölfen getanzt hatten.

know why, but the boat is much heavier tonight, and I have to row with all my might if I want it to keep moving." "What could cause that," said the youngest princess, "except the warm weather? I feel so warm all over, too." On the other side of the river stood a beautiful, brightly illuminated palace, from which could be heard a joyful band of kettledrums and trumpets. They rowed across and went in, and each prince danced with his sweetheart; the soldier, invisible, joined in the dance, and whenever a princess held a goblet of wine, he drank out of it, till it was empty when she put it to her lips; the youngest princess was frightened by that, too, but her eldest sister silenced her every time. And so they danced until three o'clock in the morning, by which time all their shoes were worn through and they had to stop. The princes rowed them back across the river; this time the soldier sat in the first boat, with the eldest princess. On the riverbank the girls took leave of their princes, promising to return on the coming night. When they were at the staircase, the soldier ran ahead of them and returned to his bed; when the twelve girls had made their slow, weary climb with mincing steps, he was already snoring so loud that they could all hear it, and they said: "This one is no threat to us." Then they took off their beautiful gowns, put them away, placed the danced-out shoes under their beds, and lay down. The next morning, the soldier didn't say a thing; he wanted to see the unusual events again, and he went along on the second and third nights. Everything occurred like the first time, and each night they danced until their shoes were ruined. But the third time he took along a goblet as evidence. When the time came for him to make his report, he hid the three twigs and the goblet in his clothes and appeared before the king, while the twelve girls stood behind the door to listen to what he'd say. When the king asked: "Where did my twelve daughters wear out their shoes dancing at night?" he replied: "With twelve princes in an underground palace"; he recounted what had occurred, and drew forth his evidence. Then the king sent for his daughters and asked them whether the soldier had spoken the truth; since they saw that they had been exposed and it would do no good to deny the facts, they had to make a full confession. Then the king asked him which one he wanted for his wife. He said: "I'm not a youngster anymore; give me the oldest one." And so, on that very day, their wedding was celebrated and he was promised the kingdom after the king's death. But the princes were enchanted again for as many days as the number of nights they had danced with the twelve princesses.

Schneeweißchen und Rosenrot

Eine arme Witwe, die lebte einsam in einem Hüttchen, und vor dem Hüttchen war ein Garten, darin standen zwei Rosenbäumchen, davon trug das eine weiße, das andere rote Rosen; und sie hatte zwei Kinder, die glichen den beiden Rosenbäumchen, und das eine hieß Schneeweißchen, das andere Rosenrot. Sie waren aber so fromm und gut, so arbeitsam und unverdrossen, als je zwei Kinder auf der Welt gewesen sind: Schneeweißchen war nur stiller und sanfter als Rosenrot. Rosenrot sprang lieber in den Wiesen und Feldern umher, suchte Blumen und fing Sommervögel; Schneeweißchen aber saß daheim bei der Mutter, half ihr im Hauswesen oder las ihr vor, wenn nichts zu tun war. Die beiden Kinder hatten einander so lieb, daß sie sich immer an den Händen faßten, sooft sie zusammen ausgingen; und wenn Schneeweißchen sagte: »Wir wollen uns nicht verlassen«, so antwortete Rosenrot: »Solange wir leben, nicht«, und die Mutter setzte hinzu: »Was das eine hat, soll's mit dem andern teilen.« Oft liefen sie im Walde allein umher und sammelten rote Beeren, aber kein Tier tat ihnen etwas zuleid, sondern sie kamen vertraulich herbei: das Häschen fraß ein Kohlblatt aus ihren Händen, das Reh graste an ihrer Seite, der Hirsch sprang ganz lustig vorbei, und die Vögel blieben auf den Ästen sitzen und sangen, was sie nur wußten. Kein Unfall traf sie: wenn sie sich im Walde verspätet hatten und die Nacht sie überfiel, so legten sie sich nebeneinander auf das Moos und schliefen, bis der Morgen kam, und die Mutter wußte das und hatte ihrentwegen keine Sorge. Einmal, als sie im Walde übernachtet hatten und das Morgenrot sie aufweckte, da sahen sie ein schönes Kind in einem weißen, glänzenden Kleidchen neben ihrem Lager sitzen. Es stand auf und blickte sie ganz freundlich an, sprach aber nichts und ging in den Wald hinein. Und als sie sich umsahen, so hatten sie ganz nahe bei einem Abgrunde geschlafen und wären gewiß hineingefallen, wenn sie in der Dunkelheit noch ein paar Schritte weitergegangen wären. Die Mutter aber sagte ihnen, das müßte der Engel gewesen sein, der gute Kinder bewache.

Schneeweißchen und Rosenrot hielten das Hüttchen der Mutter so reinlich, daß es eine Freude war hineinzuschauen. Im Sommer besorgte Rosenrot das Haus und stellte der Mutter jeden Morgen, ehe sie aufwachte, einen Blumenstrauß vors Bett, darin war von jedem Bäumchen eine Rose. Im Winter zündete Schneeweißchen das Feuer

Snow White and Rose Red

A poor widow lived alone in a small cottage, and in front of the cottage was a garden in which grew two rosebushes, one of which bore white roses and the other red; and she had two children who resembled the two rosebushes; one of them was called Snow White, and the other Rose Red. They were as pious and good, as diligent and untiring, as any two children who ever existed: only, Snow White was quieter and gentler than Rose Red. Rose Red preferred to romp about in the meadows and fields, seeking flowers and catching butterflies; but Snow White would stay home with her mother, helping her with the housework or reading aloud to her when there were no chores to be done. The two girls loved each other so much that they always held hands whenever they went out together; and whenever Snow White said: "We'll always stay together," Rose Red would answer: "As long as we live," and their mother would add: "Whatever one of you has, she should share with the other." Often they ran around in the woods on their own, gathering red berries, but no animal ever harmed them; instead they came over trustingly: the little hare ate a cabbage leaf from their hands, the roe deer grazed beside them, the stag leaped past them merrily, and the songbirds remained seated on their branches, singing every song they knew. They never had an accident: whenever they had remained too long in the woods and night overtook them there, they would lie down side by side on the moss and sleep until morning; their mother was used to that, and wasn't worried about them. Once, after they had spent the night in the woods and the dawn awakened them, they saw a lovely child in a gleaming-white little robe sitting next to their bed of moss. He stood up and gave them a very friendly glance, but said nothing and went deeper into the woods. And when they looked around, they saw that they had been sleeping right near a precipice, and would surely have fallen into it if they had taken a few more steps in the darkness. Their mother told them it must have been the angel who watches over good children.

Snow White and Rose Red kept their mother's little cottage so clean that it was a pleasure to look into it. In the summer Rose Red took care of the house, and every morning placed a bouquet of flowers in front of her mother's bed before she work up; in the bouquet was a rose from each bush. In the winter Snow White

an und hing den Kessel an den Feuerhaken, und der Kessel war von Messing, glänzte aber wie Gold, so rein war er gescheuert. Abends, wenn die Flocken fielen, sagte die Mutter: »Geh, Schneeweißchen, und schieb den Riegel vor«, und dann setzten sie sich an den Herd, und die Mutter nahm die Brille und las aus einem großen Buche vor, und die beiden Mädchen hörten zu, saßen und spannen; neben ihnen lag ein Lämmchen auf dem Boden, und hinter ihnen auf einer Stange saß ein weißes Täubchen und hatte seinen Kopf unter den Flügel gesteckt.

Eines Abends, als sie so vertraulich beisammensaßen, klopfte jemand an die Türe, als wollte er eingelassen sein. Die Mutter sprach: »Geschwind, Rosenrot, mach auf, es wird ein Wanderer sein, der Obdach sucht.« Rosenrot ging und schob den Riegel weg und dachte, es wäre ein armer Mann, aber der war es nicht, es war ein Bär, der seinen dicken schwarzen Kopf zur Türe hereinstreckte. Rosenrot schrie laut und sprang zurück: das Lämmchen blökte, das Täubchen flatterte auf, und Schneeweißchen versteckte sich hinter der Mutter Bett. Der Bär aber fing an zu sprechen und sagte: »Fürchtet euch nicht, ich tue euch nichts zuleid, ich bin halb erfroren und will mich nur ein wenig bei euch wärmen.« »Du armer Bär«, sprach die Mutter, »leg dich ans Feuer und gib nur acht, daß dir dein Pelz nicht brennt.« Dann rief sie: »Schneeweißchen, Rosenrot, kommt hervor, der Bär tut euch nichts, er meint's ehrlich.« Da kamen sie beide heran, und nach und nach näherten sich auch das Lämmchen und Täubchen und hatten keine Furcht vor ihm. Der Bär sprach: »Ihr Kinder, klopft mir den Schnee ein wenig aus dem Pelzwerk«, und sie holten den Besen und kehrten dem Bär das Fell rein; er aber streckte sich ans Feuer und brummte ganz vergnügt und behaglich. Nicht lange, so wurden sie ganz vertraut und trieben Mutwillen mit dem unbeholfenen Gast. Sie zausten ihm das Fell mit den Händen, setzten ihre Füßchen auf seinen Rücken und walgerten ihn hin und her, oder sie nahmen eine Haselrute und schlugen auf ihn los, und wenn er brummte, so lachten sie. Der Bär ließ sich's aber gerne gefallen, nur wenn sie's gar zu arg machten, rief er: »Laßt mich am Leben, ihr Kinder:

> Schneeweißchen, Rosenrot,
> schlägst dir den Freier tot.«

Als Schlafenszeit war und die andern zu Bett gingen, sagte die Mutter zu dem Bär: »Du kannst in Gottes Namen da am Herde liegenbleiben, so bist du vor der Kälte und dem bösen Wetter geschützt.« Sobald der Tag graute, ließen ihn die beiden Kinder hin-

lit the fire and hung the kettle on its hook in the hearth; the kettle was of brass, but shone like gold, it was so carefully scoured. In the evening, when the snowflakes fell, their mother would say: "Snow White, go and bar the door"; then they would sit down by the hearth, and their mother would put on her glasses and read aloud out of a big book, while the two girls listened as they sat spinning; on the floor beside them lay a little lamb, and on a perch behind them sat a white dove with its head tucked under one wing.

One evening, while they were sitting together in that loving companionship, someone knocked at the door as if seeking admittance. The girls' mother said: "Quick, Rose Red, open the door, it's probably some traveler looking for shelter." Rose Red went and pulled back the bolt, thinking it would be some poor man, but it wasn't: it was a bear, who stuck his big, black head inside the door. Rose Red gave a loud scream and jumped back; the little lamb bleated, the dove fluttered upward, and Snow White hid behind her mother's bed. But the bear began to speak, saying: "Don't be afraid, I won't hurt you; I'm half frozen and I merely want to warm up a little at your place." "You poor bear," the girls' mother said, "lie down by the fire and just be careful that your fur doesn't burn." Then she called: "Snow White, Rose Red, come out, the bear won't harm you, his intentions are good." Then they both stepped forward, and little by little the lamb and the dove approached, also, and weren't afraid of him. The bear said: "Children, beat some of this snow out of my fur"; and they fetched the broom and swept the bear's coat clean; then he stretched out by the fire, growling softly in his contented coziness. Before long, the girls regained all their confidence and played pranks on their clumsy guest. They tousled his fur with their hands, put their little feet on his back, and rolled him to and fro; or else they took a hazel wand and beat him, and laughed when he growled. The bear put up with everything, though whenever they got too wild, he'd shout: "Don't kill me, children:

> Snow White and Rose Red,
> do you want your suitor dead?"

When it was bedtime and the others went to bed, the girls' mother said to the bear: "You can remain lying there at the hearth, in God's name; that way, you'll be protected from the cold and the bad weather." As soon as day broke, the two children let him out,

aus, und er trabte über den Schnee in den Wald hinein. Von nun an kam der Bär jeden Abend zu der bestimmten Stunde, legte sich an den Herd und erlaubte den Kindern, Kurzweil mit ihm zu treiben, soviel sie wollten; und sie waren so gewöhnt an ihn, daß die Türe nicht eher zugeriegelt ward, als bis der schwarze Gesell angelangt war.

Als das Frühjahr herangekommen und draußen alles grün war, sagte der Bär eines Morgens zu Schneeweißchen: »Nun muß ich fort und darf den ganzen Sommer nicht wiederkommen.« »Wo gehst du denn hin, lieber Bär?« fragte Schneeweißchen. »Ich muß in den Wald und meine Schätze vor den bösen Zwergen hüten: im Winter, wenn die Erde hartgefroren ist, müssen sie wohl unten bleiben und können sich nicht durcharbeiten, aber jetzt, wenn die Sonne die Erde aufgetaut und erwärmt hat, da brechen sie durch, steigen herauf, suchen und stehlen; was einmal in ihren Händen ist und in ihren Höhlen liegt, das kommt so leicht nicht wieder an des Tages Licht.« Schneeweißchen war ganz traurig über den Abschied, und als es ihm die Türe aufriegelte und der Bär sich hinausdrängte, blieb er an dem Türhaken hängen, und ein Stück seiner Haut riß auf, und da war es Schneeweißchen, als hätte es Gold durchschimmern gesehen; aber es war seiner Sache nicht gewiß. Der Bär lief eilig fort und war bald hinter den Bäumen verschwunden.

Nach einiger Zeit schickte die Mutter die Kinder in den Wald, Reisig zu sammeln. Da fanden sie draußen einen großen Baum, der lag gefällt auf dem Boden, und an dem Stamme sprang zwischen dem Gras etwas auf und ab, sie konnten aber nicht unterscheiden, was es war. Als sie näher kamen, sahen sie einen Zwerg mit einem alten, verwelkten Gesicht und einem ellenlangen, schneeweißen Bart. Das Ende des Bartes war in eine Spalte des Baums eingeklemmt, und der Kleine sprang hin und her wie ein Hündchen an einem Seil und wußte nicht, wie er sich helfen sollte. Er glotzte die Mädchen mit seinen roten feurigen Augen an und schrie: »Was steht ihr da! Könnt ihr nicht herbeigehen und mir Beistand leisten?« »Was hast du angefangen, kleines Männchen?« fragte Rosenrot. »Dumme, neugierige Gans«, antwortete der Zwerg, »den Baum habe ich mir spalten wollen, um kleines Holz in der Küche zu haben; bei den dicken Klötzen verbrennt gleich das bißchen Speise, das unsereiner braucht, der nicht so viel hinunterschlingt als ihr grobes, gieriges Volk. Ich hatte den Keil schon glücklich hineingetrieben, und es wäre alles nach Wunsch gegangen, aber das verwünschte Holz war zu glatt und sprang unversehens heraus, und der Baum fuhr so geschwind zusammen, daß ich meinen schönen weißen Bart nicht mehr herausziehen

and he trotted across the snow into the woods. From that day on, the bear came every evening at the same time, lay down by the hearth, and allowed the children to have as much fun with him as they wanted; and they grew so used to him that they never bolted the door before their black companion had arrived.

When spring had come, and everything outdoors was green, the bear said to Snow White one morning: "Now I have to go away, and I can't come back all summer long." "Where are you going, dear bear?" Snow White asked. "I must go to the forest and guard my treasures from the wicked dwarfs: in wintertime, when the ground is frozen stiff, they've got to stay below, and can't work their way through; but now that the sun has softened and warmed the ground, they break through, climb up, look for booty, and steal; once something is in their hands and stored in their caves, it's not so easy to bring it back to the daylight." Snow White was very sad over his departure, and when she opened the bolt on the door for him and the bear squeezed out, he caught his fur on the door hook and a piece of his skin tore open; at that moment Snow White thought she saw gold gleaming through the rip, but she wasn't sure. The bear ran away hastily and had soon disappeared behind the trees.

Some time after that, the girls' mother sent them into the forest to gather brushwood. Out there they found a big tree that had been cut down and was lying on the ground. By its trunk something was jumping up and down in the grass, but they couldn't make out what it was. When they came closer, they saw a dwarf with an old, withered face and an ell-long, snowy-white beard. The tip of his beard was wedged into a crack in the bark of the tree, and the little man was jumping back and forth like a puppy on a leash; he didn't know how to escape. He glared at the girls with his fiery-red eyes and yelled: "Why are you just standing there? Can't you come over and give me a hand?" "What did you do to get this way, little gnome?" Rose Red asked. "Stupid, curious goose!" the dwarf replied; "I wanted to split up the tree into small pieces in order to have firewood for my kitchen; when I use thick pieces the small amount of food that we dwarfs need gets burned immediately: we don't wolf down as much food as you coarse, greedy people. I had already driven in the wedge successfully, and everything would have gone just as I wished, but that damned hunk of wood was too smooth and popped out unexpectedly, and the tree reclosed so quickly that I was no longer able to

konnte; nun steckt er drin, und ich kann nicht fort. Da lachen die albernen glatten Milchgesichter! Pfui, was seid ihr garstig!« Die Kinder gaben sich alle Mühe, aber sie konnten den Bart nicht herausziehen, er steckte zu fest. »Ich will laufen und Leute herbeiholen«, sagte Rosenrot. »Wahnsinnige Schafsköpfe«, schnarrte der Zwerg, »wer wird gleich Leute herbeirufen, ihr seid mir schon um zwei zu viel; fällt euch nicht Besseres ein?« »Sei nur nicht ungeduldig«, sagte Schneeweißchen, »ich will schon Rat schaffen«, holte sein Scherchen aus der Tasche und schnitt das Ende des Bartes ab. Sobald der Zwerg sich frei fühlte, griff er nach einem Sack, der zwischen den Wurzeln des Baums steckte und mit Gold gefüllt war, hob ihn heraus und brummte vor sich hin: »Ungehobeltes Volk, schneidet mir ein Stück von meinem stolzen Barte ab! Lohn's euch der Guckuck!« Damit schwang er seinen Sack auf den Rücken und ging fort, ohne die Kinder nur noch einmal anzusehen.

Einige Zeit danach wollten Schneeweißchen und Rosenrot ein Gericht Fische angeln. Als sie nahe bei dem Bach waren, sahen sie, daß etwas wie eine große Heuschrecke nach dem Wasser zuhüpfte, als wollte es hineinspringen. Sie liefen heran und erkannten den Zwerg. »Wo willst du hin?« sagte Rosenrot, »du willst doch nicht ins Wasser?« »Solch ein Narr bin ich nicht«, schrie der Zwerg, »seht ihr nicht, der verwünschte Fisch will mich hineinziehen?« Der Kleine hatte dagesessen und geangelt, und unglücklicherweise hatte der Wind seinen Bart mit der Angelschnur verflochten; als gleich darauf ein großer Fisch anbiß, fehlten dem schwachen Geschöpf die Kräfte, ihn herauszuziehen: der Fisch behielt die Oberhand und riß den Zwerg zu sich hin. Zwar hielt er sich an allen Halmen und Binsen, aber das half nicht viel, er mußte den Bewegungen des Fisches folgen und war in beständiger Gefahr, ins Wasser gezogen zu werden. Die Mädchen kamen zu rechter Zeit, hielten ihn fest und versuchten, den Bart von der Schnur loszumachen, aber vergebens, Bart und Schnur waren fest ineinander verwirrt. Es blieb nichts übrig, als das Scherchen hervorzuholen und den Bart abzuschneiden, wobei ein kleiner Teil desselben verlorenging. Als der Zwerg das sah, schrie er sie an: »Ist das Manier, ihr Lorche, einem das Gesicht zu schänden? Nicht genug, daß ihr mir den Bart unten abgestutzt habt, jetzt schneidet ihr mir den besten Teil davon ab: ich darf mich vor den Meinigen gar nicht sehen lassen. Daß ihr laufen müßtet und die Schuhsohlen verloren hättet!« Dann holte er einen Sack Perlen, der im Schilfe lag, und ohne ein Wort weiter zu sagen, schleppte er ihn fort und verschwand hinter einem Stein.

pull out my beautiful white beard; now it's caught there, and I
can't leave. Look, those dumb, smooth babyfaces are laughing!
Phew, are you disgusting!" The girls did their best, but they
couldn't pull out his beard, it was stuck too tightly. "I'll run and
bring some people," said Rose Red. "Crazy fools!" the dwarf cried
with a twang; "who wants to call over more people? As it is, you're
two too many. Don't you have any better ideas?" "Just don't be impatient," said Snow White; "I've got the solution." She took her little scissors out of her pocket and cut off the tip of his beard. As
soon as the dwarf sensed that he was free, he reached for a sack
that he had placed among the roots of a tree—a sack filled with
gold—picked it up, and grumbled to himself: "Unrefined people!
They cut off a piece of my magnificent beard! Get your reward
from the devil!" Then he swung his sack onto his shoulder and
made off without even giving the girls another glance.

   Some time after that, Snow White and Rose Red wanted to
catch some fish for a meal. When they were near the brook, they
saw something like a big grasshopper hopping toward the water as
if intending to jump in. They ran over and recognized the dwarf.
"Where are you off to?" asked Rose Red; "you surely don't want to
jump in the brook?" "I'm not so big a fool," yelled the dwarf; "don't
you see that this damned fish is trying to pull me in?" The little
man had been sitting there fishing, and unfortunately the wind had
caused his beard to get tangled up in the line; immediately after
that, a big fish bit, and that weak creature didn't have the strength
to pull it up: the fish held the upper hand and was dragging the
dwarf toward itself. To be sure, he caught hold of every blade of
grass and bulrush, but it didn't do him much good; he was compelled to follow the fish's movements and he was in constant danger of being pulled into the water. The girls arrived at the opportune moment; they held him tight and tried to liberate his beard
from the fishing line, but in vain: beard and line were hopelessly
tangled. There was no other remedy than to take out the scissors
and cut the beard loose, which meant sacrificing a small part of it.
When the dwarf saw that, he yelled at them: "You call that polite,
you salamanders, to dishonor a man's face? It wasn't enough for
you to trim my beard at the tip, now you've cut off the better part
of it: I can't show my face among my own kind. I hope you need to
run and you lose the soles of your shoes!" Then he seized a sack of
pearls that had been lying in the reeds and, without saying another
word, he dragged it away and disappeared behind a rock.

Es trug sich zu, daß bald hernach die Mutter die beiden Mädchen nach der Stadt schickte, Zwirn, Nadeln, Schnüre und Bänder einzukaufen. Der Weg führte sie über eine Heide, auf der hier und da mächtige Felsenstücke zerstreut lagen. Da sahen sie einen großen Vogel in der Luft schweben, der langsam über ihnen kreiste, sich immer tiefer herabsenkte und endlich nicht weit bei einem Felsen niederstieß. Gleich darauf hörten sie einen durchdringenden, jämmerlichen Schrei. Sie liefen herzu und sahen mit Schrecken, daß der Adler ihren alten Bekannten, den Zwerg, gepackt hatte und ihn forttragen wollte. Die mitleidigen Kinder hielten gleich das Männchen fest und zerrten sich so lange mit dem Adler herum, bis er seine Beute fahrenließ. Als der Zwerg sich von dem ersten Schrecken erholt hatte, schrie er mit seiner kreischenden Stimme:»Konntet ihr nicht säuberlicher mit mir umgehen? Gerissen habt ihr an meinem dünnen Röckchen, daß es überall zerfetzt und durchlöchert ist, unbeholfenes und täppisches Gesindel, das ihr seid!« Dann nahm er einen Sack mit Edelsteinen und schlüpfte wieder unter den Felsen in seine Höhle. Die Mädchen waren an seinen Undank schon gewöhnt, setzten ihren Weg fort und verrichteten ihr Geschäft in der Stadt. Als sie beim Heimweg wieder auf die Heide kamen, überraschten sie den Zwerg, der auf einem reinlichen Plätzchen seinen Sack mit Edelsteinen ausgeschüttet und nicht gedacht hatte, daß so spät noch jemand daherkommen würde. Die Abendsonne schien über die glänzenden Steine, sie schimmerten und leuchteten so prächtig in allen Farben, daß die Kinder stehenblieben und sie betrachteten.»Was steht ihr da und habt Maulaffen feil!« schrie der Zwerg, und sein aschgraues Gesicht ward zinnoberrot vor Zorn. Er wollte mit seinen Scheltworten fortfahren, als sich ein lautes Brummen hören ließ und ein schwarzer Bär aus dem Walde herbeitrabte. Erschrocken sprang der Zwerg auf, aber er konnte nicht mehr zu seinem Schlupfwinkel gelangen, der Bär war schon in seiner Nähe. Da rief er in Herzensangst:»Lieber Herr Bär, verschont mich, ich will Euch alle meine Schätze geben, sehet, die schönen Edelsteine, die da liegen. Schenkt mir das Leben, was habt Ihr an mir kleinen, schmächtigen Kerl? Ihr spürt mich nicht zwischen den Zähnen; da, die beiden gottlosen Mädchen packt, das sind für Euch zarte Bissen, fett wie junge Wachteln, die freßt in Gottes Namen.« Der Bär kümmerte sich um seine Worte nicht, gab dem boshaften Geschöpf einen einzigen Schlag mit der Tatze, und es regte sich nicht mehr.

Die Mädchen waren fortgesprungen, aber der Bär rief ihnen nach:»Schneeweißchen und Rosenrot, fürchtet euch nicht, wartet, ich will mit euch gehen.« Da erkannten sie seine Stimme und blieben stehen,

It came to pass that, shortly afterward, the girls' mother sent them into town to buy thread, needles, bodice laces, and ribbons. Their path took them across a heath, on which huge boulders were scattered here and there. Then they saw a big bird hovering in the air, making slow circles overhead; it was coming lower all the time, and finally alighted not far away, next to one of the boulders. Right after that, they heard a piercing cry of anguish. They ran over and, to their horror, saw that the eagle had seized their old acquaintance, the dwarf, and was about to fly away with him. The sympathetic children immediately got a firm grip on the little man, and tussled with the eagle until it released its prey. When the dwarf had recovered from his initial shock, he yelled in his grating voice: "Couldn't you handle me more gently? You've torn my thin little jacket, so it's in shreds and full of holes, you clumsy, awkward good-for-nothings!" Then he picked up a sack filled with jewels and slipped back under the boulder to his cave. The girls were already accustomed to his ingratitude; they continued on their walk and concluded their business in town. When they arrived back on the heath on their way home, they took the dwarf by surprise, coming upon him just as he had poured out his sack of jewels on an open spot, never thinking that anyone would still pass by that late. The setting sun was shining on the bright gems, which were glittering and beaming so splendidly in all colors that the girls halted to look at them. "Why are you standing there, gaping like imbeciles?" shouted the dwarf, and his ashen-gray face became beet-red with anger. He was about to continue his tirade of insults when a loud growl was heard and a black bear trotted over out of the forest. The dwarf leaped up in fright, but he could no longer reach his hiding place; the bear was already upon him. Then he called in deepest anguish: "Dear sir bear, spare me, I'll give you all my treasures; look at the beautiful jewels lying here. Let me keep my life; what good is a little, puny fellow like me to you? You wouldn't even notice me between your teeth; there, grab those two wicked girls, they're tender morsels for you, plump as young quail; eat *them*, for the love of God!" The bear paid no heed to his words, but gave the malicious creature a single blow with his paw, and he didn't stir anymore.

The girls had dashed away, but the bear called after them: "Snow White and Rose Red, don't be afraid, wait, I want to come with you." Then they recognized his voice and stopped,

und als der Bär bei ihnen war, fiel plötzlich die Bärenhaut ab, und er
stand da als ein schöner Mann und war ganz in Gold gekleidet. »Ich
bin eines Königs Sohn«, sprach er, »und war von dem gottlosen
Zwerg, der mir meine Schätze gestohlen hatte, verwünscht, als ein
wilder Bär in dem Walde zu laufen, bis ich durch seinen Tod erlöst
würde. Jetzt hat er seine wohlverdiente Strafe empfangen.«

Schneeweißchen ward mit ihm vermählt und Rosenrot mit seinem
Bruder, und sie teilten die großen Schätze miteinander, die der Zwerg
in seine Höhle zusammengetragen hatte. Die alte Mutter lebte noch
lange Jahre ruhig und glücklich bei ihren Kindern. Die zwei Rosenbäumchen aber nahm sie mit, und sie standen vor ihrem Fenster und
trugen jedes Jahr die schönsten Rosen, weiß und rot.

Der Meisterdieb

Eines Tages saß vor einem ärmlichen Hause ein alter Mann mit seiner
Frau und wollten von der Arbeit ein wenig ausruhen. Da kam auf einmal ein prächtiger, mit vier Rappen bespannter Wagen herbeige-
fahren, aus dem ein reichgekleideter Herr stieg. Der Bauer stand auf,
trat zu dem Herrn und fragte, was sein Verlangen wäre und worin er
ihm dienen könnte. Der Fremde reichte dem Alten die Hand und
sagte: »Ich wünsche nichts, als einmal ein ländliches Gericht zu ge-
nießen. Bereitet mir Kartoffel, wie Ihr sie zu essen pflegt, dann will
ich mich zu Euerm Tisch setzen und sie mit Freude verzehren.« Der
Bauer lächelte und sagte: »Ihr seid ein Graf oder Fürst oder gar ein
Herzog, vornehme Herrn haben manchmal solch ein Gelüsten; Euer
Wunsch soll aber erfüllt werden.« Die Frau ging in die Küche, und sie
fing an, Kartoffel zu waschen und zu reiben, und wollte Klöße daraus
bereiten, wie sie die Bauern essen. Während sie bei der Arbeit stand,
sagte der Bauer zu dem Fremden: »Kommt einstweilen mit mir in
meinen Hausgarten, wo ich noch etwas zu schaffen habe.« In dem
Garten hatte er Löcher gegraben und wollte jetzt Bäume einsetzen.
»Habt Ihr keine Kinder«, fragte der Fremde, »die Euch bei der Arbeit
behilflich sein könnten?« »Nein«, antwortete der Bauer; »ich habe
freilich einen Sohn gehabt«, setzte er hinzu, »aber der ist schon seit
langer Zeit in die weite Welt gegangen. Es war ein ungeratener Junge,
klug und verschlagen, aber er wollte nichts lernen und machte lauter
böse Streiche; zuletzt lief er mir fort, und seitdem habe ich nichts von
ihm gehört.« Der Alte nahm ein Bäumchen, setzte es in ein Loch und

and when the bear had rejoined them, his bearskin suddenly fell off and he stood there as a handsome man dressed all in gold. "I am a king's son," he said, "and I was placed under a curse by that evil dwarf, who had stolen my treasures: I was to run around in the forest in the shape of a wild bear until I was delivered by his death. Now he has received his well-deserved punishment."

Snow White married him, and Rose Red married his brother, and they shared the immense treasures that the dwarf had accumulated in his cave. This old mother lived many more years in peace and happiness with her children. But she took along the two rosebushes, which were planted in front of her window; and every year they bore the loveliest roses, white and red.

The Master Thief

One day an old man was sitting with his wife in front of their humble house; they wanted to rest a little after their work. Then all at once a splendid carriage drawn by four fine black horses came driving up, and an expensively dressed gentleman got out of it. The farmer stood up, walked over to the gentleman, and asked what his pleasure was and how he could help him. The stranger gave the old man his hand, saying: "I don't want a thing except to enjoy a country meal. Cook me some potatoes the way you usually eat them; then I'll sit down at your table and eat them happily." The farmer smiled and said: "You're a count, or a prince of the nobility, or even a duke; aristocratic people sometimes get such cravings; but your wish shall be granted." The woman went to the kitchen and began to wash and grate potatoes, intending to make dumplings of them, of the sort that farmers eat. While she was at her work, the farmer said to the stranger: "Come into my garden with me for a while; I still have something to do there." In the garden he had dug holes and now wanted to plant trees in them. The stranger asked: "Don't you have any children who could help you out with your work?" "No," the farmer replied; "it's true that I once had a son," he added, "but it's a long time now since he set out to make his way in the world. He was a wayward boy, clever and shrewd, but he refused to learn a trade, and did nothing but cause mischief; finally he ran away on me, and I never heard anything from him

stieß einen Pfahl daneben; und als er Erde hineingeschaufelt und sie
festgestampft hatte, band er den Stamm unten, oben und in der Mitte
mit einem Strohseil fest an den Pfahl. »Aber sagt mir«, sprach der
Herr, »warum bindet Ihr den krummen, knorrichten Baum, der dort
in der Ecke fast bis auf den Boden gebückt liegt, nicht auch an einen
Pfahl wie diesen, damit er strack wächst?« Der Alte lächelte und
sagte: »Herr, Ihr redet, wie Ihr's versteht: man sieht wohl, daß Ihr
Euch mit der Gärtnerei nicht abgegeben habt. Der Baum dort ist alt
und verknorzt, den kann niemand mehr gerad machen: Bäume muß
man ziehen, solange sie jung sind.« »Es ist wie bei Euerm Sohn«,
sagte der Fremde, »hättet Ihr den gezogen, wie er noch jung war, so
wäre er nicht fortgelaufen; jetzt wird er auch hart und knorzig geworden sein.« »Freilich«, antwortete der Alte, »es ist schon lange, seit er
fortgegangen ist; er wird sich verändert haben.« »Würdet Ihr ihn noch
erkennen, wenn er vor Euch träte?« fragte der Fremde. »Am Gesicht
schwerlich«, antwortete der Bauer, »aber er hat ein Zeichen an sich,
ein Muttermal auf der Schulter, das wie eine Bohne aussieht.« Als er
das gesagt hatte, zog der Fremde den Rock aus, entblößte seine
Schulter und zeigte dem Bauer die Bohne. »Herr Gott«, rief der Alte,
»du bist wahrhaftig mein Sohn«, und die Liebe zu seinem Kind regte
sich in seinem Herzen. »Aber«, setzte er hinzu, »wie kannst du mein
Sohn sein, du bist ein großer Herr geworden und lebst in Reichtum
und Überfluß? Auf welchem Weg bist du dazu gelangt?« »Ach, Vater«,
erwiderte der Sohn, »der junge Baum war an keinen Pfahl gebunden
und ist krumm gewachsen: jetzt ist er zu alt; er wird nicht wieder
gerad. Wie ich das alles erworben habe? Ich bin ein Dieb geworden.
Aber erschreckt Euch nicht, ich bin ein Meisterdieb. Für mich gibt es
weder Schloß noch Riegel: wonach mich gelüstet, das ist mein. Glaubt
nicht, daß ich stehle wie ein gemeiner Dieb, ich nehme nur vom
Überfluß der Reichen. Arme Leute sind sicher: ich gebe ihnen lieber,
als daß ich ihnen etwas nehme. So auch, was ich ohne Mühe, List und
Gewandtheit haben kann, das rühre ich nicht an.« »Ach, mein Sohn«,
sagte der Vater, »es gefällt mir doch nicht, ein Dieb bleibt ein Dieb;
ich sage dir, es nimmt kein gutes Ende.« Er führte ihn zu der Mutter,
und als sie hörte, daß es ihr Sohn war, weinte sie vor Freude, als er ihr
aber sagte, daß er ein Meisterdieb geworden wäre, so flossen ihr zwei
Ströme über das Gesicht. Endlich sagte sie: »Wenn er auch ein Dieb
geworden ist, so ist er doch mein Sohn, und meine Augen haben ihn
noch einmal gesehen.«

    Sie setzten sich an den Tisch, und er aß mit seinen Eltern wieder
einmal die schlechte Kost, die er lange nicht gegessen hatte. Der Vater

again." The old man picked up a sapling, placed it in a hole, and drove in a stake next to it; after shoveling in dirt and stamping it down firmly, he tied the trunk securely to the stake with a straw rope at the bottom, at the top, and in the middle. "But tell me," said the gentleman, "why don't you also tie that crooked, gnarled tree in the corner there, that's bent almost to the ground, to a stake like this one, so that it grows straight?" The old man smiled and said: "Sir, you speak according to your understanding; it's easy to see that you haven't devoted much time to gardening. That tree over there is old and knobby; no one can straighten it out anymore: trees have to be trained when they're young." "It's the same as with your son," the stranger said; "if you had trained him while he was still young, he wouldn't have run away; now he's probably grown hard and knobby, too." "Of course," the old man replied, "a lot of time has gone by since he ran away; he's probably changed." "Would you still recognize him if he appeared before you?" the stranger asked. "Probably not by his face," the farmer replied, "but he's got a sign on him, a birthmark on his shoulder that looks like a bean." When he had said that, the stranger took off his jacket, bared his shoulder, and showed the farmer the "bean." "Lord God," the old man cried, "you're really my son!" And his love for his child was reawakened in his heart. "But," he added, "how can you be my son if you've become a fine gentleman living in wealth and plenty? How did you achieve it?" "Oh, father," his son replied, "the young tree wasn't tied to a stake, and it grew up crooked: now it's too old, and it will never be straight anymore. How did I acquire all this? I became a thief. But don't be alarmed: I'm a master thief. For me, locks and bolts don't exist: whatever I crave is mine. Don't think that I steal like a common thief; I take only from the excess riches of the wealthy. Poor people are safe: I give to them sooner than I take anything from them. Besides that, if I can get something without effort, guile, and skill, I don't touch it." "Oh, son," his father said, "I still don't like it; a thief is a thief; I'm telling you, it'll turn out badly." He took him in to his mother, and when she heard he was her son, she wept for joy, but when he told her that he had become a master thief, two rivers of tears flowed down her cheeks. Finally she said: "Even if he's become a thief, he's still my son, and my eyes have beheld him again."

They sat down at the table, and once again he joined his parents in eating the humble fare he hadn't tasted for so long. His

sprach: »Wenn unser Herr, der Graf drüben im Schlosse, erfährt, wer du bist und was du treibst, so nimmt er dich nicht auf die Arme und wiegt dich darin, wie er tat, als er dich am Taufstein hielt, sondern er läßt dich am Galgenstrick schaukeln.« »Seid ohne Sorge, mein Vater, er wird mir nichts tun, denn ich verstehe mein Handwerk. Ich will heute noch selbst zu ihm gehen.« Als die Abendzeit sich näherte, setzte sich der Meisterdieb in seinen Wagen und fuhr nach dem Schloß. Der Graf empfing ihn mit Artigkeit, weil er ihn für einen vornehmen Mann hielt. Als aber der Fremde sich zu erkennen gab, so erbleichte er und schwieg eine Zeitlang ganz still. Endlich sprach er: »Du bist mein Pate, deshalb will ich Gnade für Recht ergehen lassen und nachsichtig mit dir verfahren. Weil du dich rühmst, ein Meisterdieb zu sein, so will ich deine Kunst auf die Probe stellen, wenn du aber nicht bestehst, so mußt du mit des Seilers Tochter Hochzeit halten, und das Gekrächze der Raben soll deine Musik dabei sein.« »Herr Graf«, antwortete der Meister, »denkt Euch drei Stücke aus, so schwer Ihr wollt, und wenn ich Eure Aufgabe nicht löse, so tut mit mir, wie Euch gefällt.« Der Graf sann einige Augenblicke nach, dann sprach er: »Wohlan, zum ersten sollst du mir mein Leibpferd aus dem Stalle stehlen, zum andern sollst du mir und meiner Gemahlin, wenn wir eingeschlafen sind, das Bettuch unter dem Leib wegnehmen, ohne daß wir's merken, und dazu meiner Gemahlin den Trauring vom Finger; zum dritten und letzten sollst du mir den Pfarrer und Küster aus der Kirche wegstehlen. Merke dir alles wohl, denn es geht dir an den Hals.«

Der Meister begab sich in die zunächstliegende Stadt. Dort kaufte er einer alten Bauerfrau die Kleider ab und zog sie an. Dann färbte er sich das Gesicht braun und malte sich noch Runzeln hinein, so daß ihn kein Mensch wiedererkannt hätte. Endlich füllte er ein Fäßchen mit altem Ungarwein, in welchen ein starker Schlaftrunk gemischt war. Das Fäßchen legte er auf eine Kötze, die er auf den Rücken nahm, und ging mit bedächtigen, schwankenden Schritten zu dem Schloß des Grafen. Es war schon dunkel, als er anlangte; er setzte sich in dem Hof auf einen Stein, fing an zu husten wie eine alte, brustkranke Frau und rieb die Hände, als wenn er fröre. Vor der Türe des Pferdestalls lagen Soldaten um ein Feuer; einer von ihnen bemerkte die Frau und rief ihr zu: »Komm näher, altes Mütterchen, und wärme dich bei uns. Du hast doch kein Nachtlager und nimmst es an, wo du es findest.« Die Alte trippelte herbei, bat, ihr die Kötze vom Rücken zu heben, und setzte sich zu ihnen ans Feuer. »Was hast du da in deinem Fäßchen, du alte Schachtel?« fragte einer. »Einen guten Schluck Wein«,

father said: "If our lord, the count up there in his manor house, finds out who you are and what you do, he won't take you in his arms and rock you the way he did when he held you at the font; rather, he'll make you swing on the gallows." "Don't worry, father, he won't do a thing to me because I'm an expert at my trade. I'll visit him this very day." When evening approached, the master thief took his seat in his carriage and drove to the manor house. The count welcomed him politely because he took him for an aristocrat. But when the stranger revealed his identity, he turned pale and was totally silent for some time. Finally he said: "You're my godson, and so I'll show mercy and treat you leniently. Because you boast of being a master thief, I want to test your skill; if you fail, you must be married to the ropemaker's daughter, and the croaking of the ravens will be your wedding music." "Count," the master replied, "think up three trials, as difficult as you like, and if I don't fulfill your assignment, do whatever you want with me." The count meditated for a few minutes, then said: "Very well, first of all you must steal my favorite horse out of its stable; next, you must take away the bedsheet from under my wife and me, after we've fallen asleep, without our noticing it, and you must take my wife's wedding ring off her finger, as well; your third and final task is to kidnap my parson and sexton right out of the church. Keep all this in mind, because your life is at stake."

The master traveled to the adjacent town. There he bought an old peasant woman's clothes from her and put them on. Then he dyed his face brown and also painted wrinkles on it, so that not a soul would have recognized him. Finally he filled a small keg with old Hungarian wine, with which a strong sleeping potion had been mixed. He put the keg in a large carrying basket, which he placed on his back, and with circumspect, wavering steps he walked to the count's manor house. It was already dark when he got there; he sat down on a rock in the courtyard, began to cough like an old woman with weak lungs, and rubbed his hands together as if he were cold. In front of the door to the stable, soldiers were lying around a fire; one of them noticed the woman and called to her: "Come closer, little old lady, and warm yourself in our company. After all, you have no lodgings for the night, and I'm sure you take them wherever you can find them." The old lady hobbled over, asked the soldiers to take the big basket off her back, and joined them at the fire. "What have you got there in your keg, you old bag?" one of

antwortete sie, »ich ernähre mich mit dem Handel, für Geld und
gute Worte gebe ich Euch gerne ein Glas.« »Nur her damit«, sagte
der Soldat, und als er ein Glas gekostet hatte, rief er: »Wenn der
Wein gut ist, so trink ich lieber ein Glas mehr«, ließ sich nochmals
einschenken, und die andern folgten seinem Beispiel. »Heda,
Kameraden«, rief einer denen zu, die in dem Stall saßen, »hier ist
ein Mütterchen, das hat Wein, der so alt ist wie sie selber, nehmt
auch einen Schluck, der wärmt euch den Magen noch besser als
unser Feuer.« Die Alte trug ihr Fäßchen in den Stall. Einer hatte
sich auf das gesattelte Leibpferd gesetzt, ein anderer hielt den
Zaum in der Hand, ein dritter hatte den Schwanz gepackt. Sie
schenkte ein, soviel verlangt ward, bis die Quelle versiegte. Nicht
lange, so fiel dem einen der Zaum aus der Hand, er sank nieder und
fing an zu schnarchen, der andere ließ den Schwanz los, legte sich
nieder und schnarchte noch lauter. Der, welcher im Sattel saß,
blieb zwar sitzen, bog sich aber mit dem Kopf fast bis auf den Hals
des Pferdes, schlief und blies mit dem Mund wie ein Schmiedebalg.
Die Soldaten draußen waren schon längst eingeschlafen, lagen auf
der Erde und regten sich nicht, als wären sie von Stein. Als der
Meisterdieb sah, daß es ihm geglückt war, gab er dem einen statt
des Zaums ein Seil in die Hand und dem andern, der den Schwanz
gehalten hatte, einen Strohwisch; aber was sollte er mit dem, der
auf dem Rücken des Pferdes saß, anfangen? Herunterwerfen wollte
er ihn nicht, er hätte erwachen und ein Geschrei erheben können.
Er wußte aber guten Rat, er schnallte die Sattelgurt auf, knüpfte
ein paar Seile, die in Ringen an der Wand hingen, an den Sattel fest
und zog den schlafenden Reiter mit dem Sattel in die Höhe, dann
schlug er die Seile um den Pfosten und machte sie fest. Das Pferd
hatte er bald von der Kette losgebunden, aber wenn er über das
steinerne Pflaster des Hofs geritten wäre, so hätte man den Lärm
im Schloß gehört. Er umwickelte ihm also zuvor die Hufen mit
alten Lappen, führte es dann vorsichtig hinaus, schwang sich auf
und jagte davon.

Als der Tag angebrochen war, sprengte der Meister auf dem
gestohlenen Pferd zu dem Schloß. Der Graf war eben aufgestanden
und blickte aus dem Fenster. »Guten Morgen, Herr Graf«, rief er ihm
zu, »hier ist das Pferd, das ich glücklich aus dem Stall geholt habe.
Schaut nur, wie schön Eure Soldaten da liegen und schlafen, und
wenn Ihr in den Stall gehen wollt, so werdet Ihr sehen, wie bequem
sich's Eure Wächter gemacht haben.« Der Graf mußte lachen, dann
sprach er: »Einmal ist dir's gelungen, aber das zweitemal wird's nicht

them asked. "A good drink of wine," she replied; "I earn my living by selling it; for a little money and a kind word I'd gladly pour a glass for you." "Out with it," said the soldier, and after tasting a glass, he called: "When wine is good, I like to have a second glass"; he asked her to pour another, and his companions followed his example. "Hey, buddies!" one of them shouted to those who were sitting in the stable; "here's a little old lady who has wine that's as old as she is; get yourselves some, too; it'll warm your stomach even better than our fire." The old woman carried her keg into the stable. One soldier had mounted the count's favorite horse, which was saddled; a second was holding its bridle in his hand; and a third had a firm hold on its tail. She poured as much as they asked for, until the spring dried up. Before long, the one with the bridle dropped it, as he slumped down and began to snore; his companion let go of the tail, lay down, and snored even louder. The one in the saddle did remain sitting there, but leaned forward with his head almost touching the horse's neck; he was asleep, puffing with his mouth like a bellows. The soldiers outside had fallen asleep long before; they were lying on the ground, as motionless as if they were of stone. When the master thief saw that he had succeeded, he put a rope in the hand of the soldier who had been holding the bridle, and gave a handful of straw to the one who had been holding the tail; but what was he to do with the man seated on the horse's back? He didn't want to throw him down, because he might have awakened and started crying out. But he had a good idea: he unbuckled the saddle girth, firmly knotted to the saddle a few ropes that were hanging on the wall from rings, and pulled the sleeping horseman upward along with the saddle; then he wound the ropes around the post and made them taut. In no time he had released the horse from its chain, but if he had ridden across the stone paving of the courtyard, the sound would have been heard in the manor house. So, before leaving, he wrapped old rags around the horse's hoofs, then led it out cautiously, jumped on its back, and dashed away.

When day broke, the master galloped to the manor house on the stolen horse. The count had just got up and was looking out the window. "Good morning, count," he called to him; "here's the horse that I successfully took out of your stable. Just look how sweetly your soldiers are lying asleep there; and if you care to visit the stable, you'll see how comfortably your guards are resting." The count had to laugh; then he said: "You've succeeded this first time, but things won't go as smoothly the second time. And I warn

so glücklich ablaufen. Und ich warne dich, wenn du mir als Dieb begegnest, so behandle ich dich auch wie einen Dieb.« Als die Gräfin abends zu Bette gegangen war, schloß sie die Hand mit dem Trauring fest zu, und der Graf sagte: »Alle Türen sind verschlossen und verriegelt, ich bleibe wach und will den Dieb erwarten; steigt er aber zum Fenster ein, so schieße ich ihn nieder.« Der Meisterdieb aber ging in der Dunkelheit hinaus zu dem Galgen, schnitt einen armen Sünder, der da hing, von dem Strick ab und trug ihn auf dem Rücken nach dem Schloß. Dort stellte er eine Leiter an das Schlafgemach, setzte den Toten auf seine Schultern und fing an hinaufzusteigen. Als er so hoch gekommen war, daß der Kopf des Toten in dem Fenster erschien, drückte der Graf, der in seinem Bett lauerte, eine Pistole auf ihn los; alsbald ließ der Meister den armen Sünder herabfallen, sprang selbst die Leiter herab, und versteckte sich in eine Ecke. Die Nacht war von dem Mond so weit erhellt, daß der Meister deutlich sehen konnte, wie der Graf aus dem Fenster auf die Leiter stieg, herabkam und den Toten in den Garten trug. Dort fing er an, ein Loch zu graben, in das er ihn legen wollte. »Jetzt«, dachte der Dieb, »ist der günstige Augenblick gekommen«, schlich behende aus seinem Winkel und stieg die Leiter hinauf, geradezu ins Schlafgemach der Gräfin. »Liebe Frau«, fing er mit der Stimme des Grafen an, »der Dieb ist tot, aber er ist doch mein Pate und mehr ein Schelm als ein Bösewicht gewesen: ich will ihn der öffentlichen Schande nicht preisgeben; auch mit den armen Eltern habe ich Mitleid. Ich will ihn, bevor der Tag anbricht, selbst im Garten begraben, damit die Sache nicht ruchtbar wird. Gib mir auch das Bettuch, so will ich die Leiche einhüllen und ihn wie einen Hund verscharren.« Die Gräfin gab ihm das Tuch. »Weißt du was«, sagte der Dieb weiter, »ich habe eine Anwandlung von Großmut, gib mir noch den Ring; der Unglückliche hat sein Leben gewagt, so mag er ihn ins Grab mitnehmen.« Sie wollte dem Grafen nicht entgegen sein, und obgleich sie es ungern tat, so zog sie doch den Ring vom Finger und reichte ihn hin. Der Dieb machte sich mit beiden Stücken fort und kam glücklich nach Haus, bevor der Graf im Garten mit seiner Totengräberarbeit fertig war.

Was zog der Graf für ein langes Gesicht, als am andern Morgen der Meister kam und ihm das Bettuch und den Ring brachte. »Kannst du hexen?« sagte er zu ihm. »Wer hat dich aus dem Grab geholt, in das ich selbst dich gelegt habe, und hat dich wieder lebendig gemacht?« »Mich habt Ihr nicht begraben«, sagte der Dieb, »sondern den armen Sünder am Galgen«, und erzählte ausführlich, wie es zugegangen war; und der Graf mußte ihm zugestehen, daß er ein gescheiter und listiger

you: if I come upon you as a thief, I'll treat you like a thief." In the evening, after the countess had gone to bed, she tightly clenched the hand on which she wore her wedding ring, and the count said: "Every door is locked and bolted; I'll stay awake and wait for the thief; if he comes through the window, I'll shoot him down." But in the darkness the master thief went out to the gallows, cut down from his rope a poor sinner who was hanging there, and carried him to the manor house on his back. There he placed a ladder against the bedroom wall, hoisted the dead man onto his shoulders, and started climbing up. When he had mounted so high that the dead man's head appeared in the window, the count, who had been lying in wait in his bed, fired a pistol at him; at once the master let the poor sinner fall; he himself dashed down the ladder and hid in a corner. The moonlight was so bright that night that the master could distinctly see the count step out of his window onto the ladder, climb down, and carry the dead man into the garden. There he began to dig a hole, in which he intended to put him. "Now," said the thief to himself, "the opportune moment has come"; he nimbly crept out of his corner and climbed up the ladder, right into the countess's bedroom. "Wife dear," he said, imitating the count's voice, "the thief is dead, but, after all, he was my godson and he was more of a rogue than a villain: I don't want to expose him to public disgrace, and, besides, I feel sorry for his poor parents. Before day breaks, I want to bury him in the garden with my own hands, so the matter doesn't spread abroad. Give me the sheet, too, to wrap the body in, and then I'll shovel the dirt over him like a dog." The countess gave him the sheet. "You know what," the thief continued, "a surge of generosity is sweeping over me; give me your ring, too; that unfortunate man risked his life: let him take it to the grave with him." She didn't want to disobey the count, and though she did it unwillingly, she took the ring off her finger and handed it to him. The thief made away with both objects and arrived home safely before the count had completed his gravedigging chore in the garden.

What a long face the count made the next morning when the master came to bring him the sheet and the ring! "Do you work magic?" he asked him. "Who took you out of the grave in which I myself put you, and brought you back to life again?" "It wasn't me that you buried," the thief said, "but the poor sinner from the gallows"; and he told him in detail what had happened; the count had to admit to him that he was a skillful and wily thief.

Dieb wäre. »Aber noch bist du nicht zu Ende«, setzte er hinzu, »du hast noch die dritte Aufgabe zu lösen, und wenn dir das nicht gelingt, so hilft dir alles nichts.« Der Meister lächelte und gab keine Antwort.

Als die Nacht eingebrochen war, kam er mit einem langen Sack auf dem Rücken, einem Bündel unter dem Arm und einer Laterne in der Hand zu der Dorfkirche gegangen. In dem Sack hatte er Krebse, in dem Bündel aber kurze Wachslichter. Er setzte sich auf den Gottesacker, holte einen Krebs heraus und klebte ihm ein Wachslichtchen auf den Rücken; dann zündete er das Lichtchen an, setzte den Krebs auf den Boden und ließ ihn kriechen. Er holte einen zweiten aus dem Sack, machte es mit diesem ebenso und fuhr fort, bis auch der letzte aus dem Sacke war. Hierauf zog er ein langes schwarzes Gewand an, das wie eine Mönchskutte aussah, und klebte sich einen grauen Bart an das Kinn. Als er endlich ganz unkenntlich war, nahm er den Sack, in dem die Krebse gewesen waren, ging in die Kirche und stieg auf die Kanzel. Die Turmuhr schlug eben zwölf; als der letzte Schlag verklungen war, rief er mit lauter, gellender Stimme: »Hört an, ihr sündigen Menschen, das Ende aller Dinge ist gekommen, der Jüngste Tag ist nahe: hört an, hört an. Wer mit mir in den Himmel will, der krieche in den Sack. Ich bin Petrus, der die Himmelstüre öffnet und schließt. Seht ihr, draußen auf dem Gottesacker wandeln die Gestorbenen und sammeln ihre Gebeine zusammen. Kommt, kommt und kriecht in den Sack, die Welt geht unter.« Das Geschrei erschallte durch das ganze Dorf. Der Pfarrer und der Küster, die zunächst an der Kirche wohnten, hatten es zuerst vernommen, und als sie die Lichter erblickten, die auf dem Gottesacker umherwandelten, merkten sie, daß etwas Ungewöhnliches vorging, und traten sie in die Kirche ein. Sie hörten der Predigt eine Weile zu, da stieß der Küster den Pfarrer an und sprach: »Es wäre nicht übel, wenn wir die Gelegenheit benutzten und zusammen vor dem Einbruch des Jüngsten Tags auf eine leichte Art in den Himmel kämen.« »Freilich«, erwiderte der Pfarrer, »das sind auch meine Gedanken gewesen; habt Ihr Lust, so wollen wir uns auf den Weg machen.« »Ja«, antwortete der Küster, »aber Ihr, Herr Pfarrer, habt den Vortritt, ich folge nach.« Der Pfarrer schritt also vor und stieg auf die Kanzel, wo der Meister den Sack öffnete. Der Pfarrer kroch zuerst hinein, dann der Küster. Gleich band der Meister den Sack fest zu, packte ihn am Bausch und schleifte ihn die Kanzeltreppe hinab; sooft die Köpfe der beiden Toren auf die Stufen aufschlugen, rief er: »Jetzt geht's schon über die Berge.« Dann zog er sie auf gleiche Weise durch das Dorf, und wenn sie durch Pfützen kamen, rief er: »Jetzt geht's schon durch die nassen

"But you're not done yet," he added; "you still have the third task to accomplish, and if you don't succeed, all the rest will have been of no use." The master smiled, but didn't reply.

When night fell, he arrived at the village church with a long sack on his back, a bundle under his arm, and a lantern in his hand. In the sack he had crabs, and in the bundle stumps of wax candles. He sat down in the churchyard, took out a crab and stuck a candle stump on its back; then he lit the candle, placed the crab on the ground, and let it crawl away. He took another one out of the sack, treated it the same way, and continued doing so until the very last one was out of the sack. Then he put on a long black garment that looked like a monk's robe, and pasted a gray beard on his chin. When he finally was completely disguised, he took the sack that had contained the crabs, entered the church, and climbed into the pulpit. The tower clock was just striking twelve; after the last echo had died away, he shouted in a loud, harsh voice: "Hear me, you sinful people, the end of the world has come; Judgment Day is nigh: hear me, hear me. Whoever wants to enter heaven with me, crawl into the sack. I am Saint Peter, he who opens and closes the door to heaven. Look! Outside in the churchyard the dead are walking and gathering their bones together. Come, come and crawl into the sack; the world is perishing." His cries resounded through the whole village. The parson and the sexton, who lived next to the church, were the first to hear them, and when they caught sight of the lights moving to and fro across the churchyard, they realized that something unusual was happening, and they entered the church. They listened to the sermon for a while; then the sexton poked the parson and said: "It wouldn't be a bad idea to make use of this opportunity to get into heaven the easy way before Judgment Day arrives." "Yes, indeed," replied the parson, "those were my very thoughts; if you feel like it, let's set out on the journey." "Yes," replied the sexton, "but you are my superior, parson; I'll follow *you*." So the parson went first, climbing up to the pulpit, where the master opened his sack. The parson crept in first, then the sexton. Immediately the master closed the sack tightly, grabbed it where it bulged, and dragged it down the pulpit steps; every time the heads of the two fools were banged against the steps, he shouted: "Now we're heading across mountains." Then he pulled them through the village in the same way; when they crossed puddles, he called: "Now we're going through moist

Wolken«, und als er sie endlich die Schloßtreppe hinaufzog, so rief er:
»Jetzt sind wir auf der Himmelstreppe und werden bald im Vorhof
sein.« Als er oben angelangt war, schob er den Sack in den Taubenschlag, und als die Tauben flatterten, sagte er: »Hört ihr, wie die
Engel sich freuen und mit den Fittichen schlagen.« Dann schob er
den Riegel vor und ging fort.

Am andern Morgen begab er sich zu dem Grafen und sagte ihm,
daß er auch die dritte Aufgabe gelöst und den Pfarrer und Küster aus
der Kirche weggeführt hätte. »Wo hast du sie gelassen?« fragte der
Herr. »Sie liegen in einem Sack oben auf dem Taubenschlag und
bilden sich ein, sie wären im Himmel.« Der Graf stieg selbst hinauf
und überzeugte sich, daß er die Wahrheit gesagt hatte. Als er den
Pfarrer und Küster aus dem Gefängnis befreit hatte, sprach er: »Du
bist ein Erzdieb und hast deine Sache gewonnen. Für diesmal
kommst du mit heiler Haut davon, aber mache, daß du aus meinem
Land fortkommst, denn wenn du dich wieder darin betreten läßt, so
kannst du auf deine Erhöhung am Galgen rechnen.« Der Erzdieb
nahm Abschied von seinen Eltern, ging wieder in die weite Welt, und
niemand hat wieder etwas von ihm gehört.

clouds"; and when he finally pulled them up the stairs to the manor house, he called: "Now we're on the stairway to heaven, and we'll soon be in the forecourt." When he reached the top, he shoved the sack into the dovecote, and when the pigeons fluttered, he said: "Just hear how happy the angels are; they're beating their wings." Then he bolted the door and left.

The next morning he went to the count and told him that he had accomplished the third task, too, and had kidnapped the parson and the sexton from the church. "Where did you leave them?" the nobleman asked. "They're in a sack up in the dovecote, imagining that they're in heaven." The count went up there in person and satisfied himself that he had told the truth. After he had freed the parson and the sexton from their prison, he said: "You're an archthief and you've won your wager. This time you're getting away scot-free, but I want you to leave my domain, because if you're ever caught setting foot here again, you can count on your elevation to the gallows." The archthief took leave of his parents and went back out into the wide world, and no one ever heard a thing about him again.

A CATALOG OF SELECTED
DOVER BOOKS
IN ALL FIELDS OF INTEREST

A CATALOG OF SELECTED DOVER BOOKS IN ALL FIELDS OF INTEREST

100 BEST-LOVED POEMS, Edited by Philip Smith. "The Passionate Shepherd to His Love," "Shall I compare thee to a summer's day?" "Death, be not proud," "The Raven," "The Road Not Taken," plus works by Blake, Wordsworth, Byron, Shelley, Keats, many others. 96pp. 5 3/16 x 8 1/4. 0-486-28553-7

100 SMALL HOUSES OF THE THIRTIES, Brown-Blodgett Company. Exterior photographs and floor plans for 100 charming structures. Illustrations of models accompanied by descriptions of interiors, color schemes, closet space, and other amenities. 200 illustrations. 112pp. 8 3/8 x 11. 0-486-44131-8

1000 TURN-OF-THE-CENTURY HOUSES: With Illustrations and Floor Plans, Herbert C. Chivers. Reproduced from a rare edition, this showcase of homes ranges from cottages and bungalows to sprawling mansions. Each house is meticulously illustrated and accompanied by complete floor plans. 256pp. 9 3/8 x 12 1/4. 0-486-45596-3

101 GREAT AMERICAN POEMS, Edited by The American Poetry & Literacy Project. Rich treasury of verse from the 19th and 20th centuries includes works by Edgar Allan Poe, Robert Frost, Walt Whitman, Langston Hughes, Emily Dickinson, T. S. Eliot, other notables. 96pp. 5 3/16 x 8 1/4. 0-486-40158-8

101 GREAT SAMURAI PRINTS, Utagawa Kuniyoshi. Kuniyoshi was a master of the warrior woodblock print — and these 18th-century illustrations represent the pinnacle of his craft. Full-color portraits of renowned Japanese samurais pulse with movement, passion, and remarkably fine detail. 112pp. 8 3/8 x 11. 0-486-46523-3

ABC OF BALLET, Janet Grosser. Clearly worded, abundantly illustrated little guide defines basic ballet-related terms: arabesque, battement, pas de chat, relevé, sissonne, many others. Pronunciation guide included. Excellent primer. 48pp. 4 3/16 x 5 3/4. 0-486-40871-X

ACCESSORIES OF DRESS: An Illustrated Encyclopedia, Katherine Lester and Bess Viola Oerke. Illustrations of hats, veils, wigs, cravats, shawls, shoes, gloves, and other accessories enhance an engaging commentary that reveals the humor and charm of the many-sided story of accessorized apparel. 644 figures and 59 plates. 608pp. 6 1/8 x 9 1/4. 0-486-43378-1

ADVENTURES OF HUCKLEBERRY FINN, Mark Twain. Join Huck and Jim as their boyhood adventures along the Mississippi River lead them into a world of excitement, danger, and self-discovery. Humorous narrative, lyrical descriptions of the Mississippi valley, and memorable characters. 224pp. 5 3/16 x 8 1/4. 0-486-28061-6

ALICE STARMORE'S BOOK OF FAIR ISLE KNITTING, Alice Starmore. A noted designer from the region of Scotland's Fair Isle explores the history and techniques of this distinctive, stranded-color knitting style and provides copious illustrated instructions for 14 original knitwear designs. 208pp. 8 3/8 x 10 7/8. 0-486-47218-3

Browse over 9,000 books at www.doverpublications.com

ALICE'S ADVENTURES IN WONDERLAND, Lewis Carroll. Beloved classic about a little girl lost in a topsy-turvy land and her encounters with the White Rabbit, March Hare, Mad Hatter, Cheshire Cat, and other delightfully improbable characters. 42 illustrations by Sir John Tenniel. 96pp. 5³⁄₁₆ x 8¼.   0-486-27543-4

AMERICA'S LIGHTHOUSES: An Illustrated History, Francis Ross Holland. Profusely illustrated fact-filled survey of American lighthouses since 1716. Over 200 stations — East, Gulf, and West coasts, Great Lakes, Hawaii, Alaska, Puerto Rico, the Virgin Islands, and the Mississippi and St. Lawrence Rivers. 240pp. 8 x 10¾.
    0-486-25576-X

AN ENCYCLOPEDIA OF THE VIOLIN, Alberto Bachmann. Translated by Frederick H. Martens. Introduction by Eugene Ysaye. First published in 1925, this renowned reference remains unsurpassed as a source of essential information, from construction and evolution to repertoire and technique. Includes a glossary and 73 illustrations. 496pp. 6⅛ x 9¼.   0-486-46618-3

ANIMALS: 1,419 Copyright-Free Illustrations of Mammals, Birds, Fish, Insects, etc., Selected by Jim Harter. Selected for its visual impact and ease of use, this outstanding collection of wood engravings presents over 1,000 species of animals in extremely lifelike poses. Includes mammals, birds, reptiles, amphibians, fish, insects, and other invertebrates. 284pp. 9 x 12.   0-486-23766-4

THE ANNALS, Tacitus. Translated by Alfred John Church and William Jackson Brodribb. This vital chronicle of Imperial Rome, written by the era's great historian, spans A.D. 14-68 and paints incisive psychological portraits of major figures, from Tiberius to Nero. 416pp. 5³⁄₁₆ x 8¼.   0-486-45236-0

ANTIGONE, Sophocles. Filled with passionate speeches and sensitive probing of moral and philosophical issues, this powerful and often-performed Greek drama reveals the grim fate that befalls the children of Oedipus. Footnotes. 64pp. 5³⁄₁₆ x 8 ¼.   0-486-27804-2

ART DECO DECORATIVE PATTERNS IN FULL COLOR, Christian Stoll. Reprinted from a rare 1910 portfolio, 160 sensuous and exotic images depict a breathtaking array of florals, geometrics, and abstracts — all elegant in their stark simplicity. 64pp. 8⅜ x 11.   0-486-44862-2

THE ARTHUR RACKHAM TREASURY: 86 Full-Color Illustrations, Arthur Rackham. Selected and Edited by Jeff A. Menges. A stunning treasury of 86 full-page plates span the famed English artist's career, from *Rip Van Winkle* (1905) to masterworks such as *Undine, A Midsummer Night's Dream,* and *Wind in the Willows* (1939). 96pp. 8⅜ x 11.
    0-486-44685-9

THE AUTHENTIC GILBERT & SULLIVAN SONGBOOK, W. S. Gilbert and A. S. Sullivan. The most comprehensive collection available, this songbook includes selections from every one of Gilbert and Sullivan's light operas. Ninety-two numbers are presented uncut and unedited, and in their original keys. 410pp. 9 x 12.
    0-486-23482-7

THE AWAKENING, Kate Chopin. First published in 1899, this controversial novel of a New Orleans wife's search for love outside a stifling marriage shocked readers. Today, it remains a first-rate narrative with superb characterization. New introductory Note. 128pp. 5³⁄₁₆ x 8¼.   0-486-27786-0

BASIC DRAWING, Louis Priscilla. Beginning with perspective, this commonsense manual progresses to the figure in movement, light and shade, anatomy, drapery, composition, trees and landscape, and outdoor sketching. Black-and-white illustrations throughout. 128pp. 8⅜ x 11.   0-486-45815-6

Browse over 9,000 books at www.doverpublications.com

CATALOG OF DOVER BOOKS

THE BATTLES THAT CHANGED HISTORY, Fletcher Pratt. Historian profiles 16 crucial conflicts, ancient to modern, that changed the course of Western civilization. Gripping accounts of battles led by Alexander the Great, Joan of Arc, Ulysses S. Grant, other commanders. 27 maps. 352pp. 5⅜ x 8½.   0-486-41129-X

BEETHOVEN'S LETTERS, Ludwig van Beethoven. Edited by Dr. A. C. Kalischer. Features 457 letters to fellow musicians, friends, greats, patrons, and literary men. Reveals musical thoughts, quirks of personality, insights, and daily events. Includes 15 plates. 410pp. 5⅜ x 8½.   0-486-22769-3

BERNICE BOBS HER HAIR AND OTHER STORIES, F. Scott Fitzgerald. This brilliant anthology includes 6 of Fitzgerald's most popular stories: "The Diamond as Big as the Ritz," the title tale, "The Offshore Pirate," "The Ice Palace," "The Jelly Bean," and "May Day." 176pp. 5⅜ x 8½.   0-486-47049-0

BESLER'S BOOK OF FLOWERS AND PLANTS: 73 Full-Color Plates from Hortus Eystettensis, 1613, Basilius Besler. Here is a selection of magnificent plates from the *Hortus Eystettensis*, which vividly illustrated and identified the plants, flowers, and trees that thrived in the legendary German garden at Eichstätt. 80pp. 8⅜ x 11.   0-486-46005-3

THE BOOK OF KELLS, Edited by Blanche Cirker. Painstakingly reproduced from a rare facsimile edition, this volume contains full-page decorations, portraits, illustrations, plus a sampling of textual leaves with exquisite calligraphy and ornamentation. 32 full-color illustrations. 32pp. 9⅜ x 12¼.   0-486-24345-1

THE BOOK OF THE CROSSBOW: With an Additional Section on Catapults and Other Siege Engines, Ralph Payne-Gallwey. Fascinating study traces history and use of crossbow as military and sporting weapon, from Middle Ages to modern times. Also covers related weapons: balistas, catapults, Turkish bows, more. Over 240 illustrations. 400pp. 7¼ x 10⅛.   0-486-28720-3

THE BUNGALOW BOOK: Floor Plans and Photos of 112 Houses, 1910, Henry L. Wilson. Here are 112 of the most popular and economic blueprints of the early 20th century — plus an illustration or photograph of each completed house. A wonderful time capsule that still offers a wealth of valuable insights. 160pp. 8⅝ x 11.   0-486-45104-6

THE CALL OF THE WILD, Jack London. A classic novel of adventure, drawn from London's own experiences as a Klondike adventurer, relating the story of a heroic dog caught in the brutal life of the Alaska Gold Rush. Note. 64pp. 5³⁄₁₆ x 8¼.   0-486-26472-6

CANDIDE, Voltaire. Edited by Francois-Marie Arouet. One of the world's great satires since its first publication in 1759. Witty, caustic skewering of romance, science, philosophy, religion, government — nearly all human ideals and institutions. 112pp. 5³⁄₁₆ x 8¼.   0-486-26689-3

CELEBRATED IN THEIR TIME: Photographic Portraits from the George Grantham Bain Collection, Edited by Amy Pastan. With an Introduction by Michael Carlebach. Remarkable portrait gallery features 112 rare images of Albert Einstein, Charlie Chaplin, the Wright Brothers, Henry Ford, and other luminaries from the worlds of politics, art, entertainment, and industry. 128pp. 8⅜ x 11.   0-486-46754-6

CHARIOTS FOR APOLLO: The NASA History of Manned Lunar Spacecraft to 1969, Courtney G. Brooks, James M. Grimwood, and Loyd S. Swenson, Jr. This illustrated history by a trio of experts is the definitive reference on the Apollo spacecraft and lunar modules. It traces the vehicles' design, development, and operation in space. More than 100 photographs and illustrations. 576pp. 6¾ x 9¼. 0-486-46756-2

Browse over 9,000 books at www.doverpublications.com

A CHRISTMAS CAROL, Charles Dickens. This engrossing tale relates Ebenezer Scrooge's ghostly journeys through Christmases past, present, and future and his ultimate transformation from a harsh and grasping old miser to a charitable and compassionate human being. 80pp. 5³⁄₁₆ x 8¼. 0-486-26865-9

COMMON SENSE, Thomas Paine. First published in January of 1776, this highly influential landmark document clearly and persuasively argued for American separation from Great Britain and paved the way for the Declaration of Independence. 64pp. 5³⁄₁₆ x 8¼. 0-486-29602-4

THE COMPLETE SHORT STORIES OF OSCAR WILDE, Oscar Wilde. Complete texts of "The Happy Prince and Other Tales," "A House of Pomegranates," "Lord Arthur Savile's Crime and Other Stories," "Poems in Prose," and "The Portrait of Mr. W. H." 208pp. 5³⁄₁₆ x 8¼. 0-486-45216-6

COMPLETE SONNETS, William Shakespeare. Over 150 exquisite poems deal with love, friendship, the tyranny of time, beauty's evanescence, death, and other themes in language of remarkable power, precision, and beauty. Glossary of archaic terms. 80pp. 5³⁄₁₆ x 8¼. 0-486-26686-9

THE COUNT OF MONTE CRISTO: Abridged Edition, Alexandre Dumas. Falsely accused of treason, Edmond Dantès is imprisoned in the bleak Chateau d'If. After a hair-raising escape, he launches an elaborate plot to extract a bitter revenge against those who betrayed him. 448pp. 5³⁄₁₆ x 8¼. 0-486-45643-9

CRAFTSMAN BUNGALOWS: Designs from the Pacific Northwest, Yoho & Merritt. This reprint of a rare catalog, showcasing the charming simplicity and cozy style of Craftsman bungalows, is filled with photos of completed homes, plus floor plans and estimated costs. An indispensable resource for architects, historians, and illustrators. 112pp. 10 x 7. 0-486-46875-5

CRAFTSMAN BUNGALOWS: 59 Homes from "The Craftsman," Edited by Gustav Stickley. Best and most attractive designs from Arts and Crafts Movement publication — 1903–1916 — includes sketches, photographs of homes, floor plans, descriptive text. 128pp. 8¼ x 11. 0-486-25829-7

CRIME AND PUNISHMENT, Fyodor Dostoyevsky. Translated by Constance Garnett. Supreme masterpiece tells the story of Raskolnikov, a student tormented by his own thoughts after he murders an old woman. Overwhelmed by guilt and terror, he confesses and goes to prison. 480pp. 5³⁄₁₆ x 8¼. 0-486-41587-2

THE DECLARATION OF INDEPENDENCE AND OTHER GREAT DOCUMENTS OF AMERICAN HISTORY: 1775-1865, Edited by John Grafton. Thirteen compelling and influential documents: Henry's "Give Me Liberty or Give Me Death," Declaration of Independence, The Constitution, Washington's First Inaugural Address, The Monroe Doctrine, The Emancipation Proclamation, Gettysburg Address, more. 64pp. 5³⁄₁₆ x 8¼. 0-486-41124-9

THE DESERT AND THE SOWN: Travels in Palestine and Syria, Gertrude Bell. "The female Lawrence of Arabia," Gertrude Bell wrote captivating, perceptive accounts of her travels in the Middle East. This intriguing narrative, accompanied by 160 photos, traces her 1905 sojourn in Lebanon, Syria, and Palestine. 368pp. 5⅜ x 8½. 0-486-46876-3

A DOLL'S HOUSE, Henrik Ibsen. Ibsen's best-known play displays his genius for realistic prose drama. An expression of women's rights, the play climaxes when the central character, Nora, rejects a smothering marriage and life in "a doll's house." 80pp. 5³⁄₁₆ x 8¼. 0-486-27062-9

Browse over 9,000 books at www.doverpublications.com

DOOMED SHIPS: Great Ocean Liner Disasters, William H. Miller, Jr. Nearly 200 photographs, many from private collections, highlight tales of some of the vessels whose pleasure cruises ended in catastrophe: the *Morro Castle, Normandie, Andrea Doria, Europa,* and many others. 128pp. 8⅜ x 11¾. 0-486-45366-9

THE DORÉ BIBLE ILLUSTRATIONS, Gustave Doré. Detailed plates from the Bible: the Creation scenes, Adam and Eve, horrifying visions of the Flood, the battle sequences with their monumental crowds, depictions of the life of Jesus, 241 plates in all. 241pp. 9 x 12. 0-486-23004-X

DRAWING DRAPERY FROM HEAD TO TOE, Cliff Young. Expert guidance on how to draw shirts, pants, skirts, gloves, hats, and coats on the human figure, including folds in relation to the body, pull and crush, action folds, creases, more. Over 200 drawings. 48pp. 8¼ x 11. 0-486-45591-2

DUBLINERS, James Joyce. A fine and accessible introduction to the work of one of the 20th century's most influential writers, this collection features 15 tales, including a masterpiece of the short-story genre, "The Dead." 160pp. 5³⁄₁₆ x 8¼. 0-486-26870-5

EASY-TO-MAKE POP-UPS, Joan Irvine. Illustrated by Barbara Reid. Dozens of wonderful ideas for three-dimensional paper fun — from holiday greeting cards with moving parts to a pop-up menagerie. Easy-to-follow, illustrated instructions for more than 30 projects. 299 black-and-white illustrations. 96pp. 8⅜ x 11. 0-486-44622-0

EASY-TO-MAKE STORYBOOK DOLLS: A "Novel" Approach to Cloth Dollmaking, Sherralyn St. Clair. Favorite fictional characters come alive in this unique beginner's dollmaking guide. Includes patterns for Pollyanna, Dorothy from *The Wonderful Wizard of Oz,* Mary of *The Secret Garden,* plus easy-to-follow instructions, 263 black-and-white illustrations, and an 8-page color insert. 112pp. 8¼ x 11. 0-486-47360-0

EINSTEIN'S ESSAYS IN SCIENCE, Albert Einstein. Speeches and essays in accessible, everyday language profile influential physicists such as Niels Bohr and Isaac Newton. They also explore areas of physics to which the author made major contributions. 128pp. 5 x 8. 0-486-47011-3

EL DORADO: Further Adventures of the Scarlet Pimpernel, Baroness Orczy. A popular sequel to *The Scarlet Pimpernel,* this suspenseful story recounts the Pimpernel's attempts to rescue the Dauphin from imprisonment during the French Revolution. An irresistible blend of intrigue, period detail, and vibrant characterizations. 352pp. 5³⁄₁₆ x 8¼. 0-486-44026-5

ELEGANT SMALL HOMES OF THE TWENTIES: 99 Designs from a Competition, Chicago Tribune. Nearly 100 designs for five- and six-room houses feature New England and Southern colonials, Normandy cottages, stately Italianate dwellings, and other fascinating snapshots of American domestic architecture of the 1920s. 112pp. 9 x 12. 0-486-46910-7

THE ELEMENTS OF STYLE: The Original Edition, William Strunk, Jr. This is the book that generations of writers have relied upon for timeless advice on grammar, diction, syntax, and other essentials. In concise terms, it identifies the principal requirements of proper style and common errors. 64pp. 5⅜ x 8½. 0-486-44798-7

THE ELUSIVE PIMPERNEL, Baroness Orczy. Robespierre's revolutionaries find their wicked schemes thwarted by the heroic Pimpernel — Sir Percival Blakeney. In this thrilling sequel, Chauvelin devises a plot to eliminate the Pimpernel and his wife. 272pp. 5³⁄₁₆ x 8¼. 0-486-45464-9

AN ENCYCLOPEDIA OF BATTLES: Accounts of Over 1,560 Battles from 1479 B.C. to the Present, David Eggenberger. Essential details of every major battle in recorded history from the first battle of Megiddo in 1479 B.C. to Grenada in 1984. List of battle maps. 99 illustrations. 544pp. 6½ x 9¼. 0-486-24913-1

ENCYCLOPEDIA OF EMBROIDERY STITCHES, INCLUDING CREWEL, Marion Nichols. Precise explanations and instructions, clearly illustrated, on how to work chain, back, cross, knotted, woven stitches, and many more — 178 in all, including Cable Outline, Whipped Satin, and Eyelet Buttonhole. Over 1400 illustrations. 219pp. 8⅜ x 11¼. 0-486-22929-7

ENTER JEEVES: 15 Early Stories, P. G. Wodehouse. Splendid collection contains first 8 stories featuring Bertie Wooster, the deliciously dim aristocrat and Jeeves, his brainy, imperturbable manservant. Also, the complete Reggie Pepper (Bertie's prototype) series. 288pp. 5⅜ x 8½. 0-486-29717-9

ERIC SLOANE'S AMERICA: Paintings in Oil, Michael Wigley. With a Foreword by Mimi Sloane. Eric Sloane's evocative oils of America's landscape and material culture shimmer with immense historical and nostalgic appeal. This original hardcover collection gathers nearly a hundred of his finest paintings, with subjects ranging from New England to the American Southwest. 128pp. 10⅝ x 9.
0-486-46525-X

ETHAN FROME, Edith Wharton. Classic story of wasted lives, set against a bleak New England background. Superbly delineated characters in a hauntingly grim tale of thwarted love. Considered by many to be Wharton's masterpiece. 96pp. 5³⁄₁₆ x 8¼.
0-486-26690-7

THE EVERLASTING MAN, G. K. Chesterton. Chesterton's view of Christianity — as a blend of philosophy and mythology, satisfying intellect and spirit — applies to his brilliant book, which appeals to readers' heads as well as their hearts. 288pp. 5⅜ x 8½.
0-486-46036-3

THE FIELD AND FOREST HANDY BOOK, Daniel Beard. Written by a co-founder of the Boy Scouts, this appealing guide offers illustrated instructions for building kites, birdhouses, boats, igloos, and other fun projects, plus numerous helpful tips for campers. 448pp. 5³⁄₁₆ x 8¼. 0-486-46191-2

FINDING YOUR WAY WITHOUT MAP OR COMPASS, Harold Gatty. Useful, instructive manual shows would-be explorers, hikers, bikers, scouts, sailors, and survivalists how to find their way outdoors by observing animals, weather patterns, shifting sands, and other elements of nature. 288pp. 5⅜ x 8½. 0-486-40613-X

FIRST FRENCH READER: A Beginner's Dual-Language Book, Edited and Translated by Stanley Appelbaum. This anthology introduces 50 legendary writers — Voltaire, Balzac, Baudelaire, Proust, more — through passages from The Red and the Black, Les Misérables, Madame Bovary, and other classics. Original French text plus English translation on facing pages. 240pp. 5⅜ x 8½. 0-486-46178-5

FIRST GERMAN READER: A Beginner's Dual-Language Book, Edited by Harry Steinhauer. Specially chosen for their power to evoke German life and culture, these short, simple readings include poems, stories, essays, and anecdotes by Goethe, Hesse, Heine, Schiller, and others. 224pp. 5⅜ x 8½. 0-486-46179-3

FIRST SPANISH READER: A Beginner's Dual-Language Book, Angel Flores. Delightful stories, other material based on works of Don Juan Manuel, Luis Taboada, Ricardo Palma, other noted writers. Complete faithful English translations on facing pages. Exercises. 176pp. 5⅜ x 8½. 0-486-25810-6

FIVE ACRES AND INDEPENDENCE, Maurice G. Kains. Great back-to-the-land classic explains basics of self-sufficient farming. The one book to get. 95 illustrations. 397pp. 5⅜ x 8½. 0-486-20974-1

FLAGG'S SMALL HOUSES: Their Economic Design and Construction, 1922, Ernest Flagg. Although most famous for his skyscrapers, Flagg was also a proponent of the well-designed single-family dwelling. His classic treatise features innovations that save space, materials, and cost. 526 illustrations. 160pp. 9⅜ x 12¼.

0-486-45197-6

FLATLAND: A Romance of Many Dimensions, Edwin A. Abbott. Classic of science (and mathematical) fiction — charmingly illustrated by the author — describes the adventures of A. Square, a resident of Flatland, in Spaceland (three dimensions), Lineland (one dimension), and Pointland (no dimensions). 96pp. 5³⁄₁₆ x 8¼.

0-486-27263-X

FRANKENSTEIN, Mary Shelley. The story of Victor Frankenstein's monstrous creation and the havoc it caused has enthralled generations of readers and inspired countless writers of horror and suspense. With the author's own 1831 introduction. 176pp. 5³⁄₁₆ x 8¼. 0-486-28211-2

THE GARGOYLE BOOK: 572 Examples from Gothic Architecture, Lester Burbank Bridaham. Dispelling the conventional wisdom that French Gothic architectural flourishes were born of despair or gloom, Bridaham reveals the whimsical nature of these creations and the ingenious artisans who made them. 572 illustrations. 224pp. 8⅜ x 11. 0-486-44754-5

THE GIFT OF THE MAGI AND OTHER SHORT STORIES, O. Henry. Sixteen captivating stories by one of America's most popular storytellers. Included are such classics as "The Gift of the Magi," "The Last Leaf," and "The Ransom of Red Chief." Publisher's Note. 96pp. 5³⁄₁₆ x 8¼. 0-486-27061-0

THE GOETHE TREASURY: Selected Prose and Poetry, Johann Wolfgang von Goethe. Edited, Selected, and with an Introduction by Thomas Mann. In addition to his lyric poetry, Goethe wrote travel sketches, autobiographical studies, essays, letters, and proverbs in rhyme and prose. This collection presents outstanding examples from each genre. 368pp. 5⅜ x 8½. 0-486-44780-4

GREAT EXPECTATIONS, Charles Dickens. Orphaned Pip is apprenticed to the dirty work of the forge but dreams of becoming a gentleman — and one day finds himself in possession of "great expectations." Dickens' finest novel. 400pp. 5³⁄₁₆ x 8¼.

0-486-41586-4

GREAT WRITERS ON THE ART OF FICTION: From Mark Twain to Joyce Carol Oates, Edited by James Daley. An indispensable source of advice and inspiration, this anthology features essays by Henry James, Kate Chopin, Willa Cather, Sinclair Lewis, Jack London, Raymond Chandler, Raymond Carver, Eudora Welty, and Kurt Vonnegut, Jr. 192pp. 5⅜ x 8½. 0-486-45128-3

HAMLET, William Shakespeare. The quintessential Shakespearean tragedy, whose highly charged confrontations and anguished soliloquies probe depths of human feeling rarely sounded in any art. Reprinted from an authoritative British edition complete with illuminating footnotes. 128pp. 5³⁄₁₆ x 8¼. 0-486-27278-8

THE HAUNTED HOUSE, Charles Dickens. A Yuletide gathering in an eerie country retreat provides the backdrop for Dickens and his friends — including Elizabeth Gaskell and Wilkie Collins — who take turns spinning supernatural yarns. 144pp. 5⅜ x 8½. 0-486-46309-5

HEART OF DARKNESS, Joseph Conrad. Dark allegory of a journey up the Congo River and the narrator's encounter with the mysterious Mr. Kurtz. Masterly blend of adventure, character study, psychological penetration. For many, Conrad's finest, most enigmatic story. 80pp. 5³⁄₁₆ x 8¼.   0-486-26464-5

HENSON AT THE NORTH POLE, Matthew A. Henson. This thrilling memoir by the heroic African-American who was Peary's companion through two decades of Arctic exploration recounts a tale of danger, courage, and determination. "Fascinating and exciting." — *Commonweal.* 128pp. 5⅜ x 8½.   0-486-45472-X

HISTORIC COSTUMES AND HOW TO MAKE THEM, Mary Fernald and E. Shenton. Practical, informative guidebook shows how to create everything from short tunics worn by Saxon men in the fifth century to a lady's bustle dress of the late 1800s. 81 illustrations. 176pp. 5⅜ x 8½.   0-486-44906-8

THE HOUND OF THE BASKERVILLES, Arthur Conan Doyle. A deadly curse in the form of a legendary ferocious beast continues to claim its victims from the Baskerville family until Holmes and Watson intervene. Often called the best detective story ever written. 128pp. 5³⁄₁₆ x 8¼.   0-486-28214-7

THE HOUSE BEHIND THE CEDARS, Charles W. Chesnutt. Originally published in 1900, this groundbreaking novel by a distinguished African-American author recounts the drama of a brother and sister who "pass for white" during the dangerous days of Reconstruction. 208pp. 5⅜ x 8½.   0-486-46144-0

THE HUMAN FIGURE IN MOTION, Eadweard Muybridge. The 4,789 photographs in this definitive selection show the human figure — models almost all undraped — engaged in over 160 different types of action: running, climbing stairs, etc. 390pp. 7⅞ x 10⅝.   0-486-20204-6

THE IMPORTANCE OF BEING EARNEST, Oscar Wilde. Wilde's witty and buoyant comedy of manners, filled with some of literature's most famous epigrams, reprinted from an authoritative British edition. Considered Wilde's most perfect work. 64pp. 5³⁄₁₆ x 8¼.   0-486-26478-5

THE INFERNO, Dante Alighieri. Translated and with notes by Henry Wadsworth Longfellow. The first stop on Dante's famous journey from Hell to Purgatory to Paradise, this 14th-century allegorical poem blends vivid and shocking imagery with graceful lyricism. Translated by the beloved 19th-century poet, Henry Wadsworth Longfellow. 256pp. 5³⁄₁₆ x 8¼.   0-486-44288-8

JANE EYRE, Charlotte Brontë. Written in 1847, *Jane Eyre* tells the tale of an orphan girl's progress from the custody of cruel relatives to an oppressive boarding school and its culmination in a troubled career as a governess. 448pp. 5³⁄₁₆ x 8¼.
0-486-42449-9

JAPANESE WOODBLOCK FLOWER PRINTS, Tanigami Kônan. Extraordinary collection of Japanese woodblock prints by a well-known artist features 120 plates in brilliant color. Realistic images from a rare edition include daffodils, tulips, and other familiar and unusual flowers. 128pp. 11 x 8¼.   0-486-46442-3

JEWELRY MAKING AND DESIGN, Augustus F. Rose and Antonio Cirino. Professional secrets of jewelry making are revealed in a thorough, practical guide. Over 200 illustrations. 306pp. 5⅜ x 8½.   0-486-21750-7

JULIUS CAESAR, William Shakespeare. Great tragedy based on Plutarch's account of the lives of Brutus, Julius Caesar and Mark Antony. Evil plotting, ringing oratory, high tragedy with Shakespeare's incomparable insight, dramatic power. Explanatory footnotes. 96pp. 5³⁄₁₆ x 8¼.   0-486-26876-4

THE JUNGLE, Upton Sinclair. 1906 bestseller shockingly reveals intolerable labor practices and working conditions in the Chicago stockyards as it tells the grim story of a Slavic family that emigrates to America full of optimism but soon faces despair. 320pp. 5³⁄₁₆ x 8¼. 0-486-41923-1

THE KINGDOM OF GOD IS WITHIN YOU, Leo Tolstoy. The soul-searching book that inspired Gandhi to embrace the concept of passive resistance, Tolstoy's 1894 polemic clearly outlines a radical, well-reasoned revision of traditional Christian thinking. 352pp. 5³⁄₁₆ x 8¼. 0-486-45138-0

THE LADY OR THE TIGER?: and Other Logic Puzzles, Raymond M. Smullyan. Created by a renowned puzzle master, these whimsically themed challenges involve paradoxes about probability, time, and change; metapuzzles; and self-referentiality. Nineteen chapters advance in difficulty from relatively simple to highly complex. 1982 edition. 240pp. 5⅜ x 8½. 0-486-47027-X

LEAVES OF GRASS: The Original 1855 Edition, Walt Whitman. Whitman's immortal collection includes some of the greatest poems of modern times, including his masterpiece, "Song of Myself." Shattering standard conventions, it stands as an unabashed celebration of body and nature. 128pp. 5³⁄₁₆ x 8¼. 0-486-45676-5

LES MISÉRABLES, Victor Hugo. Translated by Charles E. Wilbour. Abridged by James K. Robinson. A convict's heroic struggle for justice and redemption plays out against a fiery backdrop of the Napoleonic wars. This edition features the excellent original translation and a sensitive abridgment. 304pp. 6⅛ x 9¼. 0-486-45789-3

LILITH: A Romance, George MacDonald. In this novel by the father of fantasy literature, a man travels through time to meet Adam and Eve and to explore humanity's fall from grace and ultimate redemption. 240pp. 5⅜ x 8½. 0-486-46818-6

THE LOST LANGUAGE OF SYMBOLISM, Harold Bayley. This remarkable book reveals the hidden meaning behind familiar images and words, from the origins of Santa Claus to the fleur-de-lys, drawing from mythology, folklore, religious texts, and fairy tales. 1,418 illustrations. 784pp. 5⅜ x 8½. 0-486-44787-1

MACBETH, William Shakespeare. A Scottish nobleman murders the king in order to succeed to the throne. Tortured by his conscience and fearful of discovery, he becomes tangled in a web of treachery and deceit that ultimately spells his doom. 96pp. 5³⁄₁₆ x 8¼. 0-486-27802-6

MAKING AUTHENTIC CRAFTSMAN FURNITURE: Instructions and Plans for 62 Projects, Gustav Stickley. Make authentic reproductions of handsome, functional, durable furniture: tables, chairs, wall cabinets, desks, a hall tree, and more. Construction plans with drawings, schematics, dimensions, and lumber specs reprinted from 1900s The Craftsman magazine. 128pp. 8⅛ x 11. 0-486-25000-8

MATHEMATICS FOR THE NONMATHEMATICIAN, Morris Kline. Erudite and entertaining overview follows development of mathematics from ancient Greeks to present. Topics include logic and mathematics, the fundamental concept, differential calculus, probability theory, much more. Exercises and problems. 641pp. 5⅜ x 8½. 0-486-24823-2

MEMOIRS OF AN ARABIAN PRINCESS FROM ZANZIBAR, Emily Ruete. This 19th-century autobiography offers a rare inside look at the society surrounding a sultan's palace. A real-life princess in exile recalls her vanished world of harems, slave trading, and court intrigues. 288pp. 5⅜ x 8½. 0-486-47121-7

Browse over 9,000 books at www.doverpublications.com

THE METAMORPHOSIS AND OTHER STORIES, Franz Kafka. Excellent new English translations of title story (considered by many critics Kafka's most perfect work), plus "The Judgment," "In the Penal Colony," "A Country Doctor," and "A Report to an Academy." Note. 96pp. 5³⁄₁₆ x 8¼. 0-486-29030-1

MICROSCOPIC ART FORMS FROM THE PLANT WORLD, R. Anheisser. From undulating curves to complex geometrics, a world of fascinating images abound in this classic, illustrated survey of microscopic plants. Features 400 detailed illustrations of nature's minute but magnificent handiwork. The accompanying CD-ROM includes all of the images in the book. 128pp. 9 x 9. 0-486-46013-4

A MIDSUMMER NIGHT'S DREAM, William Shakespeare. Among the most popular of Shakespeare's comedies, this enchanting play humorously celebrates the vagaries of love as it focuses upon the intertwined romances of several pairs of lovers. Explanatory footnotes. 80pp. 5³⁄₁₆ x 8¼. 0-486-27067-X

THE MONEY CHANGERS, Upton Sinclair. Originally published in 1908, this cautionary novel from the author of *The Jungle* explores corruption within the American system as a group of power brokers joins forces for personal gain, triggering a crash on Wall Street. 192pp. 5⅜ x 8½. 0-486-46917-4

THE MOST POPULAR HOMES OF THE TWENTIES, William A. Radford. With a New Introduction by Daniel D. Reiff. Based on a rare 1925 catalog, this architectural showcase features floor plans, construction details, and photos of 26 homes, plus articles on entrances, porches, garages, and more. 250 illustrations, 21 color plates. 176pp. 8⅜ x 11. 0-486-47028-8

MY 66 YEARS IN THE BIG LEAGUES, Connie Mack. With a New Introduction by Rich Westcott. A Founding Father of modern baseball, Mack holds the record for most wins — and losses — by a major league manager. Enhanced by 70 photographs, his warmhearted autobiography is populated by many legends of the game. 288pp. 5⅜ x 8½. 0-486-47184-5

NARRATIVE OF THE LIFE OF FREDERICK DOUGLASS, Frederick Douglass. Douglass's graphic depictions of slavery, harrowing escape to freedom, and life as a newspaper editor, eloquent orator, and impassioned abolitionist. 96pp. 5³⁄₁₆ x 8¼. 0-486-28499-9

THE NIGHTLESS CITY: Geisha and Courtesan Life in Old Tokyo, J. E. de Becker. This unsurpassed study from 100 years ago ventured into Tokyo's red-light district to survey geisha and courtesan life and offer meticulous descriptions of training, dress, social hierarchy, and erotic practices. 49 black-and-white illustrations; 2 maps. 496pp. 5⅜ x 8½. 0-486-45563-7

THE ODYSSEY, Homer. Excellent prose translation of ancient epic recounts adventures of the homeward-bound Odysseus. Fantastic cast of gods, giants, cannibals, sirens, other supernatural creatures — true classic of Western literature. 256pp. 5³⁄₁₆ x 8¼. 0-486-40654-7

OEDIPUS REX, Sophocles. Landmark of Western drama concerns the catastrophe that ensues when King Oedipus discovers he has inadvertently killed his father and married his mother. Masterly construction, dramatic irony. Explanatory footnotes. 64pp. 5³⁄₁₆ x 8¼. 0-486-26877-2

ONCE UPON A TIME: The Way America Was, Eric Sloane. Nostalgic text and drawings brim with gentle philosophies and descriptions of how we used to live — self-sufficiently — on the land, in homes, and among the things built by hand. 44 line illustrations. 64pp. 8⅜ x 11. 0-486-44411-2

ONE OF OURS, Willa Cather. The Pulitzer Prize–winning novel about a young Nebraskan looking for something to believe in. Alienated from his parents, rejected by his wife, he finds his destiny on the bloody battlefields of World War I. 352pp. 5³⁄₁₆ x 8¼. 0-486-45599-8

ORIGAMI YOU CAN USE: 27 Practical Projects, Rick Beech. Origami models can be more than decorative, and this unique volume shows how! The 27 practical projects include a CD case, frame, napkin ring, and dish. Easy instructions feature 400 two-color illustrations. 96pp. 8¼ x 11. 0-486-47057-1

OTHELLO, William Shakespeare. Towering tragedy tells the story of a Moorish general who earns the enmity of his ensign Iago when he passes him over for a promotion. Masterly portrait of an archvillain. Explanatory footnotes. 112pp. 5³⁄₁₆ x 8¼. 0-486-29097-2

PARADISE LOST, John Milton. Notes by John A. Himes. First published in 1667, *Paradise Lost* ranks among the greatest of English literature's epic poems. It's a sublime retelling of Adam and Eve's fall from grace and expulsion from Eden. Notes by John A. Himes. 480pp. 5³⁄₈ x 8¼. 0-486-44287-X

PASSING, Nella Larsen. Married to a successful physician and prominently ensconced in society, Irene Redfield leads a charmed existence — until a chance encounter with a childhood friend who has been "passing for white." 112pp. 5³⁄₈ x 8½. 0-486-43713-2

PERSPECTIVE DRAWING FOR BEGINNERS, Len A. Doust. Doust carefully explains the roles of lines, boxes, and circles, and shows how visualizing shapes and forms can be used in accurate depictions of perspective. One of the most concise introductions available. 33 illustrations. 64pp. 5³⁄₈ x 8½. 0-486-45149-6

PERSPECTIVE MADE EASY, Ernest R. Norling. Perspective is easy; yet, surprisingly few artists know the simple rules that make it so. Remedy that situation with this simple, step-by-step book, the first devoted entirely to the topic. 256 illustrations. 224pp. 5³⁄₈ x 8½. 0-486-40473-0

THE PICTURE OF DORIAN GRAY, Oscar Wilde. Celebrated novel involves a handsome young Londoner who sinks into a life of depravity. His body retains perfect youth and vigor while his recent portrait reflects the ravages of his crime and sensuality. 176pp. 5³⁄₁₆ x 8¼. 0-486-27807-7

PRIDE AND PREJUDICE, Jane Austen. One of the most universally loved and admired English novels, an effervescent tale of rural romance transformed by Jane Austen's art into a witty, shrewdly observed satire of English country life. 272pp. 5³⁄₁₆ x 8¼. 0-486-28473-5

THE PRINCE, Niccolò Machiavelli. Classic, Renaissance-era guide to acquiring and maintaining political power. Today, nearly 500 years after it was written, this calculating prescription for autocratic rule continues to be much read and studied. 80pp. 5³⁄₁₆ x 8¼. 0-486-27274-5

QUICK SKETCHING, Carl Cheek. A perfect introduction to the technique of "quick sketching." Drawing upon an artist's immediate emotional responses, this is an extremely effective means of capturing the essential form and features of a subject. More than 100 black-and-white illustrations throughout. 48pp. 11 x 8¼. 0-486-46608-6

RANCH LIFE AND THE HUNTING TRAIL, Theodore Roosevelt. Illustrated by Frederic Remington. Beautifully illustrated by Remington, Roosevelt's celebration of the Old West recounts his adventures in the Dakota Badlands of the 1880s, from roundups to Indian encounters to hunting bighorn sheep. 208pp. 6¼ x 9¼. 0-486-47340-6

CATALOG OF DOVER BOOKS

THE RED BADGE OF COURAGE, Stephen Crane. Amid the nightmarish chaos of a Civil War battle, a young soldier discovers courage, humility, and, perhaps, wisdom. Uncanny re-creation of actual combat. Enduring landmark of American fiction. 112pp. 5³⁄₁₆ x 8¼. 0-486-26465-3

RELATIVITY SIMPLY EXPLAINED, Martin Gardner. One of the subject's clearest, most entertaining introductions offers lucid explanations of special and general theories of relativity, gravity, and spacetime, models of the universe, and more. 100 illustrations. 224pp. 5⅜ x 8½. 0-486-29315-7

REMBRANDT DRAWINGS: 116 Masterpieces in Original Color, Rembrandt van Rijn. This deluxe hardcover edition features drawings from throughout the Dutch master's prolific career. Informative captions accompany these beautifully reproduced landscapes, biblical vignettes, figure studies, animal sketches, and portraits. 128pp. 8⅜ x 11. 0-486-46149-1

THE ROAD NOT TAKEN AND OTHER POEMS, Robert Frost. A treasury of Frost's most expressive verse. In addition to the title poem: "An Old Man's Winter Night," "In the Home Stretch," "Meeting and Passing," "Putting in the Seed," many more. All complete and unabridged. 64pp. 5³⁄₁₆ x 8¼. 0-486-27550-7

ROMEO AND JULIET, William Shakespeare. Tragic tale of star-crossed lovers, feuding families and timeless passion contains some of Shakespeare's most beautiful and lyrical love poetry. Complete, unabridged text with explanatory footnotes. 96pp. 5³⁄₁₆ x 8¼. 0-486-27557-4

SANDITON AND THE WATSONS: Austen's Unfinished Novels, Jane Austen. Two tantalizing incomplete stories revisit Austen's customary milieu of courtship and venture into new territory, amid guests at a seaside resort. Both are worth reading for pleasure and study. 112pp. 5⅜ x 8½. 0-486-45793-1

THE SCARLET LETTER, Nathaniel Hawthorne. With stark power and emotional depth, Hawthorne's masterpiece explores sin, guilt, and redemption in a story of adultery in the early days of the Massachusetts Colony. 192pp. 5³⁄₁₆ x 8¼. 0-486-28048-9

THE SEASONS OF AMERICA PAST, Eric Sloane. Seventy-five illustrations depict cider mills and presses, sleds, pumps, stump-pulling equipment, plows, and other elements of America's rural heritage. A section of old recipes and household hints adds additional color. 160pp. 8⅜ x 11. 0-486-44220-9

SELECTED CANTERBURY TALES, Geoffrey Chaucer. Delightful collection includes the General Prologue plus three of the most popular tales: "The Knight's Tale," "The Miller's Prologue and Tale," and "The Wife of Bath's Prologue and Tale." In modern English. 144pp. 5³⁄₁₆ x 8¼. 0-486-28241-4

SELECTED POEMS, Emily Dickinson. Over 100 best-known, best-loved poems by one of America's foremost poets, reprinted from authoritative early editions. No comparable edition at this price. Index of first lines. 64pp. 5³⁄₁₆ x 8¼. 0-486-26466-1

SIDDHARTHA, Hermann Hesse. Classic novel that has inspired generations of seekers. Blending Eastern mysticism and psychoanalysis, Hesse presents a strikingly original view of man and culture and the arduous process of self-discovery, reconciliation, harmony, and peace. 112pp. 5³⁄₁₆ x 8¼. 0-486-40653-9

SKETCHING OUTDOORS, Leonard Richmond. This guide offers beginners step-by-step demonstrations of how to depict clouds, trees, buildings, and other outdoor sights. Explanations of a variety of techniques include shading and constructional drawing. 48pp. 11 x 8¼. 0-486-46922-0

Browse over 9,000 books at www.doverpublications.com

SMALL HOUSES OF THE FORTIES: With Illustrations and Floor Plans, Harold E. Group. 56 floor plans and elevations of houses that originally cost less than $15,000 to build. Recommended by financial institutions of the era, they range from Colonials to Cape Cods. 144pp. 8⅜ x 11. 0-486-45598-X

SOME CHINESE GHOSTS, Lafcadio Hearn. Rooted in ancient Chinese legends, these richly atmospheric supernatural tales are recounted by an expert in Oriental lore. Their originality, power, and literary charm will captivate readers of all ages. 96pp. 5⅜ x 8½. 0-486-46306-0

SONGS FOR THE OPEN ROAD: Poems of Travel and Adventure, Edited by The American Poetry & Literacy Project. More than 80 poems by 50 American and British masters celebrate real and metaphorical journeys. Poems by Whitman, Byron, Millay, Sandburg, Langston Hughes, Emily Dickinson, Robert Frost, Shelley, Tennyson, Yeats, many others. Note. 80pp. 5³⁄₁₆ x 8¼. 0-486-40646-6

SPOON RIVER ANTHOLOGY, Edgar Lee Masters. An American poetry classic, in which former citizens of a mythical midwestern town speak touchingly from the grave of the thwarted hopes and dreams of their lives. 144pp. 5³⁄₁₆ x 8¼. 0-486-27275-3

STAR LORE: Myths, Legends, and Facts, William Tyler Olcott. Captivating retellings of the origins and histories of ancient star groups include Pegasus, Ursa Major, Pleiades, signs of the zodiac, and other constellations. "Classic." — *Sky & Telescope.* 58 illustrations. 544pp. 5⅜ x 8½. 0-486-43581-4

THE STRANGE CASE OF DR. JEKYLL AND MR. HYDE, Robert Louis Stevenson. This intriguing novel, both fantasy thriller and moral allegory, depicts the struggle of two opposing personalities — one essentially good, the other evil — for the soul of one man. 64pp. 5³⁄₁₆ x 8¼. 0-486-26688-5

SURVIVAL HANDBOOK: The Official U.S. Army Guide, Department of the Army. This special edition of the Army field manual is geared toward civilians. An essential companion for campers and all lovers of the outdoors, it constitutes the most authoritative wilderness guide. 288pp. 5³⁄₁₆ x 8¼. 0-486-46184-X

A TALE OF TWO CITIES, Charles Dickens. Against the backdrop of the French Revolution, Dickens unfolds his masterpiece of drama, adventure, and romance about a man falsely accused of treason. Excitement and derring-do in the shadow of the guillotine. 304pp. 5³⁄₁₆ x 8¼. 0-486-40651-2

TEN PLAYS, Anton Chekhov. *The Sea Gull, Uncle Vanya, The Three Sisters, The Cherry Orchard,* and *Ivanov,* plus 5 one-act comedies: *The Anniversary, An Unwilling Martyr, The Wedding, The Bear,* and *The Proposal.* 336pp. 5³⁄₁₆ x 8¼. 0-486-46560-8

THE FLYING INN, G. K. Chesterton. Hilarious romp in which pub owner Humphrey Hump and friend take to the road in a donkey cart filled with rum and cheese, inveighing against Prohibition and other "oppressive forms of modernity." 320pp. 5⅜ x 8½. 0-486-41910-X

THIRTY YEARS THAT SHOOK PHYSICS: The Story of Quantum Theory, George Gamow. Lucid, accessible introduction to the influential theory of energy and matter features careful explanations of Dirac's anti-particles, Bohr's model of the atom, and much more. Numerous drawings. 1966 edition. 240pp. 5⅜ x 8½. 0-486-24895-X

TREASURE ISLAND, Robert Louis Stevenson. Classic adventure story of a perilous sea journey, a mutiny led by the infamous Long John Silver, and a lethal scramble for buried treasure — seen through the eyes of cabin boy Jim Hawkins. 160pp. 5³⁄₁₆ x 8¼. 0-486-27559-0

Browse over 9,000 books at www.doverpublications.com

THE TRIAL, Franz Kafka. Translated by David Wyllie. From its gripping first sentence onward, this novel exemplifies the term "Kafkaesque." Its darkly humorous narrative recounts a bank clerk's entrapment in a bureaucratic maze, based on an undisclosed charge. 176pp. 5³⁄₁₆ x 8¼. 0-486-47061-X

THE TURN OF THE SCREW, Henry James. Gripping ghost story by great novelist depicts the sinister transformation of 2 innocent children into flagrant liars and hypocrites. An elegantly told tale of unspoken horror and psychological terror. 96pp. 5³⁄₁₆ x 8¼. 0-486-26684-2

UP FROM SLAVERY, Booker T. Washington. Washington (1856-1915) rose to become the most influential spokesman for African-Americans of his day. In this eloquently written book, he describes events in a remarkable life that began in bondage and culminated in worldwide recognition. 160pp. 5³⁄₁₆ x 8¼. 0-486-28738-6

VICTORIAN HOUSE DESIGNS IN AUTHENTIC FULL COLOR: 75 Plates from the "Scientific American – Architects and Builders Edition," 1885-1894, Edited by Blanche Cirker. Exquisitely detailed, exceptionally handsome designs for an enormous variety of attractive city dwellings, spacious suburban and country homes, charming "cottages" and other structures — all accompanied by perspective views and floor plans. 80pp. 9¼ x 12¼. 0-486-29438-2

VILLETTE, Charlotte Brontë. Acclaimed by Virginia Woolf as "Brontë's finest novel," this moving psychological study features a remarkably modern heroine who abandons her native England for a new life as a schoolteacher in Belgium. 480pp. 5³⁄₁₆ x 8¼. 0-486-45557-2

THE VOYAGE OUT, Virginia Woolf. A moving depiction of the thrills and confusion of youth, Woolf's acclaimed first novel traces a shipboard journey to South America for a captivating exploration of a woman's growing self-awareness. 288pp. 5³⁄₁₆ x 8¼. 0-486-45005-8

WALDEN; OR, LIFE IN THE WOODS, Henry David Thoreau. Accounts of Thoreau's daily life on the shores of Walden Pond outside Concord, Massachusetts, are interwoven with musings on the virtues of self-reliance and individual freedom, on society, government, and other topics. 224pp. 5³⁄₁₆ x 8¼. 0-486-28495-6

WILD PILGRIMAGE: A Novel in Woodcuts, Lynd Ward. Through startling engravings shaded in black and red, Ward wordlessly tells the story of a man trapped in an industrial world, struggling between the grim reality around him and the fantasies his imagination creates. 112pp. 6⅛ x 9¼. 0-486-46583-7

WILLY POGÁNY REDISCOVERED, Willy Pogány. Selected and Edited by Jeff A. Menges. More than 100 color and black-and-white Art Nouveau–style illustrations from fairy tales and adventure stories include scenes from Wagner's "Ring" cycle, The Rime of the Ancient Mariner, Gulliver's Travels, and Faust. 144pp. 8⅜ x 11. 0-486-47046-6

WOOLLY THOUGHTS: Unlock Your Creative Genius with Modular Knitting, Pat Ashforth and Steve Plummer. Here's the revolutionary way to knit — easy, fun, and foolproof! Beginners and experienced knitters need only master a single stitch to create their own designs with patchwork squares. More than 100 illustrations. 128pp. 6½ x 9¼. 0-486-46084-3

WUTHERING HEIGHTS, Emily Brontë. Somber tale of consuming passions and vengeance — played out amid the lonely English moors — recounts the turbulent and tempestuous love story of Cathy and Heathcliff. Poignant and compelling. 256pp. 5³⁄₁₆ x 8¼. 0-486-29256-8

Browse over 9,000 books at www.doverpublications.com